# Second Chances

# Second Chances

## Lynne Norris

*YellowRoseBooks*
a Division of
RENAISSANCE ALLIANCE PUBLISHING, INC.
Nederland, Texas

ISBN 1-930928-29-7

First Printing 2002

9 8 7 6 5 4 3 2 1

Cover design by Linda Callaghan

Published by:

Renaissance Alliance Publishing, Inc.
PMB 238, 8691 9th Avenue
Port Arthur, TX  77642

Find us on the World Wide Web at
http://www.rapbooks.biz

Printed in the United States of America

Acknowledgments:

Special thanks go to Casey, Barb, Linda, and everyone else at RAP for all your efforts in editing and producing an awesome book.

Thank you, gj and Stephanie for all your support, encouragement and friendship along the way. Without this story our lives would have never crossed paths. Thanks for taking the journey with me.

The knowledge of this subject matter comes from my background in healthcare and my own research. Any errors or oversights are my own.

— Lynne Norris

To Catherine, my partner, who holds the other half of my heart and soul. I always said I wanted to write a love story. This one is for you.

# Chapter
# 1

Regina was hunched over the large textbook of emergency medicine, reviewing the most common procedures she would be expected to perform routinely as a resident in Saint Xavier's emergency department. Not that she didn't know them and could probably do most of them in her sleep, but that was just the way Regina was. She spent the last seven years working to get to this point. First, medical school with its long arduous hours of studying, followed by her grueling days as a lowly intern taking histories and physicals, drawing blood, running specimens to the lab for tests, and other menial tasks that residents no longer did.

She survived all that, paying her dues along the way. Now she was poised to begin the last leg of her journey and finish her final residency with a specialty rotation through emergency and trauma medicine which was why she had, much to her parents' dismay, moved to New Jersey, of all places. Regina packed her bags and left Leicester, Massachusetts a year ago and headed to Saint Xavier's Medical Center, which was well known for its emergency and trauma departments. Even more dismayed than her parents was her boyfriend, Derrick, whom she had met at the end of her last residency at the medical center six months ago.

He had been the lead-investigating officer in a horrific car accident that killed several teenagers at the local high school. The oldest had been eighteen and the others ranged in age from fifteen to seventeen. The two fifteen-year-olds ended up in the pediatric intensive care unit before they died several days later. Regina had been asked to brief the officers involved on the nature of the injuries and that had been when she had met Derrick.

He hung around after the meeting and very simply asked her out. Normally, Regina would have refused but the offer of friendship was a welcome balm to the frightening revelation she arrived at months earlier. All it took was a single pointed question from her mother about her choice of friends and why she insisted on spending so much time with one woman in particular. No, Regina hadn't been prepared for the onslaught of conflicting emotions or the outright rejection she knew she would suffer from her family. So she did what she thought was the most prudent thing at the time and buried those feelings, telling herself it would pass, and forgetting about everything but her studies.

When she met him, Regina had been up front telling Derrick she couldn't make any commitment to him at this point in her life and he'd said that he understood, at least she thought he did at the time. Lately, he had been pressuring her to change her specialty to something less demanding so they could spend more time together.

Regina picked up her head as she heard a car door slam and then heard the knock at her door a minute later. She opened the door and gasped as she saw the bouquet of red roses held out to her.

"What are these for?" she asked, taking the bouquet from him, closing her eyes, as she smelled the fragrant flowers.

"Does there have to be a reason?" he asked, leaning forward, and kissing her.

Regina walked into the kitchen to put the roses in a vase. She watched as Derrick unclipped his service revolver and set it on the table. She started to ask him to put it somewhere out of sight, but thought better of it, remembering his angry outburst the last time she brought the subject up. Involuntarily, she flexed her wrist, feeling the stiffness from where he had grabbed her.

Derrick followed her into the kitchen and leaned against the wall. "We need to talk, Regina."

She looked up at him, wondering what was on his mind. "Uh-oh. Those are probably the four most dreaded words to be heard in any relationship."

"Be serious, Regina," he snapped. "I wanted to know if you

thought about what I said the other night."

She stopped arranging the roses and set her hands on the counter. So this was what the roses were for. It was not an act of kindness or contrition, not a peace offering, but a bribe. She turned slowly toward him and her eyes flashed a warning, which he completely missed. "You mean my quitting emergency medicine before I start? Yes, I have, Derrick, and the answer is no."

Pupils dilated and his eyes darkened in anger. "I don't see what the big deal is, Reg. It's still medicine you'd be practicing."

"Derrick, you don't understand. I've spent the last seven years of my life struggling to get to this point. This is my last residency and I want to do it in emergency medicine. This is what I've always wanted to do." She turned around and leaned against the counter folding her hands in front of her. "Saint Xavier's has got a great level three trauma center. It's perfect."

Derrick pushed off the wall and walked toward her.

"Yeah, for you it is. It sucks for me. I'll never get to see you." He ran a finger through her blonde hair pushing it behind her ear. He trailed his finger along her cheek and down to her chin, turning her face to meet his. He bent his head forward and captured her lips, softly at first, and then with more force, pulling her against him.

Regina put both her hands on his hips and pushed him back. She pulled away, gasping a little for breath and looked up into his dark brown eyes. She wasn't used to this forcefulness and it left her feeling unsettled. "Derrick, this is my career." She turned to the sink and started washing her hands. "I'm not going to do my last residency in something I have no interest in."

Derrick sighed and leaned back against the counter. He ran a callused hand through his hair. "What about us, Regina? We're never going to see each other. Why is it that our relationship always takes a back seat to your damn career?"

She dried her hands and dropped the dishtowel on the counter. This wasn't going well. They had no plans to do anything today and Derrick's unannounced visit after the argument they'd had the other night irritated Regina. He had been doing more of that lately, showing up unannounced, expecting that she would just drop everything for him. She planned to spend the night alone and go to bed early since she was starting her first day tomorrow at Saint Xavier's as a third-year resident in their emergency department.

"Derrick, I told you when we first met that a relationship wasn't going to be easy. I'm not going to give up something that I've worked so hard to get." She brushed past him out of the kitchen, needing to put some space between them.

Derrick shoved the rest of the roses into the vase and set them on the table as he followed Regina out to the couch and sat beside her. He laid a hand on her thigh and squeezed it. "I don't want you to give it up. Just find something that will demand less of your time. That's all."

Regina crossed her arms. "Derrick, I have never once asked you to take a less dangerous assignment on the force or to not work the overtime you do. Why should it be different for me?"

"Because I want the woman I love to be home with me, not spending hours helping people you don't even know." Derrick reached into his pants pocket and pulled out a small black box.

Regina's mouth went dry and her heart pounded faster in her chest. "Derrick, no, please don't." She pushed herself into the corner of the couch, her pupils dilating as she watched him open the box, revealing the diamond ring sitting in the black velvet cushion. It might as well have been a ball and chain to wrap around her neck.

Derrick turned to face her and smiled. "Well, what do you say? Yes or no, Regina? I asked your father. He thought it was a great idea."

Regina's body started to tremble. "Y-You asked my father?"

"Yeah, you know, asking for his daughter's hand in marriage, all that stuff. I know your parents are into that." Derrick moved closer.

"Derrick." Regina rubbed her hands over the fabric of her denim shorts, smoothing it out over her well-muscled thighs. "I-I wasn't expecting this."

Derrick nodded his head. "I know. I figured it would help you feel more comfortable about making a decision if you knew I was serious."

Regina closed her eyes and took a long slow breath to calm her ragged breathing. Abruptly she jumped off the couch and walked to the window. She leaned her head against the glass looking out onto the lawn outside the apartment. Every fiber in her being was telling her to run. *Oh God, why does this feel so wrong?*

"Derrick, I can't do this, not now."

He looked up at her. "All right, well take some time, but my offer stands, Regina." He made it sound like a business deal.

"No, Derrick." She couldn't look at him. "I *can't* do this."

"What do you mean you can't do this? You mean now...or what are you saying?" Derrick set the box down and walked over to her. "Regina, look at me," he demanded.

She tore her eyes away from the grass and met his gaze reluctantly.

"I think you feel this way because you just haven't been in love before. I know it's scary, but you'll get used to it." Derrick reached out and ran his thumb over her pulse point, which was beating rapidly. He smiled at this and leaned over claiming her lips.

Regina pulled away. "Derrick, no. Please don't. I can't do this not now, not ever. This isn't right. You've made it clear that you don't support my career choice and that's just the tip of the iceberg."

Derrick raised his arms up, his voice getting louder now. "So you're telling me you think our relationship is a mistake?"

"Derrick, please don't be angry. It's not you, it's me," Regina said, suddenly wishing she were far away from here and Derrick.

"What do you expect me to be? Regina, in relationships you have to learn to compromise and make sacrifices. You know, Regina, I think you're just being selfish," Derrick said, his voice thick with anger.

"Selfish? Derrick, I'm just saying I don't want to jump in blindly. Can't you understand that?" Regina asked. Of course he couldn't understand. How could he understand something that she could hardly put words to herself? Regina had never been an anxious person but right now she felt like she was on the verge of a panic attack. She could hear the blood rushing in her ears and her heart was racing. God, what had she gotten herself into? If she said yes she knew without a doubt that she would be making an awful mistake, one that would most likely end up killing her one way or another.

Derrick didn't hear her words. He walked over to the table where he had set the vase of roses down earlier. Looking at them, his blood pounded in his ears. He thought the roses would tip the odds for him, nullify the fight they had had about her residency. After all, girls loved that stuff and what a perfect way to lead into popping the question. How could she tell him no? *Well, this will teach her to play games with me.*

He wrapped his hand around the neck of the vase and picked it up. Regina stood still, staring out the window, ignoring him. Derrick curled his upper lip in a snarl and hurled the vase at the doorway, striking the corner of the wall. There was a sharp, high-pitched sound of the impact and the vase shattered, sending shards of glass flying into the air.

Regina flinched when she heard the impact, but the sound didn't register fast enough for her to duck and get out of the way. She cried out as the jagged fragments of glass tore into the skin of her upper arm and back. She stumbled forward, clutching her arm and turned around staring at Derrick.

His face was twisted in anger and his chest was heaving. Regina staggered backward. Her heart pounded in her chest and her breath came in short gasps as she struggled not to hyperventilate. She could feel the growing burning sensation from the glass imbedded in her arm and her back. Regina felt something warm and sticky on her arm. Looking down she stared at the dark red blood pulsing down her arm in rivulets and dripping from her fingers, pooling on the hardwood floor at her feet. *Oh God, that's my blood.*

Suddenly, she felt very warm and the room seemed to close in around her. *Come on, Regina, it's just a few cuts. You can handle this.* She pressed her back against the cool wall in an effort to stay on her feet.

"Oh shit. Reg, I'm sorry. I'm sorry." Derrick walked toward her, holding his arms out.

Regina looked at the gash in the crook of her elbow. "You son of a...get me a dishtowel," she ordered, reining in her emotions and squeezing her upper arm tightly to staunch the continuous flow of dark, red blood.

Derrick stared open-mouthed at the growing red stain on the front of Regina's white cotton shirt. "W-what?"

"Get me a clean dishtowel," Regina said through gritted teeth. She watched as he ran to the kitchen and returned holding the dishtowel, his face turning a pasty, white color.

"Derrick, tie it around my arm. Here," she said, releasing her arm as he fumbled to wrap the towel around her biceps and cinched the knot tight.

"I-I'm sorry, Reg. I didn't mean to hurt you." Derrick's hands trembled and his brow glistened with nervous perspiration.

"You should have thought of that before you threw the vase.

Get your keys. You have to drive me to the emergency room. I need stitches," Regina said, wincing at a sharp stab of pain.

"B-but the blood...you'll get it in the car," Derrick said. He was panicking now. He hadn't bothered to drop the police cruiser off but had come straight here.

Not believing her ears, Regina pushed past Derrick. "Then get out of my way." She grabbed her keys and wallet from the kitchen table and left Derrick standing in the condo gaping at her.

Her arm throbbed and blood still pulsed slowly from the wound in her arm. Regina opened her car door and blinked as she saw the afternoon sun glint off the jagged piece of glass sticking out of her arm. Regina jammed her keys into the ignition and started the car. She closed her eyes and took a deep breath. Her hands trembled as she clutched the steering wheel.

"Come on, Regina. It's a five-minute drive down the hill to the ER. You can do this."

Regina threw her car into drive and drove down the hill toward the hospital. She glided through the yellow light ignoring the elderly couple that was crossing the street. She swung her car into the parking lot reserved for emergency department patients and families. She turned off the ignition and a fresh explosion of pain ripped through her arm as she pushed the car door open. Tiny lights wove and danced in her peripheral vision as she stumbled toward the doors of the emergency room.

❖ ⌘ ❖ ⌘ ❖ ⌘ ❖

Alex ran hard and fast. Her feet pounded over the hard-packed earth of the hiking trail that snaked around the Hawke's Nest Reservation. It was here that she found peace, running until the rhythmic thudding of her feet muted the sights, sounds, and smells of the day that replayed in her mind.

It became her daily routine after Lana died. She never slept through the night anymore so rising at dawn was a welcome diversion to staring at the shadowed ceiling in the bedroom of her modest two-bedroom condo in New Jersey. She would drive her newly repainted cobalt blue Cherokee to the park that was just minutes from the large medical center she worked at. At thirty-five, Alex was young to be the chief attending at the level three trauma center's emergency department, but she was one of the best.

It was early in the morning and the sun rose in the eastern sky sending ripples of light over the wind-blown waves of the large lake. Alex adjusted her stride and with one arm lifted her body over a fallen tree. A gray squirrel chattered angrily and shook his tail at her, indignant at the interruption. Alex wore a UMDNJ gray T-shirt and maroon shorts with white trim. There was fierceness to her personality, borne out of the years of indoctrination into a male-dominated medical profession, with its preconceived notions and prejudices towards women.

On her fourth lap around the lake, Alex dropped to the grass and furiously pumped out forty military style push-ups. Her routine complete she rolled over onto her back and sucked in the warm humid air as she gazed up at the light blue morning sky. Slowly, she stretched and pushed herself into an upright position and walked back to her Jeep.

Alex drove the relatively short distance down the narrow two-lane road, turned left onto Winding Brook Road, and arrived at the medical center in less than fifteen minutes. She pulled into a parking space reserved for the emergency department medical staff and got out of her Jeep. She armed her vehicle, listening to the double high-pitched beep as it locked automatically.

The locker room was empty as Alex showered and changed into a pair of blue scrubs. She looked at her watch and quickly braided her hair, pulling it back off her face. A quick look in the mirror and she stepped out of the locker room and into the emergency department to start her day.

Her first stop was the admission board at the nurse's station. She flipped through several charts, reviewed orders and signed off on care plans.

Alex set her pen down on the desk and closed her eyes against the bright, fluorescent lights. She felt someone sit down beside her. Alex opened her eyes to see who it was. She recognized the curly blonde-haired, fair-skinned nurse straddled on the chair next to her.

"Hi, Sandy."

A worried expression crossed her face. "Hi yourself. Drink this," Sandy ordered and shoved the cup of orange juice into her hand. "Your hands are shaking. Did you eat anything today?"

Alex shook her head, downed the orange juice and set the empty cup on the counter. She picked up her pen and started writing orders in the next chart.

Sandy turned her chair so she faced the doctor and regarded

her quietly as Alex signed off on the chart in front of her. Her physical features were striking to say the least and her intense blue eyes could cut any overly cocky resident down to size with a mere glance in their direction. Alex's dark moods and brooding nature kept most of the staff at the emergency department firmly at bay, but Sandy was thick-skinned and the doctor's dour personality didn't scare her.

She had been a nurse in the emergency room for over fifteen years and seen her share of physicians come and go. Most of them became burnt out with the high caseload of violent traumas, junkies who stumbled into the department blitzed out of their minds, and all of the AIDS patients they treated on a regular basis. Alex was more than capable of handling any situation, but when push came to shove in the wild chaos they often found themselves in, she was one of the few doctors Sandy had ever seen who could control the situation and run the trauma team like a veteran field general.

Sandy had never seen Alex look quite as haggard as she had in the past several months and it frightened her. She leaned closer to the doctor so only she would hear her words.

"It's been eight months, Alex. You hardly eat or sleep anymore." Sandy shook her head. "Don't give me that look." Icy blue eyes glared at her from underneath rumpled bangs. "You can fool the rest of the staff, but I know you better than that. Have you looked in the mirror lately, Alex? You've lost weight and, pardon my French, you look like shit. What are you doing to yourself?"

Alex sighed and shook her head, looking down at the triplicate order form folded in half in the chart. "I'm fine, Sandy," she replied, as she unfolded it. That was a lie. She knew Sandy was right. Since Lana died, she had been going though the motions, day to day, just barely keeping her head above the water. If she were honest with herself she would have admitted that she was probably close to being clinically depressed. Many nights she just didn't bother to go home and stayed in the on-call room at the hospital because she couldn't bear the stark emptiness of her house. It was a bleak reminder of a past that she would give anything to forget.

Alex rubbed her temples and winced as a sudden wave of emotion flooded her leaving an empty ache in her chest. Her senses reeled as she watched herself in her mind's eye, climbing up the stairs to the second floor. It became their ritual during that last month. Lana would lay curled up in the hospital bed waiting for her to come home. Alex would drag herself home after her shift in the emergency department was over and sit behind her in the bed just quietly holding her after she had given her another dose of morphine.

The nurse from the hospice pulled her aside the week before and told Alex that if Lana had any family the time to call them was now. Family. The only family Lana knew was Alex and Dana. And as much as Alex hated to admit it, she knew Lana still loved Dana.

*Alex opened the door to the bedroom and her skin crawled. There, sitting on the bed next to Lana was Dana. She looked up as Alex stood in the doorway trying very hard to process what she was seeing. An empty syringe lay on the nightstand next to the bed.*

*"What did you do, Dana? My God what did you do?" Alex felt her legs carry her to the side of the bed and practically collapse underneath her as she knelt down. She felt a pulse in Lana's neck and grabbed Dana's wrist with her other hand. "What did you do to her?" she growled.*

*"What you were too afraid to do, Alex." Dana pulled her arm out of Alex's grasp. "She called me two weeks ago and asked me to come down. She didn't have the heart to ask you to do this."*

*Alex stared in disbelief. "I was increasing her morphine each day. She would have..." Her words trailed away as she looked up at Dana. "You bitch."*

*Dana shook her head. "You see, Alex, it really didn't matter that you took her away from me. In the end, she wanted me by her side when she left this miserable existence. Not you." Dana stood up and pulled her leather jacket on. "Oh, and don't worry, Alex. I took care of all the arrangements. Nobody will know about this." She picked up the empty vial and syringe from the nightstand. She walked around the bed to Alex. "I'll leave you alone to say your good-byes." Dana started to walk away then stopped and turned back. "Oh, and Alex, if it hurts too much, I brought a little something to help numb the pain." She tossed a clear plastic bag at Alex and closed the door behind her.*

*Alex laid her head on the bed and held onto Lana's hand. Goddammit, it did hurt too much.*

"Alex?" Sandy shook her elbow. "Hey, where did you go off to?"

It had been so easy for her to take those pills and walk through the next several days in a drug-induced haze, one that almost ended her career two days later. Alex shook her head, keeping her eyes closed until the pain slowly ebbed away. She almost let her defenses down but somehow managed to shove the bitter memories of the past eight months far into the back of her mind.

"I appreciate your concern, Sandy, but I'm fine. Really I am," Alex said, as her attention was drawn to a figure down the hall. Her instincts prickled and Alex pushed her chair back to get a better look. She stood up from the desk and saw a blonde-haired woman walking slowly down the corridor. The woman leaned against the wall as she neared the desk. She wore a white T-shirt that was stained red with blood.

"Jesus, Alex, you haven't heard a word I said," Sandy complained.

"Sandy, get me a stretcher," Alex said.

She moved around the desk towards the woman, her arms coming up instinctively to catch her as she stumbled and fell. Alex cradled the limp form in her arms, lowering her gently to the floor.

"It's okay, I've got you," she said, as the blonde-haired woman slumped into her arms.

❖ ⌘ ❖ ⌘ ❖ ⌘ ❖

Regina was jostled awake. She blinked her eyes open and saw fluorescent lights passing overhead. She was vaguely aware of several faces looking down at her and voices talking around her.

The movement stopped suddenly and she heard a low voice behind her. "Okay, nice and easy." Regina was lifted up and settled down onto something hard.

She tried to sit up and several pairs of hands gently held her down.

"Easy there." She heard the voice again. "What's your name?"

"Regina. Regina Kingston." Her mouth was dry and the words didn't seem to come out right.

"All right, Regina. I'm Dr. Margulies. We're going to take

care of you."

Regina rolled her eyes up and saw a pair of blue ones look-ing back at her. She was aware of a very cold sensation through-out her body and the voices around her getting farther away.

A nurse with short blonde hair finished taking her blood pressure again. "Her pressure is dropping. One hundred over fifty."

"Let's get a peripheral line in and start a bag of Ringer's lactate. Sandy, we need to cut her shirt off. There's a lot of blood and I can't see anything," Alex said.

"Here, get these on." Sandy slipped the fluid shield mask over Alex's head and tied it for her.

"Thanks," Alex said, settling it on her face with one hand. "Give her five milligrams Valium in that IV, Sandy."

Taking only a moment, Sandy inserted the IV catheter into the back of Regina's hand and set up the IV drip.

"Okay, you've got her meds on board, Alex," Sandy said, as she injected sedative into the IV line.

They rolled Regina onto her side to slip the blood soaked garment off of her. Regina saw the lights blur, getting fuzzier around the edges right before everything faded out, and she slipped from consciousness as the medication took hold.

"Whoa. We've got a bleeder here." Alex clamped a gloved hand above the gash in Regina's upper arm, slowing the rush of blood. "Get me some pressure bandages. I need a syringe with ten milligrams of lidocaine so I can numb this for her." She peered closely at the cuts scattered over the young woman's back. "Sandy, I'm going to need some long-nosed tweezers. She's got glass imbedded in these cuts." Alex looked up as Sandy handed her the lap sponges. "Do we know what hap-pened?"

"A guy just came in claiming that he's her fiancée. He's pretty agitated and he's not making much sense right now," Sandy said, as she handed her the syringe.

Alex shook her head. "Give me some 3.0 silk." She held the lap sponge against the wound and soaked up the blood. She peered closer at the cut on Regina's arm. "Sandy, I need a clamp; it looks like the glass nicked an artery." While Alex waited for the instrument, she injected the lidocaine into the surrounding tissues of the wound.

Alex took the instrument that was handed to her and gently clamped the artery. She then picked up long-nose tweezers, grasped the jagged piece of glass, and gently removed it from the wound. She irrigated the wound with sterile water, probing it with her fingers, feeling for any more glass. Satisfied that there was no more glass in the wound, she sewed three stitches to close the tear in the vessel.

"Sandy, help me turn her so I can stitch up her arm," Alex said.

Together they repositioned Regina onto her back. Alex strapped Regina's arm onto a padded armrest. She pulled a rolling stool over and sat down next to her patient's outstretched arm. Alex raised her head as she heard a loud noise from outside the corridor followed by some angry shouts. The voices drew closer and closer to the trauma room door until the door banged open and a tall, muscular, brown-haired man dressed in a police uniform stormed into the trauma room. Alex set down the instruments and glanced at her patient who was still unconscious.

"Get him out of here," she barked, launching herself off the stool. Derrick was almost as tall as she was and he moved toward her, pushing Sandy out of the way and onto the floor. "Get security in here now." Alex put herself in between her patient and the man in front of her. "You can't be in here." She pointed her finger at his chest.

"The hell I can't. She's my damn fiancée. Isn't there a doctor here?" Derrick was inches from Alex's face.

Alex blinked and clamped down hard on the anger that threatened to boil over. "I'm Dr. Margulies."

Derrick's eyes narrowed as he immediately recognized her name. "I don't want you taking care of her."

"Hey—" Sandy started to protest.

"It's all right, Sandy." Alex pulled her gloves off and held out a hand to Sandy to pull her up from the floor.

"Derrick?" Regina's voice rasped. His yelling roused her and she tried to pull herself up out of the fog she was in.

He pushed past Alex and leaned over Regina. "I'm here, love. I'm getting you another doctor."

"Derrick." Regina opened her eyes and tried to focus on him. His image was fuzzy and distorted. "You're not my fiancée. Get out of here." Her voice was thick from the medication.

"Honey, you don't mean that. You're in pain. Let me take care of this." Derrick looked around the room and glared at Dr. Margulies. "What are you looking at? I told you to get out of here."

Alex crossed her arms. "It's her choice, not yours. Apparently she disagrees with you." She stepped back over to the stretcher, and stood beside Derrick. "I suggest you do what she asks."

"Like hell I will," Derrick growled.

"Derrick, please don't do this. Go away." Regina struggled to push herself up.

Alex reached out a hand and laid it gently on Regina's shoulder. "Stay down."

"Don't you touch her." Derrick tried to hit Alex's hand away from Regina.

Alex blocked it with her other hand and twisted his arm behind his back. "I've had just about enough of you," she growled twisting his arm up higher behind his back, forcing him to bend over at the waist. She guided him to the door and pushed him into the arms of two waiting security guards. "Get him out of here." Alex shut the door and walked back to the stretcher.

The doctor looked back at the woman lying on the stretcher and sighed. "Sandy, I'll see if someone else can finish this up. She's stable. I'll be right back."

"Dr. Margulies?" said a quiet voice behind her.

Alex turned around. "Yes?"

"I trust you. I don't need another doctor to take care of me," Regina said.

Alex looked down at the floor and took a breath. "All right." She sat back down on the stool.

❖ ⌘ ❖ ⌘ ❖ ⌘ ❖

Fifteen minutes later, the wound in Regina's arm was expertly stitched and wrapped securely with gauze. Dr. Margulies quietly pulled the gloves from her hands, and threw them into the medical waste container. She walked to the supply cabinet and retrieved some more bandages and antiseptic to finish cleaning and suturing the several smaller gashes on her patient's back.

Regina blinked her eyes open. She was aware of the pungent smell of antiseptic in the air around her. Suspended above her was a large domed light shining brightly. She picked her head up and groggily looked down at herself. Her shirt was gone and she was covered with a white sheet. The pillow's plastic covering crinkled as she lay her head back down. She rolled her head over to her left and saw the bulky bandage covering her upper arm. She heard a movement behind her.

"Derrick?" she called out.

"He's gone now," Dr. Margulies said.

Regina craned her head around and recognized the dark-haired woman who pushed Derrick out of the room before. She was holding several packages in her hands. Regina cleared her throat and shook her head.

"Ugh. Did I pass out?" She wiped her hand over her eyes.

"No," Alex said, chuckling softly. "It's the medication in the IV. I had to put a lot of stitches in, so it was better if you weren't awake." She sat down on the stool and unbuckled the strap from around Regina's arm. She lifted her arm up and gently laid it across Regina's stomach.

Regina closed her eyes and swallowed, trying to keep her emotions in check. She remembered hearing the vase shatter and seeing the enraged look on Derrick's face as she turned around. That looked had filled her with fear. She felt a hand on her shoulder.

"You okay?" Alex asked.

"I-I don't know," Regina answered honestly. For the first time in her life, she knew what it was like to truly be afraid of someone.

"Do you want to tell me what happened?" Alex asked.

Regina opened her mouth to try to say something but a sob choked off her words. She turned her head away and covered her face with her hand.

Alex sat quietly watching her. She shifted her weight on the stool uncomfortably, interlaced her gloved hands, and looked down at the bloodstained booties covering her sneakers. She hated these situations. Even with all her medical training, it seemed like she could never find the right words to say to some-one. But Alex quickly reminded herself that nurses and social workers could better deal with the mental and emotional stuff. She stuck with the physical; it's what she knew best.

"Listen. I've got some other cuts I need to look at. Do you think you can roll over onto your side?" she asked.

Regina sniffed and nodded her head. Slowly, she lifted her-self up off the stretcher to turn onto her side. She felt a pair of hands under her arms supporting her as she lowered herself back down. "Thanks."

Alex pulled the sheet off her back revealing several more

deep cuts, a couple of which had glass embedded in them. "You're going to feel a prick here. I'm injecting a local anesthetic so you won't feel too much pain."

Regina nodded her head and stared ahead of her. She felt the warmth of Alex's hands on her skin as the doctor tended the wounds on her back. The gentleness was in stark contrast to the ferocity of Derrick's violent attack earlier in the evening and she found herself unable to stop the tears.

Alex looked up from her work. "Do you remember what happened, Regina?"

She nodded her head and took a deep breath to calm her racing heart. "We had a fight," Regina said. She wiped more tears from her face.

Alex finished stitching up the last cut on Regina's back. She sat back on the stool and looked at the clock on the wall. "Is there anyone you want us to call to come pick you up?" Alex asked.

Regina sat up slowly wincing at the pain in her arm and her back. She rubbed her face trying to make herself feel more awake. "What time is it?" she asked.

"Almost midnight," Alex said. She was busy writing out two prescriptions for Regina.

"No. It's all right. I can drive myself home," Regina replied.

Alex stopped writing and arched an eyebrow in surprise. "You sure there's no one you would rather stay with tonight? Until things settle down, that is."

"No, it's all right. Derrick doesn't live with me," Regina said.

Alex noticed Regina looking around the room. "I'll get you a scrub top to wear home. We had to cut your shirt off of you when you came in."

"Oh," Regina said.

"Here's a prescription for an antibiotic and something for the pain. You should take it easy for a couple of days. No heavy lifting," she said as she handed both pieces of paper to Regina.

Alex stepped out of the triage room and walked to the desk. "Sandy, can you get our patient a scrub top to wear and call a cab for her too."

Sandy looked up and nodded. "Going home to the boyfriend, huh?"

"No, apparently they don't live together. Good thing for her I guess," Alex said.

"She ought to get a restraining order on the bastard. Screw giving him a second chance." Sandy shook her head in disgust. Alex shrugged and picked up a stack of charts, all patients she had taken care of today, and headed to an empty room to finish writing her notes.

❖ ⌘ ❖ ⌘ ❖ ⌘ ❖

Regina arrived home around one in the morning. Her apartment door was unlocked and she slipped inside quietly, not sure if Derrick would be waiting there or not. She was relieved when she discovered that the apartment was empty. She quickly locked the door and slid the chain into place.

She ran a hand through her disheveled hair and took a shaky breath as she surveyed the shattered vase with the mangled roses lying on the floor in a puddle of water. Carefully, she walked around the broken glass and into the kitchen where she looked at the remnants of her uncooked dinner.

"What a waste," she said as she scraped the spoiled meat into the garbage bag. Next, she put some dish gloves on and went about the tedious task of cleaning up the glass that covered a wide area of the room. As she cleaned the mess, the numbness of the events slowly receded to be replaced with a growing anger. She was angry that she hadn't seen the signs, and afraid because she knew Derrick would not give up that easily. A car door slammed outside her condo and Regina's heart rate accelerated. She peered out the blinds and sighed when she saw one of her neighbors walking up to their door. Regina went back to cleaning up as her brain replayed the echo of another door slamming years ago. She clenched her jaw to hold back the tears that threatened to fall from her eyes.

*She sat on the bed in her bedroom clutching her teddy bear as she listened to the angry voices downstairs.*

*"How dare you bring that filth into my house. You're a disgrace to your family. How could you do this to us?" Her mother's voice rose, exaggerating the already southern twang in her voice.*

*"Mom, please. Don't do this. I'm still your son. I love you," Jeffrey pleaded. "Those are just words and you don't know the meaning of them." There was the sharp staccato sound of a hand striking a face and those hateful words that she would never for-*

get. *"Get out of my house. I don't have a son anymore."*

*Regina listened to the footsteps as they climbed the narrow steps up to the second floor. They grew louder and she heard a soft knock on her door.*

*"Reggie? It's Jeff." She slid off her bed and opened the door. She bit her lip as she saw the red imprint of her mother's hand on his cheek.*

*"Hey now, don't cry." He pulled her into a big hug and held her tightly. He pulled back and looked at her. "Now you listen to me. You follow those dreams of yours. Don't let her tell you differently." He hugged her again and kissed her forehead. "I'll write you when I get settled somewhere."*

*"Where are you going?" she asked.*

*A shy smile played at his mouth. "Tom and I have a place out in San Francisco."*

*"I love you, Jeff. I'll miss you." She squeezed him tightly.*

*"Ditto."*

Regina gripped the chair next to her and swayed slightly as the raw emotions ripped through her unexpectedly. "God, where did that come from?" she asked the papier-mâché woman standing on her entertainment center. The woman remained silent holding the staff and water jug in her arms.

Regina was exhausted by the time she slipped gingerly into her bed. She tossed and turned for a while, trying to find a comfortable position that didn't cause her to wince with pain.

# Chapter
# 2

Amazingly, Regina woke up on time. She washed herself the best that she could without getting her arm and back wet. Listening to the weather report, which promised a hot and humid day, she selected a pair of khaki shorts and a white cotton blouse, and then rolled up the sleeves. Under different circumstances, Regina would have been more enthused about her first day in the emergency department, but the recently sewn up gashes in her arm and back were starting to ache and she was stiff from sleeping in an awkward position.

Regina padded into the bathroom to take some more ibuprofen before she left for the pharmacy. The memory of last night played on in her head like a broken record as she dumped the pills out into her hand. She looked into the mirror as she swallowed the pills, washing them down with a drink of water. Red-rimmed, green eyes with dark circles looked back at her.

"God, I look a mess." She ruffled her hair and splashed some cold water on her face. She stopped on her way out the door and hit the message button on her answering machine. It flashed that she had two messages. She heard the beginning of a message from Derrick and hit the delete button, let the next one begin and instantly deleted it as well.

An hour later Regina stepped out of the air-conditioned interior of her Mustang and walked into the doctor's entrance of the sprawling medical center. Regina took a breath as she stepped off the elevator and turned around to get her bearings. Her heart beat rapidly in her chest and she mentally chastised herself for feeling like a fledgling intern again.

She pushed open the door and walked down the long white-walled hallway through a set of doors leading into the emergency department. Regina's first impression as she walked into the brightly lit department was that it was much larger than she recalled. An expansive nurse's station sat in the middle of the department surrounded by twelve glass-enclosed trauma rooms. There were separate rooms set aside for fractures and sutures. She recognized the room she had been in last night. Several of the rooms were occupied with the curtains drawn to maintain the privacy of the patients. Regina could hear the soft whooshing sound of a ventilator and the repetitive beeping of the alarms as she walked toward the nurse's station.

Twelve monitors were housed on an island behind the desk displaying vital signs of the patients hooked up to monitoring equipment in the various rooms. She recognized one of the nurses as the one who had taken care of her last night. Regina walked over to her. "Hi. You're Sandy, right?"

"Yes, what are you doing here? Is everything all right, no problem with the stitches?" she asked, standing up to glance at Regina's arm.

"Oh, no," Regina said. "I start my residency today in the emergency department. Is there a locker room where I can change?"

After a moment of shocked silence, Sandy walked around the desk. "Sure. It's over here. You're early. Rounds don't start for an hour."

Regina shrugged. "I didn't want to be late."

"Good idea," Sandy said, watching the young woman walk away from her. She looked so young and innocent. *God help her*, she thought.

Regina chose a locker by the far corner of the room. She opened it and set her backpack inside the bottom. She turned around and flipped through the pile of light blue scrubs, select-ing a small top and bottom. Each department involved in patient care in the medical center was assigned a different color. Back at her locker, she unbuttoned her blouse and slipped out of her shorts, and hung them on one of the hooks in the locker. She slipped the well-starched garment over her head and pulled it down over her arms, wincing as she felt a tug on the stitches. Regina pulled on the scrub bottoms and tucked the top into the waistband. She sat down on the bench and pulled out a new pair of white sneakers from her backpack. Prior experience taught her to keep a set of sneakers to be used only at work. It didn't take more than one patient emptying their bladder or otherwise onto her feet to convince her that this was more than a good idea.

Regina slipped her white lab coat over her scrubs and clipped her ID badge to the left lapel. She dug in her backpack and pulled out several pens and her stethoscope, all of which she slipped into one of the pockets. Regina closed the locker and slipped her lock through the hole in the latch, securing her valuables inside. She then walked back out into the department and spotted another resident who had been at orientation with her the week before.

"Hi Marcus," Regina said, as she walked toward him. He was fidgeting with his clipboard and managed to drop half of its contents on the floor.

Regina stooped and gathered up several of the scattered papers. She handed them to Marcus noticing that his hand was trembling slightly as he took them from her.

"Hi Regina. Hey, do you know what attending we have for this residency?" he asked, quickly reshuffling his notes and slipping them back under the clip.

Regina shook her head. They could have Attila the Hun for all she cared. She was here and that was what mattered. "No, not yet," she said looking around the department.

"God, I hope its not Dr. Margulies," Marcus said, rolling his eyes up to the ceiling.

"Why do you say that?" Regina asked, suddenly remembering the name of the doctor who had taken care of her last night.

"Let's just say the words 'pit viper' pale in describing her personality. I think she has residents and interns for breakfast," he replied.

"Oh, I'll keep that in mind," Regina said.

She jumped as a glass door to one of the trauma rooms burst open and a tall figure dressed in blue scrubs and a bloodied isolation gown strode toward the desk. As the woman ripped off her fluid shield mask and her surgical hat, Regina realized that it was Dr. Margulies. She stepped directly in front of Regina and grabbed the phone from the desk, punching in several numbers and impatiently tapping her black sneaker on the floor.

"Radiology?" Her voice was low and menacing. "This is Dr. Margulies in the ER. I ordered a stat X-ray twenty minutes ago to rule out a C-spine fracture. I want somebody up here *now*." There was a pause as she listened and then she waved her hand in the air in front of her and slammed it down on the desk. "I don't give a damn if you're short staffed. Get someone up here or get me your supervisor." She slammed the phone down and shook her head. "Sandy, when is bio-med getting up here to fix our portable X-ray unit?"

"We've called twice, Dr. Margulies. They know we need it fixed stat," Sandy said and picked up the phone.

Alex turned her head and regarded the two residents standing beside her at the desk. She read the names on both their ID badges and looked back up at their faces. Regina took a step back from the fiery intensity radiating out of the doctor's eyes. The anger in the pale blue eyes faded and Alex focused on the shorter woman standing before her. Their eyes met briefly and there was a moment of startled recognition as Alex placed Regina and nodded her head imperceptibly at her. "Sandy, you didn't tell me the new residents were here already."

"You were busy," Sandy replied, without looking up.

Alex looked down the hallway and spied a portable X-ray cart sitting just inside the ER doors. "Come on, you two can help me get this X-ray taken." She headed off toward it leaving Regina and Marcus standing at the desk.

Sandy looked up and groaned. "Damn it, Alex, some radiology tech is going to come in here screaming that we stole his portable unit again."

"Then they should stop leaving it inside my department when they decide they're going on break," Alex said.

"She's kidding, right?" Marcus asked, turning his head to look at Regina.

"Somehow, I doubt it," Regina said, trotting off after the taller doctor.

❖ ⌘ ❖ ⌘ ❖ ⌘ ❖

Later after they finished taking the X-rays, Regina walked over to a sink. She pushed the foot pedal down and shoved her hands under the stream of tepid water. She soaped her hands and then pulled several paper towels from the dispenser. She turned her head and watched as the transporter wheeled the patient out of the trauma room; the boy was being taken up to the operating room for surgery. Regina dried her hands off and wondered if the kid realized how lucky he was that he hadn't suffered a complete spinal cord injury. He would be spending six to eight weeks in a halo brace that would prevent him from moving his neck but he would recover most, if not all, of his physical capabilities.

"Dr. Jack and Dr. Kingston." Regina jumped at her name.

Dr. Margulies was standing at the counter scribbling notes on the patient's chart. "I don't have all day to spend with you two. Let's move it." She flipped the chart shut and shoved it under the thin mattress of the stretcher as it passed by her.

Regina cast a glance over at Marcus who was busy drying his hands and muttering something under his breath.

"Dr. Jack, if you think your time would be better utilized on another service, you're more than welcome to make the transition." Alex fixed him with her steely blue eyes. "Just make sure you put the request in this week."

Marcus' mouth dropped and he stammered helplessly, "N-no, that's not what I..." He swallowed the rest of his sentence as he met her gaze.

Alex slipped her pen back in her pocket and picked up two large packets of paper. "These are sample trauma cases. Read them." She shoved them over to Regina and Marcus. "The next month, you'll each be on call every other day. There are two other ER doctors who you'll work with but I'll be primarily responsible for evaluating your performance."

Sandy walked over and handed Alex a slip with lab values on it. "Damn. When is ICU going to have that bed ready?" Alex asked as she read it and walked toward one of the rooms.

"How the hell did she hear what I was saying?" Marcus asked Regina, his eyes wide with a look of fear.

Regina shrugged her shoulders in response.

Alex turned when she realized that neither of the residents followed her. "Hey. I'm not going to shout over to you two. Move it."

Regina and Marcus left the desk and quickly caught up with her. Alex slipped on a surgical hat, mask, and gown as she talked. "While you're on this rotation it is your immediate responsibility to assess, resuscitate, and stabilize any patient brought in here. You determine if we need to call the trauma team." She stepped into the glass-enclosed room and adjusted the ventilator settings, then stepped back out. "If you're not sure, or if you're in over your head, you call me. There are no heroes in this place. We work as a team. Any questions?" she asked as she looked at them.

Regina shook her head, feeling slightly overwhelmed at the awesome sense of responsibility being laid at their feet. She looked at Marcus who was staring numbly at the packet of reading material in his hands.

❖ ⌘ ❖ ⌘ ❖ ⌘ ❖

It was late afternoon by the time Regina had a chance to escape the emergency room and walk down to the cafeteria. She selected a tuna sandwich, a piece of fruit, and a lemonade drink. She walked to the register and handed her ID badge to the cashier to be scanned. The woman was probably in her late fifties with salt and pepper hair and blue eyes that twinkled when she smiled.

"I haven't seen you before. You must be new here," she said, giving Regina an appraising look as she handed the ID badge back to her.

"I just started today. I'm working up in the emergency department. I'm Regina," she said sticking her hand out.

"Connie." The woman smiled at her and shook her hand warmly. "Good luck to you child."

"Thanks." Regina smiled and slipped her fruit into her lab coat pocket. She had seen a small pond and some picnic tables when she drove into the doctor's lot earlier in the day and decided it would be a quiet place to go and think.

Regina left through a side entrance of the hospital and walked toward the parking lot. She picked an empty table behind the pond shaded by a large oak tree. Her arm throbbed and she was exhausted. She lowered herself onto the wooden bench and closed her eyes, thankful for the momentary quiet around her. She slipped off her starched lab coat, set it on the bench beside her, and massaged her arm gently. She shook her head in disgust as she inspected the purplish bruise running down the inside of her elbow. She flexed her hand and grimaced when she realized that her fingers were swollen.

She and Marcus had spent most of the morning listening to Dr. Margulies rattle off vital information about the department, who to call for certain tests, what was acceptable practice and what wasn't. Together they saw twenty patients during the morning and admitted three to the hospital for further testing.

Regina removed her sandwich from the plastic container and started eating. She suspected she was still in shock from last night, feeling mostly numb about the situation and not having allowed herself time to think about it so far. After twisting the cap off her lemonade, she brought the bottle to her mouth and swallowed the sweet fluid. She guessed that Derrick must have tried to call her during the night. She had been so tired she hadn't even heard the phone ring.

Regina hung her head and rubbed the back of her neck, trying to ease the tension in her shoulders. Looking back at what happened last night Regina realized with a sickening clarity just how blind she had been to Derrick's controlling nature. She should have seen the signs. She was a doctor after all. At first, his need to spend as much time with her as he did was flattering, but it became a problem. When Regina asked for space, Derrick accused her of trying to break off the relationship. She shook her head in disgust, wondering how she allowed herself to get this involved with him. At the time, she had been grateful for the friendship, but Regina knew she let her own insecurities dictate the course she had set out on.

Her relationship with Derrick spiraled downward after she told him she had chosen emergency medicine as her specialty. He had been so angry, questioning her priorities, wanting to know how he could be expected to put up with "those ungodly hours and the stupid phone calls from junior residents and interns who couldn't handle splinters and hangnails." She was shocked when he brought up the issue of a family, reminding him that neither of them had even brought up the topic of commitment or marriage for that matter. Had he sensed something and used it to try to manipulate her? Regina watched as a blue jay dive-bombed a squirrel, eating a scrap of food on the wood chips. She would deal with Derrick later. Right now she needed some time to figure out how she was going to tell him she wanted out of this relationship without all hell breaking loose.

"Hey, I thought your doctor told you to take it easy for a couple of days?"

Regina snapped her head up and opened her eyes. Dr. Margulies was lowering herself down onto the bench directly across from her.

She was so distracted she hadn't even heard the crunch of footsteps on the wood chips. "Oh. Uh, yeah, you did," she said.

A flush crept up her neck as she raised her eyes to meet the doctor's.

A fleeting smile passed over the face of the woman sitting before her. "How are you feeling?"

Regina pulled her eyes away from Alex's. "My arm is pretty sore. Otherwise not bad."

"That was a pretty serious cut." Alex let her eyes rest on Regina's arm. She furrowed her eyebrows together and picked up Regina's hand, turned it over and inspected it. "You should get your arm elevated when you have a chance. Your fingers are starting to get swollen."

Regina swallowed, trying to compose herself as she felt the doctor's warm hand wrapped around her own. Maybe it was the lack of sleep or the deep ache she was feeling in her arm right now that made something so simple as that touch send a jolt through her body. She cleared her throat, finding her voice. "When I'm done here, I will. Thanks for taking care of me last night."

Alex looked up, releasing Regina's hand and shrugged her shoulders. "That's what we're there for." Her eyes took on a far away expression then focused back on Regina. "Why didn't you tell me last night that you were a resident?" Alex asked, suddenly serious.

Regina stopped chewing and stared at the doctor. She lowered her head, took a drink from her bottle, and swallowed the piece of the sandwich. "I-I don't know. It didn't seem important at the time."

Alex regarded her for a minute unsure of where the sudden sense of protectiveness had come from. "Has he ever hurt you before?"

Regina shook her head. "N-no, he hasn't."

"I know it's none of my business and you can tell me to butt out if you want, but you'd probably be better off without him. This isn't an easy rotation and I can't make any allowances for personal issues," Alex said, looking directly at Regina.

Regina was indignant. If she wanted special consideration she would have told this woman last night that she was a resident and begged off her first day. She hadn't and this doctor's assumption that she would ask for allowances pissed her off. "I wasn't expecting any special considerations, Dr. Margulies."

Out of the corner of her eye, Regina recognized a man heading toward them. "Oh no," she moaned as her heart rate picked up.

Alex saw Regina's body stiffen and looked up. "What's wrong?"

Regina swung her legs over the bench and scrambled to her feet watching Derrick approach her. She could feel the anger radiating from the rigid set of Derrick's body. She didn't want a confrontation here, not at work, and especially not in front of the chief attending.

"Regina, I've been looking all over for you. Why didn't you call me back?" Derrick demanded, walking right up to her and taking her hands in his.

Regina recoiled at his touch. "Derrick, we need to talk, but not here." She stepped away from him and pulled her hands out of his grasp. She was mortified that he had come to the hospital, essentially bringing her personal problems to work.

Derrick's eyes flashed and he swept his gaze over to the woman who sat at the table across from Regina. "You? Regina, what are you doing with her? Don't you know who she is?" Derrick reached out to pull her away from Alex.

"Derrick, Dr. Margulies took care of me last night and she's the chief attending in the emergency department." Regina glared at him.

"That piece of trash took care of you last night?" He turned to Alex. "I told you I didn't want you treating her."

The doctor stood up from the bench.

Frantically, Regina searched for something to diffuse the situation before it deteriorated any further.

"Derrick, it was my choice, not yours," Regina said.

"You and I need to talk right now." He stepped forward, took hold of Regina's arm, and pulled her away from Alex. He pointed a finger at Alex. "You stay away from her."

Alex clenched and unclenched her fists as she watched Derrick lead Regina away. She battled back her anger. *This isn't your fight. Stay out of it, Alex.* Angry with herself for letting her defenses down, she turned and walked away, feeling the sting of tears in her eyes from his hateful words. All she wanted to do right now was find a hole and crawl into it. Her long legs carried her quickly across the parking lot heading toward the safety of the hospital walls.

Regina walked far enough with Derrick to get them out of earshot of any other staff members.

"Derrick, you had no right to say that about her," she said, as she yanked her arm out of his grip. The movement caused a shot of pain across her back.

"Yes, I did. Don't you remember the kid that died last year in the emergency room? She was taking care of him." He pointed in the direction of the retreating doctor. "The hospital suspended her and put her on probation for being on a controlled substance at the time. She is trash. All the more reason for you to switch your residency."

Regina pointed a finger angrily at his chest. "I am not quitting my residency, Derrick." She remembered the incident. She had been doing her pediatric residency at the time. Her eyes narrowed as she realized that none of the details about the whole episode were released to the staff. "Derrick, that information is confidential. How did you find out she was on probation?" Regina was furious. She didn't need Derrick stirring up trouble for her.

"Come on, Regina, I'm a police officer. I just called in a couple of favors. I knew I remembered her from somewhere. The story was all over the papers for a week. It was the mayor's son, for Christ's sake. They should have yanked her license. Instead they suspended her," Derrick said, as if this justified his actions.

"Derrick, those kids were drunk and shouldn't have been driving in the first place. Besides we don't know the whole story."

Derrick's eyes narrowed and he leaned closer. "What? Has she been pleading her case with you or something?"

"Derrick, I can't believe you. You completely flip out last night, throw a vase, I end up at the emergency room and you're concerned with who I talk to at work." Regina rubbed her arm, acutely aware of the dull ache starting in her elbow.

"I know, I know. Regina, I'm sorry." Derrick tried to put his hands on Regina's arms, but she stepped away from him. "I don't know what happened, but I promise you it won't ever happen again."

Regina stared at him and laughed. "You're right about that. Just go away Derrick."

"You can't do this Regina. I didn't mean to hurt you," Derrick pleaded.

"Derrick," Regina replied, brushing his hand away from her. "You did hurt me. I needed I don't know how many stitches because of you. Please, Derrick, just leave. I don't want to see you anymore."

Derrick stepped closer to her.

"Don't." Regina held a hand up to stop him.

"Don't what?" he asked, frowning.

"Just stay away from me. Last night and today convinced me of one thing about you."

"What's that?"

"If you're going to call someone trash you should start by looking in the mirror. Good-bye, Derrick." Regina turned and started to walk away.

Derrick lunged after her, caught her arm and spun her around to him. She cried out as her stitches pulled in several places. "Regina, you don't mean that. Last night, it was an accident. I'm sorry."

"Last night was no accident." Regina lifted her head up and met his eyes. "It was a big, red warning flag screaming at me to get out of this relationship." She looked down at the hand that held her arm. "Now let go of me."

"Regina, please," Derrick pleaded.

"Now." Regina yanked her arm out of his grasp.

She walked away without looking back, weaving her way through the maze of parked cars in the doctor's lot, and headed back to the emergency department entrance. Her legs shook by the time she walked through the automatic doors and the blast of cool air was a welcome relief.

Regina walked over to the nurse's station and sat down at the desk, letting her heart rate settle back down. She looked up and saw Sandy at the other end of the desk. Relieved, she waved to get her attention.

"Hi, Sandy," Regina said.

"How are you doing?" The nurse walked over to Regina and sat down beside her.

"Okay," Regina said, but not feeling the least little bit okay.

"You've got guts coming in here after what happened to you last night. Most people would have stayed home," Sandy said. She creased her brow. "Hey, that guy was in here looking for you."

"I know. He found me outside." Regina shook her head feeling miserable about the awful things Derrick had said to the doctor. "I told him to get lost."

Sandy smiled at her. "You go girl. You deserve better than that."

"Did you see Dr. Margulies pass by here?" Regina asked,

running a trembling hand through her hair.

Sandy's eyes widened. "Boy, did she ever. She looked pissed off."

Regina groaned and lowered her head into her hands. "I'm afraid Derrick said some things that really upset her."

"Better to just stay out of her way, Dr. Kingston. Dr. Margulies is no picnic to be around even on her good days."

"Why?" Regina asked, leaning her elbow on the desk.

Sandy shook her head. "Not for me to say. She's an excellent doctor but she's had a bad time of it recently."

❖ ⌘ ❖ ⌘ ❖ ⌘ ❖

Regina finished her notes on the patients that she'd taken care of today, pulled the stat order tabs up on the charts, and then set them in the rack by the unit clerk. It was five o'clock in the afternoon and the emergency room was quiet. *The lull before the storm*, Regina mused to herself. She walked through the emergency room in search of Dr. Margulies. She wanted to tell her that Derrick had no right to say what he had, and that he was wrong. Lord knows she didn't need to have her attending upset at her for something totally unrelated to work.

Regina asked around and found that Dr. Margulies was probably outside by the ambulance bay. She stopped in the lounge and picked up the two bottles of water with her name on them she had left in the refrigerator. Experience taught her to not leave anything unlabeled; it was a sure guarantee that it would become community food. Regina walked outside and grimaced as the oppressive humidity hit her in the face. She pulled her lab coat off and slung it over her shoulder. Looking around, she recognized the lone figure sitting on the concrete wall high above the loading docks. Dr. Margulies had her elbows on her knees and head bowed forward. Regina was surprised to see a cigarette dangling between the fingers of the doctor's right hand.

Regina wondered whether or not to approach her. Maybe it was better to just leave well enough alone, as Sandy warned her earlier. *No*, she decided. She took a breath and walked up the grassy hill toward the brooding figure. Regina sat down about an arm's length away from her.

"Dr. Margulies," Regina said carefully. "I thought you might want something to drink. It's pretty hot out." Regina set the water bottle down beside the doctor and sat quietly for a moment, watching the woman. Dr. Margulies made no move to acknowledge Regina's presence. A white plume of smoke trailed up from the concrete as she sat motionless. Her dark hair, that had been braided earlier, now hung loosely around her shoulders, hiding her profile.

Alex lifted her head up, looking straight ahead. "Thanks for the water." Her voice sounded quiet and tired. She took a drag from the cigarette and crushed it out on the concrete.

Regina wasn't sure, but she thought she could see the sparkle of tears in the corners of the doctor's eyes when she brushed her hair behind her ear. Realizing she was uncomfortable sitting this high above the pavement, Regina leaned back.

She regarded her companion for a moment. "I'm sorry for what Derrick said to you before."

"Everyone is entitled to an opinion," Alex replied, without looking at her.

Regina looked up at the sky, watching the clouds billow and roll overhead, as she considered what to say to her, then lowered her head and looked down at her feet dangling over the cement wall.

"I-I just didn't want any of this to affect our working relationship."

Alex slowly nodded her head, taking the words in. "It won't unless you allow it to, Dr. Kingston."

"Well, good. I just wanted to get that, uh, settled," Regina managed. She was silent as she recalled the incident Derrick mentioned in the parking lot. She remembered seeing the doctor's picture in the paper.

"Dr. Margulies, can I ask you a question?" Regina looked back up at her.

The doctor knew this question was coming. It always did, it seemed. "Yeah."

"What happened with the kid that died last year?"

Alex looked at Regina. She took a breath and slowly let it out. "You know about the kids that were killed in the car accident?" Regina nodded her head.

Alex sighed, her shoulders slumping forward. No matter how hard she tried, it seemed like she could never leave her past behind. "I was called in to help out in the emergency room that night. There were too many critical patients and the accident took all our resources. I made the decision to crack the kid's chest and try to repair the ruptured arteries in the emergency room. There was too much damage around the heart. I couldn't control the bleeding. The trauma team was backed up and we were on our own in the ER. He bled out before the OR team could get to him." Alex realized she had been unconsciously rolling the bottled water back and forth in her hands, and stopped.

"So you weren't supposed to be there," Regina concluded.

Alex blinked. "No, a friend died and I took some time off to..." She waved her hand, dismissing her thought. "That doesn't change the fact that I put my hands on that kid and made decisions that I had no business making that night." Her voice deepened. "I took some sedatives to help me sleep before I got called in." Alex lowered her head and closed her eyes.

"Was it someone close to you, Dr. Margulies?" Regina didn't know why she asked the question, she just had to know.

Alex shook her head and wiped a tear away with her finger. "Shit." Alex's voice cracked.

Regina's eyes widened with surprise when she looked at the doctor's face. "I-I'm sorry. I didn't mean to get you upset. If you'd rather not talk about this, I understand."

Alex held up a hand. "It's all right. You might as well know the whole story. You'll hear it courtesy of the hospital grapevine soon enough. I, uh, my partner..." Alex stopped and took a breath, not trusting her voice just yet. She hadn't been prepared to talk about any of this. "Lana. She'd been sick." Alex lowered her head. "She was in remission from breast cancer. It recurred in her other breast." Her hands shook as she wiped her eyes. "They caught it too late. It had already metastasized to her liver." Her voice changed and she pushed down her emotions, falling into her safe and sterile clinical assessment of what occurred. "They started with radiation and then chemotherapy. Nothing worked; the tumors were too advanced."

Regina moved closer and laid her hand on Dr. Margulies' forearm. Alex wiped her eyes again and stared straight ahead, her jaw muscles clenching. "Lana decided she didn't want to go through with any more treatments. They were worse than the damn cancer. She died last November, two days before the accident."

Surprisingly, Regina felt anger well up inside her. "Jesus, how could they call you in to assist in a multiple trauma two days after you lost your partner?"

Alex gave a short bitter laugh. "As far as the hospital was

concerned that's a right reserved for married couples only."

Tears welled up in Regina's eyes. "I'm so sorry," she said, moving her hand down the inside of the doctor's forearm and gently squeezing it.

Alex tensed at the gesture and then forced her body to relax. It was the first time she could remember anyone consoling her after Lana's death. Even Sandy, someone that she had worked with for years, maintained a safe distance after the funeral, never quite sure what to say to her. Now someone she hardly knew was comforting her. Alex looked down at the blonde head and wondered who this woman was. How did she get beyond her carefully cultivated emotional defenses?

Regina sat beside Alex for a while, but finally she stood up. "I-I should go. I'm sorry for your loss." She felt exceedingly awkward and nervous as she looked at the back of the doctor's head. She opened her mouth to say something else, but thought the better of it and quietly walked back down the hill toward the emergency department.

❖ ⌘ ❖ ⌘ ❖ ⌘ ❖

Regina opened the door to her one bedroom condo and walked across the living room to the kitchen. She set her backpack in one of the chairs and pulled a bottle of water out of the refrigerator. She twisted the cap off, took a long drink of the cold water and padded across the living room to check her messages. She looked at the light: one blink, and one message. She sighed, knowing it was probably her mother calling. Regina listened to the message and groaned.

"Hi dear, this is your mother. You need to call us as soon as you get in. Derrick called. He was terribly upset. What happened? Please call me."

She slumped down onto the couch and stared at the wall. She couldn't believe Derrick called her parents. What did he think he was doing? Did he honestly think that by calling her parents it would make her feel any differently about what happened? Regina tilted her head back against the couch and covered her eyes with her arm.

"I don't need this, not now." Regina looked at the phone and contemplated not calling. She still had plenty of reading to do before she was on duty tomorrow. "Might as well get this over with. If I don't call, lord knows she will."

Regina picked up the cordless phone and dialed her parents'
number. It rang three times and her mother's breathless voice
answered.

"Hello?"

"Hi, Mom. It's Regina."

"Oh good. What happened dear? Derrick was an absolute
basket case on the phone last night. I could barely understand
him?"

"He called last night?" Regina asked. She felt bile rising in
the back of her throat as she thought of Derrick on the phone
with her mother while she was in the emergency room. *You
should get an academy award for your performance, Derrick.*

"Why, yes, dear. He was very worried about you."

Regina snorted. *I bet he was.* "What did he tell you?"

"He said he asked you to marry him and you two ended up
having a terrible argument," her mother said.

"That's it?" Regina asked pacing back and forth across the
carpeted living room.

"Why yes, dear. You don't sound very happy. What's
wrong?"

Regina pulled the sneaker off her left foot with the toe of
her right. She bent over, slipped the other one off and tossed it in
the corner. She decided not to tell her mother about the vase. No
need to bring that up right now.

"Regina? Are you still there?"

"I'm here, Mother," Regina said looking up at the ceiling.
"Mom, Derrick and I have broken up."

There was silence on the other end of the phone. "That's
nonsense. Why would you do that, Regina?"

"Derrick and I have different priorities right now. It's just
not going to work out," Regina answered.

Her mother sighed. "Regina, I don't understand why you
had to choose medical school, of all things. You'll never have a
normal life working those crazy hours. How will you ever have a
family?"

"Mother." Regina ran her hand through her hair and closed
her eyes. "Mom, let's not get into this again. It's what I want to
do. It's okay for Michael and Jeffrey to have careers—"

"Michael has a family to support. He should have a career,"
her mother replied sharply.

"And what about Jeffrey, Mom? What about me?" Regina
asked.

"Don't you dare throw that in my face. You know we don't discuss your brother. What he does is...is a disgrace." Her mother's voice cracked.

"Jeff's not a disgrace, Mom. He chose a different lifestyle, that's all," Regina said, biting back tears.

"Don't you dare defend what your brother does to me." Her mother's voice shook. "We just want what's best for you. Derrick loves you. He wants to take care of you. What's wrong with that?" her mother asked, having regained her composure.

Regina was silent. Hot tears ran down her face. *What's wrong with that? I don't love him, that's what's wrong.* "Mom, Derrick wants someone to be home to take care of him. He's made it clear that he doesn't want me practicing medicine, and I won't give up my career for anyone." Regina leaned against the wall and closed her eyes.

Even now it was the same old double standard she had argued about with her mother since she could remember. It was okay for the men in the family to be successful, but a woman, ha. Her mother counted success by how long you were married and how many kids you had. Regina rubbed her face wishing that she wasn't having this conversation. She was a fool to think she was going to get support from her mother, despite what had happened to her last night.

"Regina, sometimes you have to make sacrifices when you're in love." Her mother's Southern accent was beginning to annoy her.

"I know that, Mom, but I don't love Derrick, not at all."

"Don't say that, dear. You're just upset. Give it time."

"Mom, did Derrick tell you that I had to go to the emergency room last night?" Regina asked.

"I didn't think you started until today," her mother said.

"That's right," Regina said, letting her mother think about her answer for a minute.

"What are you saying, Regina?"

"Mom, Derrick flipped out. He picked up a vase and threw it at the wall when I told him I didn't want to get married. I got hit with the glass from it." A small cry escaped her lips. "I needed stitches in my arm and my shoulder."

"Oh well, now, dear, I'm sure it was an accident. Derrick wouldn't intentionally hurt you."

"How can you defend him? I can't believe you're saying this." Regina shook her head and paced around the room again.

"Whose side are you on anyway?"

Her mother was crying now and she heard muffled voices before her father's gruff voice came through the phone line. "Regina, what did you say to your mother? She's crying."

Regina sniffed and wiped her tears off with the back of her hand. "Dad."

"Oh great, you're both crying. What's going on?" he asked.

Regina rubbed her forehead, wincing at the pounding behind her eyes. "Derrick and I are finished." She heard her father start to say something, but Regina cut him off. "Dad, please, I can't talk anymore, not now. I'll call you later in the week. Bye." Regina ended the connection and set the phone down in its cradle.

She was furious with Derrick for calling her parents and manipulating the situation to his advantage. Regina walked into her bathroom and opened her medicine cabinet. She pulled out a bottle of ibuprofen and dumped two of the pills into her palm. After tossing them into her mouth, she filled a cup with water and took a swallow, closing her eyes as the pills slid down her throat.

She walked back out to the living room and snorted in disgust at the pile of reading she still had left to do. For a moment, she gave half a thought to just crawling into bed and falling asleep, but knew if she didn't read the information, she would probably pay for it the next time she was on duty with Dr. Margulies. With a resigned sigh, Regina opened the packet and started reading the trauma protocol for blunt abdominal injuries.

❖ ⌘ ❖ ⌘ ❖ ⌘ ❖

"Alex, wake up." The knocking at the door came again more insistent this time. "Alex, come on, wake up."

Alex groaned and rolled over, her arm shielding her eyes from the light in the hallway. "Ugh. Turn the damn light off," she said, her voice hoarse from just waking up.

Sandy opened the door wider, letting more light into the small exam room, and looked at the doctor sprawled out on her back on the hard exam table. She could never understand how anyone could fall asleep on those things. "We've got a trauma coming in. They're ten minutes out."

"All right, I'm coming." She was still groggy and drifting between wakefulness and sleep.

Sandy leaned her head against the door and watched as the doctor's breathing deepened and turned regular again. She sighed and hung her head, then grinned evilly.

"Hate to do this to you, friend." Sandy walked over to the sink and filled a cup with cold water, then stood of good arm's length away from Alex. "Alex, this is your last chance. Get up." She waited a second, then tossed the cup of water onto Alex's face and scooted back toward the door.

In a blur of movement, Alex exploded off the exam table wiping her face, and muttered several colorful expletives. She glared at Sandy through tousled bangs, menacingly curling her lip. "A simple hand on the shoulder would've worked nicely, Sandy."

Sandy laughed and shook a finger at her. "Oh, no. The last time I woke you up that way, you almost broke my hand off. This way, I have some time to get away from you." Sandy flicked the light switch on and let the door bang behind her she walked out.

Alex grabbed a towel off of the shelf and wiped her face dry. Noticing the V-neck on her scrub top was riding dangerously low on her chest, she reached to the back with both hands to pull it down, then, stretched her arms high over her head. Several vertebrae gave a satisfying pop as she arched her back.

"Ah. That's better." She sighed and walked out of the room, heading toward the trauma room.

Passing the nurses' station, Alex grabbed an isolation gown from one of the bins and pulled it on. Glancing over the desk, she saw a couple of medical students hovering around a computer. Alex changed directions, walked up behind them, and clamped her hands down onto their shoulders.

"Hey boys, what are you watching over here?" She peered over their shoulders at the Internet site they were looking at. "Nice anatomy." She yanked them both back, turned them around and pushed them ahead of her towards the trauma room. "I think this might be more educational for you, that is, if you're still interested in being doctors."

"I...uh, we just typed in—" Andy stammered helplessly.

"Shut up, Andy." Alex propelled them both forwards. "I'm sure your patients would love to know how you spend your downtime."

The emergency room doors banged open as the paramedics wheeled their patient into the emergency department. Alex quickened her pace and jogged over to meet them, both medical students on her heels.

"What do we have?" she asked.

"A forty-three-year-old male involved in a motor vehicle accident. He was unconscious at the scene but his vitals were stable. Pulse is thready, blood pressure is 110 over 80. His respirations are shallow. We couldn't get a line in at the scene." The paramedic rattled off the vital information as he quickly wheeled the stretcher down the hall.

"Sandy, which room?" Alex asked as she pulled a fluid shield mask over her face and grabbed a pair of gloves from a box on the nearby wall.

"Two," Sandy answered.

They wheeled the patient into room two and expertly lifted him onto the exam table. Alex then bent over him, feeling for his carotid pulse and listening to his breathing. She wrinkled her nose and shook her head.

"God, he smells like a distillery," she said in disgust.

She flipped her stethoscope over her head and adjusted the earpieces in her ears. One of the ER technicians cut the man's clothes off his body and Sandy hooked the EKG leads up to the wall monitor to record his heart's rhythm.

"I've got decreased breath sounds on the right side. Let's get a CBC, tox screen, and a blood gas," Alex ordered.

"All right, I need two large bore peripheral lines. Make them 14 gauge. Let's run Ringer's lactate wide-open and get a catheter in him. Sandy, I need a chest tube, 32 French."

"Got it." Sandy grabbed the sterile kit and turned around, bumping into one of the medical students. Glaring up at him she snapped angrily, "Andy, draw the blood. Come on, get with it here."

"Sorry," he mumbled, as he pulled on gloves and reached for a blood gas kit. Sandy ripped open the packaging and set the kit on the instrument tray next to Alex. Andy quickly drew the blood to avoid further criticism, and carried it out to the satellite lab in the emergency department to complete the tests.

Dr. Jameson, medical director, pushed open the door and strode into the trauma room. "Everything under control in here, Dr. Margulies?"

Alex nodded her head without looking up. "Yup, we're just fine in here, Dr. Jameson." She glanced at the bedraggled emergency technician. "Tommy, wake up and help me roll this guy over to his left side." The medical director watched for several seconds then turned on his heel and walked out of the room, obviously feeling snubbed.

Tommy quickly moved to Alex's side and helped her roll the man over. The doctor picked up the syringe and checked the bottle containing one-percent lidocaine. She quickly injected several sites on the patient's upper ribcage. Without hesitation, Alex took the scalpel from Sandy and quickly made a small incision through the skin above the rib. She grabbed the Kelly clamp that Sandy held out and pushed it slowly through the lining around the lung. When she felt the instrument break through the fibrous membrane, she opened the clamp to enlarge the hole.

She slid the clamp out, holding the incision open with her fingers. Blood trickled from the opening and ran down the man's back, staining the sheet red. Alex picked up the chest tube with the clamp and pushed it through, then held it still while Sandy connected the other end of the tube to suction. Then Alex sutured the tube in place, closing the skin edges of the incision around the tube and tying the suture ends around it. They watched as the bloody fluid flowed through the tubing and into the container on the wall.

Alex looked up a she finished dressing the area. "Let's get a chest, a cross table C-spine on this guy." Alex continued her evaluation of the patient, checking his pupils, and looking for any obvious signs of trauma on his body. She ran her hands along the man's head and neck, checking for any abnormalities. His reflexes were normal and he groaned when she rubbed hard on his sternum and tried to swipe her hand away.

"This guy's lucky," she said, pressing into his abdomen and getting no reaction from the intoxicated man. Alex shook her head. In all her years working in the emergency room, she had seen dozens of drunk drivers come in from serious auto accidents and walk away with barely a scrape. It seemed like that the other person involved in the accident always fared worse.

Andy slipped back into the room and handed the lab results to Sandy.

"The blood tests are back," Sandy said, looking over the results.

Alex looked at the results in the nurse's hand and nodded her head. "Blood gas is okay. Hamatocrit is good. All right, let's keep him on a hundred percent oxygen by mask." She looked up at the monitor and watched his heart rate for a minute. "Let me know when he wakes up. His blood-alcohol level is pretty high, so it'll be awhile. We're keeping him here for observation. Let me know if anything changes in his condition."

Alex walked out of trauma room two after having written several orders in the patient's chart. She looked up at the clock on the wall and rubbed her eyes. Two more hours to go, she thought. She walked over to the desk and sat down to finish writing her note on her patient.

"Alex, the police officers are here. They want to know if they can talk to the guy involved in that car accident," the unit clerk said.

"No, they can't," she said, continuing to write in the chart.

"Well, that's not being terribly cooperative now, is it?" a male voice asked.

Alex jerked her head up and stared into dark brown eyes. It took a moment, but she recognized the officer as the same man who she had forcibly removed from a room the night she had taken care of that new resident; the same one who harassed her in the parking lot. She stood, pulling herself up to her full height above the desk counter top, forcing him to look up at her.

"Here's his blood alcohol test," she said, shoving the chart under his nose. "Does that make it clearer why he's not awake yet?" She glanced at his partner.

Sensing the animosity between the two, the other officer stepped forward. "Uh, doctor..."

"Margulies," Alex said, ignoring Derrick.

"I'm Officer James and this is Officer Black."

"We've met."

"Did he say anything when he came in here?" Derrick asked, making a note in his notepad.

"No. He was unconscious at the scene and he hasn't woken up yet. How are the people in the other car?" Alex asked.

"Dead," Derrick said, not looking at her. "Do you have any coffee around here?"

Alex pointed down the hallway. "It's in the staff lounge." She looked at her watch and decided that she needed something to eat and headed down to the cafeteria to raid whatever was left over.

❖ ⌘ ❖ ⌘ ❖ ⌘ ❖

Derrick walked into the staff lounge. He spotted the coffee-pot and warily sniffed at it, then poured himself a cup and sipped at it. Not bad. He looked around the lounge, which was empty. He'd been working a lot of overtime the past week, by choice since Regina refused to return his telephone calls. She'd come around, he thought. She just needed some time to simmer down and realize that it was all just a misunderstanding. He hadn't really meant to hurt her, just scare her a little. Besides, her mother adored him.

Derrick walked over to the round table in the middle of the room, sat down, and propped his feet up in the chair next to him.

"Hi."

Derrick looked up, startled. He watched as the curly blonde-haired nurse walked over to get coffee.

"Hi," he said. She turned around. "Long shift?"

"Yeah. Almost over," Sandy said, eyeing him from across the room as she poured some coffee. She recognized the police officer as the man responsible for the new resident's injuries, and frankly, she didn't trust him.

"Did that guy wake up yet?" Derrick asked, leaning forward in his seat and removing his feet from the chair next to him, so that he could push it out to Sandy.

She ignored his attempt at politeness and headed toward the door. "No, and I wouldn't bother waiting around either. He'll probably start to feel his well-deserved hangover sometime tomorrow."

"Well, I'll leave my card at the desk," Derrick said.

"You do that."

Derrick watched as the door closed behind her. "Bitch."

❖ ⌘ ❖ ⌘ ❖ ⌘ ❖

Alex, sipping soda through a straw, walked back into the ER, and headed over to the desk to speak to the white team's resident covering the next shift. Before she got there, Dr. Jameson intercepted her and motioned toward an empty room. He was dressed in an expensive Italian suit and obviously on his way out.

"I need to speak to you about that patient who coded in here yesterday. QRM is sniffing around and I need to give them some answers so they can write their damned report." He handed her a copy of the notes from the code sequence in the emergency room.

Alex set her soda down and briefly read through them.

Frowning, she looked up. "So, what are they questioning?"

"They're concerned about our mortality rate in the emergency room, Dr. Margulies. You know how we're rated against our competitors. We've had an unusually high trend recently and corporate is on my back to do something about it." Dr. Jameson ran a hand through his graying hair.

Alex shook her head and snorted. "This guy was in full arrest when he came in. He'd been out for over forty-five minutes before we called it. I know he was young, but damn it, we did everything there was to do. Followed every procedure by the book." She fed Dr. Jameson's words back to him, recalling her meeting before the committee when they decided her fate six months ago. "What would you like me to do? Get on my cell phone to God and ask him if he can stop filling beds in the eternal care unit?" Alex threw the report on the gurney in disgust and stared at Dr. Jameson.

"Dr. Margulies." His voice was low and even. "I appreciate your frustration with corporate's perception of what is going on here, but I have to remind you that you only just got off probation and some people still consider you a liability to the institution. The only reason they decided not to bust your ass out of here was because of the stellar work you had done up until that time and your, um, extenuating circumstances."

Alex had both hands on her hips. The anger welled up inside and she stepped closer to her director until she was inches from his face. "My...*extenuating* circumstances," she slowly said the words, as the fury built inside her. "None of the other medical staff who lost a spouse would have been dragged in here two days after the funeral to assist in a multiple trauma." She stepped closer to her medical director, close enough to see his pupils dilate in response to her physical proximity. "You knew damn well I wasn't in any shape to be treating patients, but you called me in anyway."

Dr. Jameson took a step back and held up a hand. "Dr. Margulies, this will get us nowhere. Our personal lives have no bearing on the quality of care we deliver to our patients. The simple issue was that you used poor judgment in making the medical decisions that affected that boy's life. Besides, the board sided in your favor anyway. They revoked your colleague's privileges after he admitted that you told him that you had taken sedatives before you touched the kid." He spread his arms out. "So, it seems that justice was served."

Alex forced herself to take a breath, not realizing that she had been holding it. "Fine. Tell corporate we'll do a retrospective review of the mortalities in the ER over the past six months." She looked up at Dr. Jameson, the blood still pounding in her ears. "Will that satisfy them for now?"

"Yes, Dr. Margulies." He turned and headed toward the door, stopping before he opened it. "I'll need you to present that report at the next mortality and morbidity meeting."

Alex watched the door swing shut. She knew now that Jameson used the whole situation as a way to get back at her for blowing his comfortable scam with a drug company. The medical review board was incredulous at the punishment that he had called for under the circumstances. They said that it had been a no-win situation. Too many critically injured patients came in from the same accident and the trauma team had been overwhelmed. It was determined that there had been a breakdown in calling in additional staff when the call came into the ER. Alex had done everything medically within her power to try and save that boy. Even now she could remember every detail as if it had happened yesterday.

More tubes came out of the boy than she cared to remember. Once she'd recognized the abnormal heart rhythm on the monitor, she performed a pericardiocentesis, and with a large needle drew the gathering fluid out of the membranous sac around the heart. Sandy, thank God, had been there, and she'd documented the whole trauma sequence as it played out. Sandy also called the OR and notified the trauma team that they needed them as soon as possible. A frantic surgeon on the other end of the line told Sandy that no one was available. Alex and her team were essentially on their own. So, Alex did the only thing she could when the boy went into cardiac arrest: they coded him and she cracked his chest to try and repair the damaged blood vessels, and massage his failing heart. Again, the OR was called—said they would be ready in fifteen minutes. Fifteen minutes had been too long.

Afterwards, Jameson insisted that she should never have performed an emergency thoracotomy, to buy additional time, since the OR had been backed up. In the end, it was the only decision the medical review board said she could have reasonably made. The hospital's policy backed her up on it, but the damage had already been done as news of the high profile death and word of her suspension made the front page of the local newspaper. And now Jameson was doing this to her. Without looking, Alex cocked her arm and swung her hand down in a vicious arc, splattering the large cup of soda on the wall across the room.

Alex walked quickly down to the locker room. One of the junior residents saw her and tried to ask her a question. A look that shot daggers at him sent the resident scrambling for cover, mumbling something about another time being better. Alex opened her locker, pulled out her clothes and her waist pack. She shed her hospital scrubs, slipped a T-shirt over her black sports bra, and threw on a pair of black running shorts. She shoved her sneakers on her feet, balled her scrubs up, and viciously threw them into the dirty linen basket.

Alex stormed out of the hospital and headed toward the road. The sun was already up and it looked like it was going to be another hot day. She stretched for a few minutes and then jogged up the slowly rising incline of Winding Brook Road. By the time she reached the hill leading into Hawke's Nest Reservation, she was in her normal rhythm.

She veered off the divided road and trotted up the dirt embankment toward the trail she often used. Alex kept her stride loose, absorbing the shocks of the uneven ground with ease. She ran easily in the cool darkness underneath the canopy of maples far above.

The trail veered left and she hurdled over a fallen tree and headed toward the shimmering glow of the lake as the sun peeked over the treetops. Stopping by a large rock, she paced back and forth, gulping in the humid, summer air. She climbed up on top of the rock and gazed out over the water. After a moment, Alex sat down, stretched one long, muscular leg out in front of her and wrapped an arm around her other knee. She rested her head on her forearm and watched the sun rise, letting the solitude of the place soothe her jangled nerves.

Much later, after driving home in a daze mostly from exhaustion, Alex unlocked the front door to her townhouse and walked across the tile floor. There were no messages for her on the answering machine—not that she expected any—so she trudged up the stairs to her bedroom. After flopping down on the bed, Alex linked her hands behind her head and stared up at the ceiling.

She rolled onto her side, opened the drawer of the night table, and fished out the two pictures that she kept there. A sad smile creased her face as she looked at the first one. It was a picture of Alex and Lana sitting together looking very much relaxed, lounging on the benches in front of the town hall in Provincetown, people-watching. The second was taken a year later in the same spot with Lana sporting a red baseball cap over her cleanly shaven head.

Lana had shaven all her hair off the night before in a final act of defiance and control against the disease that had taken so much from her already. Alex had sat at the edge of the tub, chin on her hands watching, as the clipper neatly removed the thick brown hair in wide swaths. When she was done, Alex had taken her in her arms and hugged her. Later they had made love; Alex realized now, for the last time. That night had been the beginning of a lot of lasts in their relationship. Closing her eyes, Alex tried to shut out the lonely, desolate feeling that too often threatened to overwhelm her. It was a long time before sleep finally delivered her from the ache she felt deep inside.

# Chapter
# 3

Regina checked her watch. It was nine in the morning and she still had some time before her appointment at the follow-up clinic to have her stitches taken out. She returned the book she was reading on emergency medicine to the rack in the medical library. Regina allowed herself a small smile as she recalled several admissions that she was involved in over the past two weeks. She handled them all fairly well and even managed to get a grumbled "nice job" from her usually taciturn attending. It was a rarity to see Dr. Margulies smile and most of the staff kept their distance from her. After picking up her bag, Regina walked out of the medical library and headed up the back staircase.

Stopping by the emergency department, Regina saw Sandy standing at the desk, busily scrawling notes on one of the flow sheets. "Hi Sandy."

The nurse looked up from her work and smiled. "How are you doing?"

Regina smiled. "Pretty good. No major catastrophes."

Sandy watched as one of the guys from materials management lifted a brown carton of medical supplies off his cart and set it on the ground by the supply closet. Without a look back, he hastily pushed his cart down the hall and disappeared around the corner.

Shaking her head in disgust, Sandy looked at Regina. "He

sets it right underneath a sign that says, 'No boxes or stretchers in the hallway.'" She walked over to the box and started to lift it.

"Here, let me help you with that." Regina knelt down, took hold of the other side of the box and helped Sandy lift it up onto a chair. They carried the box into the supply closet and set it on one of the shelves to be unpacked later.

"How are you making out working with Dr. Margulies?" Sandy asked, knowing the attending's quick temper if her residents were unprepared.

Regina shrugged her shoulders indifferently. "I guess okay. I haven't had my head lopped off yet, so that must be a good thing."

Sandy laughed. "Oh yeah, you don't want to be around when she goes on one of her tirades."

"Hello, ladies."

Regina froze, the hair prickling on her arms.

She turned around and saw Derrick dressed in his police uniform, leaning against the doorframe.

His eyes roamed over Regina's body and he smiled at her. "Can I talk with you, Regina?"

Regina looked at Sandy and back to Derrick. "Uh, yeah. I have a few minutes, Derrick."

"Good. Let's take a walk then," Derrick replied. Regina squeezed by him, crossed her arms in front of her, and walked down the hallway ahead of him.

As they reached the end of the hallway, Derrick placed a hand on her shoulder and turned her around to face him. Regina looked up into his smiling face. "I missed you Regina," he said, trying hard to sound apologetic and sincere.

Regina swallowed and looked down at her feet. "Derrick, why did you come here?"

"Well, considering you wouldn't answer any of my messages, I figured this would be the best place to find you. We need to talk, Regina." Derrick lifted her face up with his fingers and studied her.

"Derrick, please don't do this." She backed away from him.

"Regina, listen to me. We could have something really good together. I made a mistake. I said I was sorry. What more do you want?" He moved closer to her, spreading his arms out in a plea.

Regina, shaking her head, took a step back. "Derrick, there's nothing that we have to say to each other." The young resident pushed the door to the locker room open and walked to her locker. She spun the lock several times and opened it, then reached inside and pulled out a black jewelry box. She turned and held it out to him. "Take it."

"No, Regina, I'm not taking it back. We belong together." Derrick took the box from her and set it on the top shelf of her locker and closed the door. "I love you, Regina." Derrick slipped his arm around her waist and pulled her close.

Regina tried to push away, but he tightened his grip. "Stop it!" she cried, struggling in his arms.

"Keep your voice down. Nobody else needs to hear our business," he hissed at her.

"Let go. You're hurting me." Regina glared up at him.

Derrick pulled her roughly against him and grabbed hold of her lower jaw between his thumb and index finger. "Regina, stop playing games with me." He put his other arm around her, pushing his mouth against hers and forcing his tongue inside.

She jerked her head away from him, and wiped her mouth in disgust. Hot tears rolled from the corners of her eyes. "You bastard. I'm not playing games. Go away."

Derrick pulled back. "You've had your fun. It's time you start paying more attention to me than you do to this damn hospital."

"How dare you think you can just order me around. I don't love you, Derrick, and I'm sure as hell not going to marry you."

Angrily, he shoved her away from him. Losing her balance, Regina stumbled back into the sink behind her, crying out as her back slammed into the corner of the porcelain sink. She slumped onto the floor in a heap, holding her back.

Derrick stood over her with his hands on his hips. "When you come to your senses, you let me know."

As he turned and walked away, she said, "I already have, Derrick."

Regina sat on the floor until the throbbing in her back and neck subsided enough for her to move without gasping.

Moments later Sandy poked her head in the door. "Dr. Kingston? I saw Derrick leave. Are you...oh my God. What happened?" Sandy ran and knelt down beside Regina.

The resident shook her head and lifted her arm up. Sandy grabbed hold of her hand and pulled her into a hug. "Oh boy, you're in trouble here, kiddo. We need to call security."

"No, please don't. I thought if I told him no, he would leave me alone." Regina sniffed, wiping the tears from her eyes.

"I have to notify security, Dr. Kingston. It's hospital policy."

"But Derrick's a police officer, Sandy."

"I know, but he can't keep doing this to you." Sandy put her
hands on Regina's shoulders, steadying her.

Regina nodded her head. "I've got to go. I'm going to be
late for my appointment at the clinic."

Sandy walked Regina down the back hallway. "Go on. I can
fill out the forms and then we'll talk to security."

"Sandy—"

"No arguments," Sandy answered, holding up her hand.

❖ ⌘ ❖ ⌘ ❖ ⌘ ❖

Regina sat in the small waiting room of the clinic. The walls
were a putrid green that was fading and in desperate need of a
new paint job. Cold air blew out of the overhead vents and she
sank down in her chair folding her arms over her chest to warm
herself. Regina tilted her head back against the wall, taking shallow breaths; her back hurt where she struck the corner of the
sink.

Listening to the giggles coming from around the corner,
Regina picked her head up and saw two boys chasing each other
around the furniture.

"Mason, Thomas, stop running around and come sit by me,"
a tired-looking, middle-aged woman told them sternly. Both boys
slowed and looked at her before they gave up their game and
crawled up onto the chairs next to her. Studying the woman for a
moment, Regina noticed the shunt underneath the skin of her
forearm and realized that the woman suffered from kidney fail-
ure and was on dialysis.

Regina looked up as another woman picked up her child and
walked toward the desk when the nurse called her name. Closing
her eyes, Regina tried to make some sense of the jumble of
thoughts whirling in her head. "Dr. Kingston?"

Regina opened her eyes and looked up. "That's me."

"You can come with me. I'm going to put you in this room."
The small blonde clerk looked in the chart as she directed Regina
into an exam room. "Let me see...oh, you're getting some
stitches removed. Okay, just take your shirt off and put that
gown on."

Regina set her bag down on the plastic chair and unbuttoned

her shirt. She winced as she brought her arms behind her back to pull the sleeves from her arms. After slipping the gown on, she sat on the exam table. She was glad the stitches were coming out. They had been itching mercilessly the past three days. An image of Derrick towering over her in the locker room flooded her mind and her heart rate accelerated. She couldn't believe that this was happening to her. Thankfully, her parents were taking their annual vacation and wouldn't be back for another week. She couldn't bear to listen to them tell her how Derrick was a good man and that she should consider settling down with him. *If only they knew what he was really like.*

Regina picked her head up as she heard movement outside the door. A knock sounded and the handle turned, and the door pushed open a crack. She heard the woman from the waiting room ask a question, and the door pulled closed slightly.

A voice she recognized as Dr. Margulies' came through the door. "Just make sure you give Jeremy the inhaler treatments two times a day. The humidity will tend to make his asthma worse, so you don't want to miss any treatments." After a pause she heard the attending's voice again. "If there's a problem, just bring him back to the emergency room."

The door pushed open and Dr. Margulies entered the exam room. She wore sneakers, blue scrubs, and a lab coat.

"So, Dr. Kingston, how are you doing today?" Alex walked to the sink and washed her hands. She looked back over her shoulder at Regina. "Bet you're glad those stitches are coming out."

Regina nodded her head as the doctor pulled out two plastic packages from the drawer next to the sink. She swallowed, feeling her throat go a little dry. She hadn't expected that Dr. Margulies would be covering the clinic. Usually the residents did the follow-up visits with the patients.

The doctor pulled some gloves out of the box on the wall and slipped them onto her hands. One ripped. She pulled it off and looked at it quizzically.

"No wonder," she said, noting its size. She opened the cabinet above the sink and pulled out a box of large latex gloves, slipped on a pair and turned around. "So which do you want me to take out first, the ones on the back or the arm?"

Regina shrugged. "It doesn't matter."

"All right. Let's do your back first. Your arm is going to take a bit longer, and those stitches on your back won't feel very good on that hard table. Go ahead and lie on your stomach," the doctor directed, as she opened the package and set the tweezers and scissors on the sterile towel that covered the metal instrument tray.

Regina rolled onto her stomach and turned her head to stare at the wall. She felt the cool air on her skin as Dr. Margulies pulled her gown open. There was a moment of dead silence in the room. Regina turned her head around to look at the doctor, and noted the odd expression on her face.

Dr. Margulies looked up at Regina and took a breath. "That's a pretty nasty bruise you've got there." She ran a finger around the edges of the purplish discoloration on Regina's skin. When she pressed down gently, she heard a sharp intake of breath as Regina winced in pain.

"You're lucky this wasn't any higher or you might have broken a couple of ribs."

Regina lowered her eyes, unable to meet the doctor's steady gaze. "I fell." She heard the wheels of the stool squeak as Dr. Margulies sat down and positioned herself next to the exam table.

Regina felt the tape peeled away from her skin as Alex removed the gauze bandage. "You're going to feel a few tugs as I do this," the attending said.

Alex snipped away at the knot and gently removed the stitches with the tweezers. When she finished, she dabbed some antiseptic on the site.

"Sorry, that was a little cold," she noted, seeing Regina flinch.

"It's okay." Regina's voice was muffled, as she had tucked her head into the crook of her elbow. She closed her eyes when she felt the tugging again as the stitches were removed from her left shoulder blade.

"Okay. Now, the arm is probably going to be a little more uncomfortable; the flesh is more sensitive there." Dr. Margulies set the tweezers and scissors on the tray. "You can roll onto your back and let your arm rest here." Alex pulled out an armrest from the side of the table.

The resident closed her eyes as Alex started to unwrap the gauze bandage from around her arm. She knew that there would be a fresh bruise from Derrick's hand gripping her there. No mistaking the old yellowish green mark from the cuts that ran down the inside of her elbow from the imprint of his fingers. It was too sore for it not to be. She felt the cool air against her skin as the bandage was removed and heard the doctor shift her weight on the stool.

"Regina," Dr. Margulies' voice was low and gentle, "what happened today?"

She jerked her head up, startled. "How—" Regina stopped, as the doctor just sat there, holding the rolled-up gauze in both hands.

"Those bruises on your back are fresh. Probably less than two hours old, I would guess."

Regina nodded her head in acknowledgement, trying not to cry. *God, don't be such a baby*, she told herself, but the tears ran down her cheeks anyway.

Dr. Margulies watched in silence, debating with herself. "Was it him again?"

Regina nodded and wiped her eyes. "Sorry. I didn't mean to get upset. I just...I told him I didn't want to see him anymore. He showed up today and..." Her voice trailed off, suddenly feeling very tired and overwhelmed.

The doctor's eyes widened in shock. "Here?"

Regina nodded her head.

"That's it. I'm calling security." Dr. Margulies stood up to walk to the wall phone, but Regina stopped her.

"Sandy already called them. I'm going to file a report after I'm done here."

Dr. Margulies turned around, nodding. "First things first. Let's get these stitches out and then we'll talk."

*Yeah, right, Alex. What am I going to say that will make a difference?*

Alex finished removing the stitches and placed a couple of butterfly strips over the areas that weren't completely closed yet. She held her hand out and helped Regina sit up. "Go ahead and get dressed. When you're done, my office is down the hall on the left. We can talk there."

Dr. Margulies washed her hands and walked into the small office. After sitting down behind the desk, she finished making some notes in the chart. She ticked through, in her head, some of the options available to Regina, sighed, and looked up as the resident appeared at her door.

"Sit down." Alex pushed her chair back to give Regina some room to sit in the chair next to her desk. She signed the note discharging Regina from her medical care, then looked up at the blonde woman and considered what to say. "Have you thought about what you want to do?"

Regina looked down at her shoes and fidgeted in her chair. "I don't know. He's a police officer. He's got a lot of connections at the courthouse."

Dr. Margulies leaned across the desk. "Regina, he doesn't have any right to do what he's done to you, no matter who he is."

Regina looked up and met clear blue eyes. "I know."

The tall dark-haired doctor leaned back in her chair, her brow creased in concentration. "Listen, Sandy's right. You should get a restraining order against him."

Regina gripped the armrest of the chair. "I'm afraid it's just going to make him angrier."

"It's better than nothing. Legally, it will give you some rights," Dr. Margulies said. "At least think about it."

❖ ⌘ ❖ ⌘ ❖ ⌘ ❖

Two days had passed since Derrick confronted Regina in the locker room. Holding the black jewelry box in her hand, she stood in front of her locker and pondered how she would give it back to him. She was sure she didn't want the ring. It had been bought for all the wrong reasons and the sooner she gave it back to him, the better. Until then it was just a bitter reminder of his need to control and manipulate her. She set the box inside, shut the door and walked down to the security office to file her complaint against Derrick.

Regina met Marcus as she walked out of the security office after completing the report. It took her those two days to get the courage together to do this. It ended up being a rather unsettling experience as the older security officer questioned her extensively. By the time Regina was finished, she felt that she was the one who had done something wrong, not Derrick.

"What were you doing in security?" Marcus asked, sensing that something was wrong from the distressed look on Regina's face.

"Uh, I can't find my car keys. I think I dropped them outside somewhere," Regina said.

Marcus took the statement at face value and left it at that.

Walking through the busy hallway by the hospital's main entrance, they heard a hospital code for a patient emergency announced over the intercom system. Seconds later their pagers beeped and the ER's stat page was visible on both their displays. Marcus cursed under his breath.

"God, she never leaves us alone," he complained.

Regina cast a wary glance at her colleague. Marcus was growing more vocal about the fact that he didn't like the emergency medicine rotation and disliked Dr. Margulies even more.

"Marcus, why did you pick this for a specialty rotation if you hate it so much?" Regina asked, as they ran up the stairs to the first floor.

He didn't get a chance to answer her as they entered the emergency department. Regina squeezed past a patient slouched in a wheelchair. One of the medical students was taking a history and she cringed at the hesitation in his voice. She looked at Marcus.

"God, were we that bad when we were medical students?"

He gave her a blank look; totally unaware of what she was talking about. "What?"

Regina waved her hand. "Never mind."

Sandy practically ran into them as she came out of the supply room, carrying a set of restraints.

"Good, you're both here. We've got a guy in trauma three who's pumped so high on cocaine he already broke one set of restraints," the nurse said, her eyes pleading for help.

"That's why you paged us? Isn't that security's job?" Marcus asked, obviously annoyed as he and Regina quickly pulled on their masks, gowns, and gloves.

Sandy ignored his comment, pushed the door to the trauma room open, and immediately ducked as a tray loaded with instruments sailed across the room and crashed against the wall.

Several curses followed and then Regina heard Dr. Margulies' voice. "Sandy, I hope those restraints you've got in your hands are leather." She was struggling to pin the wild-eyed man's arm down to the stretcher. One of the other nurses was fighting to keep his other arm pinned down to his side.

"Sorry. I brought a double set to tie him down with." Sandy warily approached the large, drug-crazed man.

"Hear you have a party going on down here, Dr. Margulies." Marcus stepped over the scattered instruments and looked distastefully around the chaotic room. One curtain hung by only a few hooks and the rod holding it to the ceiling swung precariously overhead.

"Are you here to give commentary or to help, Dr. Jack?"

Alex growled through clenched teeth as she finally pinned the patient's arm to his side.

One of the ER techs kicked the tray and scattered instruments out of the way. "Tommy, forget about that stuff," one of the other nurses in the room said. "Help me hold is arm down so I can tie it."

Regina walked up to the end of the stretcher and took a restraint from Sandy. She carefully slipped it around the man's ankle cinched the loop tight, and tied a knot around the rail of the stretcher.

"Sandy, come up here and let's try these damn restraints again. Where the hell is security anyway?" Alex ducked as the nurse on the other side of the stretcher lost control of the patient's arm and his fist sailed across, aimed at her head. "Damn it, Thomas, help Maggie hold that arm before someone gets hurt."

"They're on their way," Sandy said, as she struggled to wrap the restraint around the man's wrist. He cursed all the while as he writhed and bucked against the arms holding him down.

Marcus tied the other arm down to the bed and stepped back. "You need a line in him?"

Alex looked up at him. "That would be our usual protocol, Marcus. Make sure that restraint is secure before you stick him."

Regina stepped up beside Marcus. "Can I help with anything?"

"Help Dr. Jack put a line in this guy's arm," Alex said.

"I can get a line in without any help," Marcus snapped, as he opened the package containing the needle for the IV.

"I know you can, Dr. Jack, but you need someone to immobilize his arm, unless, of course, you can do both at once," Dr. Margulies said.

Regina grasped the man's beefy forearm as Marcus jabbed the needle in. The man grimaced and his fist clenched as Marcus searched for the vessel.

"Marcus, wait," Regina said, pulling the strap of the restraint down, trying to tighten the knot that was quickly working its way loose from the man's violent struggling.

The patient on the stretcher grunted and convulsed violently, ripping his arm out of the restraint and striking Marcus. It happened so fast that Regina hardly had time to think. On instinct, she lunged for his flailing arm as Marcus unsuccessfully tried to keep the needle in place.

Regina felt the sharp sting of the needle plunging into her forearm. Yelping in surprise, she yanked her arm back.

Everything seemed to slow down around her as Regina stepped back from the table and stared at the needle imbedded in her arm. She saw that the clear tubing was filled with blood from the patient's artery. Her heart raced and she backed up to the sink. Around her she could hear shouts and loud noises but they seemed far away now. She pulled the needle out of her arm and looked at the blood welling to the surface of the puncture site.

Marcus blinked at her as he retied the restraint. Regina could see his mouth form the words "oh shit," and she knew she was in trouble. Very slowly, she turned around to the sink and vigorously washed the small puncture site. She felt the contact of a warm hand on her shoulder and she looked up to see Dr. Margulies standing next to her, a worried expression on her face. "Let me see."

Regina turned her arm over. Strong hands gripped her forearm and squeezed hard around the site.

"Youch!" She wrenched her arm away and glared at the dark-haired woman.

"You need to make it bleed first," Dr. Margulies explained, staring hard at her.

"You could have warned me," Regina retorted, rubbing the reddened skin on her forearm gingerly.

Dr. Margulies turned away from Regina and held her hand out. "Sandy, give me his chart. Hurry up." She flipped through the record and muttered to herself angrily.

"What's wrong?" Regina asked, acutely aware of the sound of her own blood racing through her ears.

Dr. Margulies turned the chart around and pointed to some scribbled notes on the white history form. Regina read the words, comprehension dawning slowly along with a sinking feeling in her gut. The letters *HIV+* stared back at her. She swallowed, and then looked up at the doctor. "Oh no." Her mouth went dry and a chill ran up her spine.

"Come on, we need to start the post-exposure treatment." Alex put a hand on her back and started to guide her from the room.

"W-wait." Regina turned around, holding her hands out in front of her. "This is a high-risk exposure right?" She tried hard to control her voice.

Dr. Margulies' hand fell to her side. "Yes...it is." She

looked back at Marcus who stood helplessly by the stretcher. "Dr. Jack, you can finish in here. Make sure his restraints are secure before you try again." Marcus' face turned crimson at the remark. "Sandy, page Dr. Washington and get him up here now. When the IV line is in the patient, give him .5 milligrams of Narcan to sedate him."

Sandy nodded, and quickly tied off the last restraint. "Thomas, get the leads on him now so we can hook him up to the monitor. Maggie," she said, turning to her colleague, "get the IV in him, and Marcus, you hold his arm this time."

The remaining team continued doing what they needed to as Dr. Margulies led Regina from the room. Walking down the crowded corridor, Alex held her hand up stopping one of the nurses coming at her with a chart. "Get Dr. Alfonso. He can handle it." She pushed open a door to a darkened exam room, flicked the light on and held the door open, ushering Regina inside. Alex rummaged through one of the file cabinets and pulled out a couple of forms that she handed to Regina. "You need to read this and sign it. It's the consent form for treatment."

Regina took the papers and stared at them blankly.

"I'll be right back." Alex left Regina alone in an empty exam room, while she disappeared to procure the supplies that she needed.

Regina sat quietly reading the two papers. Her mind raced and her heart pounded so hard that she thought it was going to jump out of her chest.

She tried not to think about the blood inside the tubing, or how long the needle had been in her arm, releasing the infected fluid into her body. She knew the virus' unalterable course all too well. There was no grace period if she was infected. Mononucleosis-like symptoms would develop between six days to six weeks after infection and in three weeks the HIV antibodies would be detectable in her blood stream.

Regina shook her head. *Of all the stupid things to have happen...a bloody needle stick,* she thought. She picked up the pen, and held it in her hand as she read the last few lines. Her hand trembled and it took all her concentrated effort to sign her name legibly on the line at the bottom of the page.

The door opened and Regina looked up as Dr. Margulies walked in. Alex carried several empty vials for blood. Sitting down in front of Regina, she set the vials on the tray next to her. They rolled back and forth making a gentle clatter of glass on metal. Alex pulled a length of rubber tubing from her lab coat pocket and held it in both hands.

"We're going to run a complete blood count with differential, urinalysis, and chemical profile with liver function tests," Alex said, rattling off the list of standard blood tests used for blood exposures.

The door to the room opened and an ER tech walked in, oblivious to Alex and Regina sitting in the back of the room. Alex pivoted in her chair. "Hey, do you always just barge into a room like that?"

The young woman stopped in her tracks and stared at Alex. "I-I just needed to get a central line kit."

"Next time knock first," Alex snapped. The woman stood awkwardly unsure of whether she should leave or not. Alex tilted her head. "Hurry up and get what you need and get out, now."

The woman quickly retrieved the kit she was looking for and made a hasty retreat from the room.

Regina held her arm out, flinching a little as Alex slipped the rubber tubing around her biceps cinching it tightly. She flexed her hand several times and waited as Alex uncapped the syringe and felt for an artery with skilled fingers. Her eyes flicked up to the doctor's, meeting briefly, and darted back to her arm.

"Not bad for a doctor," Regina said, after the needle penetrated her skin and dark red blood ran freely into the tube.

Alex looked up in surprise. "Did I hurt you?"

"No, no," Regina said, laughing softly, trying to break some of the tension she felt inside. "Just an inside joke among the nurses. They all think we do a terrible job of drawing blood."

Regina watched the blood fill the tube then turned her face away as another thought made her catch her breath. "The lab in the hospital is going to run the tests right?"

Alex looked up as she pulled the vial off and replaced it with another one. After undoing the band, she removed it from Regina's arm. "Yeah, they do." Seeing Regina's worried look, Alex took a stab at what was bothering her. "If you want, I can run the tests myself, that way no one else has to know."

"Would you?" Regina asked, her eyes brightening. "I mean, it's not that I don't trust them. It's just that...well, you know how some things don't stay confidential even when they're supposed to." Her shoulders hunched slightly as if a weight was settling on her again.

Alex nodded her head, knowing all too well how rumors, false or not, got started and traveled like wildfire through the large medical center. "I'll take care of it. Don't worry."

"Thanks. That makes me feel a lot better," Regina said.

Alex blinked and scribbled some notes on the form in front of her. She took a breath and set her pen on the table. "Do we need to do a pregnancy test?" Alex asked quietly. She felt awkward asking the question but it was necessary.

Regina jumped at the question. "Pregnancy? No, no, I'm not pregnant."

Alex nodded and looked away. "The medication has some strong side effects. Just wanted to make sure."

Regina nodded and ran a hand through her hair. "So, what am I going to be taking?" Her voice trembled slightly as her emotions threatened to overwhelm her.

"Zidovudine and Lamivudine. They're more effective if you take them in combination," Alex explained.

"What are the chances...?" Regina's voice trailed off.

"About one in three hundred," Alex said, and then quickly added, "The research says the medicine lowers the risk by eighty percent." She stood up and walked to the door. "We'll test your blood in six weeks, then again in three and six months."

Regina looked up and took a shaky breath. "So if I make it to six months I'll be free and clear?"

Alex looked down at the floor. "Hopefully."

Regina nodded her head slowly, a faint smile lighting her face. "Then I'll chill a bottle of champagne, just in case."

Alex straightened her shoulders and looked at Regina. "You do that." She managed a small smile and walked out. She headed to the desk that ran the length of the nursing station, reached over the counter, and pulled out the labels she needed for the vials of blood. She wrote down the information and looked up, as Sandy walked over to her.

"How is she?" the nurse asked.

Alex shrugged her shoulders. "Pretty shaken up." She stared down at her hands. "Damn, I shouldn't have let Marcus put that line in. He's got such a damn cocky streak in him. Thinks he knows everything."

"Alex, don't blame yourself. That could have happened to anybody. That guy was out of his mind on drugs. It was a freak accident." Sandy sighed. "I wouldn't be surprised if that girl walked out of here today and never looked back."

Alex snapped her head around, a look of shock and worry on her face. "She seems a lot tougher than that, Sandy."

"We'll see. She wouldn't be the first resident who ditched out. Lord knows others have run from less than what she's been dealing with," Sandy said.

Alex realized that Sandy was also referring to Regina's ongoing problems with her boyfriend. The thought of him hurting Regina again made Alex think of several very painful things that she could do to him. "Let that jerk come in here again and I'll make him wish he'd never met her."

Sandy raised an eyebrow. "Since when do you care so much about your residents' personal lives?"

"I don't," Alex answered quickly. "She's a nice kid and she deserves better that that." Alex picked up the vials of blood and slipped them gently into her lab coat pocket. "If anybody's looking for me, I'll be in the lab."

Sandy stood at the desk with a thoughtful expression on her face as Alex walked away. "You say you don't care, Alex. We'll see."

❖ ⌘ ❖ ⌘ ❖ ⌘ ❖

After she left the emergency room, Regina walked numbly up the back stairwell listening to her footsteps echo on the metal stairs. *God, what a wretched day,* she thought.

She walked onto the pediatric unit to check on a little boy that they admitted the day before. After reading his chart she just leaned back in her chair and closed her eyes, trying to fight back the tears. *Damn, why did this have to happen?* It was like some cruel joke being played on her.

Thinking back, she hadn't realized how much Derrick had been manipulating her all along. That was until he proposed to her. A marriage proposal, of all the stupid things. She shook her head in disgust as she recalled him digging in his pocket for the box. She was glad she walked away before she got caught in a worse situation. Regina suspected that Derrick was capable of much worse than what he had already done. She never expected him to get so angry, thought that he would give up and walk away, but his male ego prevented such a gesture of defeat.

So, she had six months of waiting, praying to God that she didn't develop the antibodies for HIV. What the hell was she going to do if she did? Would they still let her treat patients?

How could she even tell her family? The thought struck Regina
as ironic and she stifled a harsh laugh as she pictured herself
telling her mother she was HIV positive. *Gee, Mom, you were
always so terrified your son would bring home the dreaded disease and disgrace you even more.*

"Dr. Kingston?" A voice called out behind her, by the tone
of it she could tell she hadn't heard it the first time.

Pushing her morose thoughts aside, she swiveled her chair
around and looked at the nurse. "Yes?"

"The kid you admitted yesterday is in room nine. I can't get
him to calm down. He's been crying and calling for his mother
for an hour now." By the tone of the nurse's voice Regina could
tell that she was at the end of her rope and looking for someone
to bail her out.

Regina frowned. "Have you called his mother to come in?"

The nurse folded her arms and her face darkened. "I would
but we don't know where she is. She hasn't been back and her
phone is disconnected."

"Oh." Regina stood up and walked toward the nurse. "Let
me take a look at him."

"Actually, I wanted to know if we could give him something
to calm him down."

Regina looked at her as she stepped around the corner of the
desk, carefully avoiding a young girl walking down the hallway,
dragging an IV pole behind her.

"Page his primary doctor. I can't change his medication. I'm
not on his case anymore. You know that."

"I can't get a hold of him," the nurse said.

Regina walked down the carpeted hallway and into the
cramped room, painted in a light blue color with a border of animal caricatures running around the top of the wall. Standing in
the metal crib with the rails pulled up around him like he was in
jail, was a light-skinned, curly towhead with baby blue eyes.
Both of his legs were wrapped in bulky bandages from his hips
down to his feet. His voice was hoarse and he was wheezing as
he sobbed and hopped back and forth.

"Momma!" The air whistled through his irritated throat.
"Momma!" He wailed and rattled the bars with his chubby hands.

The nurse walked to the crib and looked at him sternly.
"Justin, you have to calm down, sweetheart. You're going to hurt
yourself."

Regina pulled a pair of gloves onto her hands and walked up

to the crib. She lowered the rail down and stepped close to the distraught child, holding her arms out to him. "What's wrong, Justin?"

He teetered on his feet and then crashed into her, wrapping his arms tightly around her neck. "Momma! I want my momma!" he cried and hiccuped into her shoulder.

Regina felt the heat coming off his fever-wracked body and wrapped her arms around him, cradling him against her chest. "I'm sorry, love." Regina stroked his back, walked over to the rocking chair, and sat down. "Momma's not here, Justin. We have to try and find her for you. Okay?"

The blonde head pulled back, wise blue eyes regarding her for a moment, and Regina felt the odd sensation that the toddler she held in her arms had experienced more hardship in the few, tender years he had been alive than most children did all their lives. Justin scrunched down against her and tucked his head under her chin. His wailing slowly stopped and his sobbing subsided to a muffled whimpering.

Regina looked up at the nurse who stared at her. "Has social work called the Division of Youth and Family Service yet?" The nurse nodded her head and slipped quietly from the room, relieved that the kid was no longer screaming.

Regina tilted her head back against the chair and rocked gently. She looked down at the blonde curls resting against her chest and smiled sadly. "Oh, Justin, I think I need this as badly as you do." He snuggled closer and stuck his thumb in his mouth, clutching her around her neck with his other hand. Regina lowered her cheek to his head and let the tears roll down her face unchecked.

After Justin cried himself to sleep, Regina stood up from the rocking chair and carried him back to his crib. She bent over, unwrapping his arms from around her neck, and laid him gently onto his back. "You'll be okay, Justin," she whispered, and pressed her lips against his forehead. Justin squirmed and opened his eyes. His two chubby little hands reached up and held her cheeks.

"Flutterby kiss." He lifted his head and blew a kiss at her. She ran her hand over his curly hair and smiled sadly at him, then slid the side rail back up into place and walked out of the room.

# Chapter
# 4

After slamming the book shut, Regina jumped from her chair and walked hurriedly out of the medical library. Outside in the quiet corridor, she slipped into the staff bathroom. She vomited for the fifth day in a row since she started taking the medication over a week ago. Leaning back against the door of the stall, she waited for the wave of nausea to pass, wiping a trembling hand over her sweaty brow. She moaned softly. "Oh, I need to get something to control this better."

So far she was able to get by without anyone noticing her sudden disappearances, but she knew sooner or later that someone would catch on and then she would have to deal with the questions that would undoubtedly follow. She leaned on the sink, ran the water until it was icy cold, and cupped her hand under the stream. She splashed the water on her face, and rubbed the back of her neck with it as well. Feeling her beeper vibrating against her waist, she cursed softly under her breath.

"Dammit." Regina looked down at the display and read the ER's number. Fumbling with the button, she stopped the irritating sensation.

"Okay, okay. I'll be there," she muttered. "Just need a couple of minutes." She leaned against the cool tile and closed her eyes against the dizziness threatening her.

Downstairs in the crowded and noisy emergency department, Alex examined and triaged another patient. "When did the pain start, Sally?" Alex leaned over the rails of the gurney and pressed her fingertips into the right lower quadrant of the thirteen-year-old's abdomen.

The girl winced and curled up into a tight ball on her side. "After I ate lunch."

"That was, what, about two hours ago?" she asked, looking at the mother.

The woman nodded.

"I'm going to order some tests and keep her here to observe her for a little bit," Alex said.

"Do you think it's appendicitis?" the woman asked.

"It could be, but I don't want to assume she's a surgical candidate until I have the test results back." The attending started to leave the room when one of the surgeons poked his head in.

"Heard you've got an appy here, Dr. Margulies. I can bring her up to the OR and take it out now."

She turned around and glared at him. "I'm not finished running the tests so I'm not sure it *is* appendicitis."

"Oh, come on now." Stepping up beside the rails of the stretcher, he looked down at the sick girl. "I'm going to press on your stomach." His large hands pressed down into her tender abdomen. "Does this hurt?"

The girl cried out as he let go. "See. Classic rebound," he exclaimed. He looked down at the girl. "Do you think you could eat some apple pie?"

Alex pursed her lips and prudently stepped back. She heard the sounds of retching as the girl vomited into the emesis basin lying at her side, splattering the surgeon's sneakers.

"I'll book the OR," he said, looking down at his sneakers in disgust.

"You certainly will not." Alex grasped his elbow and led him out of the room. "You've got to be kidding me." She gestured angrily with her arms. "What kind of half-baked diagnostic test is that?" Several pairs of eyes looked up from the behind the desk in the emergency department. "You are not taking that child to the OR unless I say so." Alex leaned forward, her eyes narrowing as she stared down at the smaller, slightly bald-headed surgeon.

He shrugged his shoulders. "Have it your way. I'll be here another hour. You'll be calling me."

Alex shook her head in disgust and walked over to the desk. "Sandy, I need you to draw blood on the girl in room six. The orders are in the chart. Have the lab run a CBC with differential and a chem pro plus stat."

"Sure," the blonde nurse said, and winked conspiratorially at her. "He's an arrogant one, isn't he?"

"I can't believe he asked her if she wanted to eat apple pie. What an idiot." She looked at her watch and thumped her arm down on the desk in irritation. "Did Dr. Kingston return my page yet?"

The unit clerk looked up from the computer and shook her head. "No, I haven't heard from her yet. I'm sure she'll be down soon."

"I don't need her now. I needed her thirty minutes ago."

The phone rang and the unit clerk turned away as she answered it. "I told you I was working all weekend. We need the money."

Alex glanced down at the unit clerk and then looked at Sandy. "Would you like to tell her boyfriend to stop calling or shall I?" Alex smirked evilly at Sandy.

"No...no, Alex." Sandy strategically pulled the phone out of Alex's reach. "I'll take care of it." She waved her quickly away, knowing that if she let Alex intervene she would probably be short a unit clerk after today.

Marcus walked over to the desk and stood beside Alex. "Dr. Margulies?"

Alex looked at the resident. "What is it you want, Marcus?"

"Can you look at a patient for me?"

"Where's Dr. Alfonso? Isn't he supervising you today?"

"Yes, but he's with a trauma patient in two. He told me to come find you."

Alex took the chart from him and flipped it open. "Fine, let's go," she said, and walked down the hallway.

"Dr. Margulies," Marcus said, hesitantly as they reached the room, "I'm really sorry about what happened to Regina last week."

Alex stopped, her hand about to push the door open to the exam room. "It's not me you should be apologizing to, Marcus," she said, fixing him with an icy stare. After a moment of awkward silence Alex stepped back and folded her arms over her chest. "So, tell me about this patient before we go in there."

Alex left Marcus with his patient after a brief discussion about the woman's recent hospitalization, and the possibility that she might have a blood clot that needed to be ruled out immediately with a Doppler study. She wasn't the least bit pleased that he had needed as much guidance as he required and was beginning to wonder if he would be better off on a less demanding rotation.

Walking back down the hallway, she headed into her patient's room. Leaning over the stretcher, Alex checked the IV and felt the girl's pulse. "How do you feel, Sally?" she asked, looking at the girl lying huddled under the blankets.

"A little better since I got sick."

Alex glanced at the father who watched her with his arms crossed tightly in front of him. "Her fever's down. The blood tests will give us a better picture of what's going on clinically. We're going to observe her and see how she responds to the IV fluids. With the upper respiratory infection she had, it's quite possible that she has an inflammation of the lining around the intestines."

The man blinked and shifted his weight on his feet. "But it could be appendicitis?"

Alex nodded her head. "With her symptoms, it's a remote possibility, but I'd rather not have her undergo surgery unless we're absolutely sure about it." Alex turned to leave the room. "The nurse will be in to check on her every hour. We'll know if there are any changes that should be of concern."

After settling down behind a desk, Alex wrote some notes in the girl's chart. Deciding she needed a cup of coffee to keep her awake, she stood up and walked to the staff lounge. On her way there, she ran straight into Dr. Kingston. Backing up a step, Alex folded her arms, blocking the shorter woman's path.

"You didn't answer my page," Alex accused her, staring down angrily at the resident. She was surprised and more than a little disappointed with her. Regina was one of her better residents and it was unusual for her not to be on top of things.

"I, uh, I'm sorry. I got down here as soon as I could," Regina said, as her face flushed in embarrassment.

"That's not good enough, Dr. Kingston. When I page you, I expect that you'll at least return the call and let me know that you're on you way. Even my first-year residents know *that*."

"It-It won't happen again," Regina stammered, feeling completely inadequate at the moment.

"I don't expect that it will."

A movement caught her attention. Alex cursed under her breath, and brushed past Regina. "Hey. Where are you taking this patient?" she demanded, stepping in front of the orderly and taking hold of the stretcher.

"The OR," he said, as if this were common knowledge. "She's scheduled for surgery." He handed her the slip of paper.

After reading it, Alex crumbled the paper in her hand and threw it back at him. "Like hell she is." Her voice rose above the normal din in the emergency department. "Sandy, did those blood tests get back yet?"

"They just came in," the nurse called back to her, as she deftly avoided the man from housekeeping, who was mopping the floor around the desk.

"Let me see them." Alex snatched the lab report from Sandy, and read the lab values then picked up the phone. "Operator, page Dr. Kelly to the ER stat." She slammed the phone back down into its cradle.

"Problem?" Regina approached Dr. Margulies and looked up into the doctor's face.

"Yeah, I've got one of the surgeons poaching patients for the OR. This kid doesn't have appendicitis." Alex turned around as she heard the ER doors bang open. Dressed in blue gray surgical scrubs and an isolation gown thrown carelessly over his shoulder, the surgeon stomped down the hallway headed in her direction. "This better be good, Margulies. You pulled me out of scrubbing up for this case."

Alex bristled. "Dr. Kelly, there is no case," she said, crossing her arms and stepping in front of him. "What did you do? Sell the parents on the idea of removing the appendix to be on the safe side, and downplay the risks of anesthesia? You're trying to steal this patient as a surgical case so you can pad your numbers."

Dr. Margulies stepped closer to the surgeon, pointing a finger at his chest. "She's my patient and she needs to be observed first, not cut open. There's no fever now and her white blood cell count is normal. She had an upper respiratory infection last week and you know damn well the intestines could be inflamed from that."

"Fine, you do that and I'll speak to your medical director in the morning. You're on thin ice here, Margulies, remember that," the surgeon said, as he turned and stormed away.

"Dr. Margulies, he could be right." Regina's voice was quiet.

Alex turned around, glaring contemptuously at the young

doctor. "Dr. Kingston, I don't recall asking for your opinion."

Regina took a step back and turned away. Alex's words had been sharp and cut her deeply. She had only meant to diffuse things and ended up making them worse.

Regina picked up her stack of charts and walked toward one of the vacant triage rooms at the back end of the emergency department. She caught several people casting sympathetic glances her way and she was thankful when the door to the room closed behind her. Slumping into a chair, Regina pulled a pen out of her lab coat pocket. She stared at the wall, twirling the pen back and forth between her fingers. *Way to go, Regina. You really messed that one up.*

Shaking her head, she pulled her chair up to the desk and opened the first chart. Putting her pen to the paper, she started to write, then stopped. Regina felt like she let Dr. Margulies down, but she would be damned if she was going to be yelled at in front of the entire department. She rested her chin on her fist, and started to write.

It was several hours later before Regina was able to crawl out from underneath the mountain of paperwork she needed to complete. Most of it was filling out forms for the insurance companies and Medicare. It was amazing that, with all the forms and questions that needed to be answered, patients got treated at all.

After shuffling the papers together into an organized pile, she stacked them on top of the charts and carried them to the nurse's station. Her attention was drawn to an angry voice behind her.

"Marcus," Alex said, as she bore down on the resident from across the department.

Several staff at the nurse's station scattered out of the way, wanting plenty of distance between them and the angry doctor. The resident looked up and recoiled physically as the tall imposing doctor descended upon him in all her fury.

"Y-yes, Dr. Margulies?" he asked, trying unsuccessfully to sound confident.

Alex slammed the chart onto the desk and leaned over him, pinning him to the chair with her eyes. "Would you care to tell me about the patient in room four?"

Marcus reached for the chart to look at it, but Alex placed her hand down on the cover. "Ah, ah. Without the chart, Marcus."

He swallowed and looked down at his hands, which trembled slightly. "He's a forty-seven-year-old male. He complains of abdominal pain starting two days ago. No allergies, no recent illnesses or surgeries. I'm waiting for his lab results to come back."

Alex picked the chart up, flipped it open, and set it down in front of Marcus. "Very good, Marcus. I now know that you can copy the nurse's intake," she said, pointing to the nursing flow sheet. "Did *you* ask this patient any other questions, or did you just assume the nurses would get it all for you?" Her voice rose higher with each word until she was shouting. Patients and staff alike averted their attention, embarrassed by the angry outburst.

"I, uh, I—" he stammered.

"Enough! I want to see every single one of your history and physicals you write up before you put it in a chart." She turned to walk away, but stopped. "Oh, and Marcus, his medical history included illicit drug use *and* he's been diagnosed with hepatitis C. Next time ask the damn questions yourself."

Alex stormed back toward the desk, stopping as Sandy held the phone up and pointed to her.

"Who is it?" Alex asked, obviously annoyed at the call.

Sandy mouthed a name to her and Alex rolled her eyes in disgust.

"I'll take it in the staff lounge."

Regina listened to the heated exchange while she looked over two sets of lab results. She wrote an order in a chart for a broad-spectrum antibiotic, and handed it to the unit clerk to enter into the computer. Taking a deep breath, she walked over to where Marcus was sitting.

Slumped forward over the desk, with his hands covering his face, Marcus shook his head and groaned audibly. Regina pulled a chair over and sat down beside the dejected-looking resident.

"Marcus, are you all right?" she asked. Her voice was quiet and gentle.

"Oh yeah, just great. Let me know if you find the other half of my ass that she just chewed off."

Regina stifled a snicker and leaned back to look for the missing part. "I think everything is still intact, Marcus."

He shook his head and chuckled at Regina's joke. "How do you deal with her, Regina? I mean, do you really like what you're doing here?"

Regina sat up straighter and frowned at the question. "Well, yeah, I do, Marcus. Don't you?"

He took off his glasses and rubbed his eyes. "I used to think I did."

"What happened?" Regina rested her elbow on the desk and leaned forward.

"I'm tired of being responsible for people. I mean, I like to help them, but, I don't know, maybe I'm just burned out right now. It doesn't help having to deal with the likes of that bitch. I know I messed up in there. Its just, damn it, I can't keep up with all this paperwork. She didn't have to take me down in front of the whole department. That's not right." Marcus put his glasses back on.

Regina squeezed his forearm in sympathy. "You're a good doctor, Marcus. Don't let her get to you. Shit, we all make mistakes."

"Yeah, I guess you're right. Regina?" Marcus touched her arm as she stood up to leave.

"Yes?" She turned back to him.

"I'm really sorry about what happened last week. I should have listened to you before I stuck the guy."

Regina looked down at the floor and nodded her head. It was all the acknowledgement she could give him without becoming angry, and right now she really didn't want to think about it. It was better to keep the whole incident tucked neatly away in the back of her mind.

She walked purposely over to the desk and stood next to Sandy. "Uh oh, I know that look, Dr. Kingston. What's on your mind?" Sandy asked, while she printed out some discharge instructions for a couple of patients.

"Where's Dr. Margulies?"

"In the staff lounge, taking a phone call." Sandy looked up at Regina. "You okay?"

"I'm fine," the young doctor answered. "Marcus isn't."

Sandy nodded her acknowledgment of this. "Be careful, Dr. Kingston, she's not in a good mood."

"Neither am I," Regina replied, much to Sandy's surprise.

Sandy raised an eyebrow and shook her head. Either the girl had a set of brass ones or she was crazy.

❖ ⌘ ❖ ⌘ ❖ ⌘ ❖

"When are you coming up here, Alex? You have to settle Lana's affairs and you have power of attorney for her bank account," Dana complained from the other end of the telephone line.

Alex was leaning against the wall, arms crossed over her chest, with the phone cradled between a shoulder and an ear. "Dana, you know I'm coming up there in two weeks. What's wrong? Are you running short on funds?"

"Very funny, Alex. Maybe you should be a comedian instead of a doctor," Dana retorted as she filed a nail with an emery board.

Dana looked up as a solidly built woman with short-cropped, gel-spiked, bleached-blonde hair walked through the door of her store. She wore several studs in one ear and a labrys hanging from the other. She was dressed in tight, faded, blue jeans and a white T-shirt. The woman flipped through several of the prints that were stacked on the floor and then turned her attention to the wall. Dana kept an eye on the woman. She didn't look like she was interested in art.

"You know, you're not the only one who loved her, Alex. Remember, you took her away from me—or have you conveniently forgotten that part of the story?"

"It was her choice to leave, Dana. I didn't force her into anything," Alex said. She turned her back to the door as it started to open.

"Well, we all know how charming you can be when you decide you want something. Don't we, Alex?" Dana's attention drifted back to the woman, who'd walked to the back of the store. She was looking at the incense and candles that Dana kept on a shelf above the stereo system. The woman picked up a nearby book of matches and lit the candle at the right of the display.

Dana smiled to herself and walked over. She had a unique system for doing business. Four different colored candles stood on the shelf, each representing a specific drug: marijuana, heroin, cocaine, and ecstasy.

Dana walked past the woman and stepped through the curtained-off hallway that led downstairs to the cellar. The phone connection filled with static as she walked down the wooden steps. "Alex, I want to be there when you close out her bank account."

Dana winced as the quiet cellar erupted in a cacophony of yelps and barks as three German Shepherd puppies awoke at once and circled around each other, begging for attention.

"Shut up," Dana growled, banging the crates with the key ring she carried as she passed them.

"I can't understand you, Dana." Alex adjusted the phone. "Damn it, Dana. Are you listening to me?"

"Sorry, love, bad connection," Dana said, enjoying the fact that she was really pissing Alex off. "Give me a second and I'll be back upstairs." Dana unlocked the cabinet, pulled out a small plastic bag of cocaine, and put it into a brown paper bag. She relocked the storage cabinet and walked back up the stairs.

Alex leaned her head against the wall and closed her eyes. She should have guessed that Dana was still selling drugs despite her insistence otherwise. "How can you still do that, Dana? That store was Lana's life."

Dana slipped through the curtain and took the fifty-dollar bill from the woman and handed her the bag. "Nice doing business with you," she said. "Don't get righteous with me, Alex. Lana gave up any claim on this place the day she walked out on me. She left me to rot in jail. A dubious distinction you should have shared with me, Alex. You never paid for what you did. No, dear Alex has never had to pay for anything she's done."

"This conversation is over, Dana. I'll be up there in two weeks. Don't call me at the hospital anymore. Goodbye." Alex hung the phone up. "Do you always listen to other people's conversations?" she asked the person standing behind her as she turned around. She was surprised to see Regina there, but tried not to show it.

Regina stood at the counter with her arms crossed. "Not as a rule. Can I talk with you for a minute?"

"You're here, talk," Alex said, still feeling anger and resentment at Dana's phone call. *Damn her, she knows just what buttons to push with me.*

Regina unfolded her arms and walked to the table, putting her hands on the back of the chair and leaning into it. "I know I was wrong not getting down here right away when you paged me."

"You're right about that, Dr. Kingston. You were." Alex fixed her cool gaze on the blonde.

Regina took a breath and launched in. "What I don't agree with is the way you chose to tell me about it. I don't appreciate being yelled at in the middle of the department and in front of the other staff." She took a breath, as Alex's pupils dilated and her nostrils flared.

Knowing she just pissed the doctor off, Regina decided to go for broke. She'd be damned if she was going to let this woman walk all over her for the next four months.

"It sure as hell doesn't help anyone's confidence knowing that if you make a mistake, retribution is quick and public."

"Is that all, Dr. Kingston?"

"No. Marcus didn't deserve to have his legs taken off at the knees. You're supposed to help the residents learn, not intimidate them." Regina didn't wait for the doctor to respond. She spun on her heel and whipped the door open, slamming it into the wall, and beat a hasty retreat down the hall.

Alex stared at the door as it swung shut. She ran a hand through her hair and chuckled softly to herself. "Well, I'll be damned." Walking out of the room, she headed to the administrative wing of the hospital.

Alex stood in the door of the director's office, waiting patiently as she finished with a phone call. A blonde-haired woman waved her in and Alex sat in the leather chair facing the desk. She took the opportunity to look around the woman's office, which was littered with reams of paper detailing the hospital's vital statistics.

Dr. Cassandra Mitchard was one of the youngest vice presidents at the five hundred bed medical center. One of the first women at the medical center to break through the proverbial "glass ceiling" and wreak havoc on the old boy's club. She didn't subscribe to the fifth floor dress code to wear fashionable miniskirts and pumps that satisfied the adolescent fantasies of the over-fifty executive crowd. As Vice President of Medical Affairs, she learned quickly to play hardball, and ruled with an iron fist. Alex respected the woman from the moment she met her three years ago.

"It's been quite a while since you've blessed us with your presence, Dr. Margulies," Cassandra said, giving her an appraising look. "What can I do for you?"

Alex sat forward in her chair. "I need some help, Cassandra. Dr. Jameson wants the statistics for the emergency room's mortality rate for the last six months."

Cassandra nodded and leaned back in her leather chair. "And you want to know how you can put the little rat in his rightful place," she stated, as a wicked smile played at her lips.

"Subtle, very subtle." Alex tilted her head and smiled at how easily Dr. Mitchard could read her.

"You can't blame me for wanting a little revenge, Alex. He didn't just screw you last year with that bogus charge. He dragged the entire organization through the coals. He thinks his political connections are strong enough to protect him, but he's wrong. Dead wrong." She leaned forward and opened up a binder of reports and thumbed through the pages until she found what she was looking for. "Here, look at this. At first glance, Alex, you look like the grim reaper." She flashed her an apologetic grin. "But, look a little deeper and you, Alfonso, Torres, and Washington account for eighty-five percent of the emergency room department admissions a year. Do you know how many people came through our doors last year, Alex?"

"We had twenty-seven thousand admissions into the emergency department," Alex replied.

"Exactly." She scanned the sheets. "You and Torres take the most severe traumas, partly because you are chiefs but also due to just blind luck. Your average acuity rating is three, with the most severe traumas being rated a four. That more than justifies the mortality rate that the two of you have. Now just for shits and grins, let's take a look at what dear Dr. Jameson's stats look like."

Alex shook her head. "You're evil, Cassandra."

"No more than you, Alex. No more than you." The VP pointed triumphantly at the sheet in front of her. "Look. He sees approximately twenty-three patients a day. That's an average of nine less than the rest of you. Now look at his mortality rate and his average acuity rating."

Alex sat back in her chair and stared at the doctor. "Shit."

"How you choose to present this information is entirely up to you, Alex. You can make these numbers say just about anything you want." Cassandra booted up her computer. "Do you have access to a computer?"

"Yeah, the medical staff office has two with Microsoft Office running on it," Alex said.

"Took them long enough," Cassandra responded. She pushed a disc into the floppy drive and copied several files to the disk. "This has all the information you'll need. By the way, I'll be at the next Mortality and Morbidity meeting. I hope you'll make it worth my while to attend."

After taking the disk from Cassandra, Alex saluted her with it, and sauntered out of the fifth floor suite. Battle lines had been drawn.

❖ ⌘ ❖ ⌘ ❖ ⌘ ❖

As luck would have it, Regina was mercifully paired with Drs. Torres and Washington over the next two weeks and saw little of Dr. Margulies. When she did see the Chief Attending in passing, Regina felt invisible as Alex stared right through her. Regina wavered between seeking Alex out and apologizing for yelling at her and deciding emphatically that the witch deserved her anger for lashing out at her and Marcus. After all, this was a teaching hospital and neither of them had done anything to threaten a patient's life.

Today, after the M and M conference, the rotations would change again and she would be back with Dr. Margulies. Regina walked into the mahogany-paneled conference room and took a seat next to Marcus.

"Hi, Marcus." Regina nudged him.

"Hi, yourself. I hear we're back with the queen bitch again today," he said, and yawned without bothering to cover his mouth.

"Ooh, nice tonsils, Marcus," Regina commented.

"Sorry, I didn't get much sleep the past few nights. As soon as they turn the light off, I'm history. Wake me when it's all over." Marcus crossed his arms and sank down lower in his seat waiting for the lights to dim.

The conference room filled up with medical staff, and the hum of people talking over each other engulfed the room. After a few minutes, a rather tall, athletically built man wearing an expensive looking gray suit took the podium. He tapped the microphone and cleared his throat as if this would give him the attention of everyone gathered in the room.

"Excuse me," he said into the microphone. "We'd like to get started now."

"Ugh, he looks like a weasel with that moustache," Regina leaned over and said to Marcus. He opened his eyes and snorted.

A hand clamped down on both their shoulders and a deep baritone voice rumbled in their ears. "That weasel happens to be our medical director, Dr. Jameson."

Regina and Marcus turned to see Dr. Washington and Dr. Margulies standing behind them. Alex remained silent but her eyes met Regina's. The young resident quickly faced forward in her seat, feeling her face redden from the intensity of the doctor's look. *Oh shit, I'm in trouble.*

A moment later, Regina watched as Alex walked past them to the front of the conference room and handed a carousel of slides to the man in charge of the audiovisual equipment. Studying the Chief Attending, Regina observed that Alex was dressed in a dark blue linen suit, quite unlike her usual attire of scrubs and lab coat, and although Alex seemed oblivious to it, she made a striking impression on the crowded auditorium.

"Way to go, Kingston." Marcus nudged her, pulling Regina out of her quiet observation.

"I'm already toast with her." Regina waved her hand and sank down in her seat next to Marcus.

They turned their attention to the medical director standing at the front of the room beside Dr. Margulies. "I'll turn the microphone over to Dr. Margulies so she can get on with her presentation. I'm sure your statistics about the mortality rates in the emergency department will be most enlightening for us all."

"Oh, he is so smug," Regina said.

Marcus leaned over and whispered in her ear, "The rumor mill has it that he is trying to run Dr. Margulies out of here. Supposedly our illustrious chief attending has a notoriously high mortality rate. He's using this to put one more nail in her coffin." Marcus closed his eyes again as the presentation moved forward. "As far as I'm concerned, they can bury her alive."

Regina stared at Marcus and then focused her attention on the drop down screen at the front of the conference room. Regina glanced around the room and noted that most of the medical staff that could attend looked fairly interested, and others, mostly residents and interns, were using it as a chance to catch up on their sleep.

"I'm sure they will, Dr. Jameson," Alex drawled, taking the microphone and striding confidently to the center of the floor. "So everyone knows up front, these statistics were compiled from Information Resource Management and the Office of Medical Affairs. They required very little modification because Dr. Cassandra Mitchard oversees the project." She looked around the room and smiled at Dr. Jameson who seemed to be a shade paler than when she started. "Well, if someone will dim the lights, let's get started."

Alex calmly took the group through a quick but thorough explanation of the statistics as the slides flicked up on the screen. The atmosphere in the room seemed to intensify as the next several slides depicted each of the five doctors' mortality rates in the emergency department. Regina cringed when she saw Dr. Margulies' statistics outlined in blue showing her leading the way with thirty deaths for the previous year. A murmur went through the crowd and Regina listened intently to the doctor's strong voice as it carried through the conference room. Even Marcus roused himself from his slumber enough to focus on the doctor's words.

"I and Dr. Torres have the dubious distinction of having the first and second highest mortality rates in the department respectively. Dr. Washington and our medical director, Dr. Jameson, have the two lowest. I think what you will find most interesting is the average acuity factor combined with the number of the patients treated by each of us." Alex's voice trailed off as she advanced the slides and she set the microphone in its holder on the podium.

A snicker came from behind them and Regina turned to see Dr. Washington's shoulders shaking as he tried hard to keep from laughing out loud. Regina turned back to the screen and stared at it in shock. Marcus grabbed her arm and shook it to get her attention.

"Holy shit. Dr. Margulies just turned the tables on Dr. Jameson. Look, he's still trying to figure out what the slide says," Marcus said, looking at the incredulous look on the medical director's face.

"Jesus. He's been taking the easy cases and his mortality rate is close to Dr. Margulies'," Regina said, as she studied the screen.

Regina missed Alex walking past and slipping in beside Dr. Washington. It wasn't until she felt a light touch on her shoulder that she realized Alex was there. Regina turned around and saw the doctor's penetrating blue eyes watching her.

"I need to speak to you later, Dr. Kingston," Alex said, as she stood up from her chair.

Regina nodded her head, keeping her tongue in check, as she surely would have choked on it if she tried to answer her at that moment. She watched as Dr. Margulies walked away, her long legs carrying her confidently out of the conference room.

"*She* needs to talk to you?" Marcus asked.

"I'm dead, Marcus." Regina slumped lower in her chair. "You know that coffin you were talking about?" He nodded his head. "Well, keep it handy. I may need it later."

"Regina, *what* did you do?" he asked, growing concerned

that his one ally was in serious trouble.

"I yelled at her after she reamed you out in the department."
Regina twisted her hands and looked up at Marcus.

His mouth gaped and he stared at her. "Well, thanks, but
what the hell did you go and do that for?"

Regina shook her head. "I don't know. Call it temporary
insanity. Anyway, wish me luck."

# Chapter
## 5

Regina pressed the button on her watch, silencing the alarm she set to remind herself to take her medicine. She pulled the round metal pillbox from her scrub pocket and opened it. With a grimace, she popped two pills into her mouth and bent over the water fountain, pushing the button and sucking in the stream of cold water.

She took a break while she had the chance and walked up to the pediatric floor, heading toward Justin's room. She had become quite attached to the boy since the day she admitted him to the hospital over a month ago. Regina felt the same gut wrenching feeling now as she had that night. The police officers had told her that the boyfriend had dunked Justin in scalding bath water as punishment for crying too much. A neighbor had called 911 when he heard screams coming from the apartment next door. Neither the boyfriend nor the mother had been to the hospital since Justin was admitted to the trauma unit.

Regina stopped outside the door and peeked into the room. Justin sat in his crib with his back to the door. He clutched a small bear as he rocked back and forth trying to calm himself. Regina walked up to the crib and called his name softly.

"Justin."

The curly blonde head lifted and turned slowly. A wet tear-stained face met hers and she slid the bars down. Justin turned around on his knees and crawled to her. His little hands grabbed the lapels of her jacket, pulling up so he was face to face with her.

"Regi." He had a hard time pronouncing her name and it came out with a hard *g* sound.

"Hi, sweetheart." She gathered him into her arms and gave him a hug. "Let's you and I take a walk."

A lower lip protruded in a display of protest.

"Justin, do you want to be able to play with your friends when you go home?" Regina asked.

Blue eyes blinked back at her and he nodded his head.

"Well, that won't happen if everyone keeps carrying you around with them." She lowered him to the floor. Justin clutched her fingers and whimpered as he took a few tentative steps. Slowly, he gained confidence and he walked toward the door teetering on his still heavily bandaged feet. Regina patiently walked alongside of him as he made his way out of the room and headed to the nurse's station.

"Okay, you have to be good," she said, picking up one of the toys lying on the desk to hold his attention.

The nurse sitting at the desk turned her chair around when she saw Regina and smiled at her. "He's going to break your heart, you know."

Regina looked up and smiled sadly at her. "He's worth it. Aren't you, Justin?" She touched his nose with her finger.

He looked up at her and he stuck his fingers in his mouth, clutching the stuffed animal to his chest with the other hand. Unlike the other children on the floor who gradually came out of their shells as they got better, Justin remained quiet and withdrawn, responding cautiously to the affection that the staff displayed with him.

Regina felt a vibrating against her waist and looked down at her beeper. She tilted the screen so she could read the number. It was the emergency room. With a sigh, she picked up the phone and punched in the five-digit extension. A voice at the other end picked up.

"This is Dr. Kingston. Somebody paged me."

"Hang on, let me check." Farther away from the phone, she could hear someone shouting, "Anybody call a Dr. Kingston?" She was put on hold and she bounced Justin on her knee getting him to giggle and clutch her jacket for support.

"Dr. Kingston?" The unit clerk got back on the phone. "There's a patient coming in from a car accident. Dr. Margulies is with another patient and can't take it."

"Okay, I'm on my way," Regina said.

She looked at Justin. His blue eyes blinked at her and his lower lip protruded into his hallmark pout.

"Oh no," Regina chuckled. "You have to stay here. I'll see you later, Justin." She led him over to the nurse at the desk and handed him off to her. "Hey, any word on getting him foster parents yet?"

The nurse looked up at her and shook her head. "The mother showed up a couple of days ago. She went into drug rehab after the social worker told her they were going to find foster parents for him if she didn't. The hospital is going to release him as soon he is ready to go home."

Regina's jaw dropped. "When will that be?"

The nurse shrugged her shoulders. "That's up to the surgeons. They'll probably look at his wounds today."

"Just like that?" Regina looked down at the innocent face staring back at her.

The nurse nodded her head and scooped Justin up into her lap.

Regina walked off the pediatric unit and headed to the back stairwell. She ran her fingers lightly along the metal banister as she trotted down the gunmetal gray stairs. She made her way down to the emergency department and jogged through the double doors. The unit was busy. All the rooms were full and there were two patients lying on stretchers in the hallway waiting to be transported to one of the medical floors. She saw Sandy bent over the two-way radio frantically scribbling notes in the admission log. Slamming the phone down, the nurse waved Regina over when she saw her.

"We've got an MVA, five minutes out. The guy took the steering wheel in the chest." Sandy hustled around the desk toward one of the trauma rooms. "He was conscious at the scene but they lost his pulse." Sandy looked over her shoulder at Regina who was following her. After stopping at the board, Sandy ran down the list of names, quickly making a decision about which patient she could move out of the emergency department to free up a room.

"Excuse me." Sandy and Regina turned around to face a distraught man. "Can you tell me where my wife is? I got a call that they brought her here."

"The woman behind the desk can help you, sir," Sandy

directed, pointing down the hall toward the nurse's desk. Returning her attention to the board, she made up her mind. "Thomas!" she called out to the lanky emergency room technician. "Help me clear out room seven."

He glanced up at the charge nurse and with an aggrieved sigh pushed himself up from his chair at the desk.

"Now, Thomas," Sandy said, glaring at him. "We've got five minutes to set up for a major trauma. Get the patient into the hallway and call bed management. Tell them to get off their asses. We're not a hotel down here." Sandy looked at Regina and flashed her a grin. "Don't worry, we'll be ready for you, Doc."

Regina slipped past the charge nurse and pulled on an isolation gown, then grabbed a fluid shield mask. She could hear the wailing of the sirens grow louder as the rig turned into the hospital's drive and headed down the hill toward the ER entrance. Pulling on a pair of gloves, Regina met the paramedics at the doors.

"We need some help. We're losing this guy!" The ambulance driver shouted frantically.

Regina's pulse accelerated as her adrenaline kicked in. She caught a glimpse of dark brown hair and an ashen colored face.

"What've we got?" Regina asked, taking hold of the stretcher and running along side.

"Thirty-five-year-old male, head on collision, steering wheel to the chest, no seat belt on. He was conscious at the scene but we lost his pulse three minutes ago." The paramedic was already straddling the patient compressing his chest as he gave the vitals to the resident.

Sandy was just hooking up fresh tubing to the ventilator when they rushed the patient through the trauma room doors. The room was prepped. Two IV poles with bags of Ringer's lactate were standing at the head of the treatment table, EKG leads were laid out on a tray with a chest tube and blood gas kit nearby.

The paramedic stopped compressions and quickly scrambled off the stretcher. Five pairs of hands grasped the backboard. "On my count, one, two, three," Regina said. "Easy, easy." In one smooth motion, the patient was lifted off the ambulance stretcher and over to the exam table. The paramedic resumed compressions. Sandy disconnected the bag they were using to ventilate his lungs with and hooked the endotracheal tube to the ventilator. Immediately, the rhythmic whoosh and beeping of the ventilator took over breathing for the injured man. Thomas quickly slapped the leads on the patient's chest and connected the EKG wires to the cardiac wall monitor.

Regina slipped the stethoscope over the patient's chest, listening intently. "Stop compressions." She looked at the monitor. "We've got a normal rhythm." She could hear breath sounds on the right side, but the left was diminished.

Sliding up to the head of the table Regina loosened the tape holding the endotracheal tube in place. Withdrawing the tube a couple of inches, she grabbed hold of the paramedic's hand and clasped it around the tube.

"Hold it there." Placing the stethoscope back down over the chest, Regina confirmed her diagnosis. "He's got a pneumothorax on the left. I need a chest tube kit and get a blood gas on this guy." She readjusted the endotracheal tube and then moved the stethoscope, now listening for the heart sounds. They were distant, almost muffled sounding.

"No pulse," Sandy said, her fingers over the carotid artery in his neck.

Regina looked up at the medical student standing by the foot of the stretcher. "Andy, start compressions."

Eager to help out, the medical student ran over to the stretcher, crossed his hands over the patient's sternum and started rhythmically pumping on the chest. Dr. Washington pushed the doors open and ran into the room already dressed in his protective garb. "What do we have?"

"He needs a chest tube on the left," Regina replied quickly, continuing her exam.

"Give me a scalpel," Dr. Washington said, holding out his hand. Thomas reached across the stretcher, handing him the instrument.

"Let's get two peripheral lines going wide open," Regina ordered. "Sandy, get a Dopamine drip started. Thomas, draw blood for a CBC, lytes, and tox screen. Type and cross-match for four units. He needs a catheter and call radiology for a cross table C-spine."

Sandy ran to the code cart and broke open the plastic lock. She yanked out a handful of syringes and drug ampoules. One of the other nurses inserted the IV lines while Sandy set up the drip that would sustain the patient's blood pressure.

Regina ran her hands down the man's head and neck looking and feeling for anything that might be abnormal. She noticed the obviously distended jugular veins in the man's neck and immediately knew it meant that his heart muscle was damaged and blood was filling the sac around it, effectively choking the muscle. "Sandy I need a fifty-cc syringe with a 17-gauge needle and call the OR. Tell them we've got a possible cardiac tamponade coming."

Dr. Washington glanced up quickly. "You sure about that?"

"Yes, he's got jugular distension and his blood gases aren't responding with the chest tube."

Sandy tossed the packaged syringe to Regina then grabbed the receiver off the wall phone. Thomas leaned over and squirted betadine on the patient's chest. Regina ripped the packaging off the syringe and land marked to the left and below the tip of the xyphoid process at the end of the sternum with her gloved fingers as Sandy dialed the number for the OR.

"Here." Dr. Washington clipped the conductive monitoring cable to the chest lead with an alligator clamp and attached the other end to the needle. The cable would let them know if the needle pierced the heart muscle as she performed the procedure.

Her hands trembled slightly and she took a steadying breath as she checked the monitor again. "Andy, stop compressions." She was aware of everyone's eyes watching her and waiting. As the medical student stepped back, Regina pierced the skin, directing the syringe up towards the left shoulder. She pulled back on the plunger, guiding the needle with steady pressure from her hands.

Crimson blood spurted into the syringe, rapidly filling it, and she held the needle steady.

"Nice call, Kingston." Dr. Washington looked up from suturing the chest tube into place.

"What's his pressure?" Regina asked, feeling some of the tension slide away with the knowledge that she had made the right diagnosis and bought the patient a few more minutes. She knew the blood would keep refilling the sac around his heart.

"Eighty over fifty," Sandy said.

Dr. Washington was just finishing suturing the chest tube in place when the surgical team arrived. To Regina it seemed like forever, but in reality it had been minutes since the patient arrived in the emergency department. Within a matter of seconds, they got a quick history and then the patient was whisked away to the OR to try to repair the damage to the heart.

The quiet trauma room was in stark contrast to the chaos

that was present minutes before. Regina's shoulders sagged as the adrenaline left her body.

"Nice job, Regina." Dr. Washington stripped off his gloves and gown and tossed them into the garbage. He then walked out of the room following another stretcher as it rolled past.

Sandy walked over to her and patted her on the shoulder. "Twenty-two minutes. That's damn good, Dr. Kingston." Regina stared blankly at Sandy as she bent over to pick up the bloodied gauze and packaging that scattered on the floor. Sandy looked back up at her. "Dr. Margulies is the only one who has broken twenty minutes for getting them in and out of the ER as fast as that."

"I wasn't aware there was a competition for fastest triage and transfer to the operating room," Regina said, rolling her eyes. Thirty minutes was their cut off in the ER, anything above that and they were wasting the so-called "golden moment" and would most likely have their heads handed to them on a platter.

Dr. Jameson strode through the doors. "Dr. Washington just told me. Good pick up on the tamponade, Dr. Kingston."

"Thanks," Regina replied, as she pulled the bloodied gloves and isolation gown from her body. She threw the gown into the dirty linen bag and walked to the sink to wash her hands.

"I've known plenty of more experienced doctors who thought they could perform a thoracotomy in the emergency department. Usually it's not a good idea." Dr. Jameson walked up behind her.

Regina leaned on the sink as a wave of nausea rolled through her. She splashed some water on her face, only half listening to the medical director's words.

"Ah, Dr. Margulies." Dr. Jameson turned and eyed her as she walked through the doors. "I was just telling Dr. Kingston here about that unfortunate incident you had last year in the emergency department."

Regina looked up from the sink in surprise and saw Alex standing by the door still in her bloodied scrubs from the last admission. Her face was expressionless, arms folded across her chest as she looked at Dr. Jameson.

"Yes, I think that fiasco made it all the way to the medical examining committee." Dr. Jameson turned to Regina. "Did she share that with you yet, Dr. Kingston? Well?"

Regina looked away from Alex, suddenly feeling that she had unwittingly stepped into the middle of some battle. "I-I don't know what you're talking about."

"It's quite an interesting story. You should share it with her sometime, Alex." His eyes flicked to the attending and narrowed. "Too bad you weren't as competent as your resident here. Might have been a different outcome for the mayor's son."

A hush filled the room and the ticking of the clock and the drip of water from the faucet into the stainless steel sink seemed to grow louder. Regina moved away from the sink, muttered something about having another patient to check on, and made a hasty retreat from the room, leaving the two doctors facing each other.

Alex locked eyes with the medical director and for a moment, she contemplated sending him through the glass doors for his asinine remarks. She'd been exonerated of any wrongdoing that night. In fact, the medical review board found the charges that Dr. Jameson made to be frivolous. Alex stepped closer to the medical director fixing her eyes on him. She could see his throat work as he swallowed nervously.

"Now's your chance, Alex. Nobody else is around," he said.

"Is that what this is about?" she asked, stepping closer so he had to look up at her. "You want me out of here. Well, you're going to have to do a better job than this, Jim. Besides, that's ancient history." She turned and headed toward the door. "You know you're dead wood as far as the administration is concerned. It's just a matter of time before they ask for your resignation, you know, *invite* you to leave." She smiled over her shoulder as she let the door slam noisily behind her.

Regina walked unsteadily over to the nurse's station thankful to have escaped the unfolding drama in room seven. The hostility between the two doctors was palpable and she was sure Dr. Jameson was trying to gain her support against Dr. Margulies. She heard rumors from the nurses that his job might be on the line and he was working hard to deflect any scrutiny away from him. She made a mental note to stay as far away from that situation as possible. She entered her ID number into the computer and flicked through several screens with the penlight until she came to her list of patients. She ran through the list, clicking on several names to check on pending lab results. Grimacing, another wave of nausea swept over her. *Oh lovely, right on cue, an hour after every dose.* Regina reached a hand out steadying herself against the monitor in front of her as she broke out into a cold sweat. *Damn.*

Glancing up at the doctor, the unit clerk touched her arm. "You okay, Dr. Kingston?"

Regina nodded her head and swallowed hard. "Fine, just fine." She became aware of a warm presence at her back and turned her head slightly to see who was behind her. Her heart rate quickened as she saw the dark hair and the piercing blue eyes regarding her patiently.

"I need to talk to you," Alex said.

Regina mentally cursed herself, knowing that this was most likely her comeuppance for yelling at her chief attending. She had kept her interactions with the brooding doctor to a minimum since that episode a couple of weeks ago in the hopes that she could avoid another confrontation.

Regina braced herself for the worst. "Okay." She turned slowly around and faced Alex.

Alex lowered her eyes for a minute and then looked back up at Regina. "Not here. In the staff lounge," she said, nodding her head in that direction.

Regina's stomach dropped and her palms started to sweat. *Shit.* She waved her arm in front of her. "Lead the way." She was aware of several people giving her wary glances as she walked by them.

Alex held the door open for her and motioned her into the room. Regina walked past her and crossed her arms over her chest.

"Okay, so what did I do now?" she asked, turning to face Alex with as much bravado as she could muster. "It must be pretty bad since you didn't just fillet me out there in front of everybody."

Alex's eyes widened slightly and she took a breath. "Sit down," she said, indicating the chair next to Regina.

"I'd rather stand, thank you," Regina said, her heart pounding a little faster.

Alex shrugged and sat on the stool. "Suit yourself." She folded her hands letting them hang down between her legs. "What makes you think you did anything wrong?" Her voice was quiet.

Regina let out a nervous laugh. "Dr. Margulies, I haven't worked here for long, but I've learned one thing very quickly: You don't talk very much, but when you do it's usually because somebody's screwed up and you're here to let them know about it." Regina took a breath. *Shit, why do I have to ramble so much when I get nervous?* "So?" Her head pounded and she desperately wanted to get this over with.

Alex rolled her eyes up to Regina's. "I wanted to apologize for how I spoke to you that night in the hall. I was upset about something and I took it out on you. I'm sorry."

Regina groaned inwardly as the doctor's mouth started to move. "Excuse me?" she asked.

"I said I wanted to apologize to you. I shouldn't have spoken to you the way I did. You were right," Alex repeated, frowning as she watched Regina's complexion pale.

Regina closed her eyes and swayed slightly. Her stomach was threatening an all out revolt and she stepped back away from the chair and headed to the door. The color drained from her face as she ran past the doctor.

"Dr. Kingston?" Alex raised her eyebrows, and turned on her stool as she watched Regina's reaction in obvious confusion. The young doctor ran across the hall to the bathroom and pushed the door open.

Regina stumbled through the stall door. She braced herself over the toilet and vomited. *At least when this happened in college it was because I'd been praying to the porcelain goddess, promising I'd never drink that much again.* Regina flushed the toilet and stood up, steadying herself against the metal door. She staggered to the sink still feeling lightheaded and ran the cold water, cupped her hands and splashed it over her face with trembling hands.

"Regina?"

The resident jumped at the sound of her name, unaware that Alex followed her into the bathroom. She grabbed onto the sink to stay upright as the room spun with her sudden movement. Raising her head, she saw Alex's reflection behind her with a concerned look on her face.

Regina groaned and bent over, resting her head against the sink. "Oh God. Why is it you always see me at my worst?"

Alex stepped beside her and looked at her eyes closely. "Did...I...I upset you that much?"

Regina almost laughed. "Don't flatter yourself. No it's..." She didn't finish the words as she stumbled back to the stall and another bout doubled her over. This time strong hands were there to steady her as she stood up and walked unsteadily back to the sink. "It's the medication."

"How long has this been going on?" Alex demanded.

Regina leaned against the coolness of the tiles and closed her eyes. "A couple of weeks. I got something from one of the other doctors, but it hasn't helped much," she said weakly.

"Why didn't you tell me? I could've given you something to stop it," the taller woman said.

Regina opened her eyes and cocked an eyebrow at her. "No offense, Dr. Margulies, but you weren't top on my list of people to ask for help."

Alex fingered the ties of her scrub pants looking at them intently. "I guess I deserved that, huh?" she asked, feeling badly that Regina hadn't told her that the medication was doing this to her.

Regina nodded. "That and maybe a stronger dose of Haldol."

"Okay, point taken." Alex knew how most of the staff felt about her. She really didn't care that much. She'd never viewed any of them as friends, so if they thought she was a bitch it was their problem. "Hey!" She stepped forward and caught Regina as she slumped to the floor.

"Ungh. Oh, this feels awful. It's not usually this bad." The young doctor clutched her head, as the throbbing got worse behind her eyes.

Alex knelt down in front of her and lifted Regina's chin with her fingers, looking at her face. "You're probably dehydrated. I'm going to get you something that will take care of the nausea and then you're going home."

Regina pushed her hand away, embarrassed by the attention she had drawn to herself. "I can't go home. I've still got patients to see."

Alex shook her head. "Not today you don't. Marcus and the others can take care of them for you. Come on."

Regina reluctantly let herself be pulled up from the floor and led from the bathroom toward one of the exam rooms.

"This is stupid," she complained, still feeling woozy and stumbling as her feet refused to cooperate. Alex wrapped an arm around Regina's waist while the other held her elbow as she directed her to one of the stretchers.

"Lay down," she ordered, as she set Regina down on the stretcher. Alex rolled up the sleeve of Regina's lab coat and wiped her skin with an alcohol pad.

"Hey, what are you doing?" Regina protested, struggling to

sit up.

Alex put a hand on her shoulder and pressed her back down to the stretcher. I'm giving you some IV fluid. It'll make you feel better until I get the medication for you. Stay still." Alex felt for the vessel and slipped the needle inside holding it in place until she secured the IV catheter with some tape. "There."

Regina raised her head looking down at her arm in surprise. "You did it already?"

Alex grinned at her. "Yup. Relax." After hanging the IV bag from the pole she patted Regina's shoulder. "I'll be back in a little bit." She pulled a blanket out of one of the cabinets and tossed it over Regina's legs.

Shivering, Regina reached down and pulled the blanket up over her shoulders. The fluids from the IV made her chilly. A moment later, the door opened and Sandy walked into the room.

"Hey, you okay, Dr. Kingston? Dr. Margulies said to come check on you." She leaned over the rails of the gurney and felt Regina's forehead.

"Yeah," Regina said. Her voice was shaky.

"Dr. Margulies is getting Marcus to cover your patients for you." Sandy smiled and stepped closer. "So what happened?" Sandy leaned on the rails of the stretcher with her arms crossed. "We thought you were a dead woman when she asked you to go into the lounge with her."

Regina shrugged. "It was so weird. I thought she was going to yell at me. She actually apologized for reaming me out in front of the department."

"She what?" Sandy asked. Her jaw dropped. "My God, hell must have frozen over. The infamous Dr. Margulies apologizes?" She started to say more, but the door opened and Alex walked in carrying a white bag from the employee pharmacy.

"Here, this will make your nausea better." She thrust the bag at Regina and shot daggers at Sandy, who squeezed Regina's arm and backed quickly out of the room winking at her from behind Alex's back.

"Thanks." Regina tried to sit up, but the room tilted crazily around her and she slumped back to the pillow with a groan.

Alex stood awkwardly at the side of the stretcher. She checked the IV bag and adjusted the flow of the fluids. "I took care of getting Marcus to cover your patients."

Regina looked up at her. "You don't have to stay here, Dr. Margulies. I can take this out when it's done." She motioned to the IV and let her hand drop weakly into her lap.

"Stop with the 'Dr. Margulies,' you're making me feel old. Call me Alex." She gripped one of the rails on the gurney and looked down. "You look as white as a sheet. Besides, you didn't drive to work, did you?"

"H-how did you know that?" Regina asked.

"I saw you this morning when I came back from running. You were walking across the street. You live up in the apartments on the hill?"

"Yeah, I do." Regina was a little shocked that Alex seemed to know this much about her. She blinked and took a breath, trying to get her vision to cooperate.

"Let me get my Jeep and I'll give you a ride home," Alex said and left the room before Regina could utter a protest.

She must have closed her eyes and dozed off again, because when she opened them Alex was bending over her arm removing the IV. "I need to get my bag," Regina said, as Alex put a small adhesive bandage over the tiny hole left by the needle.

"Okay." Alex stood at the edge of the stretcher looking down at her.

Regina tentatively swung her legs over the edge of the stretcher and sat up. After a minute, the wave of dizziness passed and she tried her legs, which surprisingly held her up, even though she felt like they were made of rubber.

At her locker, Regina fumbled with her lock and managed to open it after a couple of tries. She pulled out her backpack and slipped it over her shoulder, then shut the door and let Alex guide her out to her Jeep.

It was a cobalt blue Grand Cherokee with tinted windows, not one of the newer models, Regina noted, slightly surprised. Most of the doctors on staff drove only the newest cars. She could tell what the new models from the car dealerships were by just looking in the doctors' parking lot. Alex pressed her remote and the Jeep chirped as it unlocked itself. She opened the door and helped Regina up into the leather seat. After shutting the door, Alex jogged around to the other side and got in.

"Okay, just tell me which street you live on," she said as she pulled the vehicle out of the emergency entrance and drove up around the traffic circle to the light. She waited until it turned green and accelerated across the intersection. A family of Canada Geese started to cross the road that led into the development. Alex muttered as she slowed to a stop. Drumming her fingers on the steering wheel, Alex counted five of the little things.

Regina giggled as she watched them. "They're cute."

"No, they're not," Alex said. "They're nasty, dirty, and make a mess."

"Yeah, I guess they do." Regina watched the last of the little yellow fluff balls hop up onto the curb. "I'm the third street up on the left."

Alex nodded and turned on her signal before making the left turn. Regina pointed out her driveway and Alex pulled up to the garage and turned off the ignition. Regina opened the door, and stepped down out of the Jeep, grabbing hold of the door to steady herself as her legs threatened to give out on her again. Slowly, she made her way to the door of the condo, Alex following, carrying her backpack and the medication. Regina unlocked the door, pushed it open, and stepped inside.

"You can put my bag on the couch," she said, as she walked straight into the bathroom and shut the door.

Alex winced at the retching noises from behind the door. A few minutes later, Regina walked back into the living room, wiping her face with a wet towel, holding onto the wall for support.

"It's never been this bad." Regina went to the couch and sat down holding her head between her legs.

"Where are your glasses? I'll get you some water."

Regina raised her head and squeezed her eyes shut as the sudden movement made the room swim around her again. "First cabinet on the right. Oh, I've got to stop doing that."

"Doing what?" Alex asked, looking back at her.

"Moving my head so fast. I keep getting dizzy."

She heard the sound of the cabinet door open and close, followed by the sound of running water. Footsteps approached her and the cushion beside her sank down. Alex picked up the bag off the couch and handed Regina the glass to hold.

Regina's hand trembled as she held the glass. She set it down on her legs, using both hands to keep from spilling it. Alex tore open the bag, pulled out the bottle, and tried removing the childproof lid. "They practically make these damn things adult proof," she complained as the lid flew off and skittered across the floor. She knelt down and retrieved it from underneath the chair. "Here." She shook a pill out into Regina's hand. Regina tossed the pill in her mouth and washed it down with a gulp of water. She tilted her head back and slumped against the cushion of the couch.

"I'm sorry, Alex."

"What are you sorry for?" Alex asked, turning to look at Regina's pale and sweaty face.

"I've been nothing but one problem after another since I got on the rotation. You'll probably be glad when I'm off it," Regina said. She wondered miserably how many residents had the dubious distinction of being driven home sick by their attending. She sunk down lower against the cushion of the couch at the thought.

Alex frowned and looked at the woman sprawled against the back on the couch. "That's not true. You're competent, you have good clinical instincts, and you haven't let any of this other stuff affect the quality of your work."

Regina was quiet for a minute taking it all in. "Thanks." She rested her head against her forearm and closed her eyes. They were quiet for a few minutes as Regina drifted in and out of wakefulness.

"Thanks for bringing me home, Alex," Regina said, before finally drifting off to sleep.

Alex waited until Regina's breathing became strong and even, then stood up from the couch. She knelt down beside the blonde and moved her onto her side.

She propped a pillow under Regina's head, slipped her sneakers off, and pulled the green and blue checkered afghan off the back of the couch and covered her with it.

Alex gave her one last look before she slipped out the door, shutting it quietly behind her.

Regina woke several hours later in the dark. She lifted her head up and looked around her, trying to figure out where she was. Rolling over, her legs tangled in the afghan. Regina turned on the lamp next to the couch. Blinking her eyes, she looked around and realized that Alex had covered her with the throw and taken her shoes off for her.

Regina gingerly sat up and let her body adjust to being upright. "Wow. I don't feel sick anymore." She laughed a little and proceeded to go to the refrigerator, where she raided the leftover chow mein that she had from the night before.

# Chapter
# 6

Regina picked up the phone and set it down for the third time that morning. "Damn," she muttered. "Come on, how many times have you gone over what you are going to tell him? Just do it." She walked around her living room one more time then grabbed the phone from the table. After dialing the numbers quickly, she waited as the phone rang.

She let the phone ring a fourth time. A click and she heard the familiar voice on the other end of the phone. "Police station. Officer Black speaking."

Regina waited a beat. "Derrick, it's Regina."

"Regina." He said her name like he was testing it out. "It's about time you called me."

She stuck her free hand into her pocket and rocked back and forth on her feet. "Derrick, don't start. I have your ring and I'm giving it back to you."

Regina thought about mailing it to him, but she wanted to put closure on this and not give Derrick the impression that he scared her, even though he did.

There was an audible sigh on the other end of the phone. "I think we should at least talk. It's been a few weeks and things have settled down some. Let's not rush into this."

"There is *nothing* for us to talk about," Regina insisted.

"Then keep the ring, Regina. I don't want it back." Derrick

clenched the pencil between his fingers.

"No, Derrick. I don't want it." *You're not going to have any-thing to hold over my head, you bastard.*

The pencil snapped in two and rolled across the desk. "All right, well, could we at least talk civilized, maybe get a bite to eat?" He hoped it would give him a chance to win her back.

"I'm on call tonight so I need to stay close to the hospital."

"Let's meet at the diner at the bottom of Dennison Avenue. Say one o'clock?" Derrick asked.

"Fine," Regina said and hung up the phone.

❖ ⌘ ❖ ⌘ ❖ ⌘ ❖

Regina arrived a few minutes before one and walked into the diner. She was glad they were meeting in public so Derrick would have to control his temper. She followed the waitress and sat down in a booth. She ordered a glass of lemonade, deciding that she didn't want anything to eat because she was nervous, and her stomach was already in knots. Regina folded her hands in front of her and let her thoughts wander.

She honestly hadn't given much thought to a restraining order, even though Alex and Sandy said it would be a good idea. It meant getting a lawyer and going to court, both of which she didn't really have the time or the money to deal with right now. She tapped her fingers on the table and looked out the window. *Come on, Derrick, hurry up and get here.*

"Regina?" Derrick said, and sat down across from her. He was wearing a blue button-down shirt and khaki pants.

"Hi, Derrick," she said, eyeing him warily.

"So." He put his hands on the table. "You know it doesn't have to end this way. I think we could work this out if you give me another chance."

The old defensiveness crept up inside Regina, but she pushed it aside. "You still don't get it, do you?"

"I only want what's best for you," he said, reaching out his hand to take hold of hers.

Leaning back, Regina pulled her arms off the table. "That only holds true if it doesn't interfere with what you want." She was tired of having to justify everything to him. She looked him straight in the eye. "Derrick." Her voice was steady. "I didn't come here to fight with you. It's over."

"I don't want to fight, Regina. I just want us to be together."

Regina dug into her pocket and fished out the gold ring with the oval diamond set in it. She held it between her fingers, really looking at it for the first time. She decided it was a nice ring, but it didn't change how she felt and it never would. With a gentle click, she set the ring on the laminated tabletop and pushed it across to Derrick.

"Here. Take it."

"Did you tell your parents?" he asked, picking up the ring and holding it between his thumb and index finger. "They'll be upset, you know." He twirled it back and forth watching the light dance off of it.

"I know, Derrick, but that's my decision. They have no say in what I choose to do with my life," Regina said as she took a sip of her lemonade.

"I don't think they would agree with that and you know it," he replied, fixing his eyes on hers. "Your mother—"

"My mother doesn't know who I am." Regina shook her head. "Derrick, we don't have anything else to discuss."

Mercifully, her beeper vibrated on her belt and she looked down at it. The display read the ER number with 911 following it. It was the code that the staff used in emergencies. She looked up at Derrick. "I've got to go, it's an emergency."

He stood up, a sneer crossing his lips. "Isn't it always. Let me walk you out."

Regina stood up and left some money on the table. Derrick walked out behind her and waited as she got into her car. He raised his hand and stepped back, watching her.

Regina turned the key in the ignition and heard a click. She turned it back and tried again. "Dammit." She banged her hand on the steering wheel. She looked out the window and saw Derrick walking back toward his car. She opened her door and ran after him.

"Derrick!"

"What's wrong?" he asked, turning around.

"My car won't start. Can you give me a ride back to the hospital?"

"Sure, get in."

Derrick pulled out of the parking lot and floored the gas pedal, gunning the engine. Regina pressed herself against the door, staring out the window as they drove up the hill toward the hospital.

Regina jumped out of Derrick's car and ran into the emergency room entrance. She pushed open the glass door and sprinted down the hall, just barely avoiding crashing into a patient being wheeled out of an exam room. She threw her backpack on a chair as she reached the desk. "Where's Dr. Margulies?"

"Trauma one," the unit clerk said without looking up.

She grabbed a yellow isolation gown from a cabinet, slipped it on and tied it behind her neck as she hurried down the hallway. Sandy came running out of the storage room, carrying some pediatric supplies and barely missed colliding with her.

"Sorry to call you in early, Marcus is out sick." She pushed open the glass door and Regina walked in ahead of her. Her eyes ran over the small form lying on the stretcher tethered to a multitude of lines. A small blue board was strapped to the child's arm preventing him from displacing the intravenous line from his right elbow. She could see the sprawl of the EKG wires as they ran from his small chest to the wall monitor behind the stretcher and one small catheter tube snaked down from underneath the sheet to a bag hooked to the rail of the stretcher.

Alex looked up as Regina walked through the glass doors. "Good, you're here." Alex's eyes narrowed and Regina glanced quickly over her shoulder. Derrick stood behind Sandy just outside the glass door looking at Regina.

"Do you want me to get your car towed, Regina?" he asked, his eyes flashing a challenge as he looked directly at Alex.

"No. I'll take care of it. You can't be here." Regina cringed inside, realizing that both Sandy and Alex probably thought she was still seeing him. *Oh well, no time for that now.*

She pulled a cap over her hair, tucking it in hastily. Moving around one of the medical students, she walked to the head of the stretcher. She saw the blonde hair matted to the boy's head and her stomach lurched as she recognized the bruised and mottled face under the tiny oxygen mask.

A shock coursed through her. "Justin." She covered her mouth with a hand and stepped back shaking her head in disbelief.

"You know him?" Alex jerked her head up.

Regina nodded. "He was discharged from the pediatric service last week. They sent him back home to his mother and her boyfriend." The initial wave of emotion ebbed away.

Regina turned her attention to the wall monitor that showed his heart rate was a hundred and thirty beats per minute. She looked at Alex, feeling her eyes on her.

"What are his blood gases?" she asked as she slipped a fluid shield mask over her face and squeezed the thin metal clips over the bridge of her nose.

"His oxygen's dropped down to ninety-six percent." Alex pulled her eyes away from Regina and inserted another IV. "Andy, get over here and hold his arm for me."

Regina slipped on a pair of gloves and stepped up beside her. "Jesus," she whispered as she saw the hideous purplish-blue bruises covering his chest and arms. She could see the distinct outline of an adult's hand in the form of an ugly bruise around his upper arm.

She looked up at Alex and then down at the sheet that covered his pale body. She lifted it up and closed her eyes. Recently healed burn wounds lay open and oozing from the cruel hands that had grabbed his legs in anger. "Do we have X-rays on him yet?" she asked, swallowing a surge of anger.

Alex nodded her head, keeping her eyes focused on the tiny vein she was trying to pierce with a needle. "Ah, got it. Over there." She inclined her head toward the view box.

Regina walked to the view box and flicked the light on with her elbow, careful to keep her gloves sterile. "He fractured his right arm and four ribs."

"He may be bleeding internally. His hematocrit is low. They're typing and crossing his blood right now," Alex said.

Regina walked back to the boy lying on the table. "We're going to have to put him on a ventilator if his oxygen drops below ninety percent."

Alex nodded her head slowly, looking at her. "I know. All right, Regina, this is your show. Let's do this quickly."

Regina leaned over the still form and stroked the blonde curls, leaning close to Justin's ear. "Hey, Justin, it's Regina. I'm just gonna listen to your heart, sweetie." Regina placed the stethoscope to his chest and listened as his heart beat frantically inside. She moved it to both sides of his chest and closed her eyes. "His breath sounds are diminished on the left. He's got a pneumothorax." Her eyes met Alex's. "I can't believe that bastard—"

"Not here, not now," Alex said, shaking her head.

Regina nodded her head grimly. "Sandy, I need a chest tube set."

"Got it." She opened it and set it down on the instrument

cart next to Regina.

Alex slipped her hands over Justin's shoulders and held him securely. Blue eyes opened slowly and tiny hands clutched at Alex's hand, trying feebly to push her away.

"No, no sweetie," Regina said. "She's not gonna hurt you." Alex collected both his arms and hugged them over his chest with her larger one.

"Regi." A hoarse whisper of a voice floated up from below.

"Shh. You're going to be okay, Justin." Regina looked up. "Sandy, give me a syringe with one-percent lidocaine." Taking the syringe from the nurse, Regina leaned over. "Justin, you're going to feel a prick here and...here," Regina said as she injected the sites with lidocaine. "It's going to make your skin numb."

Regina took a breath and let it out slowly trying to calm her racing heart. She knew the boy was in serious trouble.

"You okay?" asked Alex. Regina looked up and saw Alex's blue eyes peering at her through the clear plastic of the mask. She hated these cases, but now wasn't the time to let her emotions take over.

"Fine." Regina swallowed and nodded her head. "Justin." Blue eyes rolled up to her. "We're going to put a tube in your chest."

Big tears welled up in his eyes and his lower lip quivered as he looked up at Regina.

"What medication does he have on board?" Regina asked, her voice wavered and she swallowed hard. *Come on, Regina*, she coaxed herself, reining in the emotions battling inside her. *Now's not the time.*

"Six of morphine for pain," Alex said. "I just gave him two milligrams of Diazepam to sedate him."

Regina lowered her head, satisfied with the amount of medication the child had in his system. She ran her fingers along the rib, feeling for the border of the pectoralis muscle in his chest. Using the scalpel, she made a single incision over the rib.

"Give me the Mayo clamp," she said, holding her hand out. She closed her hand reflexively as she felt its weight in her palm when Sandy handed it to her. She inserted it into the incision with the tips closed using slow, steady pressure until she felt the lining around the lung give way.

"Ow, ow, ow, Regi, it hurts! Make it stop," Justin cried out, straining against Alex's arm.

"Andy, hold onto his legs," Alex directed as the boy kicked beneath her.

Regina flinched as she opened the clamp so she could have room to insert the chest tube. She removed the instrument, grasped the chest tube near the end with it, and inserted the tube into the incision she made in his chest wall.

Regina looked back down at Justin. "It's almost over, baby. I'm sorry, sweetie." Sandy connected the end of the tube to the suction container on the wall, while Regina quickly sutured the tube in place and dressed the incision with gauze.

Justin whimpered and clutched at Alex's hand.

"Do we have a blood gas?" Regina asked, stepping back and looking at the wall suction fill with bloody fluid.

"I'm getting it," Andy said, as he drew the blood.

Looking at the rapidly filling container, Regina let out a breath. Anger welled up inside her as she caught a fleeting image of a man beating the boy that now lay beneath her on the table.

"Hurry up, Andy." Regina's anger at the situation was getting the better of her.

"Easy, it's coming," Alex said as she checked the IV in Justin's arm and adjusted the flow. Blood arrived from the lab and Sandy checked the labels with one of the nurses to confirm the type and cross match. Alex hung the bag and piggybacked it with the already running IV line.

"Momma," Justin whimpered as he moved his head around restlessly on the pillow. He pulled the mask off his face and Regina bent over to retrieve it.

"Hey, sweetie. Momma's coming," Regina said, choking on the vile words that she knew were most likely a lie.

Justin looked up at Regina and reached an arm out for her mask. He grasped the plastic shield in his little fingers and pulled it down.

"Hey," Regina said, leaning over him. "What are you doing?" Regina's gloved hand gently covered his.

Alex looked up from across the room and walked back over to the stretcher. She watched the interaction, her face devoid of any emotion.

Regina let Justin pull her down to his face. "Regi."

"I'm here, Justin," Regina said. "You're gonna be okay."

"Flutterby kiss," Justin whispered and pecked her on the cheek.

"Blood gas is eighty-nine percent oxygen. His ph is seven

point four," Andy said, from across the room.

Regina closed her eyes and swallowed the sob that welled up in her throat just as the alarm on the monitor started a high-pitched beeping. Looking up at the monitor, its alarm indicating the oxygen in his blood was dropping below a safe level, Regina hit the icon on the screen angrily with her finger silencing the shrill noise.

"Dammit." She turned away from the stretcher and blinked the tears from her eyes.

"Regi?" Justin's voice was a whisper.

"Justin." Regina leaned back over his face and stroked his head. "We're going to give you something to make you sleepy. When you wake up you're going to have a tube in your mouth to help you breathe." She looked up at Alex. "Give him two more of Diazepam."

Alex nodded her head and drew the sedative into the syringe. She slipped the needle into the port on the IV line injecting the medication. After lowering the rail on the stretcher, she slipped her hands over Justin's arms to hold him again.

Regina picked up the laryngoscope and the endotracheal tube from the tray and leaned over Justin's head. Her head brushed Alex's shoulder as she positioned herself over Justin's face. Tilting his head back, she opened his mouth. Regina ducked her head and took a breath. It was a simple trick she learned in medical school to steady her hands when she was nervous. She inserted the scope, visualizing the anatomical structures in his throat as she guided it in.

"Regi...I'm...scared." Each word faded, becoming fainter as Regina inserted the scope, guiding the tube down his trachea. She inflated the balloon at its tip to hold it in place.

"Okay, I'm in." She slipped thin white cloth ribbon around the tube and tied it behind Justin's head so the tube was firmly in place. Sandy took the tubing from the ventilator and connected it to the endotracheal tube.

"Okay, let's take him to radiology. I want to scan his chest and abdomen," Alex said, walking over to the counter to pull the portable pulse oximeter and cardiac monitor off the shelf. "Come on, we're taking him up ourselves." She slipped the tiny device that monitored the percentage of oxygen in the blood over Justin's thumb. The soft red glow from its sensor reflected off the white sheets. "Stupid red light always reminds me of ET."

She stared down at the boy's pale face, and Regina

unhooked the endotracheal tube from the ventilator and attached the bag mask resuscitator.

"Yeah, me too," Regina said, as she squeezed the bag rhythmically.

Alex unhooked the EKG leads and hooked them to the portable monitor at the foot of the stretcher. "All set. Let's go." Twenty minutes later, they were wheeling the boy to the operating suite from radiology.

Regina continued to squeeze the bag mask resuscitator, ventilating the little boy's lungs. She almost bumped into Alex when she stopped short, and banged on the button that automatically opened the doors to the OR.

One of the scrub nurses looked up, startled to see the tall doctor and her smaller companion wheeling the stretcher into the large holding area. "Didn't know you switched jobs to transport, Dr. Margulies," she teased.

Alex gave her a dour look and handed her the copies of the CT scan. "He's got a lacerated spleen."

The scrub nurses took hold of the end of the stretcher and led them down the narrow hallway just outside the sterile environment of the operating suites. "We'll take over from here."

Alex turned to walk away, hesitating when she saw Regina standing by the door watching the stretcher disappear down the hallway. "Hey, are you coming?"

Regina nodded her head and slowly stepped back from the door, her eyelids blinking rapidly to quell the tears threatening to overflow. She didn't dare look up at the taller doctor as she walked back down the hallway to the emergency department, fighting the wall of emotions that hammered at her tattered defenses.

❖ ⌘ ❖ ⌘ ❖ ⌘ ❖

It was almost midnight when Regina finally walked into the locker room. She slumped heavily onto the bench and stared at the floor. She put her face in her hands and ran her fingers through her hair. She was exhausted and every joint in her body ached. At last check, there was still no word on Justin from the operating room. All they could tell her was that he was still in surgery.

After peeling off her scrubs, Regina started changing into her clothes. She looked up as the door opened and Alex walked in. The attending looked at Regina, hesitated and walked over to her locker, pulled out her clothes, and tossed them carelessly onto the bench. It was the time of day she hated most. Her shift was over and there was nothing left to do except go home to her empty house.

Regina threw her scrubs into the green dirty linen bag, sat back down on the bench and slipped her sneakers on her feet.

"You patch things up with what's his name?" Alex asked, her voice muffled as she pulled her scrub top over her head. She kicked herself mentally as the words came out more harshly than she intended. *What business is it of yours, anyway, what Regina does on her own time?*

"Huh?" Regina looked up surprised at Alex's question. "Oh, Derrick. God, I almost forgot," she said, rubbing her forehead. "No we, uh, I gave him back his ring today. My car wouldn't start so he gave me a ride back here."

Alex slipped off her bloodied scrub bottoms. "So, is that a good thing?" she asked, without looking at Regina.

Regina looked up at her and frowned, confused by Alex's tone. "Yeah. Of course it's a good thing." Regina averted her eyes as Alex bent over and picked up her shirt from beside her on the bench. Slipping her arms into it, Alex pulled it over her head.

Standing up abruptly, Regina grabbed her backpack and walked to the door. "Guess we'll find out how Justin's doing tomorrow."

Alex slipped on her shorts and glanced up at Regina. "Yeah, probably." Alex hesitated, she wasn't one for giving non-clinical advice but in this case she made an exception. "Listen, I know it was tough for you working on that kid, but you've got to learn to separate yourself from what's happening to do your job. Clinically, you were right on target with everything."

Regina looked down and nodded her head, knowing she frequently did allow herself to get too involved with her patients. "I'll see you tomorrow," she said, feeling somewhat dejected by her attending's appraisal of her performance. She pulled the door open and stopped short. Sandy was standing with her hand out, reaching to turn the handle on the door.

"'Night, Sandy," Regina said and started to walk past her.

"Wait." Sandy put a hand on Regina's arm, pulling her back inside the locker room. "I thought you two should know. The OR just called down. The little boy that you worked on earlier..."

Her voice wavered a bit and her face betrayed the emotions she was trying hard to hide. "He coded in the OR. He didn't make it."

Feeling like someone punched her in the stomach, Regina sagged back against the wall, covering her mouth with her hand. "Oh, God," she choked out.

"I'm sorry, Regina." Sandy squeezed her arm in sympathy. "He just lost too much blood."

Regina turned her head away, embarrassed by her own lack of composure and yanked the locker room door open. She walked quickly down the hallway and pushed open the doors to the ambulance bay.

Blindly stumbling down the concrete stairs, she leaned against the brick wall gasping for air. She didn't care about the wind, the rain pouring down around her, or the thunder rumbling menacingly overhead. The past few weeks had been an emotional drain and Justin's senseless death brought it all crashing down around her. Suddenly unable to stand, she slid down the wall, feeling the brick scraping her skin through her shirt. She covered her face with her hands and let the hot tears course down her face.

Shivering, Regina looked up at the black sky from her crouched position. "You son of a bitch. How can you let someone do that to an innocent child? It's just some sick game for you."

Her only answer was an increase in the downpour and Regina blinked the water out of her eyes.

She laughed sarcastically. "Like you would really answer me." Hugging her arms tightly around herself, Regina pushed up from her crouched position and started walking up the hill toward the road. She just wanted to get home, away from this wretched place with all its pain and suffering. She'd had enough and right now she felt cold and hopelessly empty inside.

She'd made it halfway up the grassy slope when she heard footsteps running toward her splashing through the ankle deep puddles. "Regina?" Alex called out as she trotted up beside her and put a hand on her arm. Rain dripped down her face in rivulets and her hair was plastered to her shoulders. Regina just shook her head, covering her face with her hand as a sob escaped her. Her body sagged against Alex as her emotions finally overwhelmed her.

Alex stood still for a moment, unsure of what to do, and then hesitantly wrapped her arms around the smaller woman's shoulders. "You did everything you could, Regina. You know that," Alex said, as she rubbed her back. *Don't do this to yourself, Regina. There're too many that you'll lose over the years. Please don't do this to yourself.*

Regina pulled away and wiped her nose with her hand. "God, he shouldn't have died."

Alex brushed the wet strands of blonde hair from Regina's face. "I know. Come on, I'll drive you home. We'll both get sick standing out here in this mess," she said, as the rain continued to pour down around them.

Alex walked beside Regina and pulled her into a hug with one arm as they walked towards her Jeep. Regina opened the passenger side door and put her foot in. "I'm soaked, Alex," she said, looking down at her drenched clothes.

Alex tilted her head and glared at her. "So am I. Just get in."

Regina slid into the seat and huddled against the passenger side door staring out the window on the short, silent drive to her condo. The tears kept coming now as she remembered Justin's sweet, trusting face looking back up at her from the stretcher.

The truck pulled into the driveway and the engine idled quietly as Alex put it in park, its headlights casting a bright light on the white garage door. The rain drummed on the roof of the Jeep and a flash of lightning lit up the pale interior. She turned to Regina.

"Hey, look at me," Alex said.

Regina shook her head. "You're right, you know. It's my own fault. I just have to stop getting so close to my patients."

Alex put a hand on her shoulder. "No, that's what makes you a good doctor, Regina. You do care and your patients know that. It just makes it harder when they die. It hurts more inside."

Regina sniffed and smiled faintly, wiping the tears from her face. "Do you still cry, Alex?"

"Not as much as I used to." *No, the bad ones just give me nightmares,* she thought wryly.

Regina shivered as a chill left goose bumps on her arms. "You must think I'm a basket case."

Alex shook her head slowly. "No, I don't. You've had a hell of a few weeks. It was bound to catch up with you sometime." She noticed that Regina was shivering. "You should get inside and change into some dry clothes before you get sick."

"Yeah, I guess. Uh...do you want to come in, Alex?" Regina asked, realizing that she didn't really want to be alone. "I don't know about you, but I could use a drink right now."

Alex decided that a drink sounded really good at the moment. "You sure you want company?" she asked, not wanting to intrude.

"Yes, I do." Regina pushed the door open and stepped out onto the pavement. Slamming the door shut, she ran through the torrential downpour to the front door, unlocked it and slipped inside, feeling with her hand for the light switch just to the left of the door. She flicked it up, illuminating the room in a soft glow. Behind her Alex stomped her feet on the mat outside the door.

"Alex, I don't think you need to worry about getting anything wet. I've already taken care of that," Regina said, as she looked at the puddle of water forming around her feet from her saturated clothes. "I'm going to get changed. I'll be right back." Regina slipped off her wet shoes and dumped them by the door. She walked to her bedroom, dropping her bag on the floor inside the room.

Alex took the opportunity to walk around Regina's living room and looked at the pictures on her entertainment center. Alex suspected from the family resemblance that the framed picture that looked several years old was of Regina's parents and a brother. She noticed the diploma hanging on the wall from the University of Massachusetts where Regina graduated from medical school.

Regina walked out of the bedroom and stood beside Alex. "Here." She handed her a pair of large scrubs. "Thought you might want some dry ones."

"Oh. Thanks." The doctor gladly accepted them.

"The bathroom is in the hallway off the bedroom," Regina directed.

Alex walked into the bathroom and shut the door. She was surprised by her reaction to Regina when she ran out of the locker room. If it had been anybody else, she would have left them to their own devices, but something inside had sent her running after the distraught resident, without a second thought about what she was doing.

Looking at her face in the mirror, Alex ran a hand through rain soaked bangs, ruffling them. She emerged a couple of minutes later wearing the blue scrubs that Regina had given her. "I hope you don't mind, I hung my wet clothes up over the shower rod."

"Not at all." Regina's nervous energy from before was wearing off and her body quickly reminded her that it had been hours since she had anything to drink or eat. She walked over to the kitchen and opened the refrigerator door.

Alex followed and leaned against the wall, watching as Regina then rummaged through the shelves. *All right, Einstein, you take the kid home because she's upset, now come up with something intelligent to say to her.* Her back tightened up from being bent over the kid for most of the evening and she stretched backwards until she heard a pop.

"Ah. What was that?" Regina stood up and looked at Alex.

"Just my back. It gets stiff sometimes when I bend over a lot."

Regina nodded, understanding. "Do you want a beer?" She held two micro-brews in her hand.

"Sure." Alex took the proffered beverage, twisted the cap off and took a drink. "Mm. This is good," she said, looking at the label on the bottle. "I'll have to remember this one. It's got a smooth taste to it, not too bitter like some of them."

"Yeah, I like this one," Regina agreed. "Sorry, I don't have much in the way of real food right now. How about some chips?"

"Anything sounds good," Alex said taking the bag that Regina handed her.

Regina opened her own beer and took a gulp as she walked past Alex and into the living room.

The young doctor flopped down onto the couch and stared up at the ceiling. She realized that this was the first time she had ever really been around Dr. Margulies outside of work, but she felt surprisingly at ease with her despite her colleague's typically unkind remarks about her. She wasn't counting the first time they'd been here, because she'd been practically delirious from being dehydrated and nauseous all day.

Regina watched as Alex walked by her and sat down on the other end of the couch.

"You okay?" Alex settled onto the cushion and leaned her elbows on her knees, holding the beer in both hands. She could sense that Regina needed to talk about the evening's events.

After years of working in emergency medicine, she had seen her share of patients die, young and old. Some died mercifully because they had been suffering, others because they had been stupid, and then there were those that made you realize for a sickening moment just how fucked up this life could be sometimes. In any case, Alex learned quickly to put those emotions in a box and move on.

Regina shook her head and looked at Alex, her eyes flashing angrily. "I want five minutes in a room with a baseball bat with that bastard."

Alex shook her head. "No, the punishment should fit the crime. He should be drawn and quartered." She saw the tears glistening in the corners of Regina's green eyes. "Is this the first kid you've had die because he was abused?" she asked carefully. She reflected upon her own reaction years ago to a similar situation. The boyfriend showed up just as Alex came storming out of the trauma room. Her mentor at the time, Dr. Washington, physically restrained her, but not before she broke the bastard's nose and sent him crashing over a stretcher. That outburst got her suspended for three days.

Regina nodded her head solemnly, tilting the bottle back and draining her beer.

"I know you don't want to hear this right now, Regina, but I'm going to tell you anyway," Alex began. "You'll find a way to dull your senses. Somehow you've got to learn to put up a wall for everything that you have to deal with in there. Otherwise, it eats you up inside. You did everything you could for him. Sometimes it's just not enough. We can't save them all." She leaned back against the arm of the couch and sighed. "You're good with the kids."

Alex knew that experiences like this sometimes left scars that haunted people and turned them away from what they were good at. She didn't want that for Regina.

Regina lifted her head, surprised at the unexpected compliment. "You think so?"

"Sure. The way that kid..." Alex raised her hand searching for his name. "The way Justin responded to you...you could tell he trusted you." Alex took a drink from her beer and toyed with the label. "You're good at that, getting patients to trust you. That's important."

Regina just looked at Alex and swallowed. "Thanks," she said quietly. She wasn't expecting the compliment and she found herself feeling shocked. "I know it's okay to get emotionally involved with your patients, but how the hell do you do that and stay objective? How do you keep that distance, Alex?"

Alex shrugged. "I don't know. I don't let them get that close, so I guess I'm not the best one to answer that question."

Regina saw something flicker in Alex's eyes that she could only describe as profound sadness. *What have you seen, Alex? What have you been through that you keep yourself so protected? I see that in you.* "Do you want another beer?" Regina indicated Alex's empty beer bottle, letting her thoughts remain silent.

"If you're having one, sure. I don't want to keep you up," Alex said, handing her the empty bottle.

Regina shrugged. "I think I'm getting a delayed adrenaline rush from earlier. I'm wide awake now."

Alex gave her a knowing smile before Regina turned away and walked into the kitchen. She closed her eyes enjoying the quiet sense of peace. It was always difficult, Alex thought, to rid yourself of the sights and sounds that imbedded themselves in your memory. Some faded quickly and others lingered, coming back and haunting you with startling clarity, opening up vulnerabilities that you didn't realize existed in your soul.

It had been a long time since Alex socialized with anyone at the hospital. Too many times conversations with her colleagues invariably led to their most current real estate deals, what luxury car they had just purchased or how the insurance companies were trying to cut into their profits. It was a game of one-upmanship and Alex had no desire to involve herself with that kind of meaningless interaction. Her experiences in the past taught her hard lessons about what that kind of money could buy you and how fleetingly transparent it all was in the end.

Regina returned with two bottles in her hand.

"Thanks," Alex said, as she took the bottle that Regina offered her. Alex leaned forward to set her beer on a coaster. The motion brought on a sharp pain in her back and her muscles stiffened immediately in response. Shifting her position on the couch, Alex winced as the muscles in her lower back clenched into a painful spasm.

Regina put a hand on her forearm. "Are you all right?" she asked, as Alex struggled to hide the pained expression on her face. "It's your back, isn't it?"

Alex arched her back. "It'll be okay."

Regina stood up and motioned for Alex to lie down. "Lie on your stomach. My brother has the same problem. I can usually work out the spasm."

Alex shook her head. "No, it's okay." Her voice was strained and she grimaced as the spasm tightened again.

"You're not a very convincing liar," Regina replied, standing before her with her hands on her hips. "Lie down. It's the least I can do considering all the times you've helped me so far."

Alex grumbled in protest as she lowered herself down onto the couch, tensing momentarily when she felt the warmth of Regina's hands through her scrub top. Regina rubbed them over Alex's lower back, slowly increasing the pressure and kneading deeper as the muscles gradually relaxed.

"So...you have a brother?" Alex asked. She hardly knew anything about Regina and she found herself curious about the young resident.

She turned her head as she felt Regina's hands stop. "Actually I have two. I'm the second oldest."

"What do they do?" Alex felt the spasm start to loosen its hold on her strained muscles.

"Michael sells real estate and..." there was a slight hesitation in her words, "Jeffrey is a lawyer."

"Wow, a lawyer, a doctor, and a real estate agent. Your parents must be proud of you all." Alex picked her head up and looked at Regina when she didn't get a response. "Did I say something wrong?"

"N-no. Relax." Alex felt a hand on her shoulder as Regina pushed her gently back down and pulled her shirt out of her scrub bottoms. "I can't get a good hold on your skin with your shirt in the way," she explained as she felt Alex stiffen beneath her.

She didn't want to tell Alex about her family. Most of the time she wished that she didn't know them. They had been so cruel to Jeffrey. In fact, she was ashamed of how they treated him when he told them he was gay. Regina wished she'd had the courage to stand up to her mother when she threw him out of the house. She still carried a lot of the guilt around with her about that time of her life. Pushing the painful memories away, Regina continued to rub and knead the tense muscles until the spasm relaxed.

Regina let her hands rest on Alex's back and peered around at the older woman's face. Smiling, she realized that Alex had fallen asleep. Regina bit her lower lip, wondering whether or not to wake her, and then shook her head when she saw the empty beer bottles on the table. She pulled the afghan off the back of the couch and draped it over the length of Alex's sleeping form.

The young doctor settled into the reclining chair across from the couch and opened the book she had been reading earlier, read several paragraphs, and then realized she'd no idea what she just read. She tried again to reread the page and felt her eyes closing.

With a promise to nap only a few minutes, Regina closed her eyes and promptly fell asleep.

❖ ⌘ ❖ ⌘ ❖ ⌘ ❖

She felt a hand on her shoulder, and opened her eyes, seeing Alex before her. "Hey," she said and shook her head fighting off a yawn.

"Hey, yourself." Alex smiled at Regina's sleepy eyes. "You should've kicked me off your couch."

Regina shook her head. "Uh, uh." She pointed at the empty beer bottles sitting on the table. "Besides you probably needed the sleep. What time is it anyway?" She stretched, arching her back.

"Just after two." Alex looked at her watch and yawned.

Regina pushed the leg of the chair down and sat up, studying Alex's slim physique. "How's your back?" Alex had changed into her shorts and top.

"Much better. Thanks," Alex replied. She started to slip on her sneakers, balancing steadily on one foot and then remembered Regina's car. "Hey, do you want me to take a look at your car?"

"At two o'clock in the morning, Alex? Are you crazy? Don't you sleep?"

Alex's response was a shrug. "I'm pretty good at fixing things, unless you'd rather get it towed in the morning."

A tingle of excitement ran up Regina's spine. "You sure you don't mind?" She gave Alex another chance to back out.

"Come on. I have some tools in the back of my Jeep."

Regina pulled her sneakers on. "You keep tools in the back of your Jeep?"

"Hey, when your odometer passes a hundred thousand, you will too," Alex said as she opened the door and stepped out into the darkness.

❖ ⌘ ❖ ⌘ ❖ ⌘ ❖

The rain had tapered off and a light breeze was blowing. Back in the now deserted parking lot, the clouds overhead were

breaking up and hints of moonlight peeked from behind them,
splashing the two vehicles intermittently in a white light. Regina
peered under the hood of her car as Alex ran the beam of light
from the flashlight over the engine. To Regina, it looked like a
mass of odd shaped containers and wires.

"Now I know why I stick to medicine," she commented as
she leaned her elbow on the edge of the car, peering into the
engine.

Alex smirked and glanced at Regina. "It's not hard to figure
out an engine. It's like making a diagnosis on a person. Just a
different type of anatomy, that's all."

She leaned farther under the hood and aimed the beam of
light deeper into the engine.

"Huh." Alex leaned over and peered at something. "What
the...? Look at this." Alex shifted and gave Regina room. Regina
bent forward and peered into the engine following Alex's finger
as she pointed.

Alex held the flashlight in her left hand and pointed down at
the distributor cap with her right. "Your distributor cap wires
were loosened."

Regina stared at the wires and then up at Alex. The breeze
shifted and Regina inhaled the perfume that Alex wore. She
blinked her eyes, opened her mouth, and suddenly forgot what
she was going to say.

"I, uh, how could that happen?" she asked finally, as her
brain started working again.

Alex looked back at the cap and reinserted the loosened
wires. "Someone had to do this. These wires don't come loose by
themselves." She clenched her jaw, having a good idea about
who that certain someone might have been.

Regina closed her eyes and sighed inwardly. "Derrick. He
came into the restaurant after I did."

Alex lowered her head and gripped the edge of the hood,
turning her knuckles white. "Does he have keys to your car?"

Regina shook her head. "No, but he could open any lock
with the tool kit he carries on his belt."

Alex turned to Regina and handed her car keys back to her.
"Try your engine."

Regina slipped into the driver's seat and stuck the key in the
ignition. The engine turned over and rumbled to life. She stepped
back out of the car, walked over to Alex as she shut the car hood,
and watched quietly as Alex wiped her hands off on a towel she

had tucked into her back shorts pocket earlier.

"It doesn't make any sense," Regina said, looking at her car as it idled quietly in the parking lot.

"Why not?" Alex turned to her. "It got your attention." *Mine too, for that matter*, she reminded herself. Alex lifted her head and let her eyes roam the darkened parking lot. Her senses prickled and she got the distinct impression that they were being watched. "We should both get home. I think we've had enough adventure for one night. What do you say?" Alex looked back at Regina who was still watching her intently.

"Yeah. Are you on this weekend, Alex?" The taller woman nodded her head as she walked over to her Jeep, which she had parked facing Regina's car.

"Regina," Alex said quietly. "I'm going to follow you home."

Regina waved her off. "You don't need to do that."

"Humor me," Alex said, but she wasn't smiling as she said the words.

Regina pulled out of the vacant parking lot and onto the main road. The Jeep remained right behind her, its headlights shining in her rearview mirror. Because the roads were deserted, the drive to her condo took half the time it usually did.

Once into her driveway, Regina hit the remote she kept tucked into the sun visor and the garage door slowly slid up. She pulled in, turned the car off, and stepped out.

Alex's Jeep sat behind her with its headlights on. Regina went out to say goodnight, hitting the switch on the wall and ducking underneath the closing door. The window lowered on the driver's side as she approached the Jeep.

"Thanks for everything, Alex," Regina said resting a hand on the car door. "I think I owe you a dinner for this."

Alex shook her head, embarrassed. "You don't owe me anything, Regina."

Regina leaned on the Jeep, her arm touching Alex's as she glanced up at the sky. "At least it turned out to be a nice night after all."

Alex eyes followed Regina's movements, coming to rest on her profile.

"Look, there's Orion's Belt." Regina pointed overhead.

Alex shifted in her seat, following her finger, until she spotted the constellation. A soft chuckle rose out of her throat and Regina turned her head. "What?" Their faces were inches apart as they looked at each other.

Alex held her gaze a moment longer and then looked away. "It's just been a long time since I bothered to look at the stars." She stifled a yawn to hide her nervousness at the growing attraction she felt toward the blonde-haired woman.

"You must be exhausted and here I am keeping you stargazing." Regina stepped away from the Jeep and stuck her hands in her pockets.

"Yeah, I should get going. 'Night, Regina." Alex shifted the Jeep into reverse and smiled at her as the truck rolled back.

Regina watched as Alex backed the Jeep out of the driveway, waving to her as she drove off. She stepped back into the house, shut the door and locked it, sighing as she thought about the day and how it ended. It's strange how things turn out sometimes.

# Chapter
# 7

Regina stepped out of the fracture room and walked toward the sink. She had just finished casting a fifteen-year-old boy's wrist fracture and was discharging him. She rolled her eyes and failed miserably at stifling a chuckle as she listened to his mother yelling at him for using his bed as a trampoline again. It reminded her of the pillow fights she used to have with her older brother when they were kids.

Sandy looked up from the lab work she was reading and smiled, hearing Regina's infectious laugh as she walked over to the desk.

"You look like you're feeling better these days." She noticed that the healthy color in Regina's face had returned.

"Mm." Regina nodded her head as she hung over the desk, reaching down to snag a piece of chocolate. One of their former patients dropped the box off as a small token of appreciation for what the staff had done for him. "The medication that Alex gave me works wonders. Just a little nausea but I haven't gotten sick in days," she said, as she popped the candy into her mouth and bit into it.

Regina was feeling exceptionally good today. Alex drew her blood two days ago for the six-week blood test and slipped her results into her locker enclosed in a white envelope with Regina's name written on it in black ink. Regina picked up the envelope as she had changed into her scrubs earlier that evening and felt a warm tingle of hope as she read the results.

"Ooh, that was good," Regina said, licking the chocolate from her fingers and eyeing another piece.

"Ah, ah." Sandy swiped the box away from her. "I will *not* have the two of you on a perpetual sugar high all night. Alex is bad enough when she gets a hold of this crap."

"Where is Dr. Margulies anyway?"

Sandy rolled her eyes and pointed down at the end of the corridor. "Jameson got a hold of her. He's been looking for someone to bail him out of doing the budget for the department."

"Ugh. Why?" Regina asked.

Sandy leaned over the desk closer to Regina. "Rumor has it there's more budget cuts coming. Guess he doesn't want to be the bad guy."

"Think she needs to be rescued?" Regina asked, a mischievous glint lighting up her eyes. Sandy leaned forward as Regina whispered to her.

❖ ⌘ ❖ ⌘ ❖ ⌘ ❖

Alex crossed her arms and let her gaze fall just over the shoulder of the medical director. He was talking incessantly about the budget due at the end of the month. It was obvious that he was looking for someone to take the burden from him. Dr. Jameson had been the medical director for ten years now and was firmly entrenched in the old school of practicing medicine. It went something like this, Alex mused: "If it feels good, do it," without too much thought given to fiscal responsibility. Once again, just like he did every year, he was talking about the upcoming budget and how difficult it would be to make the mandatory seven percent cuts that the administration handed down to all the departments.

It had been a quiet Saturday evening in the emergency department so far and he had cornered her when she stepped through the doors of the emergency department. Alex listened with half an ear, her attention focused on the torrential rain coming down outside. It had been raining hard all day and many of the low-lying roads were flooded, so people seemed to be staying indoors which meant they were staying out of trouble. *Too bad*, Alex mused; she could have been otherwise preoccupied instead of stuck here, listening to her medical director drone on.

She pulled her attention away from the rain running down the outside of the window and fixed him with an icy stare. "Listen, Jim," she said, reaching the end of her limited patience with his whining. "If you spent as much time working on the numbers as you've just spent complaining, you might be done with it by now."

He stopped mid-sentence and stared at her. "You know, Alex, you might want to be a little more cooperative than that. It might just be your job that ends up being cut."

An eyebrow arched in amusement. "I doubt that. They're looking at outcomes, numbers and productivity. I think we've already cleared up any misperceptions on that." The M and M conference the week before had made it obvious who was to blame for the poor outcomes and productivity slump.

Alex felt a vibration at her waist and looked down at her beeper. She frowned at the extension listed in the LCD display and looked in the direction of the nurse's station. Sandy was holding a phone up pointing to it.

"I've got a phone call I need to take," she said, hoping that it wasn't Dana calling again.

"This isn't over by a long shot, Margulies," he hissed following her as she walked to the desk and took the phone from Sandy.

"Who is it?" Alex asked, turning her back to the seething doctor.

Sandy gave her a weird look. "Sorry, didn't ask."

Alex frowned and put the phone to her ear. "Dr. Margulies here."

"We thought you needed rescuing." Regina's giggling voice floated through the phone line.

Alex laughed. "Thank you. I did, no, actually I still do," she corrected as she looked up and saw the doctor standing next to her. "Hang on a second." She covered the mouthpiece of the phone and looked at him. "Jim, our conversation is over. It's one of my patients."

He shot Alex a threatening look as he walked away in search of another victim. Alex watched him skulking past the trauma rooms.

She took her hand off the mouthpiece. "Where are you?" she asked, her eyes twinkling mischievously.

"Room five," Regina said.

"Get out."

"W-Why?"

"You've got three seconds," Alex said as she watched Dr. Jameson walking down the corridor. "He's looking for someone else to commiserate with about the upcoming budget he has to do." There was a squawk at the other end of the line and a click. Alex set the phone in its cradle and sat down in a chair chuckling.

Regina ducked as she saw Dr. Jameson walk by the room. She scooted over to the interconnecting door and slipped through to the next exam room. Regina waited until she saw the tall, blonde-haired doctor's head turn the corner and then made a bee-line for the nurse's station. She slid around the desk and slumped into one of the chairs, letting it roll back away from the desk, looking decidedly relieved that she had eluded the medical director. Alex winked at Regina as she met her eyes.

Regina smiled and turned her chair when she heard her name.

"Thanks, Dr. Kingston." The boy whose arm she had put a cast on waved at her as he walked past the desk. His mother was less enthusiastic, still berating him about using the bed as a trampoline.

Alex glanced at Regina. "Another happy customer."

Regina smirked. "I don't think his mother appreciated me telling him about the pillow fights I had with my brother growing up. It was a good diversion while I set the break."

"Uh oh," Sandy said, looking up from the desk.

"What uh oh?" Alex looked up dismayed. "Ah shit, he's coming back. Come on, let's get out of here." The doctor grabbed Regina's arm and pulled her out of the chair.

"Wh-where are we going?" Regina asked, completely startled by Alex.

"Away from here. I've had enough of budgets *and* him for one evening," she said nodding her head in Dr. Jameson's direction.

"Hey! That's no fair," Sandy called out. "Don't leave me here alone."

Alex turned around and waved. "We're not, you've got Marcus and Dr. Jameson to keep you company. We'll bring you back something from the cafeteria." She grinned at her.

Alex released Regina's arm as they turned the corner and opened the door to the stairwell. Regina walked through the door, trotted down the flight of gunmetal gray stairs, and held the door open at the bottom of the stairs for Alex. They entered the mostly empty cafeteria, which wasn't unusual, given the lateness of the day and the fact that it was a Saturday.

Regina headed to the self-serve yogurt machine. She checked it out earlier and noted happily that it was double Dutch chocolate, one of her favorites. Holding a Styrofoam cup underneath the dispenser, she made a neat swirl of yogurt in it. She shook some sprinkles over it then stepped aside as Alex filled her cup and poured a liberal amount of chocolate syrup over the top, followed, too, by chocolate sprinkles.

She turned and noticed Regina's look. "What?"

"Have a little yogurt with that chocolate syrup, why don't you," Regina said, with a smirk.

"Thanks, I will." Alex dug her spoon in and sucked the yogurt off of it, savoring the taste as she swallowed.

"I figured you for a health nut or something the way you run every day." Regina shrugged, walking to the register to pay.

Alex snorted and followed her to the register. "Uh, uh. My treat for rescuing me from hell." Alex handed a bill to the cashier. "Remind me to get some for Sandy before we go back up. She'll kill me if I don't."

Regina walked to a table in the back of the cafeteria and sat down. Alex sat down across from her with her back to the wall, and they both worked on their yogurts for a few minutes in silence. Sitting back, Alex crossed one of her legs over the other and regarded Regina from across the table. She suspected the resident's good mood was related to the most recent set of lab results.

"Did you get the envelope I left in your locker?" the semi-reclined doctor asked. She had been uncharacteristically nervous when she had waited in the lab for the results of the HIV-Antibody Test.

A smile broke across Regina's face and she patted the pocket of her scrubs. "Right here. Thanks. I really appreciate you taking the time to run these tests yourself."

Alex waved it off. "It's no problem. I'm glad I could do it for you. Your CD4 cells look good," she said, referring to the white blood cells in the body that played a critical role in coordinating the immune system's response to infection. If the number of CD4 cells started to decline it would be a sign that Regina had contracted the disease. She had breathed sigh of relief when she had read the lab values.

"Six weeks down," Regina said, wishing that it were six months already.

"I've got a good feeling about it." Alex scraped the bottom of the cup and looked up, catching the nervous expression on her colleague's face.

"God, I hope so," Regina said, as the uneasiness settled heavily in her chest at the prospect of having to deal with HIV. "I can't even think about what I'll do if it ends up being positive."

"Don't. We'll cross that bridge when we have to." Alex caught her breath. The words were out before she had a clue where they had come from.

Regina looked a little startled by Alex's sincere words. "Th-Thanks, Alex."

"You're welcome." The older woman leaned back against the booth and ducked her head, suddenly interested in the bottom of her cup.

❖ ⌘ ❖ ⌘ ❖ ⌘ ❖

The rain had been coming down steadily all day and, by evening, three inches had fallen and many of the roads were flooded. Orange detour signs directed the white Ford Explorer through a maze of back streets. Andy looked nervously at his wife, who was trying her best not to cry out from the strength of her contractions. He reached his hand across the console and squeezed her hand gently.

"It's gonna be all right, Laura." He wished he felt as confident as his words sounded. This was the third detour he was making to get around the flooded low-lying roads that led up to the large medical center.

The contractions had started two hours ago and had progressed much more rapidly than Laura's obstetrician had expected them to. Andy turned the wipers on high as another sudden torrential downburst marred his view of the road. He fiddled with the controls, turning the A/C on to help defrost the windows faster.

"Andy," his wife gasped as she endured another contraction. "How much farther? I feel it pressing. Oh God, it hurts," she cried out, pushing back against the seat.

"We're almost there, Laura. Just hang on another five minutes," Andy said, licking his lips nervously. He recognized a street sign through the torrents. "Finally." He turned on his left turn signal and proceeded up the steep hill.

The medical center was on the left just below the top of the steep incline. Andy couldn't be sure but he thought that he heard the wail of a siren in the distance. He couldn't tell if it was behind or in front of them. He didn't see any lights, so he signaled his left-hand turn.

As he started across the wide intersection his wife cried out. "Andy, no!" The last thing he remembered as he looked up was a large vehicle spinning out of control, heading directly toward the front side of the truck. Jerking the wheel hard, he watched in horror as time seemed to slow down.

There was an ugly noise of metal impacting and crumpling as the two vehicles collided with each other. The sheer force of the collision drove the truck up over the curb and rammed it violently into a telephone pole.

The incessant chiming of the bell telling him a door was ajar pulled him out of the blackness he was swimming in. Andy blinked his eyes and winced as he felt a sickening grinding of bones as he shifted his arm. Looking down, he almost passed out when he saw his left arm bent at an impossible angle. He heard the sound of the rain drumming on the roof of the car and felt a steady dripping of cold water on the back of his neck.

"Laura?" Pushing the deployed airbags out of his way, he turned his head and focused on his wife. "Laura, oh God, Laura, talk to me." He reached out with his right arm and touched her face.

"Mm. Oh...ah...Andy, it hurts. Oh God, my leg." More awake now, Laura clutched her stomach and cried out. "The baby, Andy. I can't feel it!"

Her cries shocked him out of his daze. "Laura, I'm gonna get us help. You hold on. I promise you'll be okay, the baby'll be okay." Andy pushed against the door but it was jammed shut. Turning his head, he saw that the back door was open on the passenger side. Painfully, he unhooked his seat belt and reclined his seat. Using his legs and his good arm he pushed himself backwards. Each movement caused a blinding hot streak of pain to shoot down his arm and he bit his lip to keep from crying out. It seemed like it took forever but finally he managed to get out of the truck.

He leaned against the side of the vehicle forcing himself to stay upright, panting from the exertion and the searing pain in his arm. Thunder rumbled continuously overhead as the storm raged on around him.

Stumbling in front of the ambulance, he glanced up at the window. He couldn't see the driver, but shattered glass from the windshield littered the pavement and spatters of rain-diluted blood glistened and rolled down the white hood of the emergency vehicle. Clutching his arm to his side, he staggered across the grass toward the glowing blue sign that pointed to the emergency entrance a hundred feet away.

❖ ⌘ ❖ ⌘ ❖ ⌘ ❖

"Please...I need help."

The unit clerk at the desk looked up, his eyes widening at the man leaning heavily against the desk. His clothing was wet and he clutched his left arm through a bloodied and torn shirtsleeve. A woman the unit clerk had been talking to backed up, her face turning ashen at the sight of the man's obviously broken arm.

One of the nurses walking down the hallway saw the woman stagger backward. Running up behind her, Maggie caught the woman as she started to pass out. "I need some help here," Maggie called out, struggling to keep the woman from falling.

Dropping the linens he was stocking, Thomas ran over to help Maggie get the woman in a wheelchair. Smelling salts quickly brought her around and Thomas wheeled her into one of the treatment rooms.

Maggie quickly grabbed a package of gauze from a cart, ripped it open, and held it firmly over the man's bleeding arm. "Let's get you into a room so one of the docs can look at this."

Meanwhile, the unit clerk looked quickly around the emergency department for help. "L-let me get one of the doctors."

"No, you don't understand. My wife..." Andy grimaced and shook his head, clutching at the desk for support. "We...had an accident. She's in labor."

"Where is she, sir?"

The man shook his head and ran a hand through his wet hair. "Outside. I-I told you we had an accident."

The clerk frowned. "She's in the car?"

"Yes! Please get a doctor." The man's voice was getting louder.

The clerk stood up from his chair looking decidedly uncomfortable. "Sir, where is your car?"

"Winding Brook Road."

"Okay. I'm going to call the paramedics." The clerk picked up the phone and started punching in the numbers.

"*What?* No, please, y-you're an emergency room. Send someone...out...she can't wait for the paramedics."

"Sir, let's get you into one of the rooms so we can take a look at the arm," Maggie urged him.

"No, my wife, please, she needs help."

"Sandy." The clerk looked around and called for the charge nurse. "I need you over here. *Now.*"

Hearing her name and the tone of the clerk's voice, Sandy stuck her head out from one of the rooms. "What's wrong?"

"This man's hurt and his wife is injured out in their car. They had an accident," the clerk said, taking a step back as Sandy approached the desk.

"Please, you've got to help my wife. She's trapped in our car. She's in labor." Andy was near tears and the pain made him feel light-headed.

"Sir, we've called the paramedics. They're on their way," Sandy assured him. "Let me get you into a room." She stepped closer to help Maggie.

He slammed his hand down on the counter rattling the plastic clipboard next to him. They both jumped back. "You've got to be kidding me. You're a damned emergency room!"

Startled by the angry voice, Regina dropped her stethoscope as she walked out of an exam room. She retrieved it, stuffed it into her pocket and headed toward the commotion.

Sandy shifted her weight from one foot to another and looked over her shoulder for one of the doctors. A wave of relief washed over her when she saw Alex and Dr. Jameson walk out of one of the rooms. She called their names. They looked up from their conversation and quickly headed over to her.

"What's the problem?" Dr. Jameson looked down at her ID badge. "Sandy."

Sandy gave them a quick explanation of what had happened, motioning to the man standing across from her.

"Did you call the paramedics?" Dr. Jameson asked.

"Yes," Sandy said, cringing. She knew the distraught man on the opposite side of the desk didn't give a damn about hospital policies. His only concern was that his wife was hurt and that their unborn baby's life might be in danger.

Dr. Jameson looked at the man's arm. "Sir, come with me

and we'll get that arm taken care of."

The man took a step forward and stopped. "I don't care about my arm. My wife is hurt out there! She needs help."

"Sir, we will take care of your wife when the paramedics bring her in." Dr. Jameson lowered his voice. "Now please, let us help you."

Regina washed and dried her hands at a sink as she listened to the man plead for his wife. She hated to watch the man go through such anguish, but the hospital's policy prevented doctors from providing medical care outside of the facility while on duty.

She decided to look outside to see if the ambulance was coming. As she stepped through the doors to the ambulance bay, she saw rain pouring down in sheets. Stepping down to the pavement, she looked out at the road. A gust of windblown rain blew her hair in her face. Wiping it away, Regina flinched as a flash of lightning illuminated the darkness. For a haunting moment, she could see the sports utility vehicle smashed up against the utility pole on the grass and the flashing light of an ambulance winking faintly as it hung precariously from its roof.

"Jesus." Stepping forward, she stopped and turned back to the emergency room door. She was torn between following the policy and the oath she had taken as a doctor. Regina ran a hand through her hair and gnawed at her bottom lip.

"Shit."

Knowing she was crossing a line, Regina sprinted toward the vehicle. *Damn, damn, damn.* She peered through the shattered window and saw the young woman slumped against the door. A quick glance at the dashboard shoved up against the seat and Regina knew that at least one of the woman's legs was likely broken, if not crushed. Leaning closer, she called out and felt the woman's neck for the carotid pulse. "Ma'am? Can you hear me?"

She got a mumbled response.

"Thank God. You hold on, we're gonna help you." Regina knew there was not much she could do without equipment. She glanced at the ambulance, ran to the passenger door and tried unsuccessfully to open it. Hopping up on the runner, she peered through the glass. All she could see was darkness and the crimson blood that was being washed down the hood of the ambulance.

Regina ran back through the drenching rain, shaking water from her hair as she ran through the entrance of the emergency department.

"Alex!" She ran up to her and laid a wet hand on her forearm.

"What?" her attending asked, turning around. She arched an eyebrow at Regina's wet hair and rain soaked clothing clinging to her body.

"I saw the wreck, Alex. It's bad. The truck is up against a pole." Regina's eyes pleaded with her.

"Regina, we can't go out there," Alex said, as she pulled her eyes away from the young resident's and turned toward Sandy. "How long until the paramedics get here?"

"They're twenty minutes out. Some of the local roads are flooded and they have to take a detour."

Alex looked down at her hands. "Shit." She closed her eyes, weighing the options. The woman was in labor, most likely badly hurt. The ambulance was twenty minutes out. *Damn, sometimes the scales are tipped for you.*

"All right." She sighed, against her better judgment. "I'm going to check on the woman."

Dr. Jameson walked out of the fracture room having turned the man with the fractured arm over to one of the residents. "Dr. Margulies, don't be a fool. You can't go out there. The hospital will be liable."

"Someone may be badly injured. What's more important?" Alex spread her arms wide as she walked backwards away from him.

Jameson started to open his mouth then stopped and an evil glint flashed in his eyes. "Fine, you go right ahead."

Regina ran after Alex. "I'm going with you."

Alex spun around. "No, you're not." She put a hand on Regina's arm. "You stay here. There's no sense in you getting in trouble too." Dr. Margulies walked away from her charge and out into the driving rain.

Regina put her hands on her hips and looked down at the floor. Taking less than a second to make up her mind, she ran into the storeroom and pulled out one of the trauma kits that the paramedics used to stock their rigs. She hoisted the bright orange bag over her shoulder and ran toward the door.

Dr. Jameson blocked her, his neck veins bulging and face turning red as he watched his chief attending defy his authority as she disappeared into the darkness. "You're stealing hospital property, Dr. Kingston. You could be terminated for that."

Regina lifted her chin defiantly. "It's not considered stealing if you're using supplies to help a patient, Dr. Jameson." She
brushed past him, knocking him in the stomach with the bulky
kit slung over her shoulder.

"Just remember I make the rules!" he shouted after her. "Go
play the hero with your friend and see what kind of trouble you
get into."

Alex was soaked by the time she ran up the hill and got to
the ambulance. It was facing the wrong way and from the looks
of it the rig must have spun into the truck and hit the street sign.
The front window was shattered. Glass crunched under her
sneakers as she jogged across the pavement. She wrenched open
the passenger side door, and crawled inside, wincing as shards of
glass bit into her ankle. She grimaced as she pressed her fingers
against the driver's neck, checking his pulse, knowing that there
was nothing she could do for him now. Backing out of the ambulance, she ducked reflexively as lightning flashed and thunder
clapped overhead.

Alex ran through the grass toward the truck.

A woman's voice filled with pain and fear reached her ears.
"Andy?"

"I'm Alex Margulies. I'm a doctor," she answered. She
flicked on the flashlight she had brought with her and directed
the beam over the interior of the sports utility vehicle. The air
bags had deployed and the woman was still in her seat belt. Alex
shrugged out of her lab coat and crawled inside the back passenger door, hunching down beside the woman. The dashboard had
been pushed in by the force of the collision and pinned the
woman's legs. "What's your name?"

"Laura...oh God," she hissed as another contraction hit her.
"It's coming. Oh God. Please, it hurts."

"Does anything else hurt, Laura?" Alex asked, noticing how
pale she looked.

"My left leg," came the shaky reply.

"Alex?" Regina was at the door peering in at her.

Alex lifted her head and shot a steely glance at the resident.
"Dammit, Regina, I told you not to come out here." Seeing the
stricken look on Regina's face and realizing that it was too late
now that she was there, she gave up. "Oh, never mind. Is there a
neck collar in that kit?"

Regina ripped open the Velcro straps and opened the canvas
pack. "Here." She handed the collar to Alex.

Alex carefully slipped the collar around the woman's neck.

The woman let out an agonized scream and clutched her abdomen. "Oh God, it hurts!"

Alex pushed herself up and spoke softly to the woman as she examined her abdomen. She felt the baby, sitting low and guessed the seat belt was restricting its movement into the birth canal. "Laura, I need to release the seatbelt. Try and stay still," she instructed, as the woman strained to lift herself back as the belt released.

"I need to lay back...baby's coming." Laura gritted her teeth against another contraction.

"Okay, Laura, listen to me. I'm going to move the seat back very slowly. I need room to be able to check on the baby." Straining, Alex reached underneath the seat and pulled the handle up. With her other arm she slid the seat back. She moved the flashlight over the woman's body and stopping when she saw her lower leg.

"What's wrong?" Laura asked.

"Your leg's broken," Alex said.

"I can't really feel my foot," Laura said quietly, closing her eyes as she rested between contractions.

"Regina, I can't get down by her legs. See if you can open the passenger side door and get down there. We need to stabilize the fracture."

Regina tried pulling on the door but couldn't budge it. "Alex, I can't get it to move," she called out. A flash of lightning crackled overhead and Regina yelped, ducking as thunder ominously rolled through the dark sky.

Alex quickly slid out of the back passenger door. Grasping the door handle and the window frame, she braced herself and pulled back with all her strength, the door groaning in protest as it gave way to her.

The doctor grabbed Regina's arm, pulling her close so the woman wouldn't hear her. "We're going to have to put a tourniquet on her leg. She's got a compound fracture and she's pumping out arterial blood. If she loses too much we'll lose the baby too."

The resident nodded and squeezed in between the dashboard and the front seat, bending over to look at the leg. She caught her breath as she saw the pearly white, jagged pieces of bone protruding through the skin of the woman's shin. Alex handed her a length of rubber tubing and Regina tied it above the gash in the woman's leg. The pulsing of blood slowed considerably and Regina slipped an air cast over the lower leg to stabilize the fracture site.

"I'll be right back, Regina." Alex ran to the ambulance, yanked open the rear door of the rig, and stepped up into the vehicle. She picked up the backboard, jumped down out of the ambulance and ran back to the truck.

Laura moaned as another contraction started. Regina looked up as Alex returned and looked in on her. "We're going to have to lay her back so we can check on the baby."

Nodding in agreement, the taller doctor held up the backboard. She crawled in the back seat as Regina pulled up on the handle to lower the seat back. Alex slid the board behind Laura to support her spine.

"I'm going to start an IV. Regina, you need to check the baby. I can't fit down there." Alex indicated the small space that Regina had wedged her torso into.

The blonde stared up at her mentor, swallowing nervously. She wiped her wet bangs out of her eyes with her forearm. It was one thing to deliver a baby in the hospital with all its modern, hi-tech equipment; this was another story entirely. Regina prayed that she would hear the sound of the sirens from the recently dispatched paramedic unit, but the only thing that reached her ears was the drumming of rain and the continual rumble of thunder overhead.

Laura cried out again as another contraction took hold.

"I need scissors, Alex," Regina said, hoping her voice didn't betray how nervous she felt. This was probably one of the few times in her life she wished that she was much taller than her five-foot-four frame.

"Here," said Alex, handing her the scissors.

"Laura." Regina waited for the woman's eyes to focus on her. "I'm going to cut your underwear. We need to get it off so we can check the baby."

"G'head." She sounded groggy and Regina realized she was quickly slipping into shock.

Regina pulled the garment away and examined the woman. She looked up at her attending. "This baby's not going to wait for the paramedics. Alex, I don't know if I can..."

"Easy. You're doing fine," said a comforting voice above her. Alex knelt in the driver's seat holding the flashlight over Regina giving her what little light she could.

Regina could see the perineum distending and knew the head would be crowning with the next couple of contractions. She could hear the woman breathing hard and felt her tense under her hands as another contraction started. "You're doing great, Laura." Regina looked up at the woman. "Okay, try and relax. I can see the head. That's it. You're doing great."

The woman screamed again and clutched at Alex's hand, making her wince as her fingers were squeezed in a vice-like grip. Rain drummed down on the roof of the truck filling it with its incessant noise, and in the distance, the wail of a siren could be heard from the approaching ambulance.

A wave of relief went through Regina as the ambulance approached. *Finally.*

Laura screamed again and Alex looked over Regina's shoulder as she watched the resident gently guide the head out. The shoulders and the rest of the body followed minutes later.

"It's a boy." Regina breathed a sigh of relief, as she leaned over and gingerly settled the baby on his mother's stomach. Laura opened her eyes briefly and mumbled something that Regina couldn't quite understand. The resident squirmed back out from the tight space, grimacing at the blood covering the front of her scrubs.

Alex looked around for something to wrap the baby in when the ambulance finally pulled up behind them. A young paramedic stuck his head in the wrecked vehicle and blanched when he saw the scene before him.

Alex pinned him with her eyes. "Get blankets, a clamp, and scissors, now."

Looking down at the infant, the attending checked his pulse and breathing, satisfied that he was all right for now. Returning seconds later, the paramedic handed Alex everything she had asked for. The dark-haired doctor quickly clamped the cord and cut it, giving orders to the resident at the same time.

"Regina, take the baby into the emergency room and call the Intensive Care Unit. I want one of the neonatologists to check him out." Alex wrapped the baby in the blanket, reached across the seat and laid him in Regina's arms. "Go on. Tell Sandy we're going to need an OR for this lady."

Sandy met Regina at the door and took the baby from her, listening as Regina told her about the woman in the truck. Within minutes the emergency room was once again chaotic as the paramedics and Alex wheeled the mother into one of the rooms and

residents from the neonatal unit arrived to take over the care of
the newborn.

Regina stood in the hallway with her arms clamped tightly
over her chest, shivering as she watched the surgical team wheel
Laura off to the operating room.

"Here." A blanket was tossed over her shoulders and a set of
dry scrubs was thrust around in front of her. Taking the scrubs,
Regina turned around to see Alex looking down at her. Blue eyes
twinkled for a moment and then turned predatory as they looked
up and fixed on someone else.

"You know, Dr. Margulies," Dr. Jameson said, his voice
oozing sarcasm, "you just solved all my problems for me. You
put the hospital at risk for the last time. I just talked to the surgeon and that woman is going to lose her leg. You were the one
who put the tourniquet on it." Regina opened her mouth to protest. "Don't interrupt me," Jameson snapped. "I've already con-
tacted the medical review committee. You are suspended starting
immediately."

"You can't suspend her." Regina jumped to Alex's defense.
"She didn't—"

"Regina, don't," Alex warned, holding a hand out to stop
her.

Looking between the two doctors, the young resident
stepped forward. "I put the tourniquet on her leg, not Dr. Margulies."

A wicked smile crossed the medical director's lips. "Fine.
You're both suspended, immediately."

Regina's mouth dropped. "B-but she didn't do it."

"She's your immediate supervisor. You both are going
down," he said triumphantly. "Have a nice day, ladies." Looking
back at his nemesis, Dr. Jameson laughed. "You won't be so
lucky this time," and walked away.

Regina turned to say something to Alex but she had already
slipped away. "W-where did she go?" she asked turning around.

Sandy, who stood at the desk nearby and witnessed the
entire scene, pointed at one of the empty trauma rooms.

Regina headed to the locker room, scrambled out of her
filthy scrubs and jumped into the shower washing off the blood
and grime from the delivery. She threw on the set of scrubs Alex
had given her and headed for the trauma room.

Regina stood by the window, looking in at the curtain that
was pulled across the room, the bright procedure light was on

over the table casting a shadow of someone sitting on the stretcher. Pushing the door open, she slipped quietly into the room, looked around the curtain and saw Alex sitting on the treatment table with her back to her. She was hunched over in an awkward position, her leg bent underneath her, and she peered intently at her ankle.

"You can come in, Regina," Alex said quietly.

"How did you know it was me?" Regina asked, as she stepped up beside the doctor.

"No one else would have followed me in here."

"Oh. Alex, I...I'm sorry. I didn't mean to get you in trouble."

"It's not your fault."

Regina hung her head, feeling miserable about the whole situation. "What happened to your ankle?" she exclaimed, at the blood seeping out from under a wad of gauze Alex held on it.

Alex shrugged. "I must have cut it on the glass getting into the car."

"Let me see." Regina pulled Alex's hands away and carefully lifted the gauze. "You're going to need stitches," she said, looking up at the woman.

"I know." Alex held up a package of 3-0 silk and handed it to Regina.

"You want me to do it?"

Alex nodded her head. "I can't reach it very well."

Regina walked to the sink, washed her hands, and pulled out a set of sterile gloves from an overhead cabinet. After filling a syringe with lidocaine, she walked back to Alex and injected the medication around the site. The resident pulled the gloves on and took the silk out of the package that Alex had opened for her.

Regina looked up at her. "You ready?"

Alex leaned back on her hands and closed her eyes.

"Don't like getting stitches, huh?"

Alex shook her head. Regina smiled to herself and started stitching the wound closed.

"You have gentle hands," Alex said, breaking the silence.

Regina looked up and their eyes met. She held Alex's gaze and then ducked her head, turning her attention back to the gash; she felt her ears turning red from the heat of the blush working up on her face.

"Thanks." Regina finished closing the wound and then wrapped it in a sterile dressing. When she was done she peeled her gloves off and stood at the end of the table looking down at her hands. "You know, what you did back there was the right thing to do. I'm just sorry I got you in trouble, Alex."

"Don't be. If I had to do it again I would." Alex smiled and leaned forward, picking her sneaker up off the table. She turned serious as she pulled it back on her foot. "Listen, Jameson wants me out. I know that." She held her hand up at Regina's protest. "Let me finish. They will probably meet with us separately in a day or two. Just tell them exactly what happened. You'll be okay. I promise."

"What about you, Alex?" Regina asked, close to tears now. *I only wanted to help and now we're both getting in trouble for this. It's not fair.*

"Don't worry about me."

Regina wished she believed her as she watched her walk out of the room.

❖ ⌘ ❖ ⌘ ❖ ⌘ ❖

The chief attending walked to the open office door and leaned on the doorframe. "What do you want, Margulies?" he asked, without looking up.

Alex walked into Jameson's office, stood over his desk, and stared at the top of his head. "You can take my privileges away, right now. No meeting. Just leave Dr. Kingston out of this. She has nothing to do with you and I."

"Hmm. Interesting." He leaned back in his chair and laced his fingers behind his head, surveying the woman in front of him. "Actually, I think it'll be fun to watch you squirm as you see your little friend get hung out to dry."

He wasn't sure how she did it. But all he saw was the door to his office slam shut and then felt his body lifted out of his chair. The two diplomas hanging on the wall crashed to the floor with the impact of his body. When the room stopped spinning, Dr. Jameson found his back pinned against the wall, with Alex's hand wrapped around his throat and her knee shoved up painfully against his groin.

Her voice purred in his ear. "I'll say this one time. You take my privileges away and leave Dr. Kingston alone. Are we clear?" She pressed harder with her hand and her knee.

She felt his throat work as he swallowed. "Crystal," he squeaked.

Alex pulled her badge off her lab coat and threw it on his desk. "Have the paperwork filled out. I'll sign it tomorrow." Without another word she left the office.

❖ ⌘ ❖ ⌘ ❖ ⌘ ❖

Regina unlocked the door to her condo and walked in, locking it behind her. Everything ached in her body and she felt like she was getting sick. She looked at the blinking light on her answering machine and headed into the kitchen, ignoring it for the moment.

Feeling thirsty, she opened the refrigerator and pulled out a can of soda. The tab opened with a pop and hiss of bubbles, and she took a long, drawn-out swallow. Alex said everything would work out but in the pit of her stomach Regina felt her guts churning and her head was starting to throb.

The message machine blinked its red light incessantly, demanding her attention. The petite, blonde woman sighed, knowing it was either her mother or Derrick calling and, truth be told, she really didn't feel like dealing with either of them right now. Blink. Blink.

"Oh, all right." Regina gave in and hit the button.

"Hi, Regina, it's Mom. I just wanted to remind you about our plans to have you come up here this weekend. Please call. We really want to see you since you won't be up for the holidays. Call us on Friday before you leave."

"Great, just great." Regina slid down onto the couch and held her head between her hands. "Gee, Mom, sorry I can't come home this weekend because I have to go to a hearing to see if I lose my privileges as a resident at the hospital." *Well, this ought to drop me right down to Jeffrey's rung of the ladder.* Regina looked up. *Jeffrey? Oh where did I put that number?*

She rustled through papers on the kitchen table. "Damn." She put her hands on her hips and looked around the room. Walking into her bedroom, she flicked on the light and yanked open the drawer to her nightstand, emptying its contents on the floor and quickly sorting through them. "Aha!" Holding the piece of paper in her hand, she looked at the clock. California was how many hours behind Eastern Standard Time?

"Come on, Jeff, pick up." Regina paced her living room, listening to the phone ring on the other end of the line.

"Uh, hello," a hoarse voice answered.

"Jeffrey? It's Regina."

"Oh, Regina. No, this is Darryl. Hang on a second." She heard muffled voices in the background.

"Regina? What's wrong?" her brother asked.

"How do you know something's wrong?"

"It's two in morning out here, Reg. Or did you just forget the time difference again?" Her older brother was awake now and sitting on the edge of his bed.

"Shit. I'm sorry. I guess both."

"Both? You're confusing me Regina. Have you been drinking?"

"No. I, uh, listen. I'm in trouble. At least I think I am." Regina motioned with her hand as she walked restlessly around the room.

"What did you do now?"

"It's a long story. Um, well, we saved a woman tonight who was in a car accident. We delivered her baby in the car, but she's going to lose her leg. The hospital is suspending us and they might take our privileges away." Regina took a breath. Silence at the other end of the phone then, "Jeff, you there?"

"Eyah. What the hell happened?" he asked. "Okay, this time give me the details and slow down."

Regina spent an hour detailing what happened earlier that evening. "I'm sorry Jeff. I know you have to go to work in the morning."

"It *is* morning. Don't worry about it. You're my sister and the only member of my family who still talks to me. Hey, thanks for the anniversary card. Darryl thought it was really sweet."

Regina smiled briefly. "You're welcome. So what do you think, Jeffrey? Can they suspend us and take our privileges away?"

"Well, based on what you told me about the hospital's policy, they could suspend you. But considering the circumstances, the weather, the ambulance being delayed, the fact that the woman was critically injured *and* in labor..." He hesitated and took a breath. "It would be a poor choice to make scapegoats out of two doctors who saved her and the baby." Jeffrey was in full legal mode now. "Hospitals revoke privileges when doctors practice bad medicine and make mistakes that, based on the situation, they shouldn't have. You know that, Regina. Do yourself a favor, get that policy before you go into that meeting and fax it to me." His upset sister agreed. "So you sound pretty upset about this Dr.

Margulies. Is he a friend of yours?"

"No. Alex is the attending I report to while I'm on the residency," Regina explained. She started to tell Jeffrey that Alex
was a woman but stopped. It wasn't relevant anyway.

"All right, well, call me later today. Let me know what happens. You have my pager number?"

"Yeah I do," Regina said, holding the piece of paper.

# Chapter
# 8

Regina fell asleep in bed still wearing her clothes. It had been a restless night filled with strange dreams and she woke up tangled in the bed covers. After several minutes of kicking and wrestling with them, she rolled out of bed, showered, dressed, and ate a quick breakfast of cereal and juice. It was still raining out so she opted to drive the short distance to the hospital, parking in the lot reserved for medical staff.

She practically ran into Marcus and Dr. Washington in her haste to get into the emergency department.

"I guess you already know about last night?" she asked, looking warily at the two of them. Marcus nodded his head but remained silent. Ever since the day of the needle-stick incident, Marcus had tried to keep his distance from Regina, succeeding more lately than in the beginning.

"Yeah, we heard," Dr. Washington said, looking grim. He looked around the department, grabbed the resident's arm, and pulled her into the staff lounge. "Listen, Regina, everyone knows that you and Dr. Margulies did the right thing. Jameson is using this as an opportunity to discredit her."

"I know," Regina said, her eyes glistening with tears.

"You have to talk to Alex before she leaves. I don't know what he said to her but she's giving up her privileges and resigning. I saw her earlier this morning."

Regina's heart skipped a beat. "You mean she's quitting? Just like that? I don't understand. Why?"

He shrugged. "I don't know, Regina. Maybe she'll talk to you." Dr. Washington smiled sadly. "You both did a great job last night." He patted her on the shoulder. "The woman was asking for you and Alex when she came out of recovery. You should go see her," he said before he left the room.

Regina walked aimlessly through the corridors of the hospital. Everyone she asked told her they had not seen Alex and she was getting worried that she had missed her altogether. She had to find out why Alex was just giving something up that she knew she loved. Regina displayed her ID badge to the security guard as she walked onto the wing of the hospital that was reserved for the newborns and their mothers. The unit clerk at the nurse's station directed her to the room where Laura was staying. Regina knocked on the door and a quiet voice told her to come in. Peeking around the multi-colored curtain, Regina saw the woman whose baby she had delivered, lying in the bed. She was hooked up to an IV, her face was still pale, and her brown eyes looked sunken and hollow. She smiled weakly when she saw Regina.

"Come here." She held out her hand to her.

Regina walked to the edge of the bed and squeezed her hand gently. Her eyes traveled down the length of the covers and her gut clenched when she noticed the blanket as it dipped down to the mattress just below Laura's left knee. Regina lifted her eyes and saw Laura's husband lying in the chair on the other side of the bed dozing. His arm from elbow to fingers was encased in a fiberglass cast, which hung at his chest in a sling.

"I'm so sorry, Laura," Regina said, looking at the heavily bandaged leg.

Laura nodded her head. "You saved my baby. Wait until you see him."

A slight rattling of the clear bassinet's wheels broke the silence as the nurse rolled the newborn into his mother's room. "Here he is, Mrs. Martin," the nurse said, as she pushed the bassinet up to the edge of Laura's bed.

Laura struggled to sit up, losing her balance momentarily as she overcompensated for the loss of her lower leg. Regina steadied her and leaned over her shoulder as Laura cuddled the infant to her chest. A light, downy fuzz covered the crown of his head and tiny blue eyes peeked out between the puffy eyelids.

"He's beautiful, Laura," Regina whispered. Laura beamed at

Regina and squeezed her hand. "What's his name?" Regina ran a
hand gently over the baby's head, staring in wonder at the little
boy she had brought into the world last night.

Laura looked at her husband who had woken up and was
leaning forward in the chair. He nodded his head and went back
to marveling at the bundle lying in his wife's arms. "Alex Reginald Martin. He wouldn't be here if it weren't for you two."

Regina was flabbergasted and stared at Laura in disbelief.
Her jaw worked several times before she could find any words to
say. "I...well, thank you," she finally managed to get out. After
hugging both of them, she left and wondered as she walked down
the hallway if Alex had come up here to see them. She had forgotten to ask before she left their room.

Regina walked into the emergency department and headed
to the nurse manager's office. The door was unlocked so she let
herself in and walked over to the shelf that held the policy and
procedure manuals. She wrinkled her nose as she read the titles
that were printed on the spine of the large three ring binders.

"Ah, administrative policies. It should be in there." She
pulled the thick manual down, opened it up and sat down behind
the desk. It took her several minutes of flipping through the
index to find the policy she was looking for. Regina pulled it out
and read it over, deciding to make a copy. Next, she picked up
the phone and dialed the number for the police department.

Regina closed the office door quietly behind her and walked
out into the department. Dr. Jameson spotted her immediately as
she stepped around the corner.

"I have the VP of medical affairs in the conference room
down the hall. We both want to speak to you now, Dr. Kingston."

Regina took a deep breath and squared her shoulders. "I
need to get something off the fax machine." Regina walked away
from the director praying the report would be there.

"*Now*, Dr. Kingston." She could hear the edge of barely contained anger in his voice.

Regina ignored him and tapped her fingers nervously as the
machine beeped and a fax started coming through. She saw the
heading on the top of the page and breathed a sigh of relief as
she retrieved the document. She folded it and slid it into her bag.

Walking slowly towards the door, her anxiety built inside as
she remembered her conversation with Jeffrey earlier in the
morning. She wished he were here to help her now.

She entered the carpeted room with its mahogany tables and

chairs lined up around the perimeter. Dr. Jameson walked to the head of the table and sat down, resting his hands in front of him on the table. A sharply dressed woman sat to his left. She wore a black pantsuit and a red silk shirt. Her short blonde hair accented her strong features and she nodded her head at Regina in acknowledgment.

"Sit down, Dr. Kingston." The medical director pointed to a chair across from the other woman. "This is Dr. Mitchard, our vice president of medical affairs. She already heard Dr. Margulies' story and I suppose yours is much the same, so let's not waste her time, shall we?"

Regina watched the woman as her eyes narrowed subtly and her jaw muscles worked as the director spoke.

"Since Dr. Margulies is your supervisor, legally she bears the responsibility for your actions. You both rendered emergency medical care outside of the hospital and caused irreparable damage to a patient." Dr. Jameson opened a folder in front of him. "We have no choice but to suspend you without pay until the medical review committee can meet and determine the appropriate course of action." He slid a triplicate document over the table and rolled the pen in her direction. Sitting back in his chair, he crossed his legs and folded his hands over one knee, looking very self-confident and smug. "This is a copy of the report. I need you to sign it."

Regina could hear the blood rushing in her head as she listened to him. *Jesus, this couldn't be happening, could it?* She pulled the paper toward her and read it over twice. "No, no. This isn't correct," she said, sitting up straighter and pushing her hair behind her ear.

"What do you mean?" The VP leaned forward, suddenly taking an interest in Regina for the first time since the meeting began.

"This says the vehicle that Mrs. Martin was in was off the hospital property. It wasn't. It was on the front lawn of the hospital." Regina pushed the paper away from her. "I'm not signing this."

"That doesn't mean a damn thing. Sign the paper." Jameson leaned forward in his seat, letting the front legs of his chair bang heavily onto the carpet.

"Like hell I will."

"You have no proof that the car was on hospital property." He stood up, put his hands on the table and leaned over her.

"I have the police report." Regina stared back at him, her eyes challenging and defiant. *Thank you, Jeffrey. I owe you one.*

Dr. Jameson paled and the vice president leaned forward, touching Regina's arm. "Dr. Kingston, may I see the police report?" She cast a warning glance at the medical director. Regina dug inside her backpack and pulled out the report. After unfolding it, she slid it across the glass-topped table.

"But the policy—" Dr. Jameson argued.

Dr. Mitchard cut him off with a motion of her hand. She studied the report and pushed it over to the medical director. "Jim, stop splitting hairs. Yes, they took a risk and the hospital will probably be liable for the woman's injuries, but it could have been much worse."

She turned her attention to the resident sitting across from her. "Well, this certainly sheds a different light on the situation since the car was on hospital property. It would look very damaging for the medical center to take the stance that we will not offer medical care to an injured or sick person because they're not inside the building. I'm afraid the suspension will stand until the committee meets."

Regina breathed a sigh of relief. "What about Dr. Margulies?"

"Obviously, you're not aware that Dr. Margulies resigned this morning due to personal reasons," Dr. Jameson said.

A cold numbness settled over Regina as she left the office and watched residents and nurses hustling in and out of various rooms taking care of patients. For the first time in her career, she felt oddly distanced and unsettled as she watched the activity that had become her life over the past couple of months.

Sandy walked up behind Regina and tapped her on the shoulder. "Hey."

Startled from her daze, Regina turned around. "Why did she leave, Sandy?" she asked, trying to fight the lump forming in the base of her throat.

Sandy lowered her head and shrugged her shoulders. "Maybe she got tired of fighting Jameson at every turn."

"I don't understand it, Sandy. She could fight this." Her voice was ragged and tears rolled down her cheeks. "Do you know where she is?" Regina wiped the tears from her face.

"No. She didn't tell me where she was going." The nurse took pity on the young woman. "Here, I have her cell phone number." She wrote it down on a piece of paper and handed it to

Regina. "Give her a call. I think she still has it."

Regina took the paper from Sandy and headed home. There was nothing left for her to do here. The hospital would contact her when the committee was ready to meet.

❖ ⌘ ❖ ⌘ ❖ ⌘ ❖

Fighting the quiet depression in her heart, Regina made the three-hour drive up to her parent's house. She had only talked to them on the phone twice since she had broken up with Derrick and could only imagine the reception she was going to get.

Turning into the dirt driveway, she slowed the car, the gravel crunching beneath her tires as she drove up to the old farmhouse. A familiar wash of memories flooded her as she stepped out of the car and shut the door.

Her father walked out of the barn carrying a shovel and a pail. He stopped and watched as she stepped out of her car and shut the door. "Hello, Regina."

"Hi, Dad." She walked up to him and kissed him on the cheek. Looking at her father, she decided he had more gray hair and the lines on his face seemed deeper than the last time she saw him.

His dark eyes regarded her carefully. "So, I guess you've made up your mind about Derrick then." He set the bucket down on the ground and leaned on the handle of the shovel regarding his only daughter carefully.

Regina nodded her head. "It's the right thing for me to do."

Her father closed his eyes and shook his head. "I don't understand your generation, Regina. You have a good man who's willing to take care of you. Why do you always want to be so independent?"

"Dad, please, I really don't want to get into this. Is Mom inside?" Regina asked. *Might as well get this over with,* she thought morosely.

"Yeah," he sighed. "She's pretty upset."

Regina nodded her head and walked up to the wooden steps. *Of course, she would be upset.* She pushed opened the screen door and stepped inside, holding her hand out behind her so it wouldn't bang when it closed. "Mom?"

She listened and heard the creak of the floorboards over head. She was in the sewing room. *Where else would she be?* It was Friday and her mother always ironed clothes on Friday.

"Up here, Regina."

Regina climbed slowly up the steep staircase, looking at the family pictures that hung on the wall. There were empty spaces where Jeffrey's pictures had been taken down. Regina had never been able to understand how her mother had shut him out of her life so completely; it was like he had never existed in this house.

Stepping onto the small landing, Regina watched as her mother poked her head out of the room. She was wearing a faded denim skirt and a brightly colored shirt.

"Hi." Regina stood in the hallway awkwardly. Part of her wanted to reach out and hug her mother, needing the reassurance that everything was okay, but she didn't. Physical displays of affection were not commonplace in her home and her mother's piercing green eyes held her at bay.

"You look thin, Regina. Aren't you eating enough?" Alice walked back into the sewing room, picked up the iron, and started pressing the creases into her husband's shirt.

"I'm fine, Mother," Regina said, pointedly avoiding any questions about her health. Regina could see her mother's jaw working as she clenched and unclenched the muscles, and she felt the butterflies start in her stomach. Quietly, she stepped into the small room and leaned her hip against the wooden desk.

Her mother lifted the shirt off the ironing board and hung it on a wire hanger. She turned and set the hanger over the door and glanced at her daughter.

"Derrick was heartbroken, Regina." It was a simple statement but it spoke volumes.

It had always been about how other people perceived the family. *Appearances are important, Regina. You'll understand that one day.* Her mother's voice echoed in her ears.

"I *don't* love him, Mother. Can't you understand that?" Regina looked down at her hands. *Oh, this was going to be a joyful weekend*, she thought.

Her mother pulled another shirt from the pile and laid it on the ironing board. She sprayed the fabric with starch and picked up the iron, pressing the button and causing steam to belch out as she ironed the shirt. "Regina, you hardly gave him a chance. Love doesn't just happen, it takes time."

Regina tilted her head up against the wall and closed her eyes. "Mom, has Dad ever laid a hand on you?"

"What kind of a question is that, young lady? How dare you?" Her mother's face reddened with rage.

"I didn't think so."

Her mother's eyes narrowed. "Just what are you saying?"

"Derrick threw a vase at me, Mom, or did you conveniently forget that?" She yanked the sleeve of her shirt up and shoved her arm out so her mother could see the red and puckered scar running up the inside of her arm. Her mother turned away. "I needed close to twenty stitches by the time it was all over."

Her mother pursed her lips. "Well, you've always had the capacity to infuriate people with your stubbornness. He shouldn't have done that though."

Regina chewed her bottom lip. "Mom, I can't love someone like that."

"Regina." Her mother turned around to face her. "You're going to end up being old and alone. Is that what you want for yourself?"

Coming to the decision that talking about this was a useless proposition, Regina walked to the door. "I'm going to bring my bags in." She walked down the stairs, fighting back the sting of the tears welling up in her eyes.

❖ ⌘ ❖ ⌘ ❖ ⌘ ❖

Dinner was a quiet affair. Regina picked at her food and excused herself after enduring the idle conversation her mother made about people Regina hardly knew anymore. She had lost contact with most of them after she was accepted to medical school.

Regina brought her plate into the kitchen and set it down in the sink. She could hear the hushed voice of her mother talking in the other room as she washed the plates and the pots. It was obvious that her breakup with Derrick was the topic of conversation. She stacked everything in the dish rack and walked back to the living room.

"I'm going to take a walk," she announced, as she went back through to the front hall.

Her parents looked up at her and her father motioned her over. "Take my flashlight and don't get lost in the woods. It's in the hall closet."

"Dad, I think I know my way around. I grew up here," Regina said testily. It was like she had never grown up and left home. Some things just never changed. *I've been here half a day and not once has either of them asked about my work. The only thing they're concerned with is Derrick.*

Regina grabbed the flashlight and her jacket from the hall closet. She stepped out onto the deck and cringed when the screen door banged loudly against the frame. "Sorry," she called out.

Wrapping her purple and green fleece jacket around her, Regina stepped down off the porch and walked to the gravel driveway. She headed up the hill, listening to the sounds of the night animals around her. In the distance, she heard the haunting sound of the barn owl calling out in the darkness.

Her feet carried her over the broken ground, down a small hill and toward the stand of pine trees she had played in as a child. This place had always been the one she had come to when she was confused or hurting. No one ever looked for her this far from the house, never thinking she would wander this far from home. Inhaling the fresh scent of the pines, Regina squeezed between their tightly woven branches. Ahead of her, she could just hear the sound of the water running through the narrow creek on the other side of the pines.

She walked quietly along the pine needle-covered trail. A shadow loomed ahead of her and she made out the dark shape of the ageless glacial boulder that sat proudly above the running water. She stepped up onto its base and felt for the familiar handholds; she lifted herself up and crawled onto her favorite spot.

Overhead, the moon was rising and the stars were twinkling brightly in the sky. Regina leaned back against the rock, pulling her knees up to her chest, wrapping her arms around her legs, and gazed up at the stars.

She scanned the darkness above and she took a breath as she saw the hazy arc of the Milky Way, the light of millions of stars reflecting back to earth from light years away.

The stars had always fascinated the young woman. They hung up in the sky like sentinels looking down over the world, connecting and binding the strands of time and space together. The same stars that people had looked upon when they gazed up at the sky thousands of years ago. She felt a profound sadness flow through her now as she sat alone in the darkness.

She had forgotten how awkward it was for her to go home. Her old friends acted weird around her after they had found out she was going to medical school. She'd finally decided they were just jealous that she had left the small town she grew up in and moved on to better things. Her mother, well, that was another story altogether.

She had always resented the fact that Regina had defended Jeffrey's lifestyle; she considered it a personal affront that her only daughter hadn't sided with her. Her father and her younger brother, Michael, although they didn't approve of it, tried to keep in touch with him after he first left home. Gradually they gave up, as the weekly battles had taken their toll on all of them. Finally, her mother had resorted to ridding the house of anything that reminded her of Jeffrey.

Regina had secretly written to him and kept in touch, knowing how hard it was for him to follow his heart even though it had destroyed his relationship with his family. When Regina had taken the MCAPS and gotten into the University of Massachusetts, her mother's reaction had been subdued at best. For Regina it was an escape and to her mother it was a betrayal. Her only daughter wasn't supposed to leave home before she was married.

She wasn't sure how long she sat on the rock. She only knew that her seat was sore and she was starting to fall asleep. Carefully, she slipped down off the rock and made her way back to the house.

Regina noticed the light was on in the study as she walked through the front door and closed it quietly behind her. She could hear her mother's voice talking but heard no one else's.

Deciding she was on the phone Regina headed for the stairs. As she started to walk up the steps, she overheard her mother's voice and stopped. The hairs stood up on the back of her neck.

"You have to come up and talk to her...Yes, I know it's all been a terrible misunderstanding, Derrick. I'm sure you two can work it out...It's all right...Good, then we'll see you tomorrow morning...Excellent."

Regina walked quietly to the door of the study and waited for her mother to hang up the phone and turn around. Her mother's eyes widened slightly and then her mouth set in a thin line when she saw her daughter standing there.

"How dare you?" Regina growled, barely able to contain the anger she felt. "I can't believe you would go behind my back and ask Derrick to come up here. You know damn well I don't want to see him."

"Regina, I'm just looking out for your best interests. You obviously aren't capable of doing that," her mother insisted. "Who is this doctor that you've been working with in the emergency department?"

*Oh shit.* "She's my supervisor." Regina crossed her arms. Warning bells went off in her head.

"After what Derrick just told me, it doesn't sound like she should still be practicing medicine at all."

"Mom, you have no idea what went on. Derrick doesn't like her because she ran him out of the ER the night he attacked me."

Her mother's eyes searched her face. "She's—" She stopped and put a hand up to her mouth.

"She's what, Mom?" Regina asked, as her heart raced. *Oh God, not now. I don't need this.*

"A lesbian." Her mother spat the word out like she had just tasted something rancid.

"So?"

"You should find another hospital to work at."

Regina laughed at her. "Don't be ridiculous mother. There are gay people everywhere."

"She's going to try and corrupt you."

Regina rolled her eyes. "Mother, that is so..." She threw her arms up. "Either you're gay or you're not. What does it matter who you fall in love with as long as they love you back?"

Her mother's eyes narrowed. "What are you saying?"

Regina's heart skipped a beat, as she realized the question for what it was. She was tired of the half-truths and she wasn't going to keep living a lie. She took a breath and let it out slowly. "I'm gay."

"You are not!" Her mother stepped up closer and pointed a finger in her face. "Don't you dare say that to me."

Regina backed up. "Come on, Mom, you knew three years ago. Why do you think you asked me about Sarah?" She stuck her hands in her pockets and looked down at the floor. "The problem was I was too scared to admit it to myself at the time." She looked back up.

"No! You are not a lesbian." Her mother sat down in a chair. "Oh God, I think I'm going to be sick."

"You know what, Mom?" Regina jammed her hands down deeper in her pockets, feeling completely alienated for the second time in a day. "I think maybe Jeff was the lucky one when he left home."

Her mother stepped up to her and slapped her hard across the face. "You bitch. I don't know who you are anymore, Regina. You've changed since you left home and I don't like the person you're turning into."

Regina restrained herself from showing how much the slap hurt. "I think it's called growing up, Mom, and finding your own way." Regina kept her emotions in check as she stood face to face with her mother. Slowly she turned and walked up the stairs away from her mother, retreating into her old bedroom.

"We are *not* finished discussing this," her mother called after her. "You are not like your brother."

After closing the door behind her, Regina leaned against it. Her heart pounded in her chest and her mind was racing. She couldn't stay here. Derrick would be here by morning and he was the last person she wanted to see. Regina brought her hands up to her face and shook her head as the reality of what she had just done hit her. *Good grief, I just came out to my mother. Oh, this is not good. What the hell were you thinking? I must be going crazy.*

Pacing across the room, Regina looked at her unpacked suitcase. Part of her wanted to grab it, run down the stairs and drive away now, but she could barely keep her eyes open and if she got into the car now she was sure she would end up in a ditch or worse. Before she climbed into the bed she looked at her watch and set her alarm for midnight. At least she could get a couple hours of sleep before she left.

Two hours later, the gentle beeping woke her from a sound sleep. Blinking her eyes open, Regina reluctantly sat up from underneath the warm covers and ran a hand through her hair, unsure of where she was for a second. *Oh, just a little more time. I feel like I just fell asleep.* It would have been so easy to lie back down and close her eyes, except her mind quickly reminded her that Derrick was on his way and that he had been the person who had disabled her car just a few nights ago. That and the thought of another confrontation with her mother was the only reminder Regina needed to get moving.

Carrying her bags, Regina slipped down the stairs. She felt catapulted back to her high school days. She and Jeffrey would frequently wait until their parents went to sleep to sneak out of the house and go sit on their special rock by the creek. They had talked for hours, forming a bond between them that most siblings their age didn't share.

Regina felt a pang of cowardice and guilt as she wrote a quick note to her parents. She would call them in a few days, but she couldn't stay. She hoped they would understand in time.

Regina locked the door behind her and got into her car. She left the lights off as she pulled out of the driveway, turning them on as she headed down the road toward the Massachusetts Turnpike.

The interstate was deserted at this hour of the night as Regina traveled east toward Boston. She hadn't really thought about where she was going, only that she wanted to get away from her home. *Ironic that I still considered it home. It certainly isn't anymore. Who was it that said that home is where the heart is, anyway?*

The young doctor just let her body go on autopilot, like it knew exactly where she needed to go even if she didn't know why. In less than an hour, Regina turned off the turnpike and headed north onto Route 93. Then it was a right turn into Sumner Tunnel and a toll to pay. After negotiating through the confusing directions at Logan Airport she left her car in long-term parking and walked toward the entrance for departing flights.

Inside she stood staring at the monitors wondering why she had ended up here of all places and why did she still have that awful sense of dread building inside of her? She dug in her pocket, pulled out a wrinkled piece of paper and headed toward a bank of phones.

# Chapter
# 9

Alex stood in the second floor apartment looking out over Provincetown Bay. By sheer luck she had stumbled across the listing in the local newspaper five years ago. It was a small rectangular lot, with the old house sitting close to the road one block up from Commercial Street. She bought it for a reasonable price and had taken her time fixing the house up to her liking. She rented out the downstairs part and kept the upstairs apartment as her own.

A separate entrance ensured her privacy. The narrow staircase led up to a small landing. A ninety-degree turn to the right, and the hallway that was bracketed by two large crawlspaces that she used for storage led to the apartment door.

The apartment itself was U-shaped. The walls were paneled with knotty pine wood and the ceiling was whitewashed with heavy wooden beams running across its length. There was a small rectangular wooden table that sat next to the bay window looking out onto the gravel driveway below. To the right of the room sat a maroon leather couch that pulled out into a bed, and a color television faced it from the opposite wall. Alex's favorite spot in the apartment was the small deck with a sliding door entrance she had built onto the side of the house. Completing the U-shape was the area that was filled with the queen-sized bed with two nightstands.

She bought the house with the intention of making it an annual vacation spot. As it turned out, Lana had gotten sick again and the vacations had never become a reality. One of the last requests Lana had made before she died was for Alex to bring her ashes back to Provincetown and spread them out in the bay. Eight months had passed since her death and it had taken her all this time to return here.

Alex sighed as she turned away from the glass door. There was no sense in delaying the inevitable.

"Well, I guess its time I get this over with," she said quietly to herself. Alex opened the box that the urn was securely packed in and slipped the metal container into her backpack. Slinging the pack over her shoulder, she stepped out of the apartment, locked the door behind her, and headed down the stairs into the warm late-night summer air.

It was a clear night and the moon was out, three-quarters full. Alex walked along the still bustling main drag in Provincetown. Weaving in and out of the crowd, she kept quietly to herself, stepping up onto the steps of some of the storefronts at intervals to keep away from the jostling crowds.

She gratefully left the noisy and raucous atmosphere behind her, heading down the narrow road toward the mile long outcropping of rocks that formed the jetty. It was high tide and she could hear the gentle sound of the water lapping up in between the rocks as she headed farther out into the darkness, picking her way carefully along the rocks. The smell of salt water and fish filled the air.

Finding a flat rock to stand on, Alex stood in the moonlit darkness and removed the urn from her backpack.

She stood quietly for a few odd moments watching the eerie trail of white moonlight flicker on the waves of the water and gradually disappear into the darkness as it reached the horizon. Alex raised her head and looked at the moon above. The man was still there looking down, but his face was only half-visible tonight. Alex closed her eyes as she was reminded of another time that she sat in the darkness with the moon the only source of light.

*"I can't save you."*

*A light chuckle rang in her ears.*

*"Alex, I didn't ask you to save me. Just help me get through this. Please?"* Lana clasped her frail hands around Alex's.

*Alex wrapped the blanket more tightly around her bare shoulders as another shudder ran through her drug-craved body. The drugs refused to let go of her, clinging seductively to her nervous system. She ran her tongue over her dry and cracked lips.*

*"What do you think I can do that a hospital up here can't?" Her breath came in short gasps as she tried desperately to catch her breath, struggling against the base craving from the withdrawal she was only beginning to experience.*

*"I don't want to die alone in a hospital. I want you to be with me when the time comes."*

*"I'm not a doctor, Lana."*

*"Yes, you are."*

*"No. Not anymore, not after this." Alex desperately tried to focus on the vision sitting before her.*

*"Sometimes being a doctor isn't about saving someone. It's about letting them go. I can't fight this anymore, Alex," Lana pleaded. "Please let this happen, let me go."*

*She leaned against Lana's shoulder and nodded her head slowly.*

Opening her eyes, she let out a heavy sigh. There was a moment of uncertainty as she looked at the container that lay in her arm, holding Lana's ashes. *No, it was what she wanted. You promised.* Alex squatted down on the rocks and unscrewed the lid, staring into the dark water below. She thought that she should feel more sadness than she did and decided that maybe she was just numb from everything that had happened over the past several months.

She held the urn out over the water and emptied its contents, watching as the gray ashes were carried off in the breeze and disappeared into the dark water below. In the distance, a foghorn sounded. *Good-bye, Lana.*

"Ooh, how touching, Alex." A harsh voice broke the stillness.

Alex lifted her head up to see a blonde-haired woman dressed in jeans and a dark leather jacket, standing several feet away, clapping her hands slowly.

"Hello, Dana."

"You know, I'm so hurt you didn't invite me to this ceremony." Dana chewed hard on her bubble gum, snapping the bubbles loudly in between her teeth.

The tall, dark-haired woman stared at the leather-clad blonde and slowly stood up, twisting the top back on the urn. *That was the whole point you self-absorbed, manipulative bitch.*

"After you didn't show up for your own sister's memorial service, I honestly didn't think you cared one way or the other what I did with her damn ashes."

"You know I cared about Lana."

Alex stared down at the water, listening to the gentle lap of the waves on the rocks as she considered her next comment. "Only when it suited your purposes."

Dana flashed her a toothy grin and crossed her arms, shifting her weight onto one leg. "Oh, that hurts, Alex."

"The truth usually does, Dana," Alex stated, her lip curling into an evil sneer.

"So, we finally get to see what Lana left the two of us. You know, Alex, I was thinking, after the lawyer does his thing with the will Sunday afternoon, maybe we can go back to the store and have us a private party for old times sake." She eyed her appraisingly.

Alex ignored the comment and picked up her backpack. She shoved the urn inside and zipped it shut. "Is that all you came out here for, Dana?" Alex asked, knowing that it wasn't.

"You never were much for conversation, were you, Alex? Come and work with me again. We'll split the profits fifty-fifty," Dana bluntly offered.

Alex brushed by her, starting to negotiate her way back toward the shore. "I'm not interested, Dana."

Scampering across several rocks, Dana caught up with Alex and placed a hand on her arm. "What's wrong, Alex, afraid you'll be tempted again?"

A look of pain crossed Alex's face. *God, I caused Lana enough pain to last a lifetime.* "Yes."

"Come on, Alex. They're no strings attached this time. You've got no one to worry about now but yourself. I'll make it worth your while," Dana said, smiling seductively.

"Give it a rest, Dana." Alex angrily shrugged her arm free.

"Well, you can't blame me for trying, Alex. Here, I brought you something to help you relax tonight." Presenting the taller woman with a bag, Dana smiled. "I know how much you've been dreading this whole thing. Sweet dreams, love." Dana shoved a brown bag into Alex's hand and winked at her, before she disappeared into the darkness. Alex stared after her wondering how in the hell she was going to keep her last promise to Lana.

Alex walked back to her apartment in the darkness. Restless and on edge, she prowled around the apartment. She opened the sliding glass door and stepped out onto the deck, folded her arms across her chest and leaned back against the railing, looking up at the sky. Seeing the stars overhead, she searched and found the constellation Regina had pointed out to her: Orion's Belt. *I wonder...does the sky look the same where you are tonight, Regina?*

*Well, you sealed your fate today,* Alex thought bitterly. For better or for worse, she severed her ties with the hospital and that was just fine with her. *I don't need any more complications, damn it.* Alex took a breath and blew it out slowly between her lips. Dropping her arms down to her sides, she looked across the apartment at the brown bag sitting on the table, patiently waiting for her. *Oh, what the hell. Who gives a crap about what you do at this point anyway?*

She walked over to one of the cabinets and pulled out a shot glass. The brown bag crinkled as she grabbed it off the table and walked over to the couch. Alex lowered herself to the floor, her back leaning comfortably against the couch with one leg pulled up in front of her and the other stretched out, resting against the leg of the table. She pulled the bottle of Green Label Jack Daniels out of the bag and set it on the table in front of her.

There was no subtly to Dana's motive; she had always been the grand manipulator. After all, Alex grossed her the most profit in the short time she worked for Dana. Why wouldn't she want her to come back?

She unscrewed the cap and filled the shot glass with the amber fluid. Lifting it up to her mouth, she tossed the alcohol back, grimacing as it burned her throat and heated up her insides on the way down. Twirling the cap on the table with her fingers, she stared at the TV screen in front of her. Briefly, she wondered how the mother whose baby Regina delivered the day before was doing. *It doesn't matter anymore; just forget about it.*

Alex picked up the bottle, refilled the shot glass and lifted it up to her mouth. Without hesitation she tossed the alcohol down and set the glass down on the table, wiping the liquid from her lips with her other hand. She could feel the warm fog settling down around her and she smiled as it numbed her aching soul. *Ah, the wonders of self-medicating. What was that saying? Healer, heal thyself?* She laughed caustically. *Yeah right.*

Her cell phone rang and she ignored it. "Oh screw off. It's

probably some asshole calling from the hospital. Doesn't realize I don't work there anymore." It rang three times and then stopped.

Alex fished in her jacket pocket for a lighter and picked up the joint she had taken out of the brown bag. *What the hell did it matter anyway what she did at this point?* She wasn't going back to the hospital. She made sure of that when she signed the papers earlier today, or was it yesterday? The past few days seemed like one big blur to her now.

She lit the end of the joint and sucked the acrid tasting smoke into her lungs. Holding her breath, Alex turned the joint, rolling it slowly between her index finger and her thumb, studying it intently as she exhaled. *The apple doesn't fall far from the tree now does it, papa?* She picked up the bottle and she poured herself another shot. Holding the glass of oily amber fluid and the joint in front of her, Alex saluted them.

"To old friends." Alex tossed the shot down and swallowed the alcohol, grimacing as it burned her throat. She took another long drag from the joint and inhaled the smoke. She was well on her way to getting completely soused and quite frankly, she really didn't give a damn one way or the other. There were no responsibilities, no obligations to fulfill anymore, so she could do what she wanted.

She wasn't sure how long she sat like that, floating in that dreamy state of consciousness, feeling comfortably disconnected from reality. At some point, she screwed the top back on the bottle of Jack Daniel's and stubbed out the joint.

It had been six years since she wandered aimlessly down this desolate road. Did she really want to open those doors again, letting those demons drag her back down? She laughed at the absurdity of it all. *God, if they only knew back at the hospital, Jameson wouldn't have had to work so hard to get her out of there.*

Her heart pounded faster, as one by one all her sins lay out in front of her. She let the noble belief that she could succeed where the other doctors failed drive her to conveniently rationalize her grossly misguided actions. There was no way that Lana could have gotten the money she needed to pay for the experimental drug to treat the aggressive cancer while she was still in medical school. Alex was terrified enough of losing her that she struck a deal with Dana, Lana's twin sister. It was simple enough and Alex willingly agreed to it. She would sell drugs for Dana and get a cut of the profits. The money was easy and she was confident that she could handle herself.

*Lana's incredulous face stared up at Alex as she handed her the prescription for the medicine that promised to shrink the tumors. "Where did you get this, Alex?"*
*"I'm doing a friend a favor. Don't worry about it."*

Alex swore Dana to secrecy. It became a game and Alex hadn't realized she was the one being played until it was too late. They made a staggering amount of money in one week and Dana insisted on having a party to celebrate their success. Alex did the one thing she promised herself she wouldn't do and by the end of the night she gave everything away, including her soul. It was a quick and dizzying descent into a nightmare of overpowering compulsion to continue taking the drugs, seeking a repeat of that initial euphoric excitement.

An image of lying in bed next to Dana nauseated her. Out of desperation she laid everything on the line, compromising her relationship, career, and her life. She did it all to keep a dear friend alive and to cheat death. It hadn't worked and in the end it was Lana's pleading that pulled Alex back from the brink of self-destruction.

*"I don't want this Alex." She threw the medicine in the garbage and took Alex's hand. "Listen to me, please. I'm dying and you're the one bargaining your life away, for what?" Lana asked. "A few stolen moments?"*

Alex shook her head as memories of the night of the accident ran through her head vivid and clear like they just happened yesterday. Alex rubbed her face as she saw herself standing next to the boy's body that lay naked and lifeless on the stretcher. Her hands hung limply by her sides as she watched, helpless to do anything else.

The blood dripped slowly from the wound where they had cut the boy's chest open and used the rib spreaders to open the chest cavity. Blood saturated the blue sheet that covered the stretcher, rolling down the metal rails, slowly dripping to the white tiled floor, staining it a dark red as it pooled and coagulated. The damage was massive. The impact of the steering wheel tore several of the vessels around his heart. It had ceased beating moments before, so blood was no longer pumping from the torn vessels with each beat of his dying heart. Alex stared down at the gaping wound, her bloodied hands, and the blood-soaked scrubs she was wearing. She saw herself stagger back against the wall, and slide limply down to the floor, over-whelmed by the loss of her lover and now the death of this boy whose name she couldn't even remember.

"Alex, do you want me to tell the boy's parents?" Sandy crouched beside her, watching as the doctor struggled to control her raging emotions.

"No, I'll do it."

Alex pulled her eyes away from the wall, dispelling the haunting image from her thoughts. She imagined Sandy standing at the desk with her hands on her hips, glaring at Alex for some sarcastic remark, no doubt. Then an image of Regina flooded her mind. The young doctor was staring up at her with a look of wonder as she lifted the newborn and set him on the mother's stomach. Angry at the strong emotions that thoughts of Regina evoked in her, Alex shoved the unwelcome images out of her mind. *Damn you, for feeling anything about her!*

Alex wrapped her arms around her knees and tucked her head down, rocking back and forth as tears unexpectedly rolled down her face. Distraught, she reached inside her jacket and pulled out the bottle of Lana's pain medication she found in her medicine cabinet at home earlier that day. She had grabbed it as she shoved clothes and toiletries haphazardly into her duffel bag, packing to leave for the Cape. She twisted the cap off and shook all the pills out into her hand, counting them methodically. There were thirty.

After unscrewing the cap from the liquor bottle once again, she poured more Jack Daniels into the shot glass. Alex wiped her eyes and leaned forward onto the table, covering her mouth with her hand as the tears rolled down her face. She didn't think she had the strength left to listen to Lana's will being read on Sunday. She'd put it off for eight months after she died, but was no more prepared to listen to it now than she was before.

All the while, she knew Dana was waiting for the right time to tempt her back into that hellish existence she struggled so hard to get out of. Of course that was no one else's fault but hers. How stupid could she have been to think she could walk away unscathed? Yeah, she got the money she needed at the time, but what had she lost in the process? Alex rolled her fingers over the white pills, listening to them clicking together on the wooden table. She was tired of waking up and hurting everyday. Staring at the glass in front of her, she decided that she desperately wanted it all to go away.

The cell phone rang shrilly again and she jumped. She reached across the table for it and knocked the glass over, scattering the pills onto the rug. "Son of a bitch," she cursed and picked the phone up. "Didn't anyone tell you I don't work there anymore?" she slurred angrily into the phone.

"Alex, is that you?" Regina's voice on the other end of the phone startled her out of her haze of self-pity.

"Shit." Alex tried to sit up straighter and collect her wildly scattered thoughts. "Regina? How'd you get this number?"

"Sandy gave it to me. Are...are you all right?" Regina asked, hearing the uncharacteristically slurred and broken speech.

"I'm fine...Regina. Never better." Alex grimaced and rubbed her forehead with her hand as the sarcastic words slipped out.

"I don't understand why you left, Alex."

Alex tilted her head back, and laid her arm over her eyes. "I don't expect you to understand why I left. It's complicated." She groped for words. "It has to do with more than just what's going on at the hospital. It's better this way."

"No, Alex. I don't accept that. What do you have to do that is so important that you would throw away your career? It's your life. It's who you are."

"It's over, Regina. There's nothing you can do." Alex wished now she hadn't picked the phone up.

"I got the police report. The car was on the hospital's property." Regina paused to let the words sink in. "It's possible we won't lose our privileges."

There was silence on the line for a few moments and Regina wondered if Alex had heard her.

"Yeah, whatever you say," Alex finally answered. "It doesn't matter. I'm not coming back." Alex leaned over and slowly picked the pills up off up the floor. Her words conveyed more meaning than she intended them to.

A shiver ran through Regina and she clutched the edge of the phone booth. "Alex, don't do this." It was obvious she was drinking and walking a very fine line emotionally. "Hey," her voice softened, "do you want to know what they named the baby?" *Just keep the conversation going*, Regina told herself.

Alex sat silently on the other end of the phone, her arm wrapped around her middle, rocking back and forth.

"I know you can hear me." Regina could hear her ragged breathing. "She named him Alex Reginald Martin."

"Yeah, well they should've put your name first." She rolled awkwardly onto her knees and put a hand on the table, pushing herself up. She took a moment to regain her balance before she slowly walked awkwardly into the kitchen and opened a cabinet. She leaned against the counter, reached inside, fumbled a little, and finally pulled out a glass. Holding it under the faucet, she filled it with water.

"Alex, where are you?" Regina heard the sound of running water in the background.

"What do you care where I am?" Alex snapped defensively. She steadied herself on the counter with her hand. "Why are you calling me anyway?"

"I care, Alex. You're a friend and you're hurting. I care," Regina said, leaning into the phone and closing her eyes at the pain she heard in her friend's voice.

Alex leaned her head against the cabinet and closed her eyes. "Damn it, Regina." Her voice was hoarse and Regina thought she might be crying.

"Alex, whatever it is, let me help you."

"It's not your problem. Besides, you're on call this week-end." Alex walked back to the leather sofa and slumped heavily into its softness. She stared at the pills on the table, sitting there mocking her cowardice.

"No, I'm not. They suspended me until the review board meets to decide what action the hospital should take," Regina said.

Alex felt her blood pressure rise, pounding in her ears, as she seethed. Jameson reneged on his promise to leave Regina out of this mess. *God damn him to hell.* She knew he used his power to sway the medical review committee to order an immediate suspension. Cassandra's hands were tied; as the VP of medical affairs, she couldn't override the committee's decision.

"Are you still there?" Regina asked.

"Yeah." Her voice was foggy and sounded far away as she struggled with the sudden wave of guilt that washed over her at what she had intended to do.

"Where are you?"

A heavy sigh. "I'm on the cape in Provincetown," came the quiet reply.

Regina looked up at the monitors blinking their departing flights information. Taking her heart in her hands, she leaned into the phone booth. "Alex, let me come out there. You shouldn't be alone. Please?"

Alex felt her resolve crumbling. She didn't want to be alone and for as much as she told herself that it was for the best to remain so, her heart was telling her differently.

"Alex?"

"Why would you want to see me?" She wiped the tears from her face.

"Because I'm afraid if I don't, I won't ever get a chance to see you again." She paused. "Please, don't do this, Alex." Regina's heart hammered in her chest.

"Where are you?" came the hoarse question. She thought hazily that she could hear voices in the background but she wasn't sure.

"I'm at Logan Airport," Regina answered hopefully.

"What are you doing there?"

"It doesn't matter. I don't quite understand why I came here, but I did. I can get a flight on Cape Air at eight in the morning. Let me help you."

"Why?" Alex whispered.

"You're my friend. I don't want to lose that."

Alex closed her eyes and the tears rolled unchecked down her face. "W-What time is it anyway?" she asked, as some of the pain ebbed away.

"Almost two thirty in the morning," Regina answered, stifling a nervous giggle as the absolute absurdity of what she was doing hit her.

"Has anyone ever told you, you're crazy?" Alex asked after she took a long swallow of water from her glass.

"Mm. Yeah, my older brother tells me that all the time," Regina said.

Alex leaned forward, putting an elbow on her knee and holding her head in her hand. "What are you going to do between now and eight o'clock?"

Regina looked around at the mostly quiet ticket area. A few people, mostly employees, walked to and from different areas of the airport. She smiled into the phone. "I can stay right here and keep talking to you, if you want."

"No. I...you should sleep," Alex said, grimacing at the not-so-subtle beginnings of a hangover announcing itself to her brain.

"Alex, are you going to be all right?" Regina didn't want to get off the phone.

"Yeah. Regina?"

"What?" she asked, feeling a wave of relief wash through her.

"I don't know...how or why." Alex put her head down and took a breath.

"You're going to be okay. Now promise me you'll be there in the morning, okay?"

"I promise, I'll be there."

"G'night, Alex." Regina listened until she heard the click of the receiver on the other end and then slowly hung up the phone. She turned around and headed to the ticket counter.

# Chapter
# 10

Regina peered out the window of the small commuter plane. Even having grown up in Massachusetts, she had never been to the Cape. Flying in from the west gave her an appreciation of the narrow peninsula that hooked around like a finger beckoning to the Atlantic. Years ago, her brother Jeffrey had shown her an aerial photo of Cape Cod that he found in a book. It showed the Cape from the air on a clear summer's night; a myriad of lights reflected up from all the vacationers that frequented the area at that time of the year. The next photo was taken in the dead of winter, again on a clear night and the number of lights dwindled to where parts of the island were bathed in darkness.

Her thoughts turned to the present as the plane turned and descended toward the small runway below. The blonde-haired woman closed her eyes and waited as she heard and felt the flaps rise, slowing the plane's air speed. There was a bump and a rumbling sound as the tires hit the tarmac, the brakes engaged, and the plane coasted to a stop. Minutes later she heard the sounds of the hatch opening.

The young doctor's mouth was suddenly dry and a flock of butterflies took up residence in her stomach as she stiffly stood up from her seat, shouldered her duffel bag, followed the few other passengers down the aisle, and ducked through the narrow door. The conversation that she had with Alex earlier that morning replayed in her mind and she experienced a sudden sickening feeling that she had done something incredibly stupid. *God, what was I thinking?* Regina ran her fingers nervously through her hair. It must have been a momentary lapse of sanity to call this woman, who was her attending at the hospital. *What if she's not here? What if she doesn't want to see me? What an idiot you are, Regina.*

The glare of the morning sun blinded her momentarily and she shielded her eyes with her hand. Holding onto the railing, she walked awkwardly down the metal steps. It was nine thirty in the morning on Saturday and the small municipal airport at Provincetown was relatively quiet. Regina stepped onto the ground and let her eyes roam around the small airport. She saw a hangar with a small airplane inside and a square building with two large windows looking out onto the airstrip.

To her immense relief, she saw the cobalt blue Jeep parked next to the office and a tall dark-haired figure leaning against the back bumper. Regina walked toward the woman, feeling the butterflies take flight as Alex pushed off the Jeep and slowly walked toward her. Regina decided that the doctor looked slightly rumpled, wearing a white T-shirt, blue jeans, and sneakers.

A pair of black sunglasses hid Alex's eyes and her hair was pulled back in a braided leather headband. Regina smiled nervously as she neared the taller woman, unsure of what to say or do. Alex pulled her hands out of her pockets, and reached out for Regina's bag as she stepped up to her. The resident felt the bag lifted from her body and then the weight of Alex's hand replaced it as she laid it on her shoulder.

"Did you sleep at all?" Alex's voice was hoarse and rough, evidence of her night of heavy drinking and smoking.

Regina looked up into the black sunglasses and could barely make out the lashes that blinked back at her from behind them. Alex's face looked pale and haggard in the early morning sun.

"Hardly." Regina couldn't help the relief she felt at seeing her friend alive and well. She wrapped her arms around Alex's waist and squeezed her tightly.

"What was that for?" Alex grunted as she was released from the exuberant embrace.

"I'm just glad you're okay." Regina held her gaze until Alex turned away and walked to the Jeep.

"I have some errands to run in town. If you want, you can

crash on the sofa and sleep for awhile," Alex offered as she set Regina's bag in the backseat and climbed in behind the wheel.

"That sounds like a good idea." *Okay, you're here. Now what?* "Um, how are you feeling, Alex?"

In response, Alex turned her head slowly and looked down over her dark glasses, arching an eyebrow. "Like shit. I'm ashamed to say I've felt worse."

Alex put the Jeep in reverse and pulled out of the space quickly. The tires crunched over the windblown sand from the dunes and the truck skidded slightly as Alex stopped and put it into drive.

"Sorry," she mumbled.

Regina looked out the window and took in the sight of the scrub pines and other plant life that grew along the winding road. In the distance, a gray tower rose up toward the sky. She glanced at Alex, noticing that the doctor had lowered her window and her arm rested on the frame, fingers idly dancing on the mirror. The Jeep rolled to a stop as the light turned yellow and then red. "Did you take anything?" Regina asked.

Alex reached down into the console and picked up a bottle of ibuprofen. She shook it in answer and then accelerated as the light turned green.

What she really wanted was a hyperbaric oxygen chamber to stick her head into. The oxygen-saturated air would help to relieve the intense pounding behind her eyes. It was a trick she learned from Dr. Washington after they went out drinking one night many years ago, following a particularly awful trauma that had come in.

Of course, they were both on the next day and staggered in to the hospital before their shifts, miserably hung over. He led her down past the morgue and opened the door to the unmarked room. Dr. Washington flicked on a couple of switches and the hiss of oxygen filled the glass chamber. Sticking their heads in, they inhaled the air, dulling the knife-like pain behind her eyes. Alex slipped back down to the room three more times that day to repeat the process.

Alex cleared her throat. "So, why were you at Logan airport at two thirty in the morning?"

Regina shifted uncomfortably in her seat and rubbed her hands over her thighs. "I, uh, went up to visit my parents and ended up leaving rather abruptly. I just got on the highway and kept driving. It's crazy, I know, but that's where I ended up."

"And then you called me," Alex said, finishing the chain of events with no comprehension of why this woman she had known for less than two months called her in the middle of the night. A call that came at a time when she had been so low and absorbed in the pain of past events that all she could think of was ending the pain.

"Yeah, I called you," Regina repeated. "I just, I got this feeling and I...I had to talk to you."

Alex looked at Regina from behind her black sunglasses. She nodded her head and turned into the gravel driveway. "Okay, we're here." Alex slipped out of the Jeep. "I'll walk you up and then I have to go into town."

She stuck the key in the lock and opened up the door. She motioned Regina to go ahead of her and carried her bag up the stairs behind her. Regina waited as Alex opened the door and let her into the apartment.

She stood in the narrow kitchen taking in her new surroundings, acutely aware of the awkward silence settling between them as Alex set her duffel bag on the floor by the couch.

"This is nice," Regina said, as she turned around looking at the apartment.

"Thanks." Alex pulled the glasses off her face and squinted as the light hit her sensitive eyes. She rubbed the bridge of her nose and winced as her headache kicked back into high gear.

"Listen, Alex." Regina hesitantly walked closer to her, feeling that she needed to explain something, anything to her. "I wanted to make sure you were okay. You sounded really...upset on the phone."

Alex turned to Regina and fixed bloodshot, pale blue eyes on her then, looked down at the floor and studied a knot in the wood before she looked back up at the smaller woman. "You were right...what you said..." She let her words trail off as a hand touched her elbow. She'd been so close.

"I thought you might be mad at me for intruding on you like this," Regina said, looking up at the painfully red-rimmed eyes.

Alex shook her head and patted Regina on the shoulder. "No, no, I'm not." Her voice was hoarse again. She thought she would be mad too, but oddly enough, it was a comfort to have Regina here. "Get some sleep. I'll be back in a couple of hours." She squeezed the shoulder under her hand and quickly walked out of the apartment, shutting the door behind her.

❖ ⌘ ❖ ⌘ ❖ ⌘ ❖

Alex walked up to one of the tellers in the bank. The woman looked up at her and smiled. "Can I help you?"

Alex nodded and pulled a paper from her hip pack. "I need to close this account." She handed the account information across the counter and waited. She watched as the woman ran the information through the computer.

"I need to see some identification please," the teller said.

Alex pulled out her driver's license and handed it across. The woman read the name on the card and frowned. "I'm sorry, but this isn't the name on the account."

Alex interrupted her, handing another document across. "Here's the power of attorney." The woman took the document and read it over.

"Okay, everything looks in order here. I just need you to sign here." She passed a document to Alex and pointed at the bottom. "This just states that we have released the funds to you and the account is officially closed."

A wave of grief swept over Alex as she signed her name. This was one more in a long string of painful things she needed to do, bringing her closer to having to really let go of all the worldly ties she shared with Lana. It left her feeling raw and vulnerable.

It hadn't been the best of relationships, fraught with its multitude of stops and starts. They never had enough time to devote to each other, giving most of their energy to their work. When Lana was finally diagnosed with breast cancer and started really getting sick, it evoked a deep, visceral reaction of fear and the painfully obvious knowledge that their time together was quickly running out.

"What did you say?" Alex looked up, realizing she hadn't heard the bank teller's question.

"How do you want the money?" the teller asked again, slightly perplexed at the large sum in the account.

"Hundreds," Alex said. It was the remainder of the money she had gotten from Dana for selling drugs. Standing here now it seemed like another lifetime ago.

She thanked the woman quietly and pulled her dark glasses down over her eyes. Alex stepped out of the cool air-conditioned building and into the thick, humid air. She took in a couple of gulps of air to clear her racing mind and focused on the busy street ahead of her. Sensing Dana's presence, Alex turned her head and regarded the woman with the short-cropped blonde hair leaning lazily against the railing.

"Hello, Dana," said Alex, as she stepped down onto the sidewalk.

Dana's green eyes traveled appraisingly over Alex's lean muscular frame as she clipped her key chain to her belt loop. Dana slid off the railing, arching her back, exposing her well-toned midriff as her tank top slid up her trunk.

"Oh, Alex, don't I get a warmer reception than that?" Dana stepped forward and laid a hand on Alex's stomach, rubbing it against her shirt, feeling the firm ripple of muscles beneath it.

She rose up onto her toes and planted a kiss on her cheek. Alex stopped the roaming hand and pushed it firmly away from her.

"Oh, you really do know how to hurt a girl's feelings." Dana pushed out her lower lip and pouted.

"One, you're not a girl," Alex said, as her eyes ran over Dana's scantily clad figure. "And two, I wasn't aware that you had feelings."

"Oh, don't be such a bitch, Alex. It's not becoming of you. So, did you think about my offer from last night?" Dana's eyes glinted at the prospect of having Alex back with her.

Alex shrugged. "Why are you so sure I want to come back to that?"

"You have nothing else, and you forget, Alex, how quickly it seduced you the last time. Once you've tasted that kind of power, it stays in your blood. It's a part of you forever."

Alex regarded Dana coolly. "This is the money from Lana's bank account. It's all of it." She shoved the envelope into Dana's hand.

"The deal was only fifty percent, Alex," Dana said, looking greedily at the wad of green bills in the envelope.

"I don't want it." Alex turned to leave.

Dana made a face and shrugged her shoulders. "Don't forget. We go to the lawyers tomorrow," Dana reminded her needlessly.

Alex shook her head and stalked off. Her feet quickly carried her through the growing summer crowd toward a more residential area off of Commercial Street. Gravel crunched under her sneakers as she turned into her driveway. She cast an uneasy glance up at the window, wondering what her unexpected guest was doing.

Her question was answered when she opened the door to the apartment and saw Regina's body curled up on the sofa. The even rise and fall of her chest told Alex that she was still asleep. Alex opened the refrigerator door and stared bleakly at the meager contents.

With a grunt of disgust, she closed the door more loudly than she intended. Regina stirred on the couch and rolled onto her back, stretching. Pushing her rumpled bangs back, she sat up on the couch and blinked in confusion.

"Where...? Oh. Wow, I was really out of it."

"Sorry. I didn't mean to wake you up." Alex picked a glass up out of the sink and filled it with water.

Regina swung her legs over the side of the couch. "Did you get your errands done?" She stifled a yawn.

Alex nodded her head and swallowed two more ibuprofen pills. She walked over to the table and picked up the shot glass and the bottle of JD. Her eyes must have darted to the ashtray because Regina looked down at the same moment and saw the half-burnt joint sitting in the bottom. Alex quickly picked up the glass ashtray and carried it over to the sink. She dumped it out into the garbage, silently cursing herself for not having cleaned it up before she picked up Regina. At least she had the presence of mind to pick up the pills before she left for the airport.

"Alex, I—"

"Regina, listen." Alex cut her off, turning back around to face her. "I...this is crazy." She paced across the room agitated at the turmoil of emotions running though her. "The person you knew at the hospital is, well, there's a lot you don't know about me and the sooner you knock me off of whatever pedestal it is you have me on, the better." Alex fixed steely blue eyes on the young resident sitting on the edge of the couch watching her.

Regina stared at Alex and then stood up. "Alex, what happened to make you so upset?"

Alex opened her mouth to speak, but found herself lacking the words. "It's...I don't want to talk about it," she finally managed to say and walked over to the window. She knew that settling Lana's estate and dealing with Dana had set her on edge, but Regina's unexpected phone call last night completely caught her off guard. Why else did she agree to pick her up at the airport this morning?

Regina narrowed her eyes and shook her head. "All right."

To Alex's relief Regina's stomach growled loudly. "I don't imagine you've eaten anything, have you?"

Regina shook her head, conceding the change in the conversation for now. She knew that if she didn't eat shortly she would turn into a bad-tempered grump. She could bring up the subject again later and find out what was upsetting Alex so much.

Fifteen minutes later they were walking through the A&P. Regina snagged a bagel and a banana and paid for it at the express register. She caught up with Alex as she was bypassing the produce aisle. Regina eyed the basket and shook her head in dismay.

"I have an idea."

"What?" Alex turned slowly, an eyebrow arching suspiciously.

"I remember telling you I owe you a dinner for fixing my car. How about I cook for you tonight?" Regina offered.

Alex shrugged in apparent indifference and relinquished the shopping cart as Regina headed off down the aisle. Later at the register, Regina looked up at Alex who was busy burying her face in a tabloid paper.

"Alex Margulies, tell me you do not read that garbage," Regina teased her.

Alex cringed and shook her head without looking up.

A high-pitched singsong voice floated across the registers. "Alexandra? Is that you? Oh girl, I haven't seen you in ages."

"Ah shit," Alex muttered. She closed the paper, shoved it back in the rack in disgust, and resigned herself to her immediate fate.

A rather tall and thin, dark-haired man with a moustache sauntered over, flashing her a brilliant smile. He wore a bright yellow tank top and snugly fitting black shorts that revealed his well-muscled arms and legs. Alex sighed as he planted himself directly in front of her.

"What's the matter, Alex? No kiss for me, darling?" he chided, turning his cheek. Alex looked at him out of the corner of her eye and pursed her lips.

"Be nice, Richard," she warned him as she pressed her lips lightly against his upturned cheek.

"Mmm. So who's your friend?" he asked, as his eyes ran appraisingly over the green-eyed, blonde standing on Alex's other side.

"I'm Regina." She stuck her hand out.

"Well, Regina," he made a face at Alex, "since tall, dark, and gorgeous here apparently has no manners, I'm Richard." He shook her hand and leered at Alex who rubbed the bridge of her nose and grimaced, her headache having suddenly gotten much worse. "Nice taste, Alex," he whispered in her ear loud enough that Regina heard and blushed red as the remark registered.

"Back off, Richard," she warned.

"Ooh, aren't we touchy. Wrong time of the month?" He swiped her shoulder with his hand. "Nice meeting you, Regina." Richard pivoted on his heel flashing them both an up-close view of the words emblazoned on the back of his shirt. Alex quickly shifted to block Regina's view, but not before she was able read the words.

"Strictly dickly?"

Alex covered her face with her hands and her shoulders shook convulsively as she laughed. Regina buried her head in her hands and groaned in embarrassment.

"Sorry about that," Alex said as they rode back toward the house.

Regina shook her head and blushed. "Well, he certainly was, um, flamboyant, wasn't he?"

Alex cleared her throat. "Uh, not really. He was actually on his good behavior."

❖ ⌘ ❖ ⌘ ❖ ⌘ ❖

Alex slept soundly on the bed. She practically collapsed after they returned from the grocery store. Regina took the opportunity to jump into the shower. She felt incredibly grungy since she had slept in her clothes last night before driving to the airport.

After stepping out of the hot shower, Regina toweled herself off. She slipped on clean underwear, stepped into her favorite pair of jeans, and pulled a sweatshirt on. It didn't matter if it was eighty degrees out; she always seemed to be cold. Pulling her hair out of the neck of the sweatshirt, she looked in the mirror and held her shoulder length hair off her neck.

The alarm on her watch beeped. Regina rummaged through her toiletry bag and pulled out her medication. She opened the pillbox, and muffled a curse as the pills tumbled to the floor, scattering over the tiles. She picked them up from around the bathroom floor, and dropped all but two of them back into the box.

She tossed the two pills back into her throat and filled a paper cup with water to chase them down. Regina started to snap the lid on the small round box when she noticed the odd looking pill. She pulled it out and examined it. *Alex must have dropped it on the floor.* She opened the lid of the toilet and dropped it into the water. Her breath caught as she looked closer and counted at least ten more of the pills lying at the bottom. *Oh, Alex. You really were that close to doing it.* Regina closed her eyes. *I don't know why or how, but I'm glad I called you. What's going on with you that would drive you to that?*

Regina stepped out of the bathroom and looked at Alex sleeping on the bed. She was curled tightly on her side with her arms tucked in around her stomach. Her face twitched and Regina could hear mumbling in her sleep. She almost reached out to touch her, but stopped just shy of touching her and pulled her hand back. *Let her sleep. She's probably exhausted and doesn't need you waking her up.*

Regina found a bag of charcoal in the pantry off the kitchen and carried it outside, where she filled up the grate with the briquettes. She covered the black coals with lighting fluid, lit a match, and watched as the flames shot up. Then she sat at the wooden picnic table and studied the flames until they burned down, leaving the coals red-hot and glowing.

Satisfied, she walked back up the stairs into the apartment, where she found Alex sitting on the couch tying her sneakers.

"Hey, you're up," Regina said.

Alex looked up and nodded. "Yeah. Sorry. I didn't mean to go off for so long."

Regina shrugged. "I lit the grill. Are you getting hungry?"

"I'm starving."

Regina coaxed Alex into eating outside. Alex didn't say much as she polished off the steak and potato on her plate. Regina knew from the hospital that Alex didn't care for idle conversation and small talk. So, for now, she was content to sit quietly and not push Alex about what was bothering her.

Regina lifted her head up. "What?" She realized that Alex had spoken to her while she had been lost in her own thoughts.

"I asked what happened with your parents that made you leave," Alex repeated.

"Oh." Regina ran her fingers idly over the condensation on her can of beer, leaving a trail of squiggly lines behind.

"It's okay if you don't want to talk about it, Regina," Alex said, watching as the expression on her face turned pensive.

Regina looked up. "No, it's okay, really. I overheard my mother talking to Derrick. She called him to come up and 'talk some sense into me,'" Regina said, crooking her index fingers to quote her mother. "I decided not to hang around for the lecture series about family values and commitments."

Alex shook her head and leaned forward. "You're kidding me? Did you tell her about what Derrick did to you?"

"Yeah. I don't think she wanted to believe that Derrick would be capable of something like that." Regina closed her eyes, suddenly remembering the angry confrontation she experienced with her mother. It left her feeling tired, and more than a little scared that she had burned a bridge with her family she hadn't planned on doing at this point in her life. With a sigh, she lifted herself up off the bench and picked up the plates. "If you don't mind, Alex, I think I'm going to go to sleep. I could really use it."

Alex shook her head, sensing that Regina hadn't told her everything that happened at her parent's house. "Thanks for dinner, Regina," Alex said, her eyes following Regina as she disappeared through the door. Alex sat alone in the waning sunlight, letting her thoughts wander to tomorrow and Lana's will.

# Chapter
# 11

Alex woke in the pre-dawn darkness, her heart pounding in her chest and her body covered in a sheen of cold sweat. She wiped a trembling hand across her brow and let out a sigh, unable to recall the dream. A sense of dread filled her in the darkness.

Pushing herself up on her elbows, she let her eyes adjust to the darkened room and looked across the apartment at the sofa bed, making out Regina's sleeping form.

Alex crossed her arms over her knees, hugging them to her. *So much for not having complications in your life, Alex.* Dana *was* wrong. She did have someone else to worry about, one very strong-willed woman, who was very slowly pulling down the barriers that Alex carefully erected around her during the past year.

With a sigh, Alex rolled out of the bed and walked around to the kitchen. Very quietly, she pulled out a bowl and filled it with cereal and milk. Sitting there in the darkness, in her oversized white T-shirt, she ate the corn flakes and then set the dish and spoon in the sink.

Filled with restless energy, she prowled around the apartment. She leaned against the edge of the sliding door and watched Regina sleep, lying curled up on her side. Shaking her head at her indulgence, she turned and looked out the door into the darkness. After a few minutes, Alex decided that standing here staring into the dark was doing her no good, so she threw on running shorts and a smaller T-shirt.

She looked at the clock. *Four-fifteen. Regina won't be up for hours.* Alex found a piece of paper and a pen, and in the light of the bathroom, she scrawled a quick note and left it on the table next to the couch. She crawled on the floor searching for her running sneakers and shoved her feet into them. Quietly, she let herself out of the apartment.

Alex drove down Route Six, passing the quiet campgrounds and the dunes with bike trails snaking through them. She turned into the vacant parking lot at Race Point beach and hopped out of the Jeep. A cool breeze blew in off the ocean and her hair lifted off her shoulders as she walked down to the beach. The tide was out and she could make out the wet hard-packed sand with the sweeping arcs of dried froth and seaweed lying on it in the waning moonlight. Her skin chilled and goose bumps traveled up and down her arms and legs as she stretched her legs, listening to the sounds of the surf breaking farther out from the beach.

Running beside the ocean, Alex turned her thoughts inward, concentrating on her pace and listening to the rush of air with each breath she took. Her sneakers sank lightly into the hard-packed sand, leaving a trail of footprints in her wake. She passed clumps of tangled seaweed, broken shells, and pieces of driftwood worn smooth by the relentless waves of the ocean. After a couple of miles, she slowed to a jog then crouched in the sand, gazing down at her hands and listening to the sound of the waves breaking in the distance. Raising her eyes, she could see the subtle changes in the dark sky just peaking above the eastern horizon, signaling the dawn of a new day.

Alex rolled back onto her hips, leaned back on her hands and stretched her long muscular legs out in front of her. She closed her eyes and lifted her head as the salty air blew in off the ocean. Her thoughts drifted and she could see the tiny apartment that she lived in with Dana for three and a half months all those years ago.

*It was dark except for the candles that flickered around the cramped room. Alex sat on the edge of the couch and lit another cigarette. Leaning over the table, she calibrated the postage scale and using a small scoop, she poured the white powder into the dish attached to the scale and waited for it to stop its gentle oscillations.*

*"Perfect," she whispered as she poured the powder into a small plastic bag and sealed it shut.*

*Hearing the sound of a key in the lock, she looked up to see Dana walk in carrying a bag of groceries. "Ah, you read my mind. I'm starved." Alex wiped her hands on her jersey and stood up from the couch.*

*Dana set the bag on the counter and blocked Alex's path. "Mm. So am I." She put her hand on Alex's chest and pressed it into her, backing her up. She wrapped her other hand around Alex's neck and pulled her head down to hers, searching for her lips and finding them. Lunch was a forgotten topic.*

Alex opened her eyes and followed the flight of a sea gull as it plunged toward the sand several feet away. It landed on its feet and ran after something, snatched it up in its beak and swallowed it. It took flight, crying out as it flew up in the air. She leaned forward and rested her forehead on her arms.

*She blinked her eyes and grimaced. "Get up."*

*Her mind acknowledged the words, but her body was too sluggish to respond. Alex felt hands grip her roughly under her arms and pull. She lurched to her feet and leaned heavily against something soft, then lifted her head and tried to focus on the blurred image in front of her.*

*"So, you're Dana's latest pet? Why, Alex?" Lana led her from that darkened room and out the back of the cellar. Alex stood in her drug-induced stupor as the passenger door to a car opened and she was guided inside.*

*She spent the next ninety-six hours in agony as her mind and body screamed to have its insatiable craving satisfied again. Death would have been a welcome relief to the psychological and physical withdrawal she experienced.*

*When she finally opened her eyes and focused on Lana, she uttered one word to her. "Why?"*

*"Because you're not the animal Dana has you convinced you are, Alex, and I need your help."*

*"No, you don't," Alex contested.*

*"Yes, I do. I'm dying and I need you to stop doing this."*

"I'm sorry, Lana."

Alex rose to her feet and ran. She stretched her legs and

allowed her body to find that stride that was fluid grace and power melded together. She ran until her lungs burned, and she tasted the tang of metal in the back of her mouth, forcing herself into a sprint as she raced back down the beach. When she made it back to the path leading up to the parking lot, her legs trembled and she struggled up the path as the sand shifted beneath her feet.

Tired, but feeling rejuvenated from the rush of endorphins, Alex slipped into the Jeep. She closed her eyes and tilted her head back against the seat, letting her heartbeat slow down. Maybe meeting with Dana and the attorney to settle Lana's estate wouldn't be so awful after all.

❖ ⌘ ❖ ⌘ ❖ ⌘ ❖

Regina rolled over in the sofa bed and stretched. Sitting up, she looked across the room and saw the empty bed with its covers thrown back in a rumpled heap.

"Hmm." Regina looked at the table beside the couch and reached for the piece of paper that had familiar handwriting scrawled on it. "Running? And she says I'm crazy."

She checked her watch and shook her head. Why anyone would get up that early to go run was beyond her comprehension. Regina quickly showered and changed, deciding she would make some coffee before Alex returned.

She was just tying her sneakers when she heard footsteps coming down the hallway. Alex opened the door and stepped into the apartment.

"You're up." Her expression softened when she saw Regina. "And you made coffee?" she asked, sniffing the air.

"I hope you don't mind." Regina's chest tightened at the sight of Alex's lean and well-toned body, glistening with perspiration. She managed to pull her eyes away to fuss with her shoelace for a second and then stand up.

"Mind? No, I don't mind," Alex said, thinking that she wouldn't have bothered to make it for herself.

"How do you like it?" Regina pulled a couple of mugs out of a cabinet.

"Milk and sugar." Alex stood next to Regina and handed her a spoon that she removed from a drawer. She pulled a glass out of the overhead cabinet, filled it with water, and quickly downed it.

Alex took the mug that Regina handed to her and sat down at the kitchen table. The young resident sat in the chair opposite the dark-haired woman. She could almost feel Alex keeping her at an arm's distance, not wanting to talk about what had brought her here. Looking at her mug, Regina swirled the light brown liquid around in it and they continued to dance carefully around the subject.

"So, why did you go into emergency medicine, Alex?" Regina finally asked, breaking the awkward silence between them with something that she thought was safe.

Alex leaned back in her chair and glanced out the window. *Okay, I can do this.* "The adrenaline rush. I like the pace. It's quick, you make decisions, kind of like living or dying by the sword."

Regina regarded her companion. "That sounds like a well-rehearsed, pat answer to me."

Alex's jaw sagged, the comment catching her off guard. "Geez, am I that transparent?"

Regina blushed at her boldness. "No. Sorry, I guess that was uncalled for."

Alex closed her eyes and tilted her head back. "Actually, you're right. That is my pat answer," she said, focusing her eyes Regina.

"Okay. So what's the real one then?" Regina leaned forward and smiled back at her, green eyes flashing a challenge.

Alex shook her head. *Someone please remind me not to play twenty questions with this one.* "I guess for me it's the pace and the quick decisions, but it's also the fact that I don't have to get involved. You know. Sew 'em up and ship them back out. Makes things less complicated." Alex's voice faded away, realizing once again she let slip something about herself that she hadn't intended to. She could almost see the next question forming behind those penetrating eyes.

"Is that why you left, because it was too complicated to stay?" Regina asked, toying with the handle of her coffee mug before she looked up again.

Alex stared at her. "It was complicated either way." She cleared her throat and looked away from Regina. "I need to meet with the lawyer. I'm settling Lana's estate today."

Regina stood up. "I'll walk into town with you."

Alex started to protest, but stopped. *What could it hurt?*

❖ ⌘ ❖ ⌘ ❖ ⌘ ❖

Alex shifted her tall frame in the uncomfortable wooden chair and glanced around the office. It was a small two-room apartment over the bank with wall-to-wall orange shag carpeting that looked like it hadn't been changed since the late seventies. Obviously the kid was just starting out and Lana, being the person that she was, tossed the young lawyer some business when she decided it was time to have her will drawn up.

It wasn't that Lana was rich; there were things that she didn't want her sister to get a hold of. For twins, they were as opposite as they could get.

If Lana said white, Dana would say black. It had always been that way between the two of them. Lana had been the sensitive and smart half of the duo. Dana had always been intimidated by her sister's confident demeanor and did her best to come off as tough and angry, vying for attention. The act became who she was today and dealing drugs was just another way to act out her anger and get attention from people.

Dana was sprawled on the couch, chewing gum and fussing with her meticulously manicured nails. The lawyer who Lana appointed executor of the will was a fair-skinned, red-haired man with bright blue eyes.

"Uh, Ms. Romano, this shouldn't take long," the lawyer said, trying to get Dana's attention. Dana yawned and stretched lazily, pulling the already brief tank top higher up on her chest. "Lana's will was very clear and straightforward." He pulled his eyes away from Dana and stared at the papers on his desk.

"Good, then let's dispense with all this legal bullshit and get to the point. What did my dear sister leave me?" Dana sat up and ran a hand through her already tousled bleached blonde hair.

Alex rolled her eyes and snorted. "Have some respect, Dana. Shut up and let him read the damn will."

Dana flashed Alex an evil look. "Always trying to take the fun out of everything, Alex. You know, I think I liked you better when you worked for me."

"Drop it, Dana," Alex warned.

"Ooh, you are testy. What's wrong? The little blonde you have with you not enough for your tastes?" Dana leaned forward, her eyes flashing as she locked glares with Alex. "Please, Alex, don't you think Richard didn't just come running to me with that little tidbit of information?"

"Back off, Dana," Alex growled.

"Ladies, please, can we just—"

"Read the damn will," Alex and Dana said to the lawyer at once.

He cleared his throat a couple of times. "Ms. Romano." He looked at Dana. "Lana has bequeathed you her art collection, her corvette, and the sum of one dollar."

Dana was leaning back with a smug, self-satisfied look on her face as she listened to the list. "W...Wait, one dollar? What's that for?" She sat forward with a puzzled expression on her face.

The lawyer coughed and reached for a glass of water. "That's for the title to the art store she gave to you."

"What? Wait a minute." Dana shook her hand in front of her. "What do you mean? She told me the store was mine." Dana jumped out of her seat gesturing angrily with her hands.

"Ms. Romano, please, sit down. What Lana may have told you and what she wrote in her will are two different things. Her will supercedes any verbal agreements she may have entered into before her death."

Alex watched Dana's face as it paled and then turned crimson as she geared herself up for a major tantrum. *Oh boy, here it comes.*

"That bitch. I'll...I'll..." Dana ground her teeth.

"You'll what, Dana? Kill her? She's already dead." Alex leaned forward in her chair. "Sit down and let him finish."

The lawyer gave Alex a pathetically grateful look and returned his attention to the papers in front of him on the desk. "Dr. Margulies."

"Doctor Margulies." Dana mimicked in a fake Boston accent.

Alex ignored her.

"Lana bequeathed you the art store and—"

"Shit." Alex uncrossed her legs and leaned forward, putting her face in her hands. *Why the hell did you leave me the art store, Lana? Of all the stupid, dumb, asinine things for you to do.*

Dana launched herself off of the couch and dove for the desk. "That can't be right. She wouldn't leave the store to Alex. She never wanted it." She yanked the papers from the lawyer's hands and read the words, her face getting redder as she glanced down the page.

She threw them back at the lawyer and stormed toward

Alex. "You godforsaken...piece of...you bitch!" She screamed and hauled her arm back, balling her hand into a tight fist.

Alex sat calmly in the chair watching Dana's arm cock back. She shifted her weight to the left and brought her hand up blocking Dana's punch using her momentum to spin her around. Dana let out a frustrated scream when she found both arms pinned firmly behind her back.

"Let me go, Alex." She struggled uselessly against her grip. She tried to stomp on Alex's feet.

Alex rose up out of the chair still holding Dana's arms and walked her back to the couch. "Sit down and shut your mouth," she growled in Dana's ear, pushing her roughly.

Dana rolled over and smiled at Alex. "You always did like to be rough, Alex," she purred.

She glared down at Dana. "Are we finished?" She looked at the attorney who was red-faced.

"Uh, just this. Lana instructed me to give this to you personally." He reached inside his coat pocket and pulled out a white envelope. "That's everything."

The doctor turned the envelope over in her hand and looked at her name typed on the white paper. It was marked "confidential." A chill went through her and she folded the envelope in half and tucked it away into her pocket. Alex cast a parting glance at Dana who was busy sulking on the couch, and walked out of the office.

Alex heard Dana running down the stairs following her out of the building. She put on her sunglasses, stepped out onto the bank steps, and looked over the crowds, searching for Regina. The tousled-looking blonde stepped up behind her and put both hands on Alex's hips, pulling her closer.

"We need to talk about the art store. Maybe we can come to some sort of an agreement...that's equitable," Dana whispered into Alex's ear.

Alex stepped away from her and looked over her shoulder at her. "I doubt that's even remotely possible, Dana."

"So, who's the blonde powder puff you have trailing around after you?" Dana breathed in her ear as she leaned against Alex.

Alex regarded her coolly through her darkened shades. "Her name is Regina and she's a friend."

"Mm." Dana tilted her head. "She's really not your type, Alex. Or maybe you're into someone who's soft and innocent while you're still getting over Lana. That's okay. I can wait."

Dana moved around her front and pressed a hand on her stomach, stretching up to plant a kiss on her cheek.

"I wasn't aware that I had a type." Alex stepped back as she caught sight of Regina, out of the corner of her eye, walking toward them.

Dana's eyes flicked past Alex and watched with interest as the youthful, innocent-looking blonde approached them.

"Hi." Regina glanced up at Alex and then at the woman dressed in a matching shorts and a sports top that looked tight enough to have required a crowbar to get over her body. The young doctor saw the woman sliding her hand over Alex's stomach as she leaned up to kiss her. Regina grinned when Alex knocked her hand away.

Alex looked at Regina. "Hi," she said quietly.

"Alex, why don't you introduce me to your *friend?*" Dana stepped into Alex's space again.

"Regina, this is Dana. She's Lana's sister," Alex explained, hoping Dana would keep her damn mouth shut for once in her life.

Sensing the tension surrounding the two women, Regina decided that whatever they were discussing she didn't need to make herself a part of it. "I found a Portuguese bakery down the street. I'm going to go check it out. Any requests?"

Alex shook her head. "No thanks. I'll catch up to you in a few minutes." She watched as Regina disappeared into the throng of moving bodies. "What do you want, Dana?" Alex returned her attention to the woman in front of her.

"Hell of a way to treat a friend, Alex." Dana bristled and folded her arms over her chest.

"You are no friend, Dana." Alex lifted the glasses from her face and brushed her bangs off her forehead.

"No, I guess I'm not." Dana played with her keys. "Look, there's a softball game on the west field today at three if you want to come by. There'll be a lot of familiar faces and I'm sure everyone would like to see you." Maybe a change of tactics would work to her advantage.

"I'll think about it." Alex started to walk away.

"Oh and Alex, you can bring Regina along if you like." Dana flashed her one of her dazzling smiles.

Alex waved in acknowledgement and walked off. She felt like she needed to take a shower. She threaded her way through the mass of bodies milling about on the crowded sidewalks,

stopped at the bakery shop and peered in over the crowd at the
counter, using her height to her advantage. When she didn't spot
Regina, she continued to walk, scanning both sides of the street.
She breathed a sigh of relief when she picked out the now familiar blonde head of the woman. She was perched on a bench in
front of the town hall.

"Hi." She sat down next to Regina and leaned forward on
her elbows, watching her munch happily on a pastry.

"This is really good, Alex. You want to try one?" Regina
offered her the bag.

Alex peered inside and grinned. "And you accuse me of
having a sweet tooth, huh?" She selected one of the nut-filled
pastries and popped it into her mouth.

Regina wiped her hands on the napkin and grinned. "Yeah,
one of my biggest vices. How did your meeting go?" she asked,
as her eyes roamed over the crowds of people walking along the
brick sidewalk in front of the town hall.

Alex sighed. *Not as I planned.* "I inherited a store."

"A store?" Regina turned and faced Alex. "Wow, that
sounds interesting. What kind of a store is it?"

*Careful Alex, you do not need to drag Regina into this.* "Uh,
Lana sold all sorts of odds and ends. Dana's been running it for
the past year." She stood up suddenly fidgety and looked around
at the busy square. "Listen, there isn't really anything else to do
today. There's a softball game later on, if you feel like going."
She looked back down at Regina, who watched her intently from
her seat on the bench.

"Yeah, I'd like that, Alex. I haven't been to a softball game
in a long time," Regina answered, wondering why Alex seemed
so nervous all of a sudden.

❖ ⌘ ❖ ⌘ ❖ ⌘ ❖

Three hours later, Regina sat on the metal bleachers at the
park watching the softball game in progress. Alex had been
vague when she questioned her about the art store. Actually, eva-
sive was a better way to describe her response, Regina thought.
It was obvious the doctor was uncomfortable talking about it and
she wondered why.

Regina shielded her eyes as she looked out onto the field.
She decided that Alex looked rather intimidating at first base.
Her long dark hair was pulled back in a single braid underneath a

white baseball cap and she wore her dark sunglasses to block out the glare of the mid-afternoon sun. Her black running shorts and red tank top showed off her well-toned body, muscles rippling subtly beneath her skin as she prowled around her territory at first base.

She recognized the pitcher as the woman Alex had been talking with earlier. Her current attire of a green T-shirt and shorts, although considerably less revealing, left little to the imagination. Regina watched as she hurled the ball toward the plate. The batter swung, hitting the ball, driving it hard between first and second base. It should have been a base hit except that Alex launched her body parallel to the ground and picked the ball out of the air with her outstretched glove. Then landing in the dirt, she rolled neatly to her feet and tossed the ball back to Dana in one graceful motion. Regina nodded appreciatively.

The next batter up swung twice, catching air on both of them. Catcalls erupted from the outfield. "Hey, just what we needed...a little breeze out here!"

The third pitch came very close to her shoulder, driving her back off the plate and Regina swore she saw Dana smirk. The woman stepped back out of the batter's box and drove the barrel of the bat into the dirt.

"Try it again, Dana, and see what happens," she yelled at her.

"Bite me," Dana shouted back.

The next pitch curled in and struck the woman in the side of the head, buckling her knees and dropping her to the ground in a heap. She lay motionless and several players quickly converged around her. Regina walked up behind the backstop and looked on, as Alex bent over the stunned player and talked to her. After a couple of minutes, two of her teammates helped the girl off the field and gave her an icepack to put on her head.

"Are you okay?" Regina asked, sitting down beside the woman on the metal bleachers.

"Yeah. I should have expected that Dana would go after me," she said, looking at Regina through slightly unfocused eyes.

"Why?" Regina couldn't understand why Dana would intentionally hit someone, especially in a pickup game.

"I'm dating her ex-girlfriend," the woman said, as she held the ice pack to the side of her head.

"Oh." Regina sat back and considered this as she watched

Alex's team trot in off the field.

"I'm Sarah." The red-haired woman stuck a hand out.

"Regina." The blonde grasped her hand and shook it. "You better keep that ice on or you're going to have one heck of a lump on your head."

Sarah smiled and nodded her head, then winked at Regina. "Ah, but it's nothing that a little beer won't take care of later."

Regina was about to tell her that a beer might not be such a good idea if she had a concussion, but was interrupted by one of the women from Sarah's team.

"Hey." Regina looked up, realizing the woman was talking to her. "Can you play? We need a left fielder, now that Sarah's out."

"I don't have a glove," Regina explained.

"No problem. Take mine." Sarah pushed the glove into Regina's hands.

"You *can* play, right?" the woman standing in front of Regina asked.

The blonde bristled slightly. "It's been a few years but, yeah, I can play." She took the glove and followed the team out onto the field, setting herself in the outfield just to the left of third base.

"Oh great," the girl in center field groaned loudly. "Might as well go sit back on the damn fence."

Regina looked over. "Why?"

"This batter." She pointed as Alex stepped up to the plate. "She sends it over the fence almost every time I've ever played against her." Regina grinned as Alex swung the bat, testing its weight and then settled into a relaxed stance to wait for the pitch.

The doctor let the first two pitches go by, not even flinching at them. She stepped back out of the batter's box and looked over the outfield for a moment.

Regina watched as she pulled her glasses down and looked in her direction. The resident couldn't keep from grinning as Alex looked back at the bleachers, and then back into left field.

"Heh, didn't expect to see me out here, did you, Alex?" Regina snickered.

On the next pitch, Alex swung, launching the ball over the infield. It was still climbing and didn't start to come down until it was well past the fence in center field. The other team went wild as Alex jogged leisurely around the bases and tied the score. Three more batters came up; two got on base and one flied out.

Dana was up next and the girl at second base turned around, pointing at Regina. "She's coming to you in left field."

Regina watched as Dana set her feet. *Oh damn, she's gonna hit it right at me. Just great.* Regina stepped back and watched Dana swing and miss. *Yup. She's coming right at you, kid.*

She bent forward, smacking her hand in her glove in anticipation. Regina heard the ball make contact with the bat and watched as it sailed high into the air. She backpedaled, determined not to let it get behind her, and then realized that she had given too much room. Switching directions, she ran forward, sliding on her hip underneath the ball with her left arm extended, as the ball fell right into the pocket of her glove.

Regina plucked the ball out and side-armed a line drive at the second baseman, who almost let herself get hit because she was so surprised that Regina even made the catch. Her throw caught the base runner in no man's land, and they completed a double play. Regina grinned. It was like she had never stopped playing.

Trotting off the field, Regina enjoyed the shouts of appreciation from her team members. She was acutely aware of Dana's openly hostile glare in her direction as she headed to the bleachers.

"You're batting second, Regina," one of the women told her as she set her glove down on the bench.

"Okay." She stood behind the batting box, picked up a bat, and stretched her arms up over her head to loosen her shoulders. She laughed as she thought about the last time that she played, which was when she was an undergraduate at University of Massachusetts. The first girl up got a single.

Regina stepped up to the plate and met Dana's challenging stare. The first ball swept by her for a strike.

"Come on, Reggie." Some of the girls shouted encouragement and rattled the metal fence behind her.

*Nice and easy. Just make contact.* She let the next ball go by her then, looked the next pitch all the way in and swung. She felt the contact in her hands as she smacked the ball solidly and took off running hard for first base. She was aware of Alex planting her foot on the base, stretching forward, waiting for the ball. Regina ducked her head and put all her effort into beating out the throw. A cheer went up from the sidelines as Alex caught the ball

a second after Regina ran over first base. Alex tossed the ball
back to the pitcher. She lowered her glasses and looked directly
at Regina. "You didn't tell me you played ball," she said, swat-
ting at her with her glove.

Regina realized that she was being teased and grinned inno-
cently at her. "You didn't ask." She planted herself firmly on
first base.

"I guess I'll have to remember to ask next time," Alex said,
as she settled herself in between first and second base.

Regina's team lost as Alex cleared the bases in the last
inning of the game with another blast over the fence. Regina
really didn't care. She had such a good time playing that it didn't
matter to her who won—well, not really; the resident always had
a competitive nature. It was another one of those things her
mother found distasteful, and the woman had artfully swayed her
daughter from spending too much time involved with sports as
she grew up. In college, Regina rekindled her passion and played
softball up until her junior year, but by then her pre-med courses
consumed all her time and she gave it up again.

"Hey." Regina looked up to find Alex gazing down at her.
"That was some catch you made out there."

Regina blushed at the compliment. "Thanks. It's been
awhile since I played. It brought back some old memories."

"Mm. We've got an invite to Sarah's houses for burgers.
You interested?" *Hell,* Alex thought, *they were suspended from
work and nothing else to do, so why not have some fun in the
meantime?*

"Yeah, why not," Regina answered.

❖ ⌘ ❖ ⌘ ❖ ⌘ ❖

Alex parked the Jeep on the road in front of the house. They
walked up the steep driveway and entered through the front door.
Sarah met them as she walked out of the kitchen holding a couple bags of ice.

"Hey, thanks for playing for me today, Regina," the red-
haired woman said. "There's beer out back. We're just lighting
the grill so we'll have some burgers on in a bit. Give me a couple
minutes and I'll show you both around."

The house turned out to be a large Cape Cod with a two-
tiered deck out on the back. From the top-level Regina could see
Cape Cod Bay in the distance. She leaned on her elbows and

watched the sun as it started its slow descent toward the horizon, and took a sip from her beer. She closed her eyes. It seemed hard to believe that less than seventy-two hours ago she was listening to her medical director tell her she was suspended. Right now, it all seemed like some surreal nightmare. Since it was Sunday, there was nothing she could do, so she might as well enjoy herself.

The flare of several torches being lit on the deck below interrupted her thoughts. She inhaled the salty air and lifted her head so the breeze lifted her bangs. Regina felt a nudge in the small of her back and turned around to find Alex grinning at her. She realized that it was the most relaxed she had ever seen the doctor.

"One medium hamburger with lots of pickles, as requested," Alex said, holding a paper plate out to her.

"Thanks." Regina set her beer on the rail and took the plate, then turned her attention to the water as she started to eat. The sun was descending through the sky, causing the sea to glow a deep orange.

"You doing okay?"

Regina looked up and blinked. "Yeah. Just thinking." She took another sip from her beer and held the empty cup down by her side as she stared into the growing darkness.

Alex regarded her quietly. "You should call Dr. Mitchard's office tomorrow and find out when the medical review board is meeting."

Regina nodded her head. "What are you going to do, Alex?" It was the first time Regina asked Alex about her plans since arriving.

Alex peered into her cup. "I don't know. I have to take care of some things up here first." The doctor motioned at Regina's cup. "You want some soda?"

"Sure. My limit's one beer with this medication I'm on."

Alex took her cup and walked into the house, and returned several minutes later with Regina's soda. "Hang on to mine for me," she said, handing Regina her cup of beer. "I'm going to help them bring in a beer ball." Regina watched the dark haired woman disappear around the corner of the house.

"Not a bad catch out there today." Dana walked up beside her and leaned casually against the railing next to Regina. Dana sipped her drink and smiled coyly at the young woman.

Regina eyed her cautiously for a moment. "Thanks."

Alex reappeared on the deck and set the beer ball down in a large tub of ice. Dana nodded to her. "So, how long have you two known each other?"

Regina straightened as her eyes traveled to Alex, who was filling cups with beer from the tapped ball. "A couple of months. We work together in the emergency room." A gust of humid air blew a lock of hair across her face and Regina brushed it behind her ear.

Dana pursed her lips. "You're a doctor?"

Regina nodded her head. "I'm finishing my last residency."

"Interesting." She brazenly looked Regina up and down. "You don't strike me as the type Alex would be interested in."

Regina choked on her soda, almost spitting it out of her mouth and nose when she realized what Dana was implying. "Oh! It's not like that," Regina replied, between spasms of coughing.

Dana reached out and took Regina's cup from her and set it on the deck rail behind her. She brought her own cup up to her lips, and a wicked smile spread across her face. *So, Alex, there still is a chance I can get you back.* She took a long drink and watched Alex out of half-lowered eyelids, letting an idea take hold. The tall, dark haired woman stood up, a full head over most of the other women around her.

Dana watched as Alex's eyes scanned the large deck and came to rest on the petite blonde. *Well, I'll just take out a little insurance so the balance weighs in my favor tonight.* Dana slipped her hand into her pocket and pulled out a dark blue capsule.

"Oh that's cute." Dana leaned closer to Regina, blocking her from seeing her hand, and skillfully slid the ends of the capsule apart; the contents spilled into Regina's soda. She then picked it up, swirled it gently, and handed it back to the doctor.

Regina turned and frowned at Dana. "What do you mean?" she asked, taking the cup from her.

Dana watched Alex talking with some of the women from the softball team. "Oh, let's just say she has a reputation for being dangerously charming and always getting what she wants." She looked Regina up and down and smirked. "I'd get out before you get burned, sweetie."

Regina took a drink and stared at Dana as she swallowed. "Listen, I don't know what you think and I really don't care, Dana. Alex and I are friends."

"Oh and you know her so well, don't you? Listen, Regina, Alex doesn't have friends. She just uses people until she gets bored with them."

"No, she's not like that," Regina protested.

Dana laughed. "You don't think so? Well, you remember that when she's screwing you later."

Regina felt paralyzed. In front of total strangers, Dana might as well have dragged her through burning coals. "Go to hell, Dana."

"Bitch. Don't you tell me what to do," Dana spat back at her and quickly stepped into Regina's space, backing her up several steps.

Regina turned and almost bumped into Alex who had walked up behind her quietly; she opened her mouth and promptly shut it, seeing the unreadable look on Alex's face as she glanced at Regina and then over to Dana. Her blue eyes darkened in the flickering torchlight. Alex ducked around Regina without a word and followed Dana as she quickly retreated down the steps to the lower level. The brunette skipped the last three stairs and caught up with her by the hot tub. She grabbed Dana's arm, spinning her around so she lost her balance and almost fell.

"What did you say to her, Dana?" Alex growled, clamping her hands on Dana's trim waist.

Dana was lifted up onto the edge of the tub. "Why, Alex, don't you trust me?" Her tongue ran over her lips as she saw Alex's eyes darken. Dana leaned closer.

"Not as far as I can throw you."

"Mm. That's too bad." Dana ran her hand up Alex's arm.

"Be careful, Dana, you may get more than you're bargaining for," Alex said, moving closer.

"Alex, wouldn't it be better if we take this inside? A bed might be more comfortable," Dana said, running her hands over her well-toned shoulders and smiling up at her.

Alex grinned evilly and slid her hands down to Dana's thighs. She stepped closer, pulling Dana against her so she was forced to look up.

"Oh no." She bent her head, bringing her lips closer to Dana's ear. "Right here is just fine, Dana." Alex laughed, as she slipped her hands underneath her legs and tipped Dana backwards into the water, cutting off her outraged shriek.

Regina walked into the house in search of a bathroom after Alex had gone after Dana. *Oh heck, what did I get myself into?*

*Alex isn't like that, is she?* She walked into the kitchen and asked one of the women where a bathroom was.

"Down the hallway, it's the second door on the left," the tall redhead informed her with a smile.

"Thanks." Regina walked down the carpeted hallway and found the bathroom easily. She flicked the light on and stopped. "Oh." She looked at the crystal bowl sitting on the vanity. Beside it lay a razor blade and a mirror.

A few minutes later, Regina walked out of the bathroom and bumped into one of the women on the other team.

"Good stuff in there? Huh?" the woman asked her.

Regina just stared up at her, wondering how someone could put that stuff in their body knowing what it could do to them. Walking around to the front of the house, Regina saw no sign of Alex, so she sat on the steps. She thought about what Dana said and wondered how well she really knew Alex. She didn't believe Dana, but the words kept replaying in her head.

A fuzzy feeling slowly enveloped her head and Regina brought a hand up to her face and winced. "Oh, this isn't good," she groaned as her vision blurred slightly. Maybe she shouldn't have had that beer in the first place. "I didn't think I had that much to drink," she muttered to herself, feeling dizzy as she sat there in the darkness.

Footsteps came around the corner and stopped. "Hey, I was looking for you. Where'd you go off to?" Alex walked over and sat down beside Regina.

Regina picked her head up and squinted. "Right here," she answered, and then groaned as her brain cells protested the foreign substance racing through her blood.

Alex tilted her head and looked in Regina's face. She put a hand on Regina's shoulder. What's wrong?"

Regina tensed and swallowed. "I think I had too much to drink."

"I thought you only had one beer? Hmm, I guess we should get you home then, huh?" The brunette stood up and held a hand out. Regina hesitated, then took the offered hand and was pulled to her feet. "Yikes." She teetered forward and bumped into Alex, who put both hands on her shoulders, looked into her eyes, and frowned at the contracted pupils.

"Alex!" Squish, squish. "I'm going to kill you, you bitch!" Squish, squish, squish. Alex turned around, keeping Regina slightly behind her.

The noise grew louder. "What is that?" Regina blinked and looked up at the taller woman standing beside her with her hands resting on her hips.

"Where are you? You're going to pay for this!" Dana stepped around the bushes and glared at Alex.

Regina snorted and fell into a fit of giggles. Dana's mascara was streaked down her face in tiny rivulets and her green tank top was plastered tightly to her chest.

"Ooh, too bad we're not having a wet T-shirt contest," Regina snickered. Alex simply looked down at her and tried not to laugh.

Dana's nostrils flared as she stood dripping, a puddle of water gathering around her feet. She yanked one of her sneakers off and threw it angrily at Alex, who easily ducked under the errant throw.

"Dana, you know, you really should start wearing some clothes that leave a little more to the imagination," Alex drawled, running her tongue across her lips.

Several catcalls erupted from the windows on the second floor and a beam of light caught Dana for all to see. "Way to go, Alex," someone shouted amid a chorus of long whistles and hollering.

Dana turned her anger at the woman holding the flashlight on her and threw her other sneaker up at the window.

"Come on. Let's get out of here before this gets any uglier." Alex guided Regina down the driveway, keeping a protective hand against the small of her back to stop her from stumbling.

Inside the car, Regina dissolved into a fit of giggles again. "Alex, what did you do to her?" She leaned against the door with a hand over her face trying to regain her composure.

Alex started the engine. "I dumped her into the hot tub," she said without looking at Regina.

"Can I ask why?"

"Because Dana likes to start trouble."

"Oh." Regina's mind drifted off and she closed her eyes as Alex drove them back to her house.

The resident was vaguely aware that Alex opened the passenger door and helped her out of the Jeep, getting her to stand on her feet. She felt suddenly awkward and vulnerable as Dana's words echoed eerily in her ears. Regina slowly negotiated the narrow slate walk, trying hard not to fall over her uncooperative feet. She stumbled over a piece of slate and strong arms caught her as she pitched forward.

"No, no," she said, pushing Alex's arms away from her. "Let go of me. I can stand by myself."

Alex backed off, hearing the anger in her voice. "O...kay." She drew the word out. "I'll go, uh, unlock the door. You just let me know if you need help." Alex walked up the stairs leaving Regina standing outside, unsure of what she had done to upset her.

Regina opened her eyes and saw the threshold of the door and the stairs leading up to the apartment in front of her. She blinked, and saw Alex seated on the bottom of the stairs, one hand supporting her head. She was looking at her and twirling her car keys around her fingers.

"Oh God, please stop," Regina groaned and held out a hand to block the twirling motion from her eyes.

Alex arched an eyebrow. "Stop what?"

"The keys. Please, don't do that." Regina shook her head and took a deep breath trying to quell her upset stomach.

Alex scooted down to the ground and leaned forward so her forehead was almost touching Regina's. "So, do you want me to help you up the stairs or do you want to sleep out here under the stars tonight?"

Regina jerked her head up. "You're making fun of me," she said, squinting with one eye so she could see just one of Alex.

"No, I just want to know if you want some help. You've been sitting out here on the ground for a little bit now." Alex placed her hand underneath Regina's chin and lifted it gently. Unfocused eyes looked back at her.

Regina surrendered. "Help, please."

Alex squatted down beside her. "Put your arm around my neck. That's it. Okay, hang on. Let's see if I can still do this. Oomph." She scooped Regina up, cradling her in her arms.

"Alex, I'm sorry." Regina slurred the words, her head resting on Alex's shoulder as she climbed up the steps.

"For what?" Alex looked down at Regina as she carried her down the hallway and into the apartment. She had pulled out the sofa bed when she had walked up to the apartment the first time. She knelt down beside the mattress and deposited Regina onto her back.

"Regina?" Alex shook her shoulder. She stepped back and scratched her head and then sat down on the bed. "Hey, I'm just going to take your shoes and socks off." She set them on the floor and decided Regina could sleep with the rest of her clothes on.

Alex rolled her onto her side and covered her with the sheet. She picked up Regina's wrist and felt her pulse, then checked her pupils, which were still constricted. "Shit," Alex cursed, wondering what the hell she was having a reaction to.

❖ ⌘ ❖ ⌘ ❖ ⌘ ❖

Alex woke in the predawn stillness as the sky turned a lighter shade of gray. She stayed up most of the night watching Regina to make sure she was all right. At some point, she had given in to her body's craving for sleep and drifted off in her own bed.

Alex stretched and rolled over. She peered around the corner of the room and saw the sleeping form in the sofa bed. She swung her feet over the side of the bed and walked across the hardwood floor to Regina. She stood next to her and listened to her breathing. *Well, she'll probably sleep most of the morning.*

Deciding that it was time to take the morning run she changed into a pair of running shorts and a T-shirt, slipped out of the apartment and walked onto the street. The air was humid and it chilled her skin. She bounced on her toes a couple of times and then stretched her legs out on the fence post.

Alex jogged slowly up the hill, allowing her legs to loosen up and get the blood flowing. Once she'd reached the top of the hill she jogged in place, as a lone car sped by.

She took a deep breath and stretched her legs out as she loped down the steep grade of the hill, then headed down toward Provinceland's Road.

Slowing to a walk, hands on her hips, Alex ambled around the circle, taking long breaths to slow her heart rate. She looked out at the dunes nearby, watching as the tide crept back in along the inlets. Her mind wandered back to Regina and she shook her head, remembering the perplexed, almost fearful expression she had gotten when she asked Regina if she wanted help climbing up the stairs. She made a face as she mentally recalled how many drinks Regina had at the party; *she couldn't have gotten that drunk off of one beer.*

Suddenly, anger stirred in her as she remembered Dana standing beside Regina on the deck. It wouldn't be the first time she had deliberately spiked a person's drink.

Alex was sweating freely by the time she climbed the stairs to her apartment. She opened the door and headed over to Regina who was now sprawled on her stomach, moaning.

"Ungh. Oh God, please tell me this is a dream." Regina buried her head in her pillow and groaned.

"Nope. Can't do that." Alex walked over to the refrigerator and returned, carrying a Coke and two ibuprofen tablets in her hands. "Here, this might help." She sat on the edge of the bed and waited as Regina pulled herself up into a sitting position.

Regina took the soda and sipped it. "Alex."

"Mm?" She turned to look at the blonde.

"Please tell me I didn't do anything stupid last night. I hardly remember anything." Regina rubbed her eyes and looked up at Alex sheepishly.

Alex shook her head and grinned. "No, but I did find out you have quite the stubborn streak in you."

Regina's face reddened and she covered her face with her hands to hide her embarrassment. "Oh no."

Alex shifted her weight on the mattress as she pulled her foot up to remove her sneaker. "Don't worry. It wasn't a big deal. You just needed some convincing that you needed help getting up the stairs."

"Oh, I'm sorry. I don't usually get like that."

Alex took off her other sneaker and leaned back on her hands. "I don't think that *you* did."

The blonde gave her a confused look.

"I think Dana may have slipped something into your drink last night," Alex explained.

"What? Oh, that is so juvenile." Regina rubbed her temples. "Why would she do something stupid like that?"

Alex shrugged her shoulders. "Probably to get back at me."

"Uh, okay, you lost me now," Regina said.

Alex ran a hand through her hair. "It's a long story, Regina." She got off the bed and walked to the other side of the room.

Regina watched her and nibbled on her bottom lip. "Alex, does Dana sell drugs out of the store?" It was a guess but based on what she had seen last night at the party and now obviously experienced, Regina guessed it was a distinct possibility.

Alex whirled around, her blues eyes flashing dangerously. "Did Dana tell you that?"

"No. I'm just taking a guess." Regina shrugged her shoulders. "I...there was cocaine in the bathroom at the house last night, quite a bit of it. Is that why you didn't want to tell me about the store?"

"Don't you have a phone call to make to Dr. Mitchard?" Alex looked away, staring out the window with her arms crossed over her chest.

Regina walked over to the window and stood beside Alex. "Alex, you can trust me. Please, let me help."

Blue eyes cut through her. "I learned a long time ago not to trust anybody." Alex turned and walked into the bathroom, shutting the door firmly behind her.

The blonde stood with her mouth agape at the doctor's biting words. She hadn't expected the sharp retort, and it hurt. She toyed with the idea of waiting until Alex got out of the shower to try talking with her but then decided against it, not wanting to anger her more. Regina pushed the sofa bed back into its place, set the cushions back on the couch, and sat down to put her sneakers on. With her dejection written plainly on her face, the young woman quietly made her way out of the apartment and walked down toward Commercial Street.

# Chapter
# 12

The narrow one-way street was packed wall to wall with people, mostly couples holding hands, meandering aimlessly along the sidewalks, walking in and out of the many shops. Funny, Regina had expected to feel a little intimidated by the overtly gay and lesbian community, but somehow it felt comforting. Maybe it was simply a gut reaction, seeing so many people here, comfortable being themselves and not afraid of someone ridiculing who or what they were. The young doctor's mind drifted to her brother and she wondered if he had felt this way when he came here in the past.

Regina found a seat on one of the empty benches along the crowded street and sat sipping the lemonade she had bought earlier at one of the cafés.

"Hey, did you lose your girlfriend, sweetheart?"

"What?" Regina jerked her head up and shielded her eyes from the brightness of the sun through her sunglasses. She found herself looking at a tall, athletically built woman wearing a bikini top and running shorts. "No, I'm fine."

"You look pretty far away from being fine," the red-haired woman said. "My name's Emily. Mind if I sit?" She settled down next to Regina, draping her arm casually over the back of the bench. "You come up here often?"

Regina groaned inwardly. It didn't matter what shape or form it came in, a pick up line was a pick up line. "No, actually this is my first time on the Cape."

Emily shifted on the bench so she was facing Regina. "So, are you up here alone?"

"No, I'm here with someone."

"Oh." Her voice was filled with disappointment. "Well, if things don't work out you can come find me. I'm at Gabrielle's." The woman stood up. "Listen, you look too nice to have someone trampling on your heart. Whoever it is, cut them loose."

Regina stared as the woman flashed her a grin and turned away, sauntering off down the street and disappearing into the crowds. She shook her head, feeling rather self-conscious about the woman's blatant attempt to pick her up. Regina had never been one to get involved in casual relationships and the whole interaction made her uncomfortable.

She made a face as she thought of her relationship with Derrick. Maybe Jeffrey was right about her being a little naïve; sometimes she couldn't see something coming at her until it was too late. Why else had she allowed herself to get that involved with Derrick and not seen him for who he truly was? *Yeah right, Regina, you were just too damn afraid to admit to yourself that you were attracted to women in the first place.*

She stood and looked up and down the crowded sidewalks wondering what to do next.

Regina spent the rest of the day ambling through the various shops. She stopped at one particular store and browsed through the books. She picked up a couple of nonfiction titles about dealing with one's sexual identity. She thought they would help her with the teenagers who came into the emergency department and were struggling with their own identities.

Regina started to turn away from the shelves of books lining the walls but stopped as she passed the section for romance. She hesitated for a moment before she finally gathered her courage, walked over, and looked at the various titles.

The young doctor pulled out a couple of books and read the back cover. Not sure if she would like them or not, she put them back and found two other books that looked promising. Flipping through the pages, she stopped and read a couple of pages out of one of them. Her pulse quickened and a shudder ran through her as she read the words.

She quickly shut the book, acutely aware that her thoughts had drifted quite unexpectedly to one blue-eyed, dark-haired woman. *Get a grip, will you, Regina?* Feeling the warmth recede from her face, she slipped the books underneath the ones she was already carrying and walked over to the counter. She could hardly make eye contact with the woman standing on the other side as she waited for her to ring up her purchase, afraid she could read the jumble of emotions running through her mind.

Regina walked out of the store feeling incredibly unsettled at her response to what she had read. It stirred something in her she hadn't really given much thought to until now. She knew she liked Alex as a friend. That was obvious enough, but a physical relationship had certainly never crossed her mind before. Now it was all she could think of.

Her thoughts flew in a dozen different directions at once. Did Alex find her attractive? Could Alex be angry with her for getting them suspended? They wouldn't be in this situation to begin with if she hadn't run out to check the pregnant woman in the truck. A sickening feeling settled in the pit of her stomach. *What a fine mess you made of everything, Regina.*

The young woman walked toward the small park that sat below the Pilgrim Monument on Bradford Street. She looked up at the tall stone tower and watched as clouds swept by overhead, turning away as the motion of the white, billowy puffs made the tower look like it was swaying above her. Regina sat on one of the stone benches and pulled out her cell phone, dialed the hospital's main number, waited for the operator to answer and then asked for Dr. Mitchard's office.

A moment later the line clicked and a harried female voice answered. "Office of Medical Affairs. How can I help you?"

Regina leaned forward, resting her elbows on her knees. "Hi. My name is Dr. Kingston. I'm calling to find out when the medical review committee is meeting."

"What is the meeting for?"

Regina shook her head. "It's about the Martin family." She cringed, knowing that by now, half the hospital had probably heard all the details and that, thanks to the grapevine, they were most likely gravely distorted.

"Let me check. I don't see it on her calendar." Regina listened to the DMX system playing music as she waited on hold.

"Dr. Kingston," the voice came back on the line, "that meeting is scheduled for next Monday."

"A whole week? Why so long?"

"Apparently Dr. Jameson isn't available until then."

*Wonderful.* "Oh. What time is it scheduled for?" she asked, brushing her hair behind her ear.

"Ten in the morning. It's in the fifth floor conference room. Is there anything else, Dr. Kingston?"

"No, no there's not. Thank—" Dial tone. "You." Regina looked at the phone and snapped it shut in disgust. She wondered why the meeting wasn't on Dr. Mitchard's calendar and why her assistant had been so short with her. Her brain ran through a myriad of possibilities. *Great, maybe it's just a formality and they already know they're going to revoke our privileges...and you think Alex is mad at you now, ha!*

Regina leaned back against the cool concrete wall and looked up at the sky. She could still see the angry look on Alex's face when she had asked her about the store. It was obvious she had hit a raw nerve with her. Now all she had to do was figure out why and how she could undo some of the damage she had done.

Regina decided she would walk along Commercial Street one last time before she headed back to the apartment. She walked several blocks lost in her own thoughts, then stopped and turned around, looking back down at the row of shops she had just passed. She recognized the tall figure standing underneath an awning of one of the stores. Regina hesitated, and then walked toward the doctor.

"Alex?" Regina saw her back stiffen as the woman heard her name and looked warily in her direction.

As she got closer, she realized that Alex had a ring of keys in her hands and had been trying to figure out which one opened the door she stood in front of.

"Alex, I didn't mean to upset you before. Please don't be mad." Regina stepped closer, looking up at the guarded expression on her friend's face.

Alex hung her head and sighed. The last thing she had expected was to run into Regina down by the store. *Idiot, what the hell did you think she was going to do, disappear?* She fiddled with the ring of keys.

"I'm not mad at you, Regina. I..." She dropped her hand to her side and looked up at the window. "This is Lana's store. It's not open today, so I figured I'd check it out and see what Dana was doing with it."

Regina looked inside the window and back up at Alex, seeing the mix of emotions on the taller woman's face. "A lot of memories tied up in there, huh?"

*You don't know the half of it.* "Yeah, something like that,"
Alex said, trying desperately to come up with an idea to keep
Regina from coming in with her.

"Let me come with you. I promise I won't get in the way."

Alex lowered her eyes. "Regina, I don't know what I'm
going to find in there. I really don't want you to be here."

"Why?"

"I've done some things in the past I'm not proud of and I'd
rather not have you be a part of this."

Regina turned and looked up into the blue eyes that stared
off into the distance. "Alex, I don't know too many people in
this life, including myself, who haven't done some things that
they wish they could change or do over."

"No, Regina, you don't understand. I've crossed boundaries
most people wouldn't think of crossing." Her voice was quiet
and resigned.

"Alex, you don't owe me any explanations. We're friends
and I'm not going anywhere."

"God, are you always so damn stubborn?" Alex groaned.

Regina just smiled and nodded at the door.

Alex unlocked the door, pushed it open and stepped up into
the darkened interior of the store. She wrinkled her nose as she
inhaled the strong scent of recently burned incense. A new age
melody played softly on the stereo system. The doctor flicked
the light switch up on the wall, and the store was illuminated
with the soft glow from the recessed lighting overhead. Alex
stood still as a wash of memories ran through her; a hand
touched her back and she opened her eyes.

Regina had an odd sense that Alex was deeply troubled and
it worried her. "Are you okay, Alex?"

She took a breath and forced her shoulders to relax. "Yeah, I
wasn't sure how it would feel to be back here after all this time."
She looked warily around the store.

Dana hadn't changed it much, she had to give her that.
Lana's tastes were always somewhat eclectic and that was what
her store had been centered around. Alex walked over to a glass
shelf and trailed her fingers along its edge as she looked at the
jewelry and gifts that adorned this corner of the store. There
were candles of every shape, color and size scattered along the
shelves, and long thin envelopes of incense were stored in the
wooden bins that were built into the wall. In the center of the
store, Dana still maintained a small collection of artwork from

the local artists that she sold on consignment for them. Alex turned around to find Regina quietly studying her. "What?"

"I always enjoyed stores like this. They have such a warm feeling to them."

Alex shook her head grimly. "This wasn't the part of the store that I had much to do with." She walked past the counter with its register sitting at the end of it. Long strings of beads still hung in the opening to the cellar. Alex's gut churned as she stepped closer, remembering the long dark hours spent in the room below, making deals, and losing a part of herself that she wasn't quite sure she would ever get back.

She closed her eyes, putting a hand up to the wall to steady herself as a vivid memory flashed by in her mind.

*She sat on the chair next to Dana, watching as she held the spoon over the open flame, liquefying the white powder. She was already in a haze from snorting cocaine earlier and she felt disconnected from everything going on around her. Richard walked up in front of her and held out the rubber tubing.*

*"Come on, Alex. What are you afraid of? We're all friends here, right?" He smiled and looked at Dana. "We'll take good care of you."*

*Hesitantly, she held out her arm as she watched Dana draw the liquid up into the syringe. The tubing bit into the flesh around the biceps and she felt the pressure building in her arm as her veins became distended.*

*Dana knelt down in front of Alex and took hold of her arm. She probed roughly for the vein and jabbed the needle into it. As she depressed the plunger, she released the band around the doctor's arm.*

*Alex remembered Dana smiling and leaning in to kiss her as her vision narrowed and her heart pounded furiously in her chest. When she finally came to much later, she was lying sprawled half-naked on the couch in Dana's apartment. She picked her head up and looked around the room. The bile rose in her throat as she saw Dana, Richard and two other people who she didn't know sprawled about the room in various stages of undress. She pushed her body off the couch and staggered to the bathroom. Collapsing in front of the toilet, she vomited.*

*She walked on unsteady legs back out to the living room and looked down at the table strewn with drugs and other paraphernalia. Alex sifted through the contents, her heart racing as she*

*confirmed her fears and stared hopelessly at the single syringe
lying next to the bag of cocaine.*

Alex let the painful memory fade and opened her eyes, gazing around the room. "Just as I remembered," she muttered quietly to herself.

"What's that?" Regina walked up to stand beside Alex.

Alex started, almost forgetting that Regina was there.
"These candles." The doctor shook her head and pointed with her
finger. "Left to right." She ran her hand across the wooden shelf.
"Marijuana, Cocaine, Heroin, Ecstasy, and Amphetamines. All
you had to do was light a candle. That was Dana's code so no one
else in the store knew what we were doing."

"We?" Regina looked up at her, realizing for the first time
what Alex had meant when she said she had done things in the
past that she wasn't proud of. Her gut twisted in reaction, wondering how involved Alex had been in Dana's world.

Alex looked down at Regina. "I don't think you want to be
here, Regina."

"No, I want to stay, Alex."

"All right. I'm going downstairs. Stay up here." She parted
the strings of beads with her hands, listening to them click softly
against each other as they swung in the air, and reached to her
left and found the switch for the light. A small circle of pale yellow light filled the darkened space below. Alex cocked her head
as rustling and then a high-pitched whimper reached her ears.
She walked down the narrow wooden steps, bending forward to
see farther into the cellar.

"What is it?" Regina asked, standing on the landing above
her.

"A puppy."

"Ooh, let me see," Regina said.

Alex made a face and stepped down as Regina squeezed past
her. The clatter of little claws on the metal tray of the crate
became frenzied as the puppy danced and whined while Regina
knelt down to investigate.

"It's a German Shepherd. Alex, look its ears aren't even
standing up yet." Regina's fingers were on the crate and she
laughed as the puppy eagerly nibbled on them.

Alex shook her head and walked over to the crate. "She
must have bred Thor," she commented as she recognized the
familiar markings.

"Thor?" Regina looked up at Alex.

"He was the guard dog that Dana kept in the store. I'd recognize these markings anywhere." She knelt down beside Regina and slid the latch over and let the puppy out. He scrambled out of the crate and playfully jumped up, grabbing a lock of Alex's hair in its mouth and tugged on it. "Hey." She pulled the now wet strands of hair from its mouth and swept it back over her shoulder. "So what's your name?" Alex asked, lifting the squirming bundle of fur up into her arms.

Regina scratched between its ears. "He's cute."

"Yeah, he's going to be huge. Look at the size of these paws." She picked one up and squeezed it with her hand. Alex stiffened as she heard the sound of a key turning in a lock. "Take him." She shoved the puppy into Regina's arms.

Whirling around at the sound of hinges creaking behind them, Alex tucked Regina behind her, backing her up into a darkened corner of the room. She pressed her fingers to Regina's mouth, silencing the question that she was about to ask. Alex brought her fingers back to her own lips, motioning for Regina to stay quiet. Squeezing Regina's shoulder quickly to reassure her, Alex glided silently in the shadows, along the back wall. She grabbed a wooden dowel off the table, listening as the heavy wooden door groaned as it was slid open. Alex stepped closer, waiting as a shadow wavered and then moved forward into the room. Grabbing a fistful of shirt, Alex spun the intruder around and pinned them up against the wall with the dowel pressed hard against their neck.

"Damn it, Alex, get off me."

"What are you doing here, Dana?" Alex demanded, shoving the dowel hard into Dana's chest.

"I might ask you the same question," Dana snarled.

"It's my store now. I'm just checking out the inventory," Alex replied smoothly, slowly releasing the pressure off the dowel.

Dana rubbed her neck and glared at her. "Bullshit. Hey, what is she doing here?" Dana jerked her head Regina's direction.

"It is my store. I can invite who I want."

Dana looked at Regina, her eyes roaming over her and licked her lips suggestively. She burst into laughter as Regina shifted her feet and found the puppy at her feet much more interesting.

"Really, Alex, I just don't understand what you see in her. After all, I know what you like in a woman." Dana pushed off the wall and ran a hand down Alex's side and rested it on her hip suggestively.

Regina's gut clenched as she watched. The touch was one of possessiveness and ownership; it reminded her of how Derrick acted toward her. She felt a wave of anger, followed instantly by a cold trickle of fear down her spine. What did Dana hold over Alex that she would tolerate the way Dana treated her now?

"So, let's get down to business here." Dana walked behind Alex, letting her hand fall away. "How much are you making a week, Alex? Two thousand? Four thousand?"

"I make enough, Dana. I already told you, I'm not interested." Alex crossed her arms over her chest and turned to face Dana. She could feel Regina standing off to the side watching her. Alex wanted to scream at Regina to get out of there. She didn't want her to hear this, not like this, not from Dana. *Shit, why did I let you come in here with me?* She looked back at Dana and her eyes narrowed when she saw the hate that this woman felt for her reflected in her eyes.

"Really? Well, that's too bad, Alex. You see, business is booming. Lana bailed you out just before things got interesting." Dana circled around her. "What was our largest take in one week? Do you remember? Oh yes, I see that you do. I see that glint in your eye. What was it now?" Dana leaned across the table and pointed at Regina. "Say it, Alex. I want to hear you say how much we sold in one week, so that little 'Miss Innocent' over there understands who you really are."

Regina knelt down, picked up the puppy, and held him in her arms as she watched the two women facing off in the center of the room. From where she stood she could see flecks of dust highlighted in the beam of the overhead light bulb. The glare hurt her eyes and she stepped back away from it. Alex lowered her head, wishing desperately that Regina wasn't with her. She decided there was no sense in lying; Dana knew the truth and would only make the situation worse if she did lie. She looked at Regina and swallowed. "We pulled in fifteen thousand dollars in cocaine and heroin in a week."

Regina's chest constricted as the words sunk in. The puppy squirmed out of her arms and jumped to the floor, sniffing around her feet. Regina stared at Alex, as the enormity of what she had done hit her. "Jesus, Alex."

"How do you feel about your dear doctor friend now, love?" Dana pulled a pocketknife out of her pocket and walked to the back of the cellar. She unlocked a padlock and pulled the metal door open, then disappeared inside. When she reappeared she held a plastic bag in her hand. Dana dropped it on the table and slipped the pocketknife through the plastic.

She leered at Regina and licked her finger. She plunged it into the white powder. "Do you want some candy, little girl?"

"Leave her out of this, Dana. This is between you and me." Alex stepped closer to Dana and blocked her view of Regina.

"Who knows, Alex, maybe she'd like it." Dana glanced around Alex's shoulder. "Want to try some, sweetheart?" Dana pulled her powder-covered finger out of the bag and sucked it into her mouth, running it over her gums. Withdrawing her finger slowly, she fixed her eyes on Regina and leered at her.

Regina stepped back. In that moment, she knew what evil was as she watched Dana toying with Alex. Her mind warred with the conflicting images she had of Alex now, the doctor who she knew, and the woman who had existed in a world terribly foreign from anything Regina had ever known. The doctor she'd spent long, countless hours working with in the emergency department, watching and learning from as they treated hundreds of patients. The successes were sweet and the losses, tragic. They had shared them both and Regina was beginning to realize why Alex had always worked so hard, trying to outrun this, her past. Regina's attention jerked back as she heard Dana's taunting voice again. Dana dug into the bag again and walked over to Alex.

"How about for old times sake? Do you remember what we used to do?" She raised her fingers up to Alex's mouth.

Alex caught her hand and twisted it painfully away from her. "Go to hell," Alex growled, as she increased the pressure on Dana's wrist.

Dana cried out in pain and grabbed hold of Alex's hand, trying to pry it away. "Stop. You're going to break it."

Alex curled her lip in a feral grin and shoved Dana away from her, knocking her to the floor. She walked over to the open door of the walk-in closet and stood at its entrance looking in. "So, this is where you keep it now."

Dana reached for the dowel and scrambled to her feet, charging Alex from behind.

"Alex, look out!" Regina shouted, realizing what Dana

intended to do.

Alex spun around and with her arms up in front, blocked the dowel with her hands. She twisted it hard, breaking Dana's hold and kicking her hard in her gut. Dana cried out as she tumbled to the floor. Alex stepped forward, reached up, felt for the short chain just inside the door and pulled on it, turning the light on.

The narrow room was lined floor to ceiling with wooden shelves. A few of them were filled with wooden crates that were unmarked. Dana sat in a heap on the floor clutching her ankle. "You son of a—"

"Shut up, Dana."

Regina walked up beside Alex and peered into the room. "My God, Alex."

Alex looked quickly at Regina. Her voice was hoarse when she spoke. "Yeah, now you know. Still like what you see?"

Regina stared up at Alex trying to come up with something intelligible to say to her.

Alex jerked her eyes away before Regina could respond. "Get out of here, Regina." She stepped into the room and picked the ring of keys up from the sawdust-covered floor. She pulled a crowbar off the nail in the wall and walked to the nearest crate; wedging the teeth underneath the lid, she pushed down on the bar with her hand. The wood creaked and splintered under the force as the lid opened, Alex reached into the crate, and pulled out a plastic bag.

"You want it, don't you, Alex?" Dana asked, nodding her head at the bag. "Go ahead and take it. I'll give it to you on the house. What do you say?"

Alex laughed and knelt down in front of Dana. "I don't want this crap. I don't want any of it. In fact, what I do want is for you to get this shit out of here before this week is over."

Dana sat back on her hands and laughed at her. "That's rich. And what if I say no? What are you going to do? Call the police? That's a laugh. The title of the store is in your name, or did you forget that minor detail? So guess who's going down if they find out what's in here?" Dana spat at her.

Alex stood up and threw the bag of powder at Dana in disgust.

"You can't stop me, Alex."

"That's what you think, Dana." She turned and bumped into Regina who was still standing behind her. Alex quickly dropped her gaze to the floor and brushed by her.

❖ ⌘ ❖ ⌘ ❖ ⌘ ❖

Alex walked along the pier with her hands shoved in her pockets. Lost in her thoughts, she was hardly aware that the blonde was at her side, until she felt a tug on the back of her shirt. Looking over her shoulder, Alex saw Regina looking up at her.

The young doctor saw that same look of ragged emotion pass over Alex's face she had seen the night they had been sitting in Regina's apartment after Justin had died. As quickly as it was there, it disappeared and that cool outer façade that Alex kept wrapped tightly around her slid back in place. Regina felt a twinge of pain as she saw the door shut firmly, keeping her at a distance.

"Alex," Regina said, not quite sure what she could say to her. Unable to face Regina, the doctor turned away and looked out over the water. She walked over to a vacant slip and sat down, leaning heavily against the wooden pilings. Regina sat down next to her, dangling her legs over the edge of the pier.

"Go home, Regina. You shouldn't be here," Alex said, looking down at her hands.

"Why, because you're afraid of what I might think about what happened back there?" Regina asked, picking up a piece of wood and toying with it.

Alex was quiet for so long that Regina wasn't sure she was going to answer her. She pulled one leg up, shifting her weight, trying to decide if she should just leave. Regina looked at her dark-haired friend and saw the pained expression on her face as she stared out over the water. She dropped her leg back down and leaned forward on her hands, trying to make sense of what she was feeling inside.

It would be easy enough to walk away and leave Alex here to deal with her own problems, but she really didn't want to. Her rational mind told her it was because of the kind of work they did that made her feel connected to Alex. Almost everything they did in the emergency department was characterized by intense short-lived periods of crisis that required quick thinking, totally committing all their resources to what they were doing at the moment. Maybe it was just a reaction to the intensity of their work and the emotional stress of the past few weeks that had brought these feelings for Alex to the surface.

Alex lowered her head and sighed. "Why are you still here,

Regina?"

It was Regina's turn to look down at the water and be silent. "Do you really want me to leave?" *Please say no, Alex.*

"I don't want you to be here. I know what I have to do to stop Dana. She'll just try to hurt you again if you stay," Alex insisted, still staring out at the water.

"I can handle myself, Alex."

"No, you can't, not with Dana," Alex snapped. "Don't argue with me about this, Regina."

"And you think that you can handle her? I saw what she did to you back there." Regina leaned forward and grabbed Alex's arm. "Alex, you're not the same person you were before." *You can't be.* "I'm not going to leave knowing that Dana is going to do everything that she can to drag you back into that life."

Alex jerked her head around and stared at Regina. "What do you know about my life? What do you care anyway?"

Regina turned, and faced Alex, sitting cross-legged next to her. Her fingers worked loose a piece of bark that curled up from the wood she held in her hands. She watched as it fluttered down into the water below, spinning slowly in the current of water washing around the wooden piling.

She had the same feeling in her chest now that she did when she stood by the window in her apartment the night she told Derrick she wouldn't marry him. She was scared, but for a totally different reason. Regina realized as she sat here, if she was really honest with herself, that her feelings for Alex over the past couple of months had slowly started to cross that invisible line between friendship and something much deeper.

Regina tossed the rest of the wood out into the water and looked up at Alex's tense profile. Taking a breath, she tried to put her thoughts into words. "I'm not sure I know what to say to you to convince you that I do care, Alex." She looked back down at her hands and laughed nervously. "You intimidated the hell out of me that first morning in the ER." Regina sighed. "I came out to talk to you later that day after Derrick showed up. I was afraid, I didn't want to start out on the wrong foot with you." Regina looked up at Alex. Her eyes were closed and she wasn't sure if Alex was even listening to her. "You're right, I don't know about your life, but I do care and I'm here if you want me to be."

Regina watched as Alex lowered her head, her shoulders rising and falling as she let out a heavy sigh, seeming to reach a decision.

"I do want you to be here, Regina." Alex met her eyes. "But promise me you won't go anywhere near that store. I need to convince Dana that I want to go back with her. That's the only way I'm going to be able to stop her."

"I don't understand. Why do *you* have to do this? Isn't that what the police are for?"

Alex nodded her head. "Ordinarily, yes."

"So what's not ordinary about this? Why are you so willing to throw everything away because of Dana?" Regina leaned back and stared at Alex, waiting for an answer.

Alex slowly raised her eyes to look at Regina.

She had a fleeting vision of kneeling next to Lana's bed and holding her hand the day that she died. "It was the last thing that Lana asked me to do. After everything, I owe her at least that," Alex whispered.

Regina reached out a tentative hand and cupped Alex's chin in her fingers. "Alex, let me help you."

"I can't let you do that. This is my problem, not yours." Alex closed her eyes and turned her face away. "Regina, I know what I am. I sold drugs and benefited from getting people hooked. Every time a kid comes into that ER strung out on drugs, I see what I did. There's not much you can do that's worse than that, so I guess when Derrick called me trash, it was an appropriate description."

"No, it's not." Regina shook her head and took Alex's hand in hers. She smiled tentatively, seeing the startled expression on Alex's face. "I know you did some really awful things, but that's not who you are now. You wouldn't have bothered to help me, if you were still that person."

Alex shook her head and turned away. "I know who I am."

"Do you? I see someone who's a good person. You went way above what anyone would have expected when you helped me these past few weeks." Regina moved closer to Alex. "I won't lie. I don't like what you did, but I didn't know you then." Then she spoke more softly. "I know you now and I'm glad I do, Alex."

Alex hung her head, incredulous as she heard the words. *God knows I don't deserve this.* "I'm glad I know you too, Regina."

Any other words seemed meaningless, so they sat beside each other listening to the water lap up against the sides of the pier. Regina could sense Alex's vulnerability lying exposed and raw just beneath the surface. She watched as Alex drew her knees up and leaned her head back against the piling, closing her eyes.

Regina kept seeing images of Alex. That first day in the ER when she came storming out of one of the rooms, and how incredibly intimidated she had been of the doctor. She remembered the day that Alex drove her home, when she'd been so sick from the medication, and the night Justin died and Alex held her in the pouring rain. That was the person she knew, the one she wanted to believe Alex was now. Regina squeezed Alex's hand and leaned closer to her. "Alex?"

"Hmm. What?" Alex had been quietly soaking up the warmth of Regina's hand on hers, afraid if she opened her eyes, she would find that this moment was just a figment of her imagination.

"Let's go back to the apartment." Regina stood up, and slipped her hand under Alex's chin, lifting her face to hers. Regina couldn't help herself as she pressed her lips gently against Alex's forehead. Alex blinked her eyes open and looked up at Regina as she pulled away.

Regina smiled at her, stepping back as Alex pulled herself up to her feet and stood facing her. "Come on," she said, as she turned and walked back down the pier.

Alex stood staring after Regina for a long moment before her brain finally got the message to her legs that she needed to start walking. She jogged a few steps to catch up with the shorter woman. The two walked quietly alongside each other, Alex trying to make some sense of the complicated emotions running through her. *Oh chill out, you idiot, she's just trying to be nice. Don't go reading anything into that kiss. Besides, you know exactly what you have to do tomorrow. Just let it go.* Alex couldn't let it go because Regina had kept gently reminding her what it felt like to be able to trust someone again with those emotions that she had locked safely away deep inside of her. She promised herself she wouldn't let anyone get that close to her again.

A smile tugged at Alex's lips as she walked behind Regina. She really was glad she knew Regina. She admired her strength and intelligence. Her stubborn resilience and gentle sense of humor drew Alex to her, and she realized that she enjoyed having Regina as a friend...or even a lover. *Lover?* She tripped over a piece of slate as they turned into the driveway, mercifully caught herself and looked down at Regina's questioning look.

"Alex?"

"What?" She blinked, trying to rein in her errant thoughts, realizing she hadn't heard her name being called the first time.

"The keys. You know, those things on your key chain, so we can get inside." Regina smiled up at her impishly.

"Oh, yeah. Sorry," Alex mumbled and unlocked the door. She followed Regina up the stairs and into the apartment. She desperately needed something to occupy her mind, so she walked over to her bag and pulled out a pair of scissors and tweezers. Alex turned around to find Regina watching her.

"Uh, what are you doing with those?" Regina pointed to the instruments in her hands.

"I'm taking my stitches out." Alex walked over to the couch, sat down and pulled her sneakers off.

"It hasn't been ten days yet."

"I know, but it's healed." Alex awkwardly tried to reach the spot on her ankle with the tweezers where the stitches were.

Regina sat down beside her. "Let me take them out."

Alex stopped and looked up. "Why?"

"Because you couldn't reach down there to put them in. You'll just cut yourself," Regina pointed out, and took the tweezers from her hands. Several minutes later, Regina sat back and looked up at Alex, realizing Alex had been watching her the whole time. Regina set the tweezers down behind her on the table. "That was simple, wasn't it?"

Alex nodded her head slowly. "Thanks."

"For what?" Regina asked, her mouth going dry as Alex studied her intently.

"For caring about me." Alex's voice was quiet as she leaned forward, reaching out a hand and tracing her fingers down Regina's jaw. "And for being my friend." Alex cupped her fingers underneath Regina's chin, raising her face to hers, searching her eyes.

Regina felt like her heart was going to hammer its way through her chest, as she looked back at Alex. Alex leaned closer, pressing her lips to Regina's, tentatively at first, then slowly deepening the kiss as Regina's lips parted in invitation. She traced the curve of her lips with the tip of her tongue. Pulling back, Alex looked into Regina's green eyes, so close she could see the starburst of color around her pupils.

Regina looked back at Alex through slightly unfocused eyes. She circled a trembling hand around Alex's neck, feeling her silky hair flow between her fingers as she drew Alex's mouth down to hers.

They kissed slowly, again and again, exploring and tasting each other. Alex slipped her arm around Regina's waist, easing her back onto the couch. Lowering her body onto the smaller woman, Alex watched the blonde woman's eyes, as their bodies came together. Regina shuddered beneath her at the contact and Alex buried her face in Regina's hair, inhaling the fragrance of her, as she kissed her throat and nuzzled the skin beneath her ear.

"Oh God, Alex," Regina whispered, as she felt a powerful stirring of desire deep inside her. The intensity left her feeling vulnerable and she pulled back, looking up uncertainly into Alex's eyes.

"It's all right," Alex whispered, holding onto her.

Regina pressed her body against Alex, slipped her arms around her waist, and slid her hands up over her back, pulling her tightly against her.

Pressing up on her elbows, Alex raised her hands to Regina's face, running her fingertips over her eyebrows, tracing the gentle contours of her cheekbones, memorizing each detail as she went. She tilted her head and grazed her lips along Regina's jaw, sending tiny electric shocks racing up and down Regina's spine. Alex heard the woman moan softly and wrapped her arms tightly around her, pulling her close, feeling the heat between their bodies as they touched.

She lowered her mouth to Regina's, tasting her, as she kissed her way across her lips. Alex tugged gently on her lower lip, pulling it into her mouth and running her tongue across it.

The taller woman shifted her weight and unfastened the buttons on Regina's shirt. She ran her fingers down Regina's throat and brushed the cotton shirt back off her shoulders. Her tongue followed her fingers and Regina arched against her, moaning into Alex's throat.

Regina tugged Alex's shirt from her jeans and slipped her hands underneath, running her palms over her back, feeling the strength beneath her hands. Her hands trailed down over her ribs, as Alex raised up and looked down at her.

Alex moved her hands over Regina's body, gently caressing her hips and thighs. She ran her hand up her inner thigh and pressed her palm against her, through the fabric of her jeans, watching as Regina gasped and closed her eyes, arching against her hand and whimpering at her touch. When she opened her eyes and focused on her, Alex leaned over her.

"What's wrong?" Alex asked, seeing the flicker of fear in them. She rested her hand on Regina's hip.

Regina bit her lower lip and turned her head away, closing her eyes. "I'm sorry, Alex." She took a breath, trying to control her pounding heart. "It's just..." Regina lowered her head, pulling her eyes away from Alex and giving herself a moment to collect her thoughts. She remembered the bloody needle piercing her skin, the pills she'd forgotten to take today and her desire ebbed away as she looked up at Alex and realized what they were about to do. "Alex, we shouldn't do this."

"I thought you..." Alex stopped, thinking. "Am I making you uncomfortable?" she finally asked, pulling her hand back and looking seriously at Regina.

Her voice was a whisper. "No. It's just, well, I don't know what's going to happen with the rest of the tests. I know six weeks is a good sign, but that could change. We both know that."

Alex hung her head and took a breath, and let it out slowly, feeling the desire in her body fade painfully into a vague ache. "It'll be all right as long as we don't," she hesitated, "have oral sex." She lay down beside Regina and looked at her.

Regina nodded her head. "I know." She closed her eyes. "I'm sorry, Alex. I just, I can't." Her gaze traveled back up to Alex's face. "I don't want anything to happen to you," she said, wondering if Alex believed her or thought she had just strung her along. Regina rolled away from Alex and sat up. Her hands trembling, she buttoned her shirt and leaned against the arm of the couch, staring out the window into the darkness.

Alex watched as Regina turned away from her. Truth be told she hadn't even thought about the damn needle stick. She ran her finger over the cushion tracing an abstract design as she lay there on her side thinking. *Damn. You're such an idiot, Alex. Maybe next time you should ask before you leap. First, she finds out you used to deal drugs and then you come on to her like that. What the hell were you thinking?*

Alex looked up at Regina, sitting with her back to her. She pushed herself up and sat next to her on the couch. She hesitated, then leaned over her and brushed a tear from Regina's cheek. "Hey, it's okay, Regina. I didn't even think about it. Some doctor I am, right?" Alex joked, trying to get Regina to smile without success. *Oh boy. You really messed this up.* She reached for Regina's hand, interlacing their fingers together. "Regina?" She leaned forward to see her face.

The blonde stood up, walked over to the sliding door, pulled it open and stepped outside. Alex followed and stood quietly beside her. "Regina, are you all right?"

"Yes." Her voice was hardly more than a whisper.

"No, I don't think you are."

"I'm okay. Really." Regina turned away from Alex. Her emotions were raw and she swallowed, trying to push down the tears that threatened to fall.

The doctor stood very still behind her. Tentatively she reached out a hand and rested it softly on Regina's shoulder.

The touch completely undid her resolve. Regina took a breath and a sob escaped unbidden from her throat. The flood-gates opened and her shoulders shook with the intensity of the emotions running through her.

"Come here." Alex turned Regina around and pulled her into a hug. "I'm sorry. I thought you wanted...I'm sorry."

Regina nodded her head against Alex's chest. "No, Alex, it is what I want." Regina fingered the front of the tear-stained sweatshirt covering Alex's body.

Alex moved her hand over Regina's back in a comforting motion, holding her until she felt her breathing return back to normal. "Feel better?" She bent her head forward, brushing her lips against Regina's hair, as the smaller woman relaxed against her.

"Yeah, I do, thanks," Regina whispered, feeling the barest pressure against her head as she closed her eyes.

"We should get some sleep." Alex hesitated, looking down at Regina. "I'll hold you while you sleep if you want me to."

Regina tightened her arms around Alex's waist. "I'd like that," she said, and let herself be led into the apartment.

Regina disappeared into the bathroom to change, while Alex slipped into her T-shirt and crawled into bed. She lay on her back with both arms behind her head, staring up at the ceiling, wondering what twist of fate brought them together. Alex turned her head as Regina lay down beside her and smiled shyly. "I'm sorry."

"No, don't say anything. It's all right." She waited until Regina was settled and then turned the light off on the night-stand. "Goodnight, Regina."

The bed shifted and Regina slowly nestled in against her, resting her head on Alex's shoulder. "Goodnight, Alex."

They lay that way, both slowly drifting off to sleep.

# Chapter
# 13

Alex's mind slowly roused her from her slumber. Opening her eyes, she blinked and groaned inwardly as she saw the sun streaming in the through the sliding glass window. She had every intention of getting up and going running this morning, figured it would be a good way to give her some time to think before she needed to face the realities of the new day. *So much for that idea,* Alex thought, as she reached out and groped for her watch lying on the night table. Staring at it, she realized that it had been a long time since she slept this late, let alone through the night.

Shifting her body, aware of the comforting warmth pressed up against her side, Alex glanced down at Regina, lying nestled against her shoulder. After last night, she wasn't sure how Regina would feel if she woke to find her body draped over Alex, one arm wrapped snuggly around her waist and her leg thrown intimately over Alex's thigh. Not that she minded, Alex thought wryly; nope not one bit at all, the rest of her body gladly chimed in.

*Oh quit that.* She knew that her own feelings were deeper than just physical attraction. She really did like Regina. That was the problem. *Well, Regina was involved with a man before she met you. You've been with straight women before. Uh huh. No way. Been there, done that, moved on. You're not making that mistake again.* It was safer for her to tell herself that it was nothing more than a fleeting interest and the feelings she had would pass with time. Alex quickly decided as Regina shifted in her sleep that neither of them needed to deal with the fact that they had quite comfortably curled up around each other during the night. As gently as she could, trying not to wake her, Alex disentangled herself from Regina's snug embrace and sat on the edge of the bed.

She looked over her shoulder at the blonde and shook her head, wondering what in hell it was that the younger woman saw in her. Yes, she managed to get her life back on track, barely. She knew she was a good doctor, but that certainly didn't change who she was or what she'd done in her past. In fact, based on the little that she knew, she and Regina were about as opposite as two people could get. With a shake of her head, Alex stood up and stretched. She walked into the bathroom to take a shower, a nice, long, cold shower.

A few minutes later, Regina woke up to the sound of running water coming from the bathroom. She stretched and yawned, rolling over onto her stomach. Yesterday seemed like it happened an eternity ago. She pulled a pillow under her shoulders, crossed her arms over it and buried her face in its softness, as she stifled another yawn. Closing her eyes, she inhaled deeply, and the scent of Alex's perfume filled her senses. The memory of sitting on the couch as Alex touched her face, her eyes looking right through her, replayed in her mind and made her shiver involuntarily.

Her body remembered Alex's gentle touch and soft kisses, and the intense feeling that flowed through her and settled in the pit of her belly startled Regina. *Okay, obviously you're attracted to her.*

It wasn't a foreign concept to Regina. She knew that she could love a woman. She'd been attracted to other women in the past, and endured the usual assortment of crushes on some of her female friends growing up, but she never acted on any of the feelings that she experienced. When she thought about a relationship with a woman in the context of how it would impact her family, friends, plans for her career, indeed every facet of her life, she found herself holding back; until now, that is. Despite everything that she was afraid of and everything that she knew about Alex, Regina still was irresistibly drawn to the doctor.

The blonde lifted her head and her gaze fell outside the window, as she remembered Alex lying there beside her in the bed.

It was so easy to just curl up next to her and fall asleep once she got over her initial shyness. She hadn't even given it a second thought when she felt the older woman slip her arm over her shoulder and pull her closer.

Thoughts of Alex, her now familiar gestures, the strength that carried through in her every movement, and an image of her crystal blue eyes, lit up by that dazzling smile filled Regina's mind. She shook her head and flopped over onto her back and stared up at the ceiling. *Well, you certainly don't have a wealth of experience in this department, Regina,* she thought wryly, *and your timing couldn't possibly be any worse.*

"You're up." Regina lifted her head to see Alex dressed in jeans and a white shirt standing at the foot of the bed, watching her, as she towel dried her hair.

Alex shook her head and draped the towel over her shoulder. Her damp hair framed her angular face and her eyes sparkled in the morning sunlight that was streaming through the window.

"Uh, yeah." Regina realized she was staring and pulled her eyes away, wondering how long Alex had been standing there at the foot of the bed before she said something. She quickly pushed herself up and sat over the edge of the bed, staring down at the floor.

"Alex, I'm sorry about last night." Regina brought a hand up to her throat and rubbed the front of her neck. It was a nervous gesture that she did automatically, but she stopped as she felt an uncharacteristic tenderness on both sides of her neck, just under her jaw. Her heart fluttered in her chest and she sat very still as her world suddenly closed in on her.

"You don't need to explain anything to me, Regina." Alex walked over and sat down on the edge of the bed. "I understand." *You're probably the first person I've ever met who's worried about that. Doesn't say much for me. With all I've done, you have more to worry about from me than I do you.* "Listen." Alex stared down at her hands. "If you want to talk later, let me know." She looked at Regina and smiled faintly. "Hey, are you okay?" She looked closely at her face. "You're as pale as a ghost."

Regina nodded her head absently, dropping her hand down into her lap. "Yeah, yeah I'm fine," she said, glancing quickly up at Alex.

"Okay, well," Alex stood up and turned around, "I have to go over to Dana's store."

Regina shifted her attention outward and looked up at Alex. "Why?"

"Regina, I told you what I have to do." Alex looked down at her. "I'm probably going to be gone most of the day." She dug into her pocket and held out her hand to Regina. "I'll leave the keys to the truck, if you want to go down to the beach or something today."

Regina stood up from the bed. "Let me come with you."

"No." Alex shook her head and stepped back. "You're not coming with me, Regina, so don't even try and argue with me about it."

"But—"

Alex cut her off. "No. You promise me you won't go there today. I don't want Dana to be able to hurt you."

"What about you?" Regina asked, suddenly wondering if Alex just didn't want her around because of what happened between them last night.

"I'll be fine," the taller woman assured her, before she left the apartment.

❖ ⌘ ❖ ⌘ ❖ ⌘ ❖

Regina sat in the silence of the apartment and stared at the wall. After Alex left, she took a shower. She had no appetite but forced herself to eat something so she could take the AZT and 3TC in the hopes of reducing the chances that her body would develop the HIV antibodies. She tried so hard not to be angry with Marcus, realizing that it was an accident, but right now she wanted to scream at him and if he had been standing in front of her she would have beaten him senseless with her fists. She walked out of the bathroom and grabbed Alex's keys off the table. After running down the stairs, Regina hopped into the truck and squealed the tires as she pulled out of the driveway. In a daze, she followed the signs to Race Point Beach.

There were a fair number of people at the beach already, so Regina walked for a long time until she found a deserted place far away from the sounds of people playing touch football and generally having a good time. Regina slumped down on the sand and leaned back against a large piece of driftwood and stared out at the waves, watching them swell and curl, breaking on the beach in a wash of foam. If she ever felt lower in her life, she couldn't remember.

"Son of a bitch. I can't believe this is happening." Her voice cracked and the tears fell. She covered her mouth with her hand and rocked back and forth. The raw emotion passed after a time and she wrapped her arms tightly around herself. Her body ached and she noticed she was sniffling. *Maybe I'm just getting a bad cold. It was possible, right? Yeah right, Regina. Seven years of college, three years of residencies and you haven't missed one goddamn day because you've been sick. All right, come on. Be rational. You're a doctor. So what! You're twenty-nine years old,* her mind screamed back. *This can't be happening. Oh God, please don't let this happen!*

Regina pulled her legs up to her chest and closed her eyes. Twenty-nine and it felt like her world was spinning wildly out of control. Her life was completely out of balance and there wasn't one facet of it that she felt she was in control of right now.

Her family? *If* they were still talking to her it would be a miracle. She'd left in the middle of the night after an ugly fight with her mother, leaving a note, telling them that she couldn't stay. Who knew what her mother told to her father? She hadn't meant to say anything to her mother about her feelings. There was no reason to; except that she was tired of living up to her mother's expectations of who she thought her daughter should be.

Professionally, she stood on a tight rope until Monday. It was anybody's guess what the board would decide. She hoped Jeffrey was right about the hospital not wanting to make them into scapegoats.

She stared out at the water as another sudden realization came to her making her heart skip a beat. *Derrick.* He had been driving up to her parent's house and that meant he knew she had left there. Would he try and find her here? Could he find her?

Regina looked up, realizing for the first time that the sun was beginning its descent into the western sky. She'd been at the beach for hours and run the gamut of emotions, which left her exhausted as she walked back to Alex's Jeep. She slid into the driver's seat, settled back into the leather and closed her eyes, wondering if Alex was back at the apartment yet. She said if she wanted to talk to let her know. Regina shook her head. She did, but she wasn't even sure she knew what she would say to Alex, knowing what she did.

❖ ⌘ ❖ ⌘ ❖ ⌘ ❖

Alex walked along the street heading toward the West End of town. She needed to make one stop before she went to the store. Even though it surprised her that Regina didn't put up more of a fight, she was glad that she hadn't. The truth was she couldn't bring herself to do the things she would have to do if Regina was with her. She didn't want her to have to see that side of her. It was bad enough that Dana slipped something into her drink the other night. No, she couldn't let Regina get any closer than she was already. Maybe it was better that nothing happened, leaving no tangled emotions to deal with later. *Best to just get the kid home.*

Alex turned down a narrow side street and stopped in front of the gray two-story cape that sat at the end of the cul-de-sac. She walked up the worn concrete steps to the front door. The doorbell was broken and exposed wires poked through the faded shingles. Alex knocked loudly on the door with her knuckles and waited. When there was no answer, she banged on it again with her fist. She stepped back off the front porch, and looked up at the second story window; frowning, she climbed the steps again and turned the doorknob. It was unlocked so she pushed the door open.

The brunette stepped inside, shutting the door quietly behind her. She looked warily around the first floor of the house. All the shades were pulled down and the downstairs was hidden in a blur of gray shadows. She wrinkled her nose at the heavy scent of stale beer and marijuana as she walked through the living room and stepped over a pile of dirty laundry.

*Damn it, Richard, why did you have to tie one on last night? Well, I hope you're not too hung over because I'm coming up there anyway.* Alex checked out the rest of the rooms on the first floor. They were all empty. *You must be getting old, Richard. In earlier years, it wouldn't have been just dirty laundry lying scattered on your floor.*

Quietly, Alex walked up the darkened stairwell to the second floor. There were two bedrooms at the top, one to the left of the stairs and the other to the right. Both the bedroom doors were closed. She opened the door to the one on the left and looked in. Empty. *Come on. Be here.*

She turned the knob to the door of the other room and found Richard sprawled naked on the bed. Alex shook her head and walked over to him. She clamped a hand on his shoulder and shook him roughly.

"Wake up."

He grunted and rolled away from her.

"Come on, Richard. I don't have time for you to nurse your damn hangover." Alex nudged him roughly in the middle of his back.

The sleeping man moaned and rolled onto his back, his hand reaching up for her. She slapped his groping hand away. "Open your eyes you idiot. I'm not your damn boyfriend."

"Jesus." He blinked his eyes open and realized he wasn't alone. "Don't you knock, Alex?" Richard scrambled up in the bed and pulled the covers up over his waist.

Alex folded her arms over her chest. "I did. You were passed out, so I let myself in." She watched as he fumbled around for something else to throw on his naked body. "Do you need a moment to, uh, get yourself together, Richard?" She couldn't keep herself from smirking at his obvious discomfort.

"You're such a bitch, Alex," he whined.

"Really, and you're just figuring that out now? I'm disappointed, I thought you were quicker than that." She pulled out a piece of paper from her pocket and shoved it in his face. She waited as he read the words scribbled on it. "Do you have it?"

He looked up at her and tilted his head. "I didn't think you were into that kind of stuff, Alex."

She ignored his remark. "Do you have it?"

"Yeah, yeah. Give me a minute to put something on. I'll meet you downstairs." He pulled the comforter off the bed and wrapped it around himself as he stood up and walked over to his closet.

Alex rolled her eyes, walked downstairs and waited in the kitchen, staring out the window into the tiny yard. As Richard entered the room, she turned her head, pushed off the wall and walked over to him. She reached her hand out to take the glass ampoule and the syringe he held.

"How much?"

"A hundred dollars."

Alex pulled her wallet out and handed the money to him.

"So, what *are* you doing with this?" he asked, as he tucked the money she handed him into his pocket.

"None of your business."

His eyes gleamed and he leaned closer. "What's wrong, the

little blonde one not submitting to your charms, Alex?"

Alex carefully set the vial down on the table and slowly turned around. Her eyes were dark with anger when she faced him and instinctively he stepped back.

"You pathetic piece of shit." She grabbed him around his throat and shoved him up against the wall. "Don't you ever talk about her that way."

Richard's eyes bulged and he clutched at Alex's fingers trying to pry them away from his throat. "I was only joking," he croaked, as she let him go. He slumped against the wall, gasping for air and rubbing his throat.

"You would joke about it, Richard. Sex is just a game to you, it always has been." Alex grabbed his shirt and pulled him to her. "Regina knows more about caring for someone than you'd figure out in three lifetimes."

He stared at the dark-haired woman for a minute and then smiled. "Go to hell, Alex. You're no better than I am."

"I didn't say I was." She pushed him away from her, picked up the vial from the table and walked out of the house, slamming the door behind her. She could hear glass shattering against the door as he threw something after her.

❖ ⌘ ❖ ⌘ ❖ ⌘ ❖

It was late afternoon by the time Alex walked down the alley that bordered the store Lana had left to her. The brunette leaned against the side of the building, hidden in the shadows, waiting until several couples that had been walking behind passed her by. Nervously, she slipped the syringe and vial out of her pocket and twisted the cap off, holding it between her teeth as she tipped the vial and filled the syringe with the clear fluid. Alex recapped the syringe, slid it into her back pocket and walked up the alley. The store was empty when Alex opened the door and slipped quietly inside. She immediately spotted Dana perched on a stool behind the counter, reading a paperback. A pack of Marlboros lay open on the glass countertop and several cigarette butts already littered the ashtray.

Alex let the door shut behind her, not bothering to keep it from banging as it did. "Slow day, Dana?" she asked, walking slowly over to the counter, keeping her eyes trained on Dana the whole way.

Dana looked up over the cover of her book and raised an

eyebrow. "Well, well, look at what the cat dragged in." Dana
tilted her head to the side and peered behind Alex. "So, where's
the little blonde?" she asked, setting the book down on the glass
countertop, regarding Alex with feigned disinterest.

Alex shrugged her shoulders, stopping on the other side of
the counter directly in front of Dana. "Not here." She leaned an
elbow on the glass. Alex picked up the pack of Marlboros and
shook one of the cigarettes out into her hand. "You're smoking
again."

"Yeah. So what?"

"You shouldn't be, not after Lana."

"Give it a rest, Alex. You are not my keeper." Dana
snatched the pack of cigarettes back from her.

Holding the cigarette between her lips, Alex lit the end, and
took a drag, slowly exhaling the smoke into Dana's face. "You
didn't need to slip that pill in Regina's drink the other night.
That was a pretty stupid thing to do."

"Like I give a crap. Quit the lecture, already." Dana waved
her hand in irritation. "Why are you here?"

Alex leaned forward, resting her elbows on the counter and
tapped the ashes from her cigarette into the ashtray. "I was
thinking that maybe we could discuss the store." She ran a finger
up the bare skin of Dana's arm. She lifted her head and looked
into Dana's eyes. "See if we could come to some sort of
an...equitable solution."

Dana eyed her suspiciously. She pulled her arm away from
Alex's touch and slid off the stool. "Don't bullshit me, Alex. The
only person you were ever good about looking after was yourself." She looked Alex over and crossed her arms in front of her.

Alex pushed off the counter and walked over to the shelf at
the back of the room. "Well, you did extend the offer of a private
party, Dana. So, I'm taking you up on it." She picked up a book
of matches, ripped one off from the cover and dragged it across
the black strip. It flared, and the smell of sulfur dissipated as the
small flame sputtered to life. Alex turned, casually leaning back
against the wall and looked at Dana with a smile on her face. She
twirled the lit match back and forth between her fingers. "Or did
you change your mind?" She waited as Dana walked out from
behind the counter. "Business is slow. Why don't you lock up for
the day?"

Alex turned back to the shelf and lit the second candle from
the left. She smiled to herself as she heard the latch click in the

lock and the lights dimmed at the front of the store. *Now we'll see how you like it when the tables are turned, Dana.*

She was aware of Dana walking up behind her, as she pursed her lips and blew the match out. Alex turned around and looked at her for a moment. Dana was a good-looking woman, but the years of abusing her body were beginning to show. Short, spiky blonde hair framed her small face and green eyes sparkled back at her, as the candlelight flickered from behind Alex's shoulder. Alex took Dana's hand and led her up the stairs to the small apartment above the store.

Dana slipped the key into the lock and opened the door; Alex let her walk past her and followed her inside to stand in the middle of the small kitchen. The brunette slipped her jacket off and hung it on the back of one of the chairs. She watched as Dana walked over to one of the kitchen cabinets and fished around in the back of it, pulling out a mirror and a razor blade. The woman then sat down at the small table and poured some of the white powder onto the mirror, efficiently cutting a few lines of cocaine.

"Come on, Alex, you know you want it. Go ahead, take it." Dana slid the mirror over to Alex and smiled up at her. "I won't tell."

The doctor recognized the look as one of those sexy and seductive smiles that Dana used on her so many times before when she let herself be lured in. The line was clearly drawn and Alex could feel the old demons rising and tugging at her, inviting her to cross over again. For a few seconds, she held Dana's gaze, then slowly reached a trembling hand out and pushed the mirror away from her.

"No, that's not why I'm here." Alex leaned away, closing her eyes, forcing herself to breathe slowly. *You don't need this. Just get done what you need to do and get the hell out of here.*

"Oh, what? Is the good doctor all reformed now? Maybe it's just all an act for Regina to buy until you're finished with her." Dana sneered, enjoying the fact that Alex was still tempted by the lure of the drugs.

Alex's eyes snapped open at the mention of the blonde's name. "No. I don't need that stuff anymore, Dana. It almost killed me last time."

"Yeah, whatever, Alex." Dana pulled the mirror back to her, bent forward and quickly snorted the lines of crystalline powder.

Alex felt like someone hit her across the back of the head

with a two by four as memories flooded her mind. She stared at Dana's face, seeing the white powdery residue around the outer edge of one of her nostrils.

"So why are you here?" Dana leaned forward on her elbows and stared at the woman sitting across from her. She sniffed and wiped her nose with her fingers, reveling in the intense high she was experiencing.

"I already told you." She stood up and walked around the table toward Dana. She pulled Dana to her feet and slipped a hand behind her neck. She pulled her mouth to hers and kissed her roughly. Dana moaned and pressed into Alex, responding to her own body's rising desire.

The doctor led Dana down the short hallway and into the bedroom, where she wrapped her hands around the blonde's waist, turned her around, backed her up to the bed, and let the mattress buckle the smaller woman's knees. She lowered the woman onto her back and pinned her underneath her weight, as she continued to kiss her.

Alex pressed her body into Dana, spreading her legs and sliding her thigh up against her. Dana clutched at her shoulders and rose up against her body, and in response Alex ducked her head and nipped at the skin on her throat. Alex quickly tugged Dana's shirt free from her pants and without hesitation ran her hand up the soft skin of her stomach and over her breasts, eliciting a moan from the woman. Dana tried to reach down to pull Alex up to her for another kiss, but the brunette grabbed her hand and pushed her arm back down to the mattress roughly.

"No."

The blonde growled in frustration, bucking her hips as Alex undid the buttons on Dana's pants, bent over her and kissed the sensitive skin beneath her navel. Dana moaned and rolled her head back and forth, clamping her hands down on Alex's shoulders in response.

Alex ran her hand down Dana's thigh. Then calmly, she reached into the back pocket of her jeans, pulled out the hypodermic needle and twisted the cap off easily with her fingers. She distracted the woman easily by ducking her head, to kiss her neck again, pressing her thigh up in between her legs and rubbing against her.

Alex raised her body up and looked down at Dana; the woman's eyes were closed and her neck was arched, burying her head back into the pillow. It was so easy.

The doctor ran her palm up the inside of Dana's arm, stopping at her elbow and circling the sensitive skin with her fingertips. Dana grunted as the small needle penetrated expertly into the vein. Alex smoothly depressed the plunger, and then watched with satisfaction as Dana's body relaxed into the quick effect of the drug.

Alex carefully pushed herself back off the bed, picked up the cap from the sheets and quietly replaced it on the used needle. She slipped the hypodermic into her jacket pocket and scowled at Dana's prone form. *That's for Regina, you bitch.*

The dark woman walked out of the bedroom and over to the sink in the kitchen where she leaned heavily against it, her legs trembling from the adrenaline running though her system. She turned the cold water on and cupped her hands under the stream to bring a drink to her mouth; instead of drinking it, however, she sucked the water into her mouth and spat it back out into the sink, attempting to spit out Dana's taste. She then washed her hands and her face, trying to rid her skin of the stench of Dana's perfume. But she curled her lip in disgust when she raised her arm to her nose and smelled the perfume clinging to her clothes, assaulting her senses and refusing to let go, just like Dana.

The brunette turned and walked back to the bedroom to stand at the door looking in at the woman sleeping obliviously on the bed. Alex studied her briefly, watching her chest rise and fall in a normal rhythm. Now, all she needed to do was find the book that she knew Dana kept hidden in the apartment.

It took her most of the afternoon and early evening to find what she was looking for: the little black book filled with all of Dana's contacts. One thing about Dana was that she always had connections, and apparently, they had broadened significantly since Alex worked for her years ago. When she finally uncovered the book, she ran her finger down the entries and found a familiar name. She picked up the phone, dialed the number and listened to it ring three times before the answering machine picked up.

The message was simple and Alex desperately hoped as she set the phone back in the cradle that Dana still set her drug deals up the same way. She walked back to the bedroom to check the passed out woman's pulse and breathing—she would be fine, if a little groggy when she woke up, and completely devoid of any memory of today's events. Alex bent over and untied Dana's shoes, pulled them off and dumped them on the floor. *Well,*

*Dana, when Tommy comes to pick up his stuff tomorrow, the cops will be right behind him. They always knew you were dealing drugs out of this store, but could never prove it. One more phone call and it's all over. Hope you enjoy the accommodations in the state penitentiary.*

Alex sat back down at the table. She looked down at the bag of cocaine lying there and picked it up, quietly fingering the plastic baggie that held it. That very subtle base craving nudged at her seductively.

*Come on, Alex, you know you want it. Go ahead, take it.* She could hear Dana's voice tempting her and she gripped the bag, and threw it angrily down on the table. Alex stared across the room, wondering if it really was ever going to be over. She lifted her body out of the chair and walked out of the apartment.

As she shut the door behind her, she felt an overwhelming urge to get back to Regina. The thought of just being with her made some of the pain Alex felt inside fade away. She ran down the steps and headed back to the apartment.

❖ ⌘ ❖ ⌘ ❖ ⌘ ❖

Regina returned to an empty apartment. Still feeling emotionally dragged out and tired, she collapsed on the bed and fell into a fitful asleep. It was dark out and raining when she woke hours later, still alone in the apartment. Regina had a vague, unsettling feeling that something was wrong as she sat up from the bed.

The young doctor stood up from the bed, walked into the bathroom, and turned the light on. She looked at her face in the mirror and leaned heavily on the sink. "Shit." She could feel fever attacking her body; her face was flushed and her movements were slow and clumsy. *Oh Alex, please get back here. I need you. I'm scared.*

Regina gave up trying to be patient, telling herself that Alex would be back anytime now. She paced anxiously across the wooden floor, and then stopped at the sliding glass door to stare at her reflection. She listened to the rain as it pelted the ground outside and watched it run down the outside of the glass.

She sighed heavily. Alex did say she would be gone most of the day. Well the day had come and gone, and she still wasn't back.

"Damn it, Alex, where are you?" Regina asked aloud. Decision made, she turned and grabbed the spare keys off the kitchen counter.

She locked the apartment door behind her and walked down the narrow hallway to the stairs before she heard the hinges of the screen door squeak open and the sound of a key turning in the lock. *Thank God.* Turning the corner, Regina stepped down onto the small landing.

"Alex, what took you so long?"

Regina stopped dead in her tracks, as her heart jumped up into her throat. She froze, staring like a deer caught in the headlight of an oncoming car.

"Hello, Regina." Derrick leered up at her from the bottom of the steps. He was a terrifying sight. His hair was plastered to his forehead with rain and his blue sweatshirt from the police academy was soaked and clinging to his muscular shoulders. "Sorry to disappoint you, but Alex isn't with me," Derrick drawled, slowly climbing the stairs toward Regina, pinning her down with his eyes.

Regina's body finally responded to her brain's frantic message to take flight and run. She pivoted on her feet, and fled back down the hallway toward the apartment door. Her hands shook and she cursed as she fumbled for the right key. She finally got it and put it in the lock just as she heard Derrick reach the top of the staircase and call her name in a singsong voice. She pushed the door open, and stepped quickly into the kitchen.

She turned to close the door, hearing Derrick's pounding footfalls sprinting down the hallway after her. Regina felt the rush of air behind her, just before he tackled her through the open door. The impact against the molding cracked her chin, splitting the skin open. Blood welled and oozed out. Her legs turned to jelly and she crumpled to the floor, gasping for breath. Rough hands grabbed the keys away from her and tossed them across the room, far out of reach. Regina watched helplessly as they clattered across the wooden floor and slid underneath the couch. She grunted, struggling against him as he pinned her, face down, on the hard floor.

"Did you think I couldn't find you, Regina? You used your credit card to buy the plane tickets to get here. Stupid, very stupid." Derrick's breath was hot on her face, as he straddled her body, pinning her arms painfully behind her back. He hauled her to her feet and spun her around, slamming her up against the wall. "You should be thankful I didn't tell your parents where I found you. Your mother would be devastated. Is that what you want?" He yanked her face to his.

"Derrick, let me go." Regina struggled against his grip. She winced as his hands clamped painfully down on her wrists in a vice-like grip. Biting back tears, she slammed her foot down onto his instep. He immediately grunted and loosened his grip, just enough for her to wrench away from him. She staggered backwards, putting the kitchen table between them.

Regina held onto a chair and pressed the palm of her other hand against her bloody and swollen chin. Dazed, she stared incredulously at the blood on her hand.

Derrick curled his lip menacingly as he advanced on her. "What did she do to you? Give you drugs or something to get you to come to her? What spell does she have you under, Regina?" he asked, as he slowly closed the distance between them.

Regina's eyes darted to the door. "Stay away from me, Derrick." Her voice trembled, her terror betraying her. She needed to get to the door, but the space between her and Derrick was too narrow for her to get by him.

He edged closer, watching her eyes and laughing as he realized what she was thinking. He lunged at her quickly. Regina ducked to avoid him, but got caught as his arm snaked out and wrapped tightly around her waist.

"Not so fast." Despite her struggles, he dragged her back to the couch and she knew with frightening certainty what he intended to do to her.

He pushed her roughly onto the couch and pinned her down with his hands. "You never complained when we were together, Regina. Did your tastes change or do you just like it both ways now?" he asked, leering down at her.

"Go to hell, Derrick," Regina snarled back at him, struggling against his weight. A wave of anger washed over her as she saw him working his belt buckle loose. Regina braced her heels against the couch and slammed her knee up between his legs with all her strength. Her knee caught him high up on the inside of his thigh.

Derrick yelped and folded over, crumpling to the floor, moaning in pain with his hand clutching his crotch. Regina's mind screamed at her to move. She pushed off the couch, and stumbled over his grasping hand toward the door.

Fear and adrenaline pumped through her veins, propelling

her forward. She ran down the hallway, grabbing the wall and whipping around the corner. She almost lost her balance as she missed the first step, except that she clutched desperately at the railing, catching herself and wrenching her shoulder painfully in the process.

"Regina! Get back here," Derrick shouted from inside the apartment.

*Move!* Regina found her feet and fled down the steps, slamming the screen door open against the side of the house. She barreled headlong into Alex, knocking her off her feet and into a puddle.

"Hey!" Alex rolled over and scrambled to her feet, catching Regina's arm and spinning her around. "What the hell is going on?" Her voice trailed off when she saw the fear etched on her face and heard the angry voice from inside the apartment.

Alex let go of Regina's arm and turned, cocking her head as she recognized the now familiar male voice. She was edgy and in a foul mood anyway. Now, she had an excuse to vent her frustrations.

Alex heard Derrick running down the stairs and she slipped up beside the door, standing in the shadows. As he burst through the screen door, she stuck her foot out, sending him crashing headlong into the fence. Alex let out a deep laugh as she watched him roll over and climb unsteadily to his feet. He staggered as he turned around to face her.

"You know, you've got to watch that last step, Derrick." Alex smiled wickedly at him. "It really is a bitch." She caught Regina standing on the outskirts of her peripheral vision, clutching the mirror of her Jeep, and breathing heavily. The light from inside the stairwell reflected off Regina's face and Alex could see the blood staining her chin and the front of her shirt. Her eyes flicked back to Derrick and she clenched her fists as anger welled up and boiled over. "You bastard. What did you do to her?"

Derrick growled and lunged at her. Alex easily sidestepped him and hooked him under his arm, using his momentum to slam him into the side of the house. Derrick pushed himself up and swung blindly, catching Alex by surprise and cracking his fist into her jaw.

She shook her head to clear her vision and blocked his next punch with her forearm. Countering, she punched him hard in the side, doubling him over. Alex smiled as she heard the satisfying crunch of ribs breaking. He grunted and stumbled back, clutching his side. Alex stepped forward without hesitation, unleashing a powerful sidekick into his chest. Derrick stumbled backwards as she planted her foot, pivoted her hips and slammed her heel into his jaw, snapping his head backward.

"You can end this now, Derrick. Just walk away and leave Regina alone." She stood with her hands hanging loosely by her sides and bounced on the balls of her feet. Her nostrils flared and she inhaled the scent of rain and blood.

Derrick lifted his head and glared at her. "Go to hell, you bitch. I don't know what you did to her, but I'm taking her back home."

He dove at Alex, tackling her around her ankles and driving her back against the side of the house.

The impact knocked her down, slamming her head to the ground. Derrick got up and looked at Alex, lying sprawled out on the ground. "Bitch." He kicked her hard in the stomach, before he turned around.

He walked around the Jeep. "Regina?" He listened for her as he walked on the gravel.

"I'm not going anywhere with you, Derrick. Not now, not ever." Regina walked out from behind the Jeep, having retrieved the baseball bat from inside it.

Derrick turned around and took a step back. "Put the bat down." He smiled at her. "Come on, Regina, what are you going to do? Hit me? You wouldn't do that." He laughed, lifting a hand up to reach out for the bat.

Regina edged back, gripping the bat tightly in her hands. Derrick just smiled and kept advancing on her. "Back off. You tried to rape me, you bastard." Regina shifted her hands on the bat.

"Come on, Regina. You wouldn't hit me."

Regina swung the bat down, clipping his ankles and neatly sweeping his feet out from underneath him.

"You bitch. You're going to pay for that." Derrick started to scramble back up to his feet, but Alex tackled him to the ground. They rolled over each other, with Derrick finally pinning Alex onto her back. She planted her feet and pushed her hips up, knocking him off balance. Using her arms, she shoved him to the ground and pounced on top of him.

"I don't think so, you bastard." Her fist sailed in, catching him across his face, knocking him senseless.

❖ ⌘ ❖ ⌘ ❖ ⌘ ❖

Regina sat on the bottom step, resting her head in one hand and holding a small icepack against her mouth in the other hand. Her head pounded from the collision with the kitchen cabinets and her lip felt like it would burst. The flashing lights from the police cruiser alternately bathed the house in red and blue, making her headache that much worse.

She watched as Alex talked to the officer who arrested Derrick. The woman wasn't much taller than Regina, but she easily hauled Derrick to his feet. She read him his rights as she stuffed him roughly into the back seat.

"This isn't over, Regina," he shouted as he struggled against the handcuffs. The door slammed shut, silencing his angry voice. Moments later an ambulance rolled up behind the police car. She shuddered and glanced up as a shadow moved in front of her and blocked out the flashing lights.

"Let me take a look at that cut." The paramedic stooped down and examined her.

Regina winced and pulled her head away as he pressed a wad of gauze against the broken skin to stop the bleeding.

"Here, let me do that." Alex grabbed the gauze from his hands and motioned him to move out of the way.

"B-but," he protested.

"Just go," Alex growled at him. He hesitated and the taller woman curled her lip. "What didn't you understand? Go. We don't need you."

Regina watched as the young man backed up and walked away. She looked up at her friend with a worried expression on her face. "Alex, what's wrong?"

"You're already hurt. He didn't have to be that rough with you." The taller woman frowned as she tilted Regina's head back. "I can use a couple of butterflies to close that up."

"Shit," Regina groaned.

Alex stepped back and held out her hand. "Come on, Doc, we need to take care of that." Regina followed Alex up the stairs and into the apartment. She was led over to the couch. "Sit down." Alex disappeared and returned with a wet washcloth and a tube of antiseptic.

"Oh no, you are not..." Regina backed warily away from her.

Alex raised an eyebrow. "What do you think I'm going to

do? Scrub it? Come here." She held the warm cloth in her hand
and laid it over the cut on Regina's lip. "Just hold it there. It'll
loosen the blood so I can clean it."

Regina closed her eyes and tilted her head back on the
couch. She felt Alex get up and then return several minutes later.
The warm washcloth was lifted off her mouth.

"Cold," Alex warned her, as she touched an ice cube around
the edges of the cut. Regina opened her eyes and watched as
Alex rubbed the ice cube over her chin and caught the water with
the washcloth.

She sat up off the back of the couch, pushed Alex's hand
away, and took the bloodied washcloth from her. "Don't. I'll do
that," Regina said softly.

Alex frowned as Regina took the bloody ice cube from her.
"I-I'm sorry, I didn't mean to make you feel uncomfortable." She
went to stand up, cursing herself silently, until a hand on her
forearm stopped her.

"You didn't, Alex. It's just, we don't know." She lifted the
bloody washcloth in her hand.

Realization dawned, and Alex looked down at her bruised
hands. Turning them over, she looked at the bloody cuts on her
knuckles. She looked back down at Regina. "I've got some
gloves in my bag."

Regina shook her head and smiled faintly. "Alex, you don't
have to."

"I know that." She walked away and rummaged through the
small kit she carried with her and pulled out a couple of latex
gloves. Pulling them over her hands, she sat down next to Regina
and took the ice cube back. "Here," she said, and moved the ice
over Regina's lip and chin again. "I doubt anything would happen though, even if you were."

"You don't know that."

"You're right." Alex concentrated on moving the ice over
Regina's lip, avoiding the eyes she knew were watching her. Her
heart pounded as she struggled to maintain control over her emotions. *If I was any later getting back here, God knows what Derrick would have done to you.* "I'm sorry, Regina."

"For what?" Regina stared incredulously at Alex.

Alex stared over Regina's shoulder a far away look in her
eyes. "Just...everything. You didn't have to be here at all."

"No, don't say that, Alex." Regina shook her head.

A hand against the side of her head stopped the movement.

"Did he hit you?"

"No. He tackled me into the cabinets. I didn't get my hands up in time." Regina cringed as she remembered the sound of the impact.

Alex shook her head, as anger coursed through her once more, wishing she'd done more damage to the bastard when she had the chance. She touched Regina's lip with her thumb. "Numb?"

"Yeah, I can't feel anything."

Alex applied the salve to her chin and then covered the cut with two sterile strips of tape to hold the cut closed. The dark-haired woman peeled the gloves off her hands.

Alex shifted her position so that one leg was curled underneath her on the couch. Regina sat very still, running her finger back and forth underneath her chin. A hand gently pulled her fingers away from her face. Alex frowned and lifted her hand to Regina's face.

"You're hot." She shifted closer and looked at Regina's glassy eyes.

Regina pulled her eyes away and tilted her head back, unable to look at Alex. She swallowed a lump in her throat and sank back into the couch.

"Regina, you've got a fever. What's going on?" There was concern in Alex's voice.

Regina shook her head and folded her arms over her chest. "My lymph nodes are swollen in my neck." She choked on the words. "The fever started this afternoon."

Alex sat frozen for a moment as her thoughts raced haphazardly in her head. She could see the fear in Regina's eyes and she took her hand, gently squeezing it.

"Listen to me." She slipped an arm around Regina and pulled her close to her as the tears rolled down the woman's face. "This could be a reaction to the medication or it could be the flu, or mononucleosis. You need to get it checked. The sooner the better."

Regina nodded her head. "I know," she cried through the tears.

Alex looked at her watch. "We could get to Boston in about three hours. You could take a nap on the way."

Regina looked up at Alex. "Boston?"

"I know a guy, he's an infectious disease specialist."

"What about Dana?"

Alex closed her eyes and held onto Regina giving herself a chance to calm her racing thoughts. She hated leaving loose ends. She did what Lana asked her to do in the letter, setting Dana up to fall hard. It was a payback for ruining the store with her vile and reckless habit of selling drugs. Alex shook her head. "What's done is done. This is more important."

# Chapter
# 14

Alex ran back up the stairs. "Okay. That's it." She jogged back into the apartment and rounded the corner, stopping when she saw Regina standing with her back to her, staring out the window. She walked up behind Regina and laid a hand on her shoulder, peering into her tearful green eyes. "Regina, are you ready to go?"

Regina nodded her head. "I guess so." She wiped her face with her hand. It was weird, she thought, that she didn't feel scared or nervous; it was almost a sense of being on the outside looking in at all this happening to somebody else, not her.

"You can sleep in the back if you want," Alex offered.

"That sounds like a good idea. I feel wiped out."

They walked down the stairs together and Alex locked the door behind them. She waited as Regina crawled into the back of the Jeep and lay down, covering her body with the blanket Alex handed to her. The doctor shut the door behind her, slipped in behind the steering wheel and turned on the engine. She looked up into the rearview mirror and tilted it so it was focused on Regina's huddled form, lying across the back seat. *Just relax. It could be something else,* Alex kept telling herself. She pulled out of the driveway and headed west on Route Six toward Boston.

After driving for about ten minutes, Alex dialed a number on her cell phone and waited for the operator to pick up. "This is

Dr. Margulies. Page Dr. Ivez for me. It's an emergency."

She waited impatiently for David to pick up as she negotiated through the sparse traffic.

"Alex? It's been a long time; I can't believe you're calling me. What's up?" It had been almost a year since he had last heard from Alex. The last time he had seen his friend was at the memorial service for Lana. He tried to offer what support he could to Alex but she kept everyone at a distance that day.

"David, I need your help. I've got a friend who's in trouble and I need you to look at her."

"Sure, when?"

"Tonight."

"Well, I'm here all night so come on in."

Two-and-a-half hours later, Alex turned the Jeep into the emergency department parking area at Boston Medical Center. She looked over her shoulder into the back of the darkened interior of the Jeep and could see Regina's sleeping form curled up on the back seat, underneath the blanket.

"Hey." Alex reached over and touched her shoulder. "Time to get up. We're here." Regina blinked and sat up slowly. "How do you feel?"

Regina brushed strands of hair out of her face and looked up at Alex. "I've been better."

"A friend of mine I know from medical school works here. He's going to take a look at you," Alex said, as she held out a hand to her.

Regina nodded her head and let Alex help her out of the Jeep. They walked through the doors of the emergency department where Alex looked at the desk and spotted the scruffy looking, brown-haired man whom she'd formed a friendship with during her last two residencies in New Jersey. He was thinner than she remembered and his hair was graying around the temples.

"That's him over there." She pointed the doctor out to Regina. "David Ivez." She put her arm over Regina's shoulder as she shivered against her. "Do you want a wheelchair so you can sit down?"

Regina shook her head vehemently and stepped away from Alex. "No. I can walk."

Alex held her tongue and led Regina over to the desk. She knew her stubborn streak well enough by now to realize that arguing the point would be futile.

"David?"

"Alexandra." He smiled as he stood up and walked around the desk. "You always hated when I called you that." He pulled her into a hug.

"I still do," Alex said, as she broke off the embrace.

"So I see." He grinned back at her and directed his attention at her smaller companion.

"David, this is Regina."

He frowned and brought a hand up to her face, glancing quickly up at Alex. "What happened here?"

"It's a long story," Alex offered quickly.

"Well, let's go in the back, Regina. I've got a booth set up for us."

Regina looked back at Alex as David took her arm. "Wish me luck," she said, trying to ease some of the nervousness she felt inside.

"You're going to be all right, Regina." Alex stepped forward as if to follow.

"I've got her, Alex. I'll come out and get you when I'm done."

Alex felt a pang of helplessness, coupled with jealousy, as David took Regina from her. He glanced back at Alex as he led Regina down the hallway.

"Alex, there's some paperwork she needs to fill out for insurance. Maybe you could do it for her while you wait?"

"Sure." She nodded her head and watched as they turned the corner and disappeared from her sight. *So what did you think he was going to do, ask you to go in with them? You asked for his help.* Alex stood in the middle of the hallway, staring at where Regina had just been standing a second ago, oblivious to all the activity that was going on around her.

"Hey, lady, get out of the way," a paramedic yelled as he pushed past Alex, with a stretcher in tow.

"Sorry." Alex awkwardly stepped back away from paramedics, who ran past with a patient strapped securely to the stretcher. She was vaguely aware of a loud rushing noise in her ears and a hand touching her arm.

"Ma'am are you all right?" a young twenty-something nurse with bright green eyes, asked.

"Yeah, yeah. I'm fine." *Ma'am? Shit, I'm not that old.* Alex pulled her arm away, irritated by the nurse's close physical presence. *Come on, get a grip here, Alex. You work in a hospital, what's your problem?* She turned to the woman. "I...I need to fill out some paperwork for a friend."

"Sure, no problem. Let me get you a clipboard and a pen."

Her heart beat rapidly in her chest and she felt slightly nauseated as she sat staring at the pale blue walls in the empty waiting room. *This sucks being on the other side. I hate hospitals. No, face it, you just can't stand not being in control.* The doctor stared at paperwork and decided she answered all the questions that she knew about her young friend. Regina would have to answer the rest of them later. She stood up and walked over to the desk. The nurse who spoke to her earlier looked up and smiled a little too brightly at her. "All done?"

Alex shook her head. "No. There are some questions my friend is going to have to answer. Can I go back and see her?" she asked, knowing what the answer would most likely be.

The woman's smile faded. "I'm sorry, but only family members are allowed back to see the patients."

*All right, let's try a different attack.* "Listen, none of her family is here with her. I brought her in."

"I'm sorry, but the doctor will come out and talk to you when he's done examining your friend," the nurse said, her tone more official now.

Alex bristled. *Okay, fine. Two can play at that game, sweetheart.* Alex smiled at her and took the papers off the clipboard. "Is there a bathroom around here?"

"Sure, first door down on your left."

Alex made a quick detour out to her Jeep and returned with her backpack. She walked down the hallway, found the linen room and picked up a set of scrubs. Five minutes later she emerged from the bathroom dressed in blue hospital scrubs and a lab coat. She clipped on her ID badge and flipped it over so her picture was hidden from view.

With her clothes rolled up and tucked neatly into her backpack, Alex headed down the hall to the emergency room doors. She tapped the button on the wall and walked inside as the electric doors slid quietly open and headed directly over to the nurse's station. "Where's Dr. Ivez? He asked me to meet him down here to consult on a patient."

"He's in booth ten with some AIDS patient," the nurse said without looking up from her paperwork.

Her heart leapt up into her throat at the nurse's response. "Excuse me?" She leaned over the desk and roughly pushed the paperwork away from the nurse with her hand. She barely restrained herself from grabbing hold of the nurse's scrub top. "Since *when* do you give out *any* information on a patient?" The nurse stared back at Alex with a look of shock on her face. "What if someone from her family was here? Then what? And how the hell do you know what's wrong with her anyway?" Alex asked, bringing her face to within inches of the stunned nurse. "Well?"

The nurse's jaw worked several times. "I, uh, I don't know. I'm sorry."

"You're damn right you don't know," Alex practically shouted at her.

"I'm sorry, really I am." The nurse nervously gathered up her paperwork and backed quickly away from Alex's hateful stare.

Alex stood, holding onto her desk for a minute waiting for her legs to stop shaking. *Goddamn, son of a bitch, I can't believe she just said that. Regina would freak out if she heard that.* The brunette walked to the back of the ER, letting her senses filter out the familiar noises from all the activity going on around her. She heard David's voice through the curtain as she approached and a muffled response that could only be Regina answering him. She rapped her knuckles on the wall dividing the booths.

"David?"

"In here, Alex." He looked up as she walked into the booth. "No luck getting past the front desk in your street clothes, huh?"

Alex cuffed him on the shoulder. "Funny, very funny, David. Yeah, all it took was a pair of scrubs, a lab coat, and a bad attitude." She walked past him, trying very hard not to be angry with him. There was only one way that nurse knew why Regina was here and that was David. She set her backpack on the floor and walked over to Regina. "Hey, how are you doing?" She leaned over and squeezed her shoulder affectionately.

Regina shook her head, trying her best to muster a grin. "Okay. We were just talking…about options." Regina closed her eyes, still feeling like the fever was sucking the energy out of her, and not wanting Alex to see how close to tears she was.

Alex turned around and looked at David. "So, do we have an idea about what is going on yet?"

He closed the chart he was writing in and looked back at her. "We drew some blood, so we're waiting for the test results to come back. We should know something in the morning.

Regina tells me she had a pretty severe reaction to the medication early on, so it's possible it could be happening again. Obviously we'll check to see if she's developing the antibodies." He
looked at both of them. "In the meantime, we hope for the best."

"Are you going to admit her tonight?" Alex asked.

David shook his head. "I can't, Alex. I wish I could, but the
hospital is full. We've got no beds available." He looked at
Regina. "I guess you'll be bunking in down here tonight. Sorry."

"That's okay. Thanks for doing this, David." Regina lowered her head to the pillow and closed her eyes again.

"Alex, I can show you where the on call room is if you want
to crash there," David offered.

She shook her head. "Thanks, but I'd rather stay here."

"No problem. Besides, I got a chance to trade stories about
you. Just between us, right Regina?" He laughed and nudged
Alex in the ribs.

Alex rolled her eyes at Regina, who looked back up at them.
"Great, there he goes tarnishing my stellar reputation again."

"Never," Regina said, grinning as she recalled one of the
stories David told her.

David snorted. "Yeah, I think that halo of yours needs pol-
ishing, Alex."

"Mm, thanks for the reminder. I'll get right on it," Alex
replied sarcastically. "David, can I have a word with you?" She
motioned with her hand. "Outside."

"Sure." David looked at her uncertainly and walked out of
the booth. He turned around. "What's up?" he asked, holding the
chart in front of him as he crossed his arms over his chest.

Alex walked past him. "Not here."

David walked after her, seeing the line of tension in her
shoulders. "What's going on?"

"You." She turned around and jabbed a finger into his chest,
making him flinch. "Breaking Regina's confidence is what's
going on." Alex stood in front of him with her hands on her hips.
"The nurse at the desk told me you were in booth ten with some
AIDS patient." Her eyes darkened as anger swept through her.
"How the hell did she know that, David? The only answer I see is
the one standing in front of me right now."

David stepped back against the wall. He started to say
something but stopped. "I must have let it slip after you called
me." His voice was a whisper. He rubbed his face with his hand.
"I'm sorry, Alex. I had no idea someone would repeat that, let

alone to you."

"That kid has been through hell the past few weeks. She doesn't need any more bullshit to deal with. You should know better, David." Alex gave him one last cursory glance as she headed back to the booth where Regina was.

"Hey, what took so long?" Regina pushed herself up onto her elbows.

Alex gave her a half grin. "What's wrong, did you miss me or something?"

"Yeah, I did." Regina looked up at Alex. "David is nice. I like him."

"He's a good doctor," Alex replied, trying not to let her anger slip through.

"Alex, why don't you go to sleep in one of the on call rooms? You must be exhausted after everything." Regina could see the dark circles under Alex's eyes and the normally startling blue color seemed subdued.

"I'm fine." Alex walked out and rolled a vacant recliner back into the booth next to the stretcher. "Do you need anything?" Alex sat down facing her.

Regina opened her eyes and shook her head. "Can you lower this?" She rattled the rail on the side of the stretcher. "I feel like I'm in jail."

"Sure." Alex lowered the bed rail, resting her hands on the thin mattress.

Regina sat up and rubbed her temples, grimacing at the dull pounding behind her eyes. She looked down at Alex's hand. "Did you put any ice on your hand? That looks awful." She brushed her fingers over the swollen and bruised knuckles of Alex's right hand.

"Quit worrying about me. I'm fine." Alex pulled her hand away, all too aware of Regina's touch and the tingle of sensation that ran up her spine from it.

Regina clucked her tongue. "You need to take care of yourself, Alex. It might be broken."

Alex sighed. "It's not." She flexed her fingers and made a fist to show Regina that it wasn't broken. Unimpressed, Regina rolled her eyes. "You're not going to quit on this are you?"

"Nope, go get some ice. I'm not going anywhere with this leash attached to me." She waved her arm that the IV was in. She pulled the blanket up over her shoulder and motioned at Alex to leave. "Go on."

"Fine," Alex groaned with an exasperated sigh. "I'll be right back." She pushed her body out of the chair and walked out of the booth in search of an ice machine.

Alex returned a short while later, carrying a plastic bag filled with crushed ice. Regina opened her eyes as she heard Alex step into the booth and close the curtain behind her.

"Alex?"

"What?"

"I never got to thank you for, um, taking care of Derrick."

Alex looked at Regina as she sat down in the recliner. "Somehow I don't think Derrick would think of it that way." She gingerly placed the bag of ice over her swollen knuckles, hissing as the plastic and the cold made the raw skin sting. "He deserved it. How did he manage to find you, anyway?"

Regina shook her head. "He checked my credit card and found out I bought an airline ticket."

"Slick. Nothing like using his position to get information now, huh?" Alex asked, settling back into the recliner and closing her eyes.

"It wouldn't be the first time he's done it," Regina said, thinking back to the day he confronted her outside the hospital and told her about Alex's suspension six months earlier.

"He's an asshole, Regina. How'd you get involved with him in the first place?" The words were out before she could pull them back. *Shit.* Alex looked up and saw the surprised look on Regina's face. "Ah, I'm sorry. I, uh, I don't censor what comes out of my mouth very well sometimes."

Regina shook her head, a sad expression covering her face. "It's all right. He is an asshole." She was quiet as she lay back, looking up at the ceiling. She let out a sigh. "I'm scared, Alex."

Alex looked at Regina lying on the stretcher. *I am too, Regina. Damn, I wish I knew what to say to you.* She tossed the bag of ice on the recliner behind her and moved over to sit on the edge of the stretcher next to Regina. She was used to being able to do *something:* change a medication, order a test, or recommend surgery. In this case, as much as she hated to admit it, she could do nothing except wait and hope, neither of which she was very good at. Alex touched Regina's face and brushed her hair back over her shoulder. She sat quietly for a moment, looking at Regina and rubbing her hand over her back. "Your parents don't live far from here, right?"

Regina nodded her head. "Why?" She was enjoying the

comforting touch of Alex's hand and the question brought her
back from her quiet reverie.

"Do you want to call them and let them know that you're
here?" Alex inquired. She immediately regretted her question
when she saw the look on Regina's face. *She's not a kid, Alex. If
she wanted them here she would have called them herself.*

"They wouldn't understand, Alex. They think HIV and
AIDS are only something that my brother Jeffrey could get."

"What do you mean?"

Regina glanced up at Alex quickly. "He's gay."

"Oh." She was beginning to realize some of the pressure her
young friend was getting from her family about her lifestyle.
"Does he live around here?" Alex asked, probing carefully. She
wasn't sure by Regina's response if she was uncomfortable about
her brother's lifestyle or her parent's rigid beliefs.

"No, he's in San Francisco. He hasn't lived at home since he
was seventeen. My parents," Regina looked at Alex and shook
her head, "they're not very liberal-minded. When he told them
he was gay, it was like world war three. My mother threw him
out of the house and told him never to come back."

"That must have been pretty awful," Alex said, feeling
badly that Regina had seen that happen to her brother.

"It was. I still keep in touch with him, but my mother acts
like he never existed. Pictures, awards, clothes, books—she
threw all of it out." Regina recalled the fight she had with her
mother only a couple days ago. *She's probably filling up the
trash bags with my stuff as we speak.* "I miss him."

"Can I ask you a personal question, Regina?" Alex looked
down at the floor. "You don't have to answer it if you don't want
to."

"Yeah." Regina rolled onto her side and fiddled nervously
with the sheet. She had an idea where Alex was going with this
and she wasn't sure if she really wanted to answer the question.

"Well, the other night in the apartment, when I kissed you,
and we, um..." Alex looked up at Regina. *Just ask her will you?*
"Have you ever been with a woman before?"

Regina ran her fingers over the sheet and shook her head
slowly. "No, I-I haven't. I, um, when I realized I was attracted to
women, I was in college." She looked up at Alex nervously. "I
mean I knew before then, when I was in high school, but after
what Jeffrey went through with my parents, I just pushed it
aside. I couldn't deal with it or what it would do to them."

"Yeah, I can see how you might not want them to know." *My parents hardly cared what I did when I was younger. Dad was too busy drinking himself into oblivion, and my mother wanted to pretend that everything was fine.* She pushed the errant thoughts out of her head and looked back up at Regina. "But, what about you? How come you never got involved with anyone, Regina?"

"I had some friends who were gay in college that I hung out with, but I wasn't interested in anyone." Regina shook her head. "Besides, some of them went through relationships like water and I didn't want that. I don't want that."

"I know what you mean." Alex had a feeling that she fit those particular criteria Regina was referring to at one point in her life. There had been a time, Alex remembered, when she thought she would find that one person she could share her life with, but then things happened that altered her beliefs, and she gave up hoping that she could ever find that one person. Regina flopped back down onto the pillow and covered her face with her hands as she flushed a deep red. "I can't believe we're having this discussion here," she groaned, in embarrassment.

"I'm sorry. I shouldn't have brought it up." Alex stared at the cuts and bruises on her hand.

"No, it's all right." Regina rolled over and looked at Alex. "I'm glad we have a chance to talk. This week has been crazy. So much has happened since we left the hospital."

"Regina." Alex leaned forward resting her elbows on her knees. "It can stop right here if you want it to. I shouldn't have pushed you, and I'm sorry if I made you uncomfortable the other night."

"Alex, you didn't push me." Regina touched Alex's face, and stroked her cheek. "And...I don't want us to stop," she lowered her head, "unless you want to."

Alex swallowed and shook her head. "No, I don't want us to stop, Regina." Despite all the reasons why she thought she shouldn't get involved—having lost Lana just less than a year ago, the differences between herself and Regina, and the reason they were in the hospital tonight—Alex realized with startling clarity that she didn't want to lose the bond that was growing between them.

Regina flicked the IV tubing in disgust. "This sucks." Tears ran down her face.

Alex was still absorbing what Regina had said to her when she realized what Regina was trying to do. "Hey, don't do that."

Alex tried to take hold of Regina's hand but the woman yanked it away from her.

"This...fucking...sucks!" Regina cried through her tears. She started ripping the tape off of her arm.

"Oh no, you don't." Alex jumped up, grabbed her arm and stopped her from pulling the needle out.

Regina struggled against Alex, trying to shove her away.

"Let go of me, damn it." Regina struggled as the taller woman held her hand firmly over the IV. "All because of some stupid needle stick," Regina cried as she finally gave up and leaned against Alex.

Alex held onto Regina as she cried in her arms. She tilted her head back and closed her eyes. *Oh God, please, please, don't let this happen to her. She doesn't deserve this.* She felt a flash of panic rising in her chest that left her feeling weak-limbed as it passed. Alex hastily wiped her eyes with her hand. She placed Regina's hand over the IV line.

"Easy now. Hold this for me, Regina. I just want to re-tape it so I don't have to get Nurse Sunshine to come in here." She turned away to look for tape.

Regina held her arm out as the doctor re-taped the IV. She looked up at her and laughed softly through her tears. "You mean the one with the green eyes that lit up when she saw you when we first walked in here?"

Alex shot her a look. "You noticed?"

"I'm sick, Alex, not dead. Of course I noticed. It was kind of hard to miss her reaction when we walked up to the nurse's station before."

"Yeah, well somebody can tell her to save the effort." Alex smoothed the tape down over Regina's arm, idly stroking her thumb over the soft hairs on her skin.

Regina shifted on the stretcher and groaned. "Ugh, I'm going to get bed sores lying on this damn stretcher all night."

"So switch with me. This lounge chair is pretty comfortable."

After a minute of finagling with the IV pole and moving it around in the crowded booth, Regina settled herself in the chair with Alex's help. She closed her eyes and dozed fitfully for a few minutes. The waiting was awful and for as tired as she was, Regina couldn't stay asleep. *Oh, somebody needs to invent an off key for the brain,* she thought to herself as she shifted in the chair.

So much had happened this week; between their suspensions, Alex almost committing suicide, and Derrick's attack, it
hardly seemed real. Regina turned her head and looked at the
brunette stretched out on her side, head propped on her hand
with her eyes closed.

"Alex, are you sleeping?"

A slight grin crossed the dark-haired woman's lips. "No.
Why aren't *you* sleeping? It's late," Alex chided her as she
looked at her watch and shook her head. "It's two in the morning. Go back to sleep, Regina."

"I can't." Regina huddled down into the chair and drew her
legs up to her chest. All the sounds she hardly noticed when she
was working in the hospital seemed magnified tonight. She heard
every beep from the IV pumps, the nervous whispering of the
patients and families around them in the other booths, and the
soft buzz from the fluorescent lights overhead.

Alex reached out and felt her forehead. "How do you feel?"

Regina burrowed farther under the thin blanket. "I keep getting chills."

Alex looked down at the blonde from her perch on the
stretcher. "Gee, I wonder why? Let's see, we've got cold IV fluid
running into you, a fever, and a flimsy gown, in a lovely shade of
faded blue, I might add. Too bad they don't have it in green. It
would bring out your eye color."

Regina's shoulders shook as she stifled a giggle. "I'm glad
you're here with me, Alex."

Alex stifled a yawn. "Me too. Do you want me to get you
another blanket?"

Regina nodded her head and shivered again under the blanket she already had. Alex slid off the stretcher and disappeared,
returning several minutes later with another blanket and a pair of
scrubs. "Here, I thought these might make you feel warmer
instead of that gown." She handed the blonde the bundle.

"Oh, thanks." Regina sat up in the chair and slid the pants
on over her bare legs. The blonde stood up, fumbled with the ties
on the pants, then reached back and undid the tie holding the
gown closed.

Alex backed up, realizing that Regina was going to just drop
the gown onto the floor. "Uh, let me step outside while you do
that." She hastily slipped out of the curtain and leaned up against
the wall. She heard Regina snicker. "What are you laughing at?"
Alex realized that Regina was enjoying her obvious discomfort

with this.

"You're a doctor. If you've seen one set of breasts, you've seen them all."

"Uh, not quite." Alex rolled her eyes and banged her head back against the wall. *We almost made love the night before and I really don't need to see you half naked now, Regina, because I'll never get to sleep tonight. Shit, what is wrong with me? I shouldn't be thinking like this. She's sick.* "Are you decent yet?" Alex growled through the curtain.

"Yes, I'm decent, Alex." Regina pulled the blanket back up over her body as she sat in the chair.

Alex walked back into the booth, feeling Regina's eyes following her as she sat down on the stretcher. She slipped her lab coat off and draped it over the front of her as she lay back on the stretcher and closed her eyes.

"What are you doing?"

"I'm going to sleep." The woman crossed her ankles, folded her arms over her chest, then turned her head and opened one eye. "Which is exactly what you should be doing."

"I know. I always have a hard time sleeping in a strange place."

Alex could hear Regina shift in the recliner as she settled down. *Well, this is about as strange of a place you can be in.* She opened her eyes and looked at Regina's huddled form under the blankets. *Bright fluorescent lights that don't turn off, loud noises, strange smells, and not even a decent bed to sleep in. Hmm, I think I will take David up on his offer of using the on call room. He owes me at least that.* Alex slipped quietly off the stretcher and went in search of the doctor. She found him in the staff lounge working on a pile of charts.

"David."

"So, you're still talking to me, huh?"

"Yes, I am." Alex ran a hand through her hair and sat across from him. "Can I still take you up on that offer for the on call room?"

"Sure, let me get the key." David stood and walked past Alex, hesitating as she grabbed his arm.

"You know, I never thanked you for being there...at the service."

He smiled sadly at his friend and patted her shoulder. "I know. I-I didn't know what to say to you. You were hurting so bad." David turned his head away at the tears in Alex's eyes.

He pulled the chair around the table and sat next to his friend. "You didn't break your hand did you?"

Alex smirked and shook her head. "No."

"You were always quick with your fists. Hit first, ask questions later."

"I guess deep down I'm still that angry, pissed off kid you met in college."

David leaned closer and wrapped an arm around her shoulder. "That angry, pissed off kid saved my life from a bunch of thugs that night." Alex hung her head, refusing to meet his gaze. "This woman, Regina, she means a lot to you."

Alex smiled sadly. "You know, I've never met anyone in my life like her. She's special."

David nodded his head and stood up. "Let me get you that key."

A short while later, Alex returned to the booth where Regina was now sleeping. She knelt down beside her and brushed her hair back behind her ear. "Regina?"

"Mmm. What? I just fell asleep." Sleepy green eyes peered up at her.

Alex put a finger to her lips. "I'm sorry. I got you a room to sleep in," she said, and helped Regina into the wheelchair.

"Where are we going?" Regina blinked at the bright lights overhead and pulled the blankets up around her shoulders.

"You'll see." Alex wheeled her down one of the hallways and stopped in front of an unmarked door. She unlocked it and pushed the door open. The room was small, the size of a closet in fact, and there was just enough room for a single bed. She flicked on the light next to the bed. "I thought you might be able to sleep better in here. It's quiet and you can turn out the light," she explained as she helped Regina out of the chair and into the room.

Regina sat down on the single bed and smiled up at Alex. "Thanks."

"I'll come back and check on you later. Get some sleep." Alex turned and reached for the door.

"Bu—wait."

"What?" Alex turned back around.

"Don't go. Stay with me."

"You sure? That bed is awfully small."

"Please, I don't want to be alone." Regina held out her hand.

Alex looked down at Regina, a smile playing at the corners of her lips. "All right, let me get in behind you, that way you're not up against the wall." Alex crawled onto the bed lying down on her side, stretching out next to the concrete wall. "There's not a lot of room. Are you sure you want me to stay?"

"Yes." Regina lay down and snuggled up with her back pressed tightly against Alex. "Thanks for taking care of me today *again*, Alex."

"Anytime, my friend." Alex pulled the blankets up over the both of them. "Are you warm enough?"

Regina mumbled something Alex couldn't understand then reached behind her, finding Alex's hand and pulling it forward over her stomach.

❖ ⌘ ❖ ⌘ ❖ ⌘ ❖

Several hours later, Alex awoke. She lay there next to Regina, who was still sleeping peacefully, listening to her breathe. The smaller woman stirred slightly as Alex lifted herself up on her elbow. Neither of them moved during the night, which surprised her because she was always a restless sleeper. She removed her hand from Regina's grasp and felt her forehead. *Good, it feels like the fever broke while she slept. That has to be a good sign.*

She reached up and felt for the light switch, turning on the light. From the hallway she heard a voice coming through on the paging system. *Might as well get up,* she thought, and slipped out of the bed. She looked down at her rumpled scrubs and shrugged her shoulders. *Oh well, at least I'll fit in. I'll look like any other resident in the hospital who was on call last night.*

"Alex." She turned as Regina rolled over and stretched out onto her back. "What are you doing?"

"I figured I would try and find us something to eat that resembled real food. Any requests?" Alex ran a hand through her tousled hair.

"No oatmeal. I hate lumps," Regina mumbled.

"No oatmeal," Alex repeated. "Just sit tight. I'll be back in a little while." Alex pulled the blanket away from Regina's face and shook her head when she saw that the resident had already fallen back to sleep.

The doctor negotiated her way through the maze of corridors, following the signs that led the way to the hospital cafeteria. It was still early so only a few employees that worked the early shift were wandering around and looking at the possibilities for breakfast.

She picked up a tray. "Let's see what's safe in here." She walked past the counters of hot food and stopped at the grill. She ordered two cheese omelets, figuring that was a safe bet since she wasn't sure what Regina liked. While she waited, the doctor selected a couple of bananas, two muffins, and milk and juice for both of them.

She paid at the register and headed back towards the on call room. Alex opened the door, slipped inside and sat on the edge of the bed.

"Regina?"

"Mm. I'm awake." Regina rolled onto her side and curled her body around Alex. She closed her eyes and snuggled against the taller woman, causing Alex to catch her breath at the sudden surge of heat that flowed through her belly.

"Sure you are. Wake up sleepy head. David said he would come down and talk to you before he starts rounds."

"Oh, why can't mornings start later?" Regina grumbled from beneath the covers.

"It's the best time of the day. Come on, you need to eat."

"It's the best time of day for who, the birds?" Regina protested.

Alex regarded her in silence and raised an eyebrow.

"Oh God, don't tell me you're one of those morning people." Regina untangled herself from her cocoon and sat up. "Boy, I must look awful." She brushed her hair back behind her ears. "Hey, I think my fever broke."

"No, you don't and yes, it did," Alex said. "Here, eat this." She handed her the paper plate with the omelet on it. "I hope cheese is okay. I wasn't sure what you liked."

"This is fine," Regina said in between bites. She scooted back so she was leaning against the wall and set her plate in her lap. "Ugh, I'm eating too fast."

"Slow down, nobody's going to steal it from you," the doctor teased gently. She eased back so she sat next to the blonde.

"You never ate a meal with my brothers. They were awful when they were teenagers. If you turned your head they'd swipe something off your plate."

"You're kidding me," Alex laughed.

"No. I got them back though."

"On no what did you do?"

Regina sat up straighter and snickered before she started to tell Alex the story. "My parents weren't home one night so I made brownies and slipped a powdered laxative into the ingredients. It was easy, all I had to do was tell them not to eat them because they were for school the next day."

Alex stared at Regina silently for a second and then broke into laughter. "Oh my God. That is cruel."

"Yeah, but they never touched my food again after that."

They sat side by side, eating in silence. Alex stole a couple of glances at her younger companion and wondered how Regina felt about her. *We're so different, Regina. I wonder, do we really have a chance at being together?*

"That was good." Regina reached in front of Alex, and snatched one of the muffins off the tray.

Alex stared at her empty plate with an amused look on her face. "I guess you were hungry, huh?"

There was a knock on the door. They heard David's voice on the other side.

Regina stopped eating. "Oh, I think I just lost my appetite," she said, her face paling slightly.

Alex tenderly squeezed her arm. "Whatever it is, we'll deal with it. You're not going to have to go through this by yourself, Regina."

Regina nodded her head. "Thanks, Alex. You don't know how much that means to me."

"Come on in, David."

The door opened and the scraggly-looking doctor stepped into the cramped room. "Boy, I forgot how small these rooms were." He leaned up against the wall and crossed his arms over his chest. "Not bad, room service. I wish I were that lucky." He cocked his head, looking at the blonde thoughtfully. "How do you feel, Regina?"

"Better. My fever broke during the night. Did you get the results of the test back?"

"I did. The good news is there's no sign of the antibodies yet in your system."

Regina leaned back against the wall and closed her eyes. "Thank God. So, what's going on with me then?"

"Well, that's where the problem is. The drugs you're taking to prevent your body from developing the HIV virus are doing some bad things to your system. For one, your red blood cell

count is low. That's one of the side effects of the drugs you're
on. The other problem is that your white blood cell count is dras-
tically low as well. That concerns me because the drugs which
are protecting you from developing the antibodies are essentially
killing your ability to fight off any infection you might get."

"So, what should I do?" Regina asked, looking first at Alex
and then at David.

"If it was me, I'd stop taking the drugs, Regina." He held up
a hand to stop her sentence. "I know what you're thinking. It's a
calculated risk. You've been on the drugs almost three months
now. There's a better than sixty percent chance you won't
develop the antibodies."

Regina stared down at her hands. "How much better than
sixty percent? Sixty-one, seventy percent?"

"I don't know. I'm sorry I can't give you a better answer."

"David, what's the bottom line if she stays on the drugs?"
Alex asked.

David shook his head. "Here, look at the lab values yourself."

She took the papers from him. Running her finger down the
list of numbers she frowned, not liking what she saw.

"What do you think, Alex?" The blonde leaned closer to
read the lab values.

"You're liver function tests are up. That's not good. And
look," she pointed farther down the page, "your kidneys are
being affected too."

"If I stop taking the drugs will my liver and kidneys start to
function normally?"

"If you stop now I would say they probably will," David
replied cautiously. "The other issue is if you stay on them, they
could make you infertile. I don't know if that's a concern for you
or not but that's something you need to think about as well."

She stared up at him. "So if I stay on the drugs I could have
permanent liver and kidney damage, be prone to infections, and
possibly become infertile. On the other hand, if I stop taking the
medicine I could still develop the antibodies. Great choice."
Regina groaned and slumped back against the wall.

"I wish I could have better news for you. The choice is ultimately yours to make. Give yourself some time and think about
it, but don't take too long. I'll write the discharge order so you
can leave whenever you want."

"Thanks for doing this, David. At least now I know what's

going on," Regina replied.

Alex stood up and held out her hand. "Thanks, David. I owe you one."

"Don't mention it, Alex." He looked at his watch. "I've got to go. Listen, stay in touch, Regina. Good luck." He slipped out of the room, leaving the two of them alone.

Alex turned around and looked at Regina.

"It could have been worse, right?" Regina looked back at Alex.

"Yeah, it could have been, but it wasn't." Alex sat down beside her, her hands resting on her thighs.

"Do you think I'm making the right decision if I stop taking the drugs?"

"I don't think there's much of a choice. If it was me, I'd stop taking them."

"I wish I had been able to stay on them longer before I started having the side effects."

Alex turned and faced her. "Do you want me to see if I can find out if there's anything else you can take? We can check out the Internet and look at the latest research if you want."

"No, no more pills. I'm sick of taking them. You know I forgot to take them yesterday?" Regina shook her head, then looked up at Alex. "How's your hand feeling?"

Alex turned it over and made a fist. "It's fine, just a little stiff."

Regina leaned over and looked at it. "Wow, the swelling is almost gone. You heal quickly."

Alex made a face and nudged Regina with her elbow. "Nah, just a good doctor looking after me, that's all."

Regina couldn't help the smile that crossed her lips. She shook her head and rubbed her face with her hands. "Ugh, I feel gross. I need a shower and then I have to get my car back." She looked up at Alex and her eyes widened in alarm. "What, why do you have that look on your face like something's wrong?"

"Uh, with everything that happened last night, I didn't get a chance to tell you."

"Tell me what?"

"Derrick had your car towed back to New Jersey and impounded," Alex said, casting a wary glance at Regina.

"Oh, that son of a bitch! How the hell am I going to get home? Ah shit!" She put her face in her hands.

"Hey, easy, I'll drive you home. Don't worry about it. We'll get your car back on Monday after the meeting."

Regina snapped her head up and stared at Alex. "Wait. Does that mean you're going back to the hospital?"

A smile tugged at the corner of Alex's mouth. "Dr. Mitchard won't accept my resignation so it's up to the board if they want me back or not."

Regina stared at Alex. "Why didn't you tell me?" She grabbed the woman's arm, shaking it in her excitement.

"I didn't get a chance until just now." Alex smiled at the expression on Regina's face. "I take it you think that's a good thing, huh?"

Regina stood up facing Alex, put her hands on her shoulders and pushed her back so the taller woman had to look up at her. "Of course it is." Regina resisted the urge to just lean in and kiss her. "So, any chance we can take a shower before we head home?"

"I think we can find a shower." Alex stood up and reached for the younger woman. "Regina?"

"What?"

"Everything is going to work out." Alex pulled her into a hug, wrapping her arms around her tightly. "Let's go find the locker room so we can get the hell out of here."

# Chapter
# 15

The ride home from Boston was a blur for Regina. As always the engine vibration and warmth of the sun streaming in the passenger side window lulled her to sleep minutes after they were on the highway. She didn't wake up until they were coming off their exit from the parkway in New Jersey and Alex shook her gently. Regina decided, as she looked out the window at the familiar scenery, that coming back home was strange, especially after the crazy week she and Alex had spent together.

Not surprisingly, Alex retreated farther into herself by the time she pulled into Regina's driveway. Regina suspected that Alex felt much the same as she did. Tired and nervous about the meeting on Monday, both of them wondered what they would do with the feelings they had for each other now that they were going back to the hospital. That is, if they didn't lose their privileges on Monday.

Regina retrieved her bag from the back of the Jeep and found the taller woman standing in front of her. Alex tilted her head and gave her a crooked grin.

"What?"

Alex simply leaned forward and gathered Regina in her arms, holding her tight. Regina started to pull away but the doctor held her close and whispered in her ear, "Thank you."

Regina wanted to ask for what but decided against it, and

just enjoyed the moment for what it was. There was a strength she found wrapped in those arms, a sense that no matter what happened, they would endure and go on together.

After finally releasing her, Alex picked the blonde's bag up and followed Regina into her condo. She set the bag down and waited nervously as Regina turned on the lights. A part of the doctor wanted desperately to stay, but the other half was terrified even to ask; afraid that now they had returned to reality, Regina would have second thoughts about any kind of a relationship with her. So lost in her battle of self-recrimination, Alex didn't realize that Regina had walked up behind her until strong arms slipped around her waist and pulled her close. She gasped at the contact.

The sharp intake of breath wasn't lost on the young woman and she laid her head on Alex's back, kissing her through the cotton shirt. She loved the feel of the woman she held in her arms and pressed closer, savoring the contact. Regina felt the brunette relax slowly in her embrace and she realized how much effort it had taken for Alex to let her into her life. She released the taller woman as she turned in her arms and watched the flicker of raw emotions in her companion's eyes.

"I should go. You must be tired." Alex ran her thumb gently over Regina's lip, then leaned in and kissed her gently on her lips. The younger woman's hand timidly rested on her hip and she backed off, letting her forehead touch Regina's. *Oh boy, come on. Leave before you start something she's not ready for.* The dark woman stepped back and let her hand fall away. "I'll see you Monday, Regina." Alex turned and walked quickly out of Regina's house.

The blonde watched sadly as her friend left. She felt Alex pulling away from her and it made her heart ache in a way she never felt before. Just when she thought she was beginning to understand the woman better, Alex turned around and did something like this. Too tired to think about anything, Regina slipped out of her clothes and crawled into bed falling asleep as soon as her head hit the pillow.

❖ ⌘ ❖ ⌘ ❖ ⌘ ❖

The shrill ringing of the alarm roused her from her sleep. Confused, Regina slapped her hand at the clock radio on the night table, knocking it to the floor. The irritating noise stopped and then started again a moment later. Through her sleepy haze, Regina finally realized it was the phone and not the alarm. She rolled out of bed, stumbled across the room to pick up the phone and mumbled a barely intelligible hello.

Her mother's voice on the other end of the line brought her instantly awake.

"Where the hell have you been?" her mother asked testily.

Regina sat down on the edge of the bed rubbing her face, trying to wake up. "I spent some time with a friend who needed me."

"You were with that doctor." Her mother's voice was full of accusation.

*So Derrick did tell you where I was. Damn him.* After a moment of shocked silence, Regina found her voice. "Mother, who I choose to spend my time with is no concern of yours."

"I can't believe you just left like you did. That was a terrible thing to do to us."

"You didn't leave me a choice. You should never have called Derrick in the first place." Regina stood up, slipped into her robe and walked out of the bedroom. She'd been wondering when or how she would talk to her mother after the argument she had with her. *Guess this is it. Wonderful.*

"You could have at least stayed and talked with him after he drove all that way to see you," her mother continued.

Regina almost laughed at this. "Mother, you don't get it. I don't have anything to say to him." Regina pulled open the refrigerator door. She wrinkled her nose at the meager contents.

"He cares about you, Regina."

"Oh bullshit!" She remembered with satisfaction the sound of Alex kicking him in the ribs and wishing it had been herself doing it, instead. "You have no idea what he's really like. Besides, it doesn't matter anyway."

"What are you talking about?" her mother snapped.

Regina rolled her eyes. "Mom, this is going nowhere. Why did you call me?"

"Have you thought anything about what this is going to do to your career? Do you think anyone is going to want a...a—"

"The word is lesbian," Regina interjected.

"I know what the word is. Do you think anyone is going to want you to take care of them when they find out what you are? Have you thought about that at all?" Her mother's voice was thick with anger.

Regina turned around and leaned up against the wall. "Mother, just stop it. I'm the same person I was before and I don't need to justify my life to anyone," she snapped. The past three months, and more specifically the last forty-eight hours, had more than convinced her of that. "I've spent the last ten years lying to myself and to everyone around me. I'm not going to do that anymore."

There was silence on the other end of the phone. Her mother's voice, when she did speak, was cold and callous. "Well, I guess we don't have anything else to discuss, then."

"Mom." Regina put her hand down on the counter to steady herself against the empty ache building in the center of her chest. "Please, don't do this," she pleaded, but the line was already dead, "Shit."

She started to dial her parent's number but stopped, setting the phone down on the counter. Regina knew her mother was upset. It was bad enough when Jeffrey came out to her and now it wasn't just one child she thought she lost, but two. Why should her mother's reaction to her be any different than it was for Jeffrey?

Wiping the hot tears running down her face, she walked out of the kitchen. She couldn't believe her mother was doing this. She'd sacrificed a relationship with her oldest son for the past seventeen years and now it seemed like she was willing to do the same to her daughter.

Depressed, Regina crawled back into the bed and pulled the covers up, gratefully letting her body drift back to sleep.

❖ ⌘ ❖ ⌘ ❖ ⌘ ❖

In between mundane chores and mindlessly watching television, Regina ended up sleeping her way through most of the weekend back at her condo. Monday morning arrived too quickly and the resident was more than a little nervous as she sat across from the four doctors that made up the medical review committee.

Her eyes focused on the wall behind them as she waited. She knew two of them. One, Dr. Samuels, was the head of radiology and the other was Dr. Timmons, the head of pediatrics. The other two she had seen on a couple of occasions around the hospital but had no interactions with.

The door opened and her heart sped up as Dr. Jameson

walked in. He made a point of greeting the other doctors and all but ignored Regina as he sat down at the end of the table. When he finally did look up, he made a show of checking his watch and sighing loudly.

"So, where is Dr. Margulies?" He looked pointedly at Regina and she met his gaze trying hard to hide her own nervousness. "Maybe she has decided to spare us all the aggravation and not show up today. That would be nice, wouldn't it gentlemen?" he asked, as a self-satisfied smirk crossed his face.

"Oh, I wouldn't miss this for the world, Dr. Jameson." Alex stepped through the door and walked into the room, followed by Dr. Cassandra Mitchard and a man dressed in a three-piece, black, pinstriped suit. Regina guessed he was an attorney for the hospital.

Regina watched with interest as Alex walked over and pulled out the chair next to her and sat down. She wore a pair of black pants with thin suspenders crossed in the back of a white mandarin-collared shirt. Her expression was hard and focused as she made eye contact with the medical director. The doctor's facial expression softened slightly as she glanced down at the young woman who looked back up at her.

"Well, now that we're all here," Dr. Jameson began, "let's get started. It's no surprise that the Martin family has named the hospital in a lawsuit. They are suing for damages suffered as a result of the accident and the medical care rendered by this facility."

"You're talking about two different issues, Dr. Jameson," said the attorney, as he leaned forward in his chair. "The police investigation already proved the ambulance driver was speeding and lost control of the rig. As for the autopsy report, well, suffice it to say that someone with epilepsy should not have been driving in the first place." He sat back and scribbled a note on his pad. "By the way, Dr. Jameson," he looked pointedly at the medical director, "aren't you directly responsible for overseeing the hiring of the paramedics for the medical center?" The attorney tapped the tip of his pen slowly on the pad of paper and glanced up at the medical director with a predatory gleam in his dark eyes.

Cassandra leaned back in her chair, her eyes narrowing as she listened to the verbal posturing between the medical director and the hospital attorney.

Dr. Jameson shifted in his seat, his face reddening slightly.

"We've been over that already. His condition wasn't listed in his history and physical."

"Yes, well, that's not why we're here. I think we can address that later."

Regina leaned closer to Alex and whispered, "Sounds like he's been taking some heat for this."

Alex nodded her head, her attention focused on Dr. Jameson who did his best to appear unruffled by the question.

"Let's get to the issue of why these two doctors were out there in the first place," one of the doctors across the table said.

"Yes, Dr. Kingston, as senior resident you know the hospital's policy. Why did you go out to the car?" Dr. Jameson asked snidely.

Regina ignored Dr. Jameson's attempt to rattle her and leaned forward looking at the doctor who spoke first. It was a split-second decision and she'd followed her instincts that night. "The husband was frantic. I wanted to see if the paramedics were there yet. I thought if he knew his wife was getting the help she needed, he would feel better."

"So, why *did* you go out to the car, Dr. Kingston?" The doctor across the table repeated the question, obviously not satisfied with her answer.

Regina stared at him. "I'm sorry I didn't get your name."

"Dr. Newsome."

"Dr. Newsome, are you married?"

"That has nothing to do with this, Dr. Kingston," Dr. Jameson snapped testily from the other end of the table.

"I don't think so," Regina said, ignoring him as she continued to look at the solidly built brown-haired doctor sitting across from her.

"Yes, I'm married," the doctor replied.

"Good. Then put yourself in that man's place, Dr. Newsome. Your wife's in labor and you have a serious car accident on the way to the hospital." Regina set her hands on the table and leaned forward. "You run into an emergency room to get help and the staff tells you they have to call 911. Wouldn't you want the hospital to do what it could to save your wife and your unborn child or would you rather stand by helplessly waiting for the paramedics to arrive and hope it's not too late when they do?"

"That's quite enough, Dr. Kingston." Dr. Jameson slammed his hand on the table. "The fact remains you and your cohort here broke with hospital policy. You left the building to provide medical care you are not trained to provide."

"Dr. Jameson." Alex twisted around in her chair so she faced him. "We might not be paramedics but we sure as hell are doctors trained in emergency medicine, so we are *more* than capable of handling a trauma outside in the field."

He glared at her from across the table. "So well trained, in fact, that the woman lost her leg because of your actions," he shouted at her.

Regina reached her hand out to touch Alex's arm, seeing the doctor's whole body tense at the obnoxious remark. Regina thought Alex was going to go over the table at Dr. Jameson.

"If we didn't stop the bleeding, she would have bled out and died, along with her baby, long before the paramedics would have gotten to her," Alex shot back. "I made the decision to use a tourniquet so we could save her life and give that baby a chance. If I had to do it again, I would."

"You see!" Jameson was out of his chair waving his hand in Alex's direction. "She puts the medical center at risk and admits she'd do it again. What the hell are you waiting for? There's no question she should have her privileges to practice medicine here revoked." His jugular veins were bulging and his face was flushed red by the time he finished his tirade.

"Enough!" Cassandra said, slamming her fist down on the table. There was silence as everyone stared at her in surprise. She glared at both of them. "Jim, sit down. Everybody, just calm down."

Dr. Jameson huffed angrily and dropped into his chair, sulking.

Alex leaned back in her seat. Regina's grip relaxed on her arm as she took a couple of breaths to calm her racing heart. "I hate that bastard," she muttered under her breath.

Cassandra looked at Regina and Alex. "The board needs to ask both of you some questions and then we'll take a break. Dr. Samuels, why don't you start?"

"Dr. Margulies, what did you find when you got to the truck?" the gray-haired doctor asked.

Alex leaned back in her chair and focused on the man sitting across from her. "Mrs. Martin had a compound open fracture of her tibia and fibula. She was losing arterial blood and was going into shock. We controlled the bleeding using a tourniquet just below the knee and started an IV using Ringer's lactate to start fluid resuscitation."

"I thought you said you didn't have any medical equipment with you?" Dr. Timmons interjected, leaning forward across the table.

"She didn't," Regina jumped in. "I took a trauma kit from the storeroom and brought it out to the truck."

"Who applied the tourniquet?" Dr. Samuels asked, leaning forward as he read over some notes in front of him.

"I did," the resident answered.

"Did you monitor the pulse in the foot while it was on?"

"I checked it once a couple of minutes after I put it on. The pulse was still strong at that point. Mrs. Martin was well into the second stage of labor by the time I examined her, and her labor was progressing quickly at that point," Regina explained.

"Why didn't you monitor the pulse, Dr. Margulies?" Dr. Samuels asked turning back to Alex.

"I couldn't reach down to where her foot was because the dashboard was pushed up into the middle of the console. Dr. Kingston could just barely fit in between the seat and the dash herself to deliver the baby." Alex nodded to a manila folder of pictures sitting next to the attorney. "You can see for yourself in the pictures what the truck looked like after it was hit by the ambulance and spun into the utility pole."

"When did the paramedics arrive?" one of the other doctors asked.

"I just delivered the baby and was checking its vital signs when they got to the truck," Regina responded.

"What happened after they arrived?" Dr. Timmons asked.

"Dr. Kingston brought the baby to the ER and turned him over to the neonatologist. I stayed with Mrs. Martin until we brought her into the emergency department and transferred her to the OR."

Alex leaned back in her chair and looked at the doctors sitting around her. She knew all of them; in fact, one of them trained her during her own critical care rotation. Under the circumstances, she knew they did everything medically possible. It was going to be a decision based on whether the hospital was willing to change its policy or not.

Dr. Mitchard broke the silence. "I think we have enough from the both of you for now." She looked down at her watch. "Meet us back here at one o'clock."

Regina looked up at Alex. She was already standing and

turned to leave without another look back at the committee. Regina followed her out the door. The cool air of the hallway was a welcome relief from the heated atmosphere inside the conference room.

Alex turned around and looked at Regina. "You did great in there." She rested a hand on Regina's shoulder. "Are you hungry?"

"Starving, in fact." Regina hardly ate all weekend, choosing instead to boycott reality and sleep more than half the time away.

Alex shook her head. "Come on, let's get out of here."

They rode the elevator down from the fifth floor in silence. Regina followed Alex through the back hallway into the cafeteria. She picked up a sandwich, a bottle of water, and frozen yogurt, then waited by the door for Alex to appear with her tray of food. The doctor checked her watch as she waited in line to pay for her food.

"Why don't we just eat in here?" Alex offered as she walked up to Regina.

Regina nodded her head and walked with her to an empty table in the back of the cafeteria. It was crowded and Regina saw several residents whom she recognized from the various rotations. Most of them gave her a cursory glance and ducked quickly over to their own tables. She realized, as she ate her sandwich, that they probably knew about the meeting today and were uncomfortable about seeing her here, unsure of what the final outcome would be.

Alex leaned across the table. "You really threw them in there by making it personal. That was a good idea. I would have never thought to do that."

Regina looked up and shrugged. "It should be personal. That could have been any of them that night. They needed to know that. What's with Jameson?" she asked in between bites from her sandwich. "He was ready to blow a gasket in there."

"He wants me out." Alex speared a piece of meat with her fork.

"Why? You never told me what happened between you two." Regina looked up at Alex's face. The dark-haired woman looked tired and despite the cool outer façade, Regina could see the nervous tension outlined in her face.

Alex shrugged her shoulders and sat back, pushing her food around on her plate with her fork. "It's old history," Alex explained as she looked up at Regina. "Some drug company offered Dr. Jameson a research grant to trial a new drug. He asked the doctors in the ER to take part in it. Every time we administered the drug we filled out some paperwork for the study." .

Alex gestured with her hands. "I know it doesn't sound like much, but then we started to get these 'gifts' from the company. First, it was tickets to basketball games, then as the volume picked up so did the size of the gifts. I backed out of the study along with some of the other physicians in the ER. Since I was the first to back out, Jameson blamed me when the hospital administration came down on him for accepting the gifts."

Regina pushed her tray away from her and leaned across the table. "That's Medicare fraud."

Alex sighed and nodded her head. "I know. It was a long time ago and the laws weren't as strict then as they are now. Today, it would be a whole other ballgame. He got a slap on the wrist for what he did, but he still blames me for the trouble he got into."

"Nothing like holding a grudge, huh?" Regina looked at Alex, her mind straying from their conversation.

She decided she really liked the outfit Alex was wearing, especially the suspenders and how they accented her shoulders and narrow waist.

Regina realized she was staring as Alex tilted her head and gave her a questioning look. She shook her head, trying to clear her thoughts. "Uh, sorry I just went off there for a minute. I guess we should get back," the blonde quickly mumbled, looking down at her watch. "It's almost one." *Went off? Yeah, right. Good thing she can't read your thoughts, Regina.*

"Right," Alex said, gazing back at her. She leaned forward, ignoring the questioning glances from around them as she looked into Regina's eyes. "Listen, whatever happens when we go back, don't you ever think what you did was wrong. I told you the night that this happened that I'd do it again and I still mean that."

Regina ducked her head as a heated blush crept up her face. "Thanks, Alex."

Alex straightened and picked up their trays. She dumped them on the conveyor belt and walked out of the cafeteria with her colleague.

They could hear angry voices shouting as they stepped off the elevator and walked down the carpeted hallway toward the conference room. Regina looked back at Alex, uncertain if they should go in, but Alex shrugged her shoulders, stepped forward, and opened the door.

Dr. Jameson sat at the end of the table, his eyebrows knitted together and jaw muscles clenched in anger. Dr. Mitchard stood at the opposite end, leaning on the table with her hands, staring at him. She looked up as Alex and Regina walked in and took their seats at the long mahogany table.

"Well, gentlemen. I think we have reasonably covered all the issues." She glanced at Dr. Jameson and then spoke to Alex and Regina. "Do either of you have anything you want to say or ask before we go on?"

"I do, Cassandra," Alex said.

"Doesn't that figure," Dr. Jameson said, condescendingly.

Alex shot him a withering look. "Do you remember the fifteen-year-old boy that was shot outside a medical center in Chicago about four years ago?" Alex asked, turning her attention back to Dr. Mitchard.

"I remember." Cassandra nodded her head. "Go on."

"His mother pleaded with the medical staff to come out and take care of him. They said they couldn't because their hospital policy didn't allow them to. So instead, they called 911 and transported him to another facility. He died before he got there."

"What's your point, Dr. Margulies?" Dr. Jameson asked, looking bored as he stared down at his hands.

"My point, Dr. Jameson, is that we did the right thing. That hospital in Chicago changed its policy *after* the fact. But a life had to be lost to do so. I don't think you would want that kind of publicity here," Alex explained.

"What's that supposed to mean?" Dr. Jameson asked, his upper lip curling into a snarl.

"I'm just saying that maybe we need to look at the policy this hospital has before something like that happens here."

"So you want us to rewrite the policy so you can keep your ass out of trouble. Isn't that convenient?"

Dr. Mitchard put her hands up. "Stop it, both of you. I don't want a repeat of what happened earlier. We already covered all this, Jim. It's a moot issue. If they didn't go out there, the woman would have died along with her child. There's no question in my mind or anyone else's here that these two doctors did the right thing." She looked at Alex and Regina. "The vote was four to one against revoking both your privileges."

Dr. Jameson slammed his hand down on the desk and stood up, causing his chair to bang into the wall behind him. He threw his pad of paper across the table in disgust. "Like that was a surprise. Cassandra, you'll regret this, mark my words."

Cassandra leaned across the table and glared at him, her eyes darkening as her anger built up inside her. "Dr. Jameson." Her voice was low and quiet. "I suggest you find someone to update that policy. Last time I checked, we were still in the business of taking care of people, not bickering over whether we do it in or out of the hospital."

The medical director shoved the chair out of his way as he stormed toward the door and yanked it open.

She watched the door close behind him and shook her head. "Well, we're finished here. Nice to have you back, Dr. Margulies, Dr. Kingston."

"Thanks." Alex stood up from her chair and walked to the door.

"Dr. Kingston, a moment please."

Regina hesitated and walked over to the vice president. "I know Dr. Jameson suspended you without pay, but we're reversing that decision. You'll get that paycheck this week," Dr. Mitchard said.

"That's great. Thanks, Dr. Mitchard." A sense of relief flowed through her. At least that was one less thing to worry about.

Alex held the door as Regina walked out of the room. "Shall we check out the unit and see what's up?" She grinned, knowing what Regina's answer would be. They walked together to the elevator.

"Absolutely."

They walked down the corridor strewn with stretchers and wheelchairs, and passed through the double doors into the emergency department. It was in its usual state of organized chaos, a code cart stood outside one of the rooms, a baby cried in another, and a drunken man shouted obscenities at an intern trying unsuccessfully to draw the man's blood.

Regina stopped at the desk and looked up at Alex. "Feels good to be back, huh?"

"Yeah." Alex stopped at the vacant desk and leaned against it, looking at Regina. "You had a big part in that, you know."

Regina frowned and then her expression softened as she read the serious look on Alex's face. "Alex."

Alex held a hand up. "Later. We have company."

Regina turned around and saw Sandy and Dr. Torres heading toward them. Both had a hesitant but hopeful expression on their faces.

"Please, tell me that you're down here because you're coming back," Sandy pleaded, giving Alex a wary look.

Alex folded her hands, looked down at the floor and didn't say anything.

"Well?"

"We're back," Regina said, and yelped as Sandy wrapped her in a big hug.

"Oh thank God. That's the best news we've had all week. This place has been a madhouse. A couple of us are going out for drinks, Friday night. You should come with us." Sandy squeezed Alex's arm and pulled her into a hug. "Damn it, I've worked with you for how many years now, Margulies? Give me a hug."

Alex made a face and squeezed her back.

"So, what's going on?" the dark-haired woman asked, breaking away from Sandy.

"What's not, is more like it." Sandy crossed her arms, taking in the thoughtful look on the doctor's face. "When's your first shift?"

Alex grinned. "Tomorrow. I already checked the schedule. Guess we'll see you all then." She turned to Regina and put a hand on her shoulder. "Come on, let's go get your car."

# Chapter
# 16

The following night it seemed things returned to relative normalcy as Regina walked down the hallway from the ambulance bay. A brown-haired boy about four years old was cradled on one hip, and walking next to her holding her other hand was his older brother.

Sandy looked up as she walked past the desk. "Hey, who do you have there?" She peered over the counter top at the two boys.

Regina shifted the boy in her arm, settling him higher up on her hip. "This is Mason." She nodded her head to the one holding her hand. "And this is his brother, Thomas. Their mom's in room five. The ambulance driver brought them in with her. Nobody to take care of them at home."

"Hi Mason. Hi Thomas." Sandy smiled down at them.

"Who are you?" Thomas asked, standing up on his toes to get a better look at her.

"I'm Sandy." Thomas nodded his head as if satisfied with her answer. "Guess they're staying with us for awhile, huh?"

"Yeah, they may be admitting their mother." Regina lifted Mason up onto the counter, giving her arm a rest. "Anything special we need to do?"

Sandy thought about it for a minute. "There's no family we can contact?"

Regina shook her head. "No, the mother has custody of the boys and there's no other family in the state."

"I'll call a volunteer and see if they can come sit with them." Sandy drummed her fingers on the desk, thinking. "We won't do anything until we know if mom's being admitted."

Regina looked up at the clock. "You're not going to get a volunteer at this hour."

"Nine o'clock? Ooh, I didn't realize it was that late. You're right." Sandy looked around the ER. "Well, we're not too busy right now. I think we can handle them for the time being."

Sandy turned away, her attention drawn toward Alex as she walked out of one of the exam rooms shaking her head.

"What are you laughing at?" the nurse inquired curiously, seeing the wry grin on the doctor's face.

The dark-haired attending leaned on the desk, her braid falling over her left shoulder as she rested on her elbows. "I just got propositioned by an eighty-six-year-old man." Alex was about to give a less than flattering description of the man when she caught Regina out of the corner of her eye standing at the desk with two young boys.

Sandy crossed her arms and grinned. "Lucky you. What did you tell him?" She couldn't resist teasing Alex since opportunities arose so infrequently.

Alex smirked, leaned across the desk, and whispered in her ear. Sandy glared back at her and smacked her hard on the arm.

"You jerk. Great. Just great. And now I have to go in there and put a catheter in him?" She stalked around the desk and grabbed Alex's arm. "You're coming with me."

"Hey lady." The young boy standing next to Regina pulled on Alex's lab coat. "What's a prop?" He stopped and frowned. "A proposition?" he asked, sounding out the word.

Alex stopped and peered down at the inquisitive eyes peering up at her. "Uh." She looked up at Regina who scowled back at her, arms crossed over her chest, waiting for Alex's response. "Um, it's an offer," she explained.

"For what?"

Alex swallowed and looked at Sandy for help and got none. "It could be for anything."

Regina snorted and shook her head. "All right, show's over guys. We need to go find your mom." She lowered Mason back down to the floor and started to turn away.

"No. I want to know," Thomas demanded, tugging impatiently on Regina's arm.

"Nope. Come on, let's go." Regina glared back at Alex.

Sandy snickered at the predicament Alex managed to get herself into and elbowed her in the ribs. "Ooh, you just pissed her off."

"Yeah, thanks for jumping right in and helping me out there, friend."

"Ah, but it was so much fun to watch you try and get yourself out of trouble."

❖ ⌘ ❖ ⌘ ❖ ⌘ ❖

"Mrs. Frank." Regina leaned over the stretcher and touched the woman's shoulder. "Your boys are here. I know you wanted to see them before you went down for your tests."

The frail-looking, dark-haired woman rolled over and peered down at the two boys standing beside Regina. "Ah, Thomas, come here."

The older of the two boys stepped closer. "What, Momma?"

"I need you to look after your brother while I'm here. You're both going to behave yourselves, right?"

"Yes, Momma." Thomas leaned up against the stretcher and took hold of her hand.

"Mason?"

"I don't want you to go," Mason cried.

"Now, there's nothing to cry about. The doctors just need to check some things and I'll be back in a while. Promise me you'll be good."

Mason nodded his head, wiping the tears off his face. "I promise."

Moments later the transporter appeared and wheeled the stretcher out of the room, taking the woman down to the radiology department. Regina turned around and looked down at the two boys standing beside her. She had to keep them occupied and out of trouble until Sandy found someone to watch them.

"Let me see. I want to listen," Thomas said, reaching up for the instrument hanging around Regina's collar.

"Okay." Regina pulled the stethoscope from around her neck. She held the metal prongs open, letting him grasp the ear pieces and stick them in his ears. Thomas walked over to his brother.

Regina sat back and watched them, enjoying the comedy

being played out between them. She glanced up at the clock. It was already ten o'clock and their mother wouldn't be back from radiology for a while yet.

"Let me listen to your heart, Mason." Thomas placed the stethoscope on his brother's stomach. "I don't hear anything." Thomas looked back at Regina. He frowned and tapped the plastic covering, blinking in surprise as the sound registered loudly in his ears.

Regina stifled a giggle. "Thomas, where's your heart?" Very seriously, he pointed to his stomach. "That's a little low, don't you think?"

He threw his head back, letting out a loud laugh. Regina grinned, slid off her stool, and knelt down beside him.

"Here." She lifted the piece up and placed it over his brother's heart. "Do you hear it now?"

Mason looked up at his brother. "What's it sound like?"

"Thud-thud, thud-thud," Thomas said, as he listened intently and moved the piece around his brother's chest. Mason's lower lip started to quiver. "Hey, why you crying?" Thomas pushed his brother in the shoulder.

Regina looked up at the younger boy. "Mason, what's wrong?"

"Mom's heart's broken. Is it going to sound like that anymore?"

Regina cocked her head, suddenly confused. "Mason, your mom's heart is fine," she said reassuringly.

"No, it's not. She told me so." Tears rolled down the boy's face.

Regina sat back on her heels and reached out for the boy. She heard the door open to the room and turned around to see Alex looking in at her. Their eyes met for a moment and Alex gave her a quick smile of apology. "Sandy is trying to find someone who can stay with them."

The dark-haired doctor walked over to the stretcher and sat down, watching the two boys warily. "Everything all right?"

Regina shrugged her shoulders and looked back at Mason. "What did your mom say about her heart, Mason?"

He sniffled and wiped his nose on his sleeve. "S-she said that daddy broke it when he left." Mason threw himself against Regina and wrapped his arms around her neck, holding her tightly in his grasp.

"Stop crying, Mason," Thomas said.

"Thomas, it's all right if he cries," Regina said, ruffling the older boy's hair.

Regina wrapped her arms around Mason and lifted him up. She walked over to Alex and deposited the smaller boy into her lap. "Here, hold him. I'm going to see if there's a room I can get them settled in."

Taken aback, the doctor's blue eyes widened in surprise. "I-I think the room across from the nurse's station is open," Alex finally managed to get out, holding the boy as if he were a piece of china.

"Good. I'll be back." Regina turned and disappeared out of the room.

Alex peered down at the little boy. He curled up against her, one hand clutching her lab coat and the other wrapped around her upper arm, holding her tightly. Thomas climbed up onto the stretcher and sat cross-legged, peering up at Alex. "Are you going to make my mother better?"

"We're going to try," Alex said carefully.

A little while later, Regina walked back into the trauma room carrying a couple of stuffed animals and two small gowns from the pediatric floor. "You two ever sleep over at a friend's house?" She looked at Thomas and Mason. They both nodded, staring back at her. "Well, that's what this is going to be like tonight." Regina looked at Alex. "Sandy got a couple of beds from the hallway so they can sleep in the empty room."

"Did she find anyone to watch them?"

"Not yet and Jameson is already giving her a hard time about keeping them here."

Alex's brow creased at the worried expression on Regina's face. "The Division of Youth Services isn't open now so he can't call them until the morning. We'll figure something out."

Alex stood up, cradling Mason awkwardly in her arm, and headed to the door. "Let's go, guys. It's bedtime." She pushed the door open and held it for Thomas and Regina to walk through.

"Since when do we run a day care center?" Dr. Jameson asked, as he met them in the hallway. He stared down at the two boys in contempt.

"Since their mother is having testing done, and there's no family for them to stay with." Alex glared back at him defiantly.

"There has to be someone. Make sure you call family services as soon as you know she's being admitted. We can't keep them here indefinitely." Giving them both a cursory glance, he walked quickly down the hallway.

Regina gave Alex a worried look. "He can't do anything, can he, Alex?" The young doctor followed the taller woman into the room Sandy set up for them.

"He can't do anything unless she's going to be admitted and then it's up to the mother if she'll give consent to place them temporarily," Alex reassured her.

"Hey, Doc?"

"What?" Regina looked down at the serious expression on Thomas's face.

"Mason can't go to sleep unless Mom tells him a story."

"Oh." Regina scratched her head and looked at Alex.

"Don't look at me. I sure don't know any." Alex set Mason down on the bed next to his brother. She patted Regina on the back. "Good luck."

"Thanks." Regina looked back at Thomas. "Okay, I think I can do this."

Alex listened for a minute as Regina started to tell them a story and then quietly shut the door behind her. She walked over and leaned against the desk at the nurse's station, looking back through the window in the door.

"Alex."

"What?" Alex asked without turning around. Regina sat cross-legged on the hospital bed talking to the boys. One of them tilted his head back and laughed, falling over onto his side in a fit of giggles.

"Why don't you go in there? We're not busy and your shift is over," Sandy said. "They're just kids."

Alex turned her head and scowled at the nurse. "Very funny, Sandy. You know kids aren't my forte."

Sandy looked up at Alex and chewed on the end of her pen. "Hmm."

"If the mother needs to be admitted we're going to have to call family services in the morning." Alex looked back inside the room. She hated the thought of having them placed in a foster home, even temporarily, but she hadn't figured out a way to get around that particular problem yet.

Sandy stood up and put a hand on Alex's shoulder pulling her close to her. "I don't think it's the kids that are bothering you."

"What are you talking about?" Alex quickly shrugged

Sandy's hand off in irritation.

"I think you're scared of her. She got in there, didn't she?" Sandy leaned forward and tapped Alex's chest.

"Yeah right, Sandy." Alex pulled away from the nurse, giving her a puzzled, almost angry look.

"Oh don't bullshit me, Alex. How long have we worked together, now?" Sandy saw the look of surprise on Alex's face and smirked. "You bring the kid home when she got sick, you did the blood work for her tests. Ha! You even resigned your damn position so Jameson wouldn't go after her."

"You know you are so full of shit." Alex clamped her mouth closed as Regina appeared at the desk and looked up at the two women.

"Hi." She was surprised to see the scowling blue eyes. "What's up?"

Alex glared back at Sandy. "Nothing. Not a damn thing." She pushed away from the desk and stalked off down the hall.

"Ooh, what got into her?" Regina asked, watching Alex disappear into the staff lounge.

Sandy shrugged indifferently and walked off to check on a patient.

Regina stood at the desk for a moment, trying to figure out what happened, and then walked down the hall. She opened the door to the lounge and stuck her head inside. She saw Alex sitting at the table, hunched forward, idly spinning an empty can of soda between her hands. The resident stepped inside and quietly closed the door behind her.

"Do you mind the company?"

Alex raised her head and sat back in her chair. "Hi."

"Mm. Hi yourself." Regina walked over and sat down in the chair next to the doctor. "You okay?" She watched as the woman fidgeted nervously with the tab on the top of the soda can.

"Yeah, I'm just tired." Alex rubbed her eyes.

"Did Sandy say something to upset you?" Regina leaned forward, trying to see past the guarded expression on Alex's face.

Alex stared at her then dropped her eyes down to the table. "You're getting the restraining order tomorrow, right?" she asked, ignoring Regina's question.

Regina gave Alex a puzzled look. "Yeah, I go to the courthouse at ten in the morning."

"You want me to come with you?" Alex broke the tab off the

top of the can and dropped it inside.

"I didn't think you could."

"I might be able to get someone to cover for me at the meeting."

Regina studied her companion from across the table. Something was bothering the older woman but for the life of her she couldn't figure out what it was. "Alex..." Suddenly, the lights went out and they sat in total darkness.

"They're just checking the emergency generator. The lights will come back on in a second," Alex explained quietly.

"Oh."

Seconds later, the emergency lights flickered on, dimly illuminating the lounge.

"I'm going to go check on Mason and Thomas. Hopefully they're already sleeping." Regina stood up and walked out into the hallway.

She heard Mason calling out for his mother before she even got to the room. Regina walked over and picked him up off the stretcher. "Hey, you're okay. Your mother will be back when she's finished with her tests."

The boy would hear none of it and continued to cry inconsolably.

"Geez, who's got the set of lungs I can hear all the way down the hall?" Alex pushed the door open and walked inside behind the younger doctor. Mason hiccuped and reached his arms out for the taller woman.

Regina laughed. "Well, we know who his favorite is."

Alex rolled her eyes and gathered Mason up in her arms. "God only knows why," she replied as Mason wrapped his arms tightly around her neck and held on for dear life.

Regina frowned, hating when Alex put herself down. "Hey, isn't your shift over now?"

The taller woman shrugged her shoulders. "I've got a ton of paperwork to catch up on. Figured I'd stay and get some of it done." She looked down at the boy hanging off her hip. "You want to help me?" Brown, tear-filled eyes looked back at her and Mason nodded his head. "You agree now, but wait thirty years or so." Alex chuckled wryly.

The blonde quietly watched the interaction between the doctor and the boy, then walked past the dark-haired woman. "I'm going to call radiology and see what's taking them so long." Regina slipped out of the room, glancing back as Alex gathered a pile of charts in one arm and set them on the counter.

The doctor sighed as she looked down into the brown eyes. "Listen, Mason, you need to go to sleep." Alex placed him on the hospital bed behind her and glanced at his sleeping brother. *Who are you kidding? You're just staying here so you have a chance to be around her. You just can't admit it now, can you?* With a sigh, Alex sat down on the stool and opened the first in a huge stack of charts she needed to review.

Moments later, two hands touched her shoulder, and Alex glanced up to see Mason standing on tiptoe in the bed, leaning over the railing and peering over her shoulder.

"What are you doing?"

"Reading."

"What are you reading?"

"Work stuff," Alex sighed. "Mason, you're supposed to be asleep."

"I'm not tired," he announced and rocked back and forth on his feet restlessly.

"Uh-huh." Alex spun around on the stool and regarded him seriously. "Do you know what happens if you don't go to sleep?"

"I don't believe in the boogey-man."

"You don't?"

"Nope."

Alex rubbed her eyes. *Shit, now what?* "Come here." She lifted her arms up, expecting the boy to just lean forward. Instead he jumped from the mattress and she scrambled to catch him in mid-flight. "Whoa, what do you think, you can fly?"

"I like to fly," he giggled, balancing on her muscular thighs.

"And how do you manage to do that?" She frowned, holding him firmly in her grasp.

"On a swing and then I jump."

Alex chuckled as she got an idea. "I'll make a deal with you. You get to fly once and then you go to bed. Deal?"

Mason eyes sparkled and he nodded eagerly.

"Okay, here goes, Champ." Alex stood up off the stool and lifted him up high over her head. He squealed and laughed as she turned him in her arms and held him upside down, before setting him back on his feet.

He smiled back up at her. "That was fun. One more time, please?" Mason tugged her hand impatiently.

The dark-haired woman glanced out the door then quickly scooped the boy back up into her arms. Mason giggled as he was lifted overhead and then set back down on the floor.

"Oh sure, Miss 'Kids Aren't My Forte.' You're just an over-grown version, yourself."

Alex jerked her head up to see Sandy standing in the door-way with her arms crossed over her chest. "I-I was just bribing him to go to sleep."

The curly-headed nurse rolled her eyes and walked over to the doctor. "I could think of better ways." She pursed her lips and regarded the doctor coolly. "Don't stay too late, Alex. I let the next shift know about our two visitors here so someone can come in and watch them when you're ready to leave."

Alex nodded and sat down on the stool, feeling rather fool-ish for having been caught with her guard down. "Sandy, do you know if that nurse up on pediatrics still takes foster kids?"

"Sheila?"

"Yeah."

"I think so, why?"

"Their mother probably isn't going to agree to being admit-ted if she has to give these kids over to youth services. There's no guarantee they'll keep them together in foster care."

"So, you want to see if Sheila will take them for a few days?"

Alex leaned back against the desk and blew out a breath. "Yeah, I do."

Sandy looked at the two boys. Thomas was curled up on his side fast asleep and Mason was leaning against Alex, his arms draped over her thigh. "He's taken a liking to you."

Alex glanced down at the curly brown head and then rubbed his back affectionately. "He reminds me of my brother."

The nurse ran a hand through her hair and sighed. "I'll give Sheila a call and see what she can do."

"Thanks, Sandy." Alex watched her walk out of the room. She looked down as two small hands pulled on her lab coat. "What, Mason?"

"Can you do it again?"

Alex smiled crookedly at the boy. "Sandy was right. There has to be a better way to get you to go to sleep. All right, just one more time."

By the time Regina extracted herself from the sudden influx of patients, it was well after one in the morning. She finished writing the orders on her last patient, pulled the order tab up, and slipped the chart into the cart next to the unit clerk. On her way to the on call room, she stuck her head in the room across from the nurse's station to check on the two boys. She couldn't help the surprised smile that spread across her face when she saw Alex sprawled out on her back on the hospital bed, sleeping. A pile of charts lay untouched at her feet and Mason was curled up next to her, his head resting on her shoulder and a hand clutching the lapel of her lab coat.

The image stuck in the young doctor's mind long after she left the hospital that night and headed home from her shift.

❖ ⌘ ❖ ⌘ ❖ ⌘ ❖

Regina sat in the courtroom leaning back against the hard wooden bench, silently praying that Derrick wouldn't show up today. It wasn't unusual for him to spend at least one or two days a week in court waiting to testify for cases he was involved in.

Regina closed her eyes, wishing that Alex had been able to come with her. She got held up at the medical center at the last minute and left Regina a message that she probably wouldn't make it over to the courthouse in time. Not that there was anything the doctor could do, but she just wanted her presence and moral support.

The resident sighed as she thought about Alex. It was so hard to read her. The older woman kept everything inside closely guarded and despite the time they spent together, Regina wondered where their friendship was ultimately headed. She really wanted to get to know the woman better but it was almost impossible to get her to open up since they had been back from their suspensions.

She closed her eyes trying to calm her nervousness. A part of her still couldn't believe she was actually doing this. She had never been afraid of someone hurting her until Derrick changed all that several months ago. Her last violent interactions with him convinced her to stop making excuses for him and to get a restraining order.

It was a simple enough process and without Derrick to argue his side of the story, the judge quickly granted the restraining order after he read over the police and hospital reports Regina brought with her to the court.

The somber, gray-haired man looked over the ornate desk at Regina.

"You understand that he can't come within five hundred feet

of you. The only complicating factor is his job. Once his suspension is over, and he is reinstated to active duty, I can't restrict his access to the hospital if he has reason to be there. Any questions?"

Regina shook her head, taking the papers from the judge.

"Well, good luck then."

The resident slipped on her trench coat and walked hastily out of the courtroom. A slight breeze blew and the first autumn leaves swirled down from the trees, fluttering around her feet. Regina tugged her coat closely around her as she walked along the broken sidewalk. A car door slammed shut somewhere ahead of her as she approached her own car and she heard her name being called.

Looking up, she stopped in her tracks. "Shit."

Derrick pushed off of his police cruiser and stepped around, blocking Regina's path. He looked her up and down, his dark, angry eyes boring into her. "You bitch. I can't believe you did this."

"Get away from me, Derrick." Regina summoned as much anger as she could to hide the fear she felt inside her. Her heart hammered in her chest as she moved to step around him.

"You got me fucking suspended!" He blocked her again. "They stuck me with desk duty for a month." Derrick stared down at Regina. "Do you know what that'll do for my chances of getting promoted?"

Regina stepped back. "I don't care. Just leave me alone." She heard another car door slam shut and footsteps came running up behind her.

"You better back off, Derrick," Alex growled as she stepped up beside Regina protectively.

"What's wrong? Didn't I beat your queer ass enough last time?" Derrick taunted, his upper lip curling in a snarl as he glared at taller woman.

"I'm not the one nursing broken ribs, now am I?" Alex retorted sharply.

Derrick glared at her. "Get lost. This is between Regina and me."

"I'm not going anywhere."

"You need to drop the charges, Regina," Derrick growled, turning away from Alex.

"Like hell I will. I've got a restraining order, Derrick. Stay the hell away from me." Regina stepped around him.

"What the hell are you talking about?" He reached out to grab Regina's arm and yelped in surprise as Alex stepped forward and grabbed his wrist, twisting it painfully behind his back.

"Derrick, one last time. Back off, unless you want a matching set of ribs. Believe me, I'll gladly accommodate if you like," she hissed in his ear.

"Let go of my wrist," he snarled.

She yanked his arm up higher, forcing him to bend over. "You leave her alone, you sick bastard."

"I meant it when I said I got a restraining order against you." Regina glared at him, feeling braver now that Alex was there. "A month is nothing. If you keep harassing me, you're going to end up in jail again and next time you won't just be suspended."

Derrick blinked and hesitantly looked around them aware of several curious stares from people walking by. He shrugged away from Alex as she released his wrist. "You're a damn fool for getting involved with this bitch, Regina."

"Save it. I don't care what you have to say."

"Yeah? Well, why don't you ask her about her dyke friend who deals drugs? That's right." He took in Alex's surprised expression. "It's amazing who you meet when you spend a night in the slammer. Go ahead and enjoy your time with this one, Regina. When that bitch gets out of jail, Alex, she's coming for you and there isn't going to much left when she's finished."

"Go to hell, Derrick." Regina stepped closer and put her hand on Alex's arm.

Looking at the two of them in disgust, he spat at their feet and walked away. Alex slipped her arm around Regina's shoulder. "You okay?"

"I didn't think you were coming."

"Dr. Ortiz covered for me at the meeting. Are you all right to drive back to the hospital?" Regina trembled under her arm.

"Yeah, I just need a minute." Regina steadied herself and walked slowly toward her car. "What's going on with Dana?"

The dark-haired woman stared down at the ground as they walked, knowing she needed to tell Regina what was going on. "I can't get into it now, it'll take too long. We'll talk Friday night." She saw the doubtful expression on the blonde's face. "I promise." She knew she'd been keeping her distance from Regina since they got back, mostly trying to sort out her feelings for the younger woman. The doctor squeezed her shoulder and walked with the resident to her car.

Alex held the door open as Regina slipped behind the steering wheel. "I thought you'd want to know, one of the nurses on pediatrics is taking the boys for a couple of days. The mother gave her consent this morning," Alex commented quietly, leaning against the side of the car as Regina settled in her seat.

"How did you manage that?" Regina darted a surprised glance up at the blue eyes that were looking back at her.

The dark-haired woman shrugged casually. "I know a couple of the nurses on pediatrics take foster kids. I just got lucky that one of them could take Mason and Thomas for a few days."

"So the mother is staying to get the procedure done then?"

"Yes, she should be ready to go home in a few days." Alex nodded her head, wondering how something as simple as Regina's smile could make her feel this warm inside. "I've got to get back or Dr. Ortiz is going to have a fit. Are you going to be okay?"

"I'm fine, Alex." Regina grabbed her hand. "Thanks for finding a place for those kids to stay."

"It was luck it worked out that way." Alex smiled down at her. "I'll see you tomorrow night."

# Chapter
# 17

Regina sat on the rolling chair, hunched forward over the stretcher. She had spent the last ten hours totally immersed in patients with hardly a chance to breathe in between. She chewed on the end of her pen as she worked out the last calculation for a patient's medication before she wrote it on the order sheet. Closing the chart, she sat back in her chair and stretched her arms over her head. *Done.* She smiled to herself.

It had been a good week overall, she reflected in the relative quiet of the empty trauma room. No one died in the ER this week, which meant there were no grieving families that she had to tell the heartbreaking news to. Her fever had been gone since Sunday. So the most unpleasant thing the young doctor dealt with was getting the restraining order against Derrick. His suspension didn't come as a surprise, since he was arrested, but if anything it left Regina feeling that he was becoming more unbalanced and desperate since his job was on the line.

Unexpectedly, the door swung open and Alex poked her head into the room Regina had hidden herself away in. "There you are. I thought you might have left already."

Regina looked up and smiled at Alex's slightly disheveled appearance. Her rumpled lab coat hung limply around her shoulders and there were a variety of suspicious looking stains scattered over the front of it.

"No, I needed a quiet place to finish up these notes. It was a zoo out there today." Regina pushed the chart away from her and leaned back in the chair, as Alex stood hesitantly inside the brightly lit room. Her usual outwardly cool demeanor seemed to waver momentarily as she shifted her feet and glanced over her shoulder nervously. Finally, as if coming to some decision, Alex walked over and sat on the corner of the desk.

Alex regarded Regina for a second. "Do you still want to go out to the bar with these guys?"

"Of course. You didn't change your mind, did you?" Regina asked, hoping that Alex hadn't. Regina and Sandy had spent the greater part of the week cajoling and coaxing the doctor into going out with the small group from the ER Friday night.

"No, no I haven't. Just wanted to make sure you were still up for it."

"I am," Regina said, cheerfully. She was looking forward to the time they would be spending together even if it was in a group.

"I'll meet you over there then. I've got a couple of things to finish up yet."

"Anything I can help with?" Regina asked.

Alex shook her head. "No, just boring administrative stuff. Thanks for offering, though."

Regina smiled as Alex turned and walked to the door. If she hadn't known better, it seemed like Alex was nervous about going out to the bar. *What's going on in that head of yours, Alex?*

The blonde waited until she was alone in the room and then picked up the phone. She dialed her number at the condo and waited until the second ring, then typed in the access code. There was only one message from Jeff returning her call, congratulating her on having her privileges reinstated at the hospital. "Damn." Regina set the phone back down in the cradle, a sad expression crossing her face. She'd left two messages on her parents' answering machine during the week asking her mother to please call her. They'd both gone unanswered.

Knowing her mother could shut her out like this hurt her deeply. Even though she didn't get to see them much they were still her family, and potentially losing that was hard to bear. Regina blinked back tears as she picked up the chart, walked out of the trauma room and slipped the chart into the rack by the unit clerk.

She walked into the locker room to shower and change her

clothes. From what Sandy told her, the bar was an old local establishment where the medical staff often went to forget about work, engaging in what the residents affectionately called "liver rounds."

❖ ⌘ ❖ ⌘ ❖ ⌘ ❖

Regina stepped into the darkened, smoky interior of the restaurant and walked past the crowded bar, ignoring some of the leering stares she got from the businessmen hunched over their drinks. She headed over to the room where the pool tables were.

Sandy was leaning up against one of the tables as Regina approached, watching intently as Dr. Washington lined up a shot. Regina watched as he sank the eight ball in the corner pocket. He hung his head and banged the edge of the table with his fist in frustration. The nurse let out a triumphant shout and danced around the floor.

"Ha! You're buying the next round, Jon. That'll teach you to tell me I don't know how to play pool," Sandy crowed as she taunted the tall, lanky doctor from across the table.

"Shit." He set the pool stick on the table and flopped dejectedly into his chair. His face brightened when he looked up and saw the fair-skinned resident watching the commotion. "Hey, Regina. Come on over." He pulled a chair out at the table for her. He glanced over her shoulder. "Where's Alex?"

"She's still at the hospital. She said she'd be here after she finished up." Regina sat down in the chair and slipped out of her jacket.

Sandy set her mug of beer down on the table. "Hey, do you play pool, Regina?" Her face was flushed and Regina figured that Sandy already had one or two beers in her.

"Be careful, Regina. She's a shark, just like Alex. Don't let her fool you," Jon warned playfully.

Sandy stuck her tongue out at him. "You're just a sore loser. Why don't you make yourself useful and go get us another pitcher of beer?"

Jon balled up a napkin and tossed it at Sandy before he walked over to the bar. "I've played once or twice." Regina turned to the nurse.

"Well, come 'ere then." Sandy tugged Regina off the chair and pulled her over to the pool table. "I'll teach you, before the others get here." She racked up the balls and set the cue ball down at the opposite end of the table. "This is how you break."

Regina watched in quiet amusement as Sandy sent the balls scattering in several directions.

"Why don't you try?" Sandy handed her the pool stick and reset the balls up in the rack.

Regina lifted the cue stick in her hands and looked dubiously at it. "I haven't done this in years."

"It's easy. Just like riding a bike." A warm, familiar voice floated down from behind her.

Startled, Regina turned around to see Alex standing at the table behind her. Her dark hair hung loosely around her shoulders and the black leather jacket contrasted nicely with the white shirt and faded jeans she wore. "Oh, hi," Regina said, her face brightening. "I didn't know you were here."

"Just walked through the door." Alex smiled back at her. "This is Tina." She nodded to the woman standing beside her. "She works up in labor and delivery."

"Hi, Regina." Tina walked up, shook Regina's hand, then glanced at Sandy who leaned against a table and drained her mug of beer. Regina watched as Tina walked over to the nurse and brushed her hand over the back of Sandy's shoulder as she stood next to her.

"I take it Sandy is trying to teach you how to play?" Alex walked up beside Regina, eyeing the balls neatly corralled in the rack. She glanced at the two nurses. "You have no shame, do you?"

"What did I do?" Sandy asked, giving Alex an innocent look.

"You'll teach her all of your bad habits and then challenge her to a game. I know your style, Sandra." Alex looked back at Regina and winked at her. "She won't admit it, but I taught her everything she knows."

"Good thing you're here to keep her in line, Alex," Tina chimed in from the table as she poured herself a beer.

"No. Good thing you're here. She's your responsibility now, not mine," Alex replied cheerfully.

Sandy swatted her hand at Alex as she walked past her. "Don't listen to her, Regina. She's just jealous because I beat her last time we played."

"That was a fluke. Besides, we're about to change that as of tonight." Alex hefted a pool stick in her hand and balanced it easily on two outstretched fingers.

Jon walked back over and set the pitchers of beer down on the table. "Oh boy, I sense a challenge here."

"Hi, Jon." Alex looked up at her colleague. "Where's Chris? I thought she was coming out with you tonight," she said, referring to his wife.

"She got called in to help out in the OR. A couple of people called in with the flu. It's going to be one hell of a winter with this strain." He looked at his watch. "I'm going to head over there and catch her in between surgeries. Hey, it's good to have you both back." He walked past Alex and patted her on the shoulder.

"Thanks, Jon." Alex turned to Regina after he left. "Let's see you break 'em." She pointed at the balls on the table and stepped back to watch.

Regina leaned over, and sent the cue ball careening across the table. With a loud crack, the tightly packed balls scattered. "Ooh, I think we have solids, Alex."

"Indeed, we do." Alex grinned mischievously at Sandy.

"'Oh, I've only played once or twice,'" Sandy said in a mocking voice, and gave Regina an evil look as she strode past her. "You are both in serious trouble. We're playing best two out of three."

Tina rolled her eyes. "Can't we just make it one game?" she pleaded.

Sandy shot her a look. "No."

"Ugh." Sulking, Tina sat down on one of the empty stools. "Don't get me wrong," she said, leaning closer to Regina. "I like the company but I hate straight bars."

"Say it a little louder, why don't you?" Alex walked over to her and twirled the stick menacingly in front of her. "We'll be using these sticks to fight our way out of here."

Tina snorted and rolled her eyes. "Like I said, I hate straight bars. Sandy promised me we'd go dancing after this. I have to go make sure she still remembers she made me that promise."

"While you're at it, why don't you two break first," Alex said. "I wouldn't want Sandy to think that we have an unfair advantage or anything." She settled down next to Regina and smiled at her, resisting the urge to brush a strand of blonde hair behind her ear. "How are you doing?"

"I'm okay." Regina stared into the beer she held. They had spent most of the week literally passing each other in the corridors, catching bits and pieces of disjointed conversations, settling back into a routine that made Regina fear that what small, tentative steps they made in getting to know each other the week before would quickly be lost.

"Just okay?" Alex asked, searching her face.

"I missed you," Regina said, looking up at her.

Alex's blue eyes widened in surprise, and then she stared down at the table. She wasn't prepared for Regina's blunt honesty and it caught her completely off guard.

Regina thought she could see Alex's face flush in the dim light from the overhead fluorescent bulbs. For a long moment, they were silent, until Alex finally met Regina's steady gaze.

Sandy looked up from the pool table and cleared her throat loudly. "Hey, are you two going to sit there all night or are you going to play?"

Alex sighed and stood up slowly from the stool. "Why? Are you in a rush to get your ass kicked?" She picked up a cue stick and leaned down next to Regina's head as she scraped chalk on to end of the long tapered wooden rod. "I missed you too, Regina," she whispered softly in her ear.

Regina felt the warmth from Alex's breath tickle her ear. A tingle of electricity ran up her spine as Alex brushed past her and walked over to the table.

Alex lined up the shot, nailed the cue ball, and sent two solids into a corner pocket. She cleared two more balls from the table as Sandy looked on in disbelief.

"That is not fair," Sandy complained as Alex handed her the cue, after finally missing a shot, and sauntered back to the table.

"No, not fair would be if I chose to clear the entire table on my first attempt."

Regina couldn't help the smile and warm flush she felt as Alex winked at her. She heard the stool scrape on the floor as her companion pulled it forward to sit down behind her. Regina turned to face her.

"Nice shot."

"Thanks." Blue eyes twinkled back her. "I think you're up." Alex gently nudged her from her chair as Sandy missed her shot.

Sandy stepped back as Regina stood holding the cue stick, looking at the disarray of balls on the table. "Great. You didn't leave me anything, Sandy."

"That would be the idea, Dr. Kingston." Sandy picked up her mug of beer. "Hey, what are you doing?"

Tina smiled and wagged a finger at Sandy while snatching

the mug from her reach. "You promised me we'd go dancing if I came here. If you keep drinking, you'll just fall asleep like you did last time."

Regina laughed at the pitiful look on Sandy's face. Shaking her head, she leaned over and stared bleakly at the table. Alex walked up beside her and looked over her shoulder. She studied the balls scattered over the table and then pointed at the green ball. "There. You can get that one in the corner pocket."

Regina turned her head and straightened. "Yeah, *you* might be able to make that shot."

Alex grinned at her. She walked over to the ball and held her finger next to it. "Hit it right here. Not too hard. It'll go right in."

Regina looked at Alex and bent over, setting her shot up. She tapped the white cue ball lightly and heard Sandy smack her forehead and mutter several choice words as she watched the green ball roll smartly into the corner pocket and rattle down into the cup. Alex just smiled confidently at Regina and sat back down on the stool to watch as she cleared two more balls from the table.

They played two more games, splitting the last two. "My condolences, Sandy," Alex teased as she set the cue stick on the table.

"Just wait until next time. That was just beginner's luck," she said, pointing in Regina's direction.

"Hey! Who said anything about beginner's luck?" Regina protested.

"Not me." Sandy grinned. "We're going to go dancing. You two want to come along?" she asked ignoring the elbow Tina quickly jabbed into her ribs.

Alex shrugged indifferently and looked at Regina. "What do you want to do?"

"Can we take a rain check? I think I've had enough of bars for one night." She was tired of the noise and the thought of another hot, crowded bar was not very appealing to her.

They walked outside to their respective cars and Tina ushered Sandy over to hers, and opened the passenger door. She waved to Alex and Regina as she slid into the driver's seat.

Alex turned to Regina. "What are you up to now?" she asked, fiddling with the keys on her key ring. She felt like a nervous teenager and wished she could come up with something more original than that to say to this woman.

Regina lowered her eyes and shook her head, stifling a laugh. "Nothing." She looked back up at Alex and smiled. "I thought maybe we could just spend some time together." She hoped her voice didn't sound as nervous as she felt.

"I think we can arrange that." Alex smiled down at Regina. "It's nice out." She looked up at the sky. "Why don't we go for a walk by the reservoir?"

"Sure. Lead the way." Regina waved her hand out in front of her.

Alex hesitated, looking back at Regina's car. "How about we drop your car off at your condo first?"

"Why?"

Alex glanced down at Regina, raising an eyebrow. "So you still have one tomorrow. Unless of course, you're trying to get rid of it."

"Oh, I didn't think of that." Regina laughed.

"Come on."

❖ ⌘ ❖ ⌘ ❖ ⌘ ❖

"Where are we?" Regina asked, as they stepped out of the Jeep. She shut the door and looked at the darkened landscape around them.

Alex walked around the Jeep and stood close behind Regina. "It's just one of the parks that runs through the reservation. There's a reservoir down there through that trail." She pointed over Regina's shoulder.

"What trail?" Regina squinted, trying to make out what Alex was pointing to in the darkness.

"Come on, I'll show you." Alex stepped forward, taking Regina's hand in her larger one and leading her toward the dark shadows that slowly transformed into trees, as they walked closer. She led the way through the darkness, picking her way down the winding trail that she frequently ran on.

As the trees thinned out Regina saw the dark outline of the water and heard the waves lapping gently up against the shoreline. She glanced up at her now silent companion. *There she goes again,* she thought to herself as she recognized the quiet pensive expression that frequently came over Alex's face.

"Hey, where'd you go off to?" Regina squeezed Alex's hand.

The taller woman glanced down at her, a smile twitching at

the corner of her mouth. "Just thinking." The brunette slipped her hand out of Regina's and walked beside her companion in silence for a bit. She was nervous, wondering how Regina would react to what she had to tell her.

Regina stopped at one particular point to watch the moon starting to peak over the treetops on the other side of the reservoir.

"It's beautiful, isn't it?" Regina turned, hearing Alex's voice from somewhere above her in the dark.

"It is. The moon looks so close tonight." She turned, looking around her. "Hey, where did you go?"

Alex chuckled softly. "Up here."

"Oh, well that helps." Regina yelped and jumped away as Alex dropped down beside her from a perch on top of a large boulder. "That was mean." Regina glared at Alex.

"Sorry, I thought you heard me climb up there. Come on up and sit with me." Alex scrambled back up the boulder and reached down to help Regina up.

The doctor sat down, leaning back against the smooth face of the rock behind her and guided Regina down in front of her. "You okay sitting like this?" she asked, as Regina sat down between her outstretched legs.

"Yeah, I'm fine."

The smaller woman shivered as a faint breeze rustled the leaves overhead. Alex leaned closer, her breath warm against her ear. "Are you cold?"

"Just a little." Regina wrapped her arms around herself.

"Lean back." The taller woman slipped her arms over Regina's and rubbed her hands up and down. "Is that better?"

"You're like a hot coal." Regina relaxed against Alex, feeling the softness of her breasts pressing against her back. She felt Alex's chest expand as she took a deep breath and let it out.

"Mm. Just warm blooded." Alex pulled Regina against her, inhaling the scent of her hair as she rested her cheek against the top of her head.

Regina closed her eyes enjoying the warmth of Alex's strong arms wrapped around her. She felt safe and secure sitting here with her. Her thoughts drifted around their friendship and Regina decided that in the short time that she had known Alex, the doctor had come to mean a great deal to her.

The younger woman tilted her head back to look up at Alex. "Do you come out here a lot?" She touched her palm to Alex's face, feeling her smile and pressed into the touch.

"Yeah, it's quiet and peaceful at night."

"I think I'd be afraid to come out here by myself." Regina clasped her hands over Alex's arms.

Alex glanced down at Regina. "Are you uncomfortable being here?"

"No, I like it, Alex. I like being here with you."

Alex smiled at the last remark. There was no denying the bond growing between them. Since Lana's death, she allowed herself to drift aimlessly, hardly caring that the world and everything in it passed her by. It just hadn't seemed worth the effort to take back her life until now. "Regina, have you thought about what you're doing after this residency?"

"I'm not sure yet. I've had a couple of offers. One was in Boston at a family practice. I thought I might go back home at one point, be closer to my family."

Alex tried not to let her disappointment come through in her voice. "Is that what you're still planning to do?" She looked down, biting her lower lip as she waited for Regina's answer.

Regina rested her head back on Alex's shoulder. "I don't think it really matters anymore if I go home or not."

"Why would you say that?" Alex asked, peering down at Regina's face.

Regina sighed. "I had a fight with my mother and it just came out...about my lifestyle. It wasn't exactly the best way to break the news to her and I haven't heard from her since."

"So, they're not talking to you?" She wasn't sure why she was so surprised considering what Regina's mother had done to her older brother.

Regina shook her head. "Nope, they won't return my calls. Hey, I don't really want to talk about it." Regina looked up at her friend. "What about you, Alex? You've never talked about your family."

Alex gave Regina a surprised glance. "Not much to tell. My father was an alcoholic. He was a mean son of a bitch when he was drunk, which was most of the time." Alex shrugged her shoulders. "My mother just endured it. I guess she didn't think she deserved better at the time. The best thing that happened was when she gathered me and my brother up one night and walked out."

Regina squeezed Alex's hand. "I'm so sorry, Alex."

"It was a long time ago." Alex looked away from her. *Damn,*

*I can still hear them yelling at each other. Where the hell is this coming from?*

"How old were you?" Regina could see Alex clench her jaw, turning her face away at the question.

"I don't know, maybe thirteen or fourteen." Alex closed her eyes trying to clamp down on the painful memories of what became a vicious cycle of going from one shelter to another as her mother tried many times to break away from her father's abusive nature. When her mother lost her job and couldn't pay the rent, Alex and her brother, John, were separated and sent to different foster families. The whole thing had been one agonizing nightmare that seemed like it would never end at the time.

"Where's your mother now?" Regina asked, keeping a firm hold on Alex's hand. Alex tensed at the question.

"Last I knew she was out west in Arizona," Alex said. "I...we don't really talk to each other that much anymore."

Alex squeezed Regina against her and was quiet for a time, lost in her own thoughts. She decided that night in the hospital as she lay next to Regina while she slept, that regardless of the consequences, even if it meant losing her friendship, she needed to be honest with her. She cared about her young friend and she at least deserved to hear the truth about what happened with Dana and Lana.

"Regina, I need to tell you something."

"What?" She twisted around, hearing the catch in Alex's voice.

Alex pulled her hand away and let her arms rest on her knees. "Listen, you know I sold drugs for Dana when I was in medical school."

"Alex, you don't owe me any explanations. It was a long time ago," Regina said quietly.

"Just let me say this. Please?" It would be so easy to simply omit the events that took place then.

Regina nodded her head, not quite sure that she wanted to hear what Alex had to tell her.

"I wasn't stupid, Regina. I knew what I was getting into and I was just desperate enough to do it so I could help Lana get the medicine she needed." Alex's throat muscles worked as she swallowed. "The medicine I *thought* she needed because I was so full of myself...thought I knew what was best for her at the time. I was too damn blind to see that all she wanted to do was to let go and die."

"Alex, you don't have to tell me this," Regina protested feebly. She wasn't sure if she was trying to protect herself or Alex
from hearing what she had to say.

"Yes, I do," Alex insisted quietly. "If I don't tell you now,"
she looked up at the sky and took a breath, "you'll just find out
later."

"What are you talking about?" Regina asked, frowning up at
her friend.

"I've done some pretty fucked up things in my life, did
more drugs than I care to think about, had sex just for the hell of
it, and used people because it suited my purposes at the time."

Regina was quiet as she absorbed all that Alex was telling
her.

"There's something else. I-I set Dana up last week."

Regina turned around so she could see her friend's face in
the moonlit darkness. "What are you talking about? I don't
understand."

Alex closed her eyes, unable to look at Regina as the shock
slowly registered on her face. "I set up a drug deal the day I was
at Dana's store. The police had a hunch that she was dealing
drugs out of the cellar, but didn't have enough to get a warrant. I
just helped them along."

Regina's jaw worked several times before she uttered a single word. "You what? But, wait a minute, what about the store? I
thought it was yours now. Doesn't that connect you?"

Alex shook her head. "I never inherited the store." She
reached into her jacket and pulled out the envelope that the lawyer had given her. "You can read it later, if you want to."

Regina took the envelope and held it loosely in her hands.
"You told me that you inherited it, Alex." Regina wasn't sure
what hurt more, the fact that Alex lied to her or that she didn't
trust her enough to tell her what was going on.

Alex felt Regina pull away from her. "I know I did." The
doctor stood up and jumped down to the ground. She walked
over and leaned against a tree by the water's edge. Somehow the
physical distance made it easier to tell Regina what she had
done.

"The title to the store was always in Dana's name, not mine.
Lana arranged it with the lawyer before she died. It was all a set
up so Dana would get caught, if I kept my promise. Lana made
sure of it."

"What did you promise to do, Alex?" Regina broke the

silence.

"It's complicated." Alex turned around in the dark. She could see Regina's body silhouetted in the moonlight, still sitting on the rock, her arms wrapped tightly around her knees, watching her.

"Well, why don't you try and explain it to me, because I'd really like to try and understand." Regina stared back at her.

Alex sighed and shoved her hands in her pockets. "Lana turned the store over to her sister when she got too sick to run it herself. When she found out what Dana was doing with the store, it just made a bad situation worse."

"Didn't she try and stop her?"

"Of course she did, Regina." Alex turned around angrily. "It was her kid sister who'd been a screw up for half of her life. Lana kept trying to give her the benefit of the doubt. She always believed that Dana would turn around somehow."

"I guess she never did." Regina carefully slid off the boulder and walked toward her brooding friend.

Alex was quiet for a minute. "No, and when Lana found out what I'd done to get the medication for her...I might as well have stuck a knife in her back."

"So what happened?"

Alex focused on Regina for the first time since she started talking. "Before she died I promised Lana I'd take care of her sister, get her out of the store and off the drugs. It was Lana's last request." Alex stared down at her hands helplessly. "I would have done anything to make it all up to her. I messed everything up between us."

"So you set Dana up? What was that supposed to accomplish?" Regina stared up at Alex, seeing the tense outline of her profile in the darkness.

"I already tried everything else. You can't force an adult into drug rehab and Dana couldn't handle stopping cold; she always went back to it. I figured if she lost the store and got thrown in jail, it would be hard, but she would be forced off the drugs and away from dealing them."

"Why didn't you tell me what you were doing, Alex?"

Alex ran a hand through her hair and stared out into the darkness. "I didn't know what was going to happen, what I would have to do that day." Her voice trailed off. "To Dana, sex and drugs have always meant power and control. She's an expert at manipulation."

Regina dropped her eyes, a knot starting in the pit of her stomach, as she realized what Alex was referring to. "Did...did you sleep with her?" Regina stammered.

Alex jerked her head up and looked at Regina. "No, no. Regina, please believe me. I just got her involved enough to let her think that we were going to. I injected her with Rohypnol so she wouldn't remember anything afterwards. I needed time to find her book that had all of her contacts in it."

Regina shook her head in disbelief and ran both her hands through her hair. "You what? How? Where did you get it? I mean, Jesus, Alex, that stuff is illegal."

"So is selling drugs."

"Damn it, you know what I mean," Regina snapped.

"I bought it from someone. Enough money can buy you just about anything you want today."

"Alex, didn't you think about what could happen if you got caught?" Regina peered up at the woman, her pale eyes hidden by her dark bangs. She could see the walls rising up, one by one, slowly pushing her away and shutting her out. The blonde leaned forward, gently cupped Alex's cheek with her hand, lifting her head. Alex's eyes closed and a single tear ran down her face. Regina brushed it away with her thumb.

Alex let out a caustic laugh and wiped her face with her hands, pulling away from the smaller woman's touch. "At the time, I really didn't care any more. By rights I should have lost my license to practice medicine and been thrown in jail." She let out a breath and turned away, crossing her arms over her chest. "You were the last person I ever expected to be on the other end of the phone that night you called me." Alex's voice was a hoarse whisper. She leaned back against the tree wishing it would just mercifully swallow her up and let her disappear.

"When you said you weren't coming back, I knew you were talking about more than just the hospital." Regina took hold of Alex's arm and squeezed it. "I couldn't let you do that, Alex."

Alex shook her head. "You weren't supposed to be there. If something went wrong, I didn't want you involved."

"And what did you expect me to do if something did go wrong, just walk away? I couldn't do that if I wanted to, Alex."

The taller woman shook her head. "Regina, don't do this," she pleaded. "Please I-I'm not...Shit." Her voice cracked and she pulled her face away from Regina's touch. "I don't know why you'd want to be involved with me. All I've ever managed to do is hurt people." Alex turned her head away and angrily wiped the tears from her face.

"Damn it, that's not true. And I already told you I didn't know you then. I only know the person you are now. Alex, please don't shut me out," Regina whispered to her. *Can't you see I've been falling in love with you since we met?*

She stepped up in front of her and slipped her arms around Alex's waist, pulling her into a hug. She could hear the hammering of Alex's heartbeat beneath her ear. Slowly it calmed, as the tension in Alex's body relaxed ever so slowly. Alex slid her arms around the blonde holding onto her tightly. She buried her face in Regina's shoulder, and her body shuddered as a sob quietly escaped her lips.

A blanket of peacefulness fell over them. Regina could have stayed like that forever, wrapped securely in Alex's arms, her head resting comfortably on her shoulder, listening to her heartbeat.

After some moments, she pulled away and took Alex's face in her hands feeling the soft strands of Alex's dark hair. She smoothed her bangs and smiled wistfully. When Alex finally opened her eyes and looked at her, Regina wondered when her heart crossed that invisible line between friendship and something much deeper. She realized that she couldn't walk away from Alex. Just the thought of it tore at her heart in a way she never imagined possible.

They both leaned closer, slowly closing the space between them. It was the barest of touches as their lips brushed together. Alex pulled back and looked at Regina, touching her face with trembling fingers. The taller woman ducked her head again to kiss Regina, pulling her into a fierce embrace.

Regina hardly remembered the walk back to the Jeep in the dark. She just remembered Alex handing her the keys and slumping down into the passenger seat, staring numbly out the window. She cast a couple of wary glances at Alex on the drive back to her condo and wondered what it had taken for the woman to confide in her.

Regina couldn't shake the image of Alex leaning against the tree, eyes closed, with tears running down her face. It was obvious that Alex had been deeply hurt by Lana's death and her involvement with Dana. It was as though a part of her had been destroyed and even now a piece of her was still missing.

Regina stepped out of the Jeep and tucked Alex's keys in

her pocket, firmly shaking her head as Alex reached her hand out for them.

"You're not driving home like this, Alex." Despite her protests, Regina took hold of Alex's arm and guided her to the condo. The blonde closed the door behind them and set the keys on the table.

Alex walked over to the couch and slumped down, resting her head in her hands.

"Alex, are you okay?" Regina walked over and sat down next to her, resting a hand on her knee. The brunette straightened her shoulders and pulled away from Regina. She never revealed to anyone what she told Regina tonight, and it left her feeling raw and vulnerable. She expected the woman to tell her to just get lost, and she wouldn't have blamed her if she had.

"Yeah, I'm fine." She mentally slammed the doors closed on the emotions. Alex stood up, avoiding Regina's eyes. "I'm sorry, Regina, I don't usually get like that. I should go." She started to walk away, looking for her keys.

"Alex, wait." Regina grasped Alex's hand, turned her palm over and brought it to her lips. She kissed the soft skin as she looked up at Alex's face, watching as the dark-haired woman closed her eyes, swaying slightly as she stood in the middle of the floor.

Regina stood up and ran her fingers lightly over Alex's lower lip. The taller woman leaned into Regina's touch, closing her own hand over the smaller one and resting her cheek against it. She stood silently, not trusting her voice.

"Stop running away from me," Regina whispered, wrapping her arms tightly around Alex's waist. "I want you to stay."

They held onto each other until Alex finally opened her eyes, and looked down into trusting green ones. Regina gently captured Alex's lips with her own. It was a long slow exploration, their desire building as they melted against each other's caresses.

Alex felt an electric current rush through her, followed by a sense of panic that she was doing the wrong thing. She didn't want to force Regina into anything she didn't feel comfortable with, and having made that mistake once already, she didn't intend to repeat it. The doctor broke off the kiss and gently unwrapped Regina's arms from around her waist. She leaned forward touching her forehead to Regina's.

"Oh God, you have no idea what you're doing to me."

"Then stay." Regina's hand drifted down and clasped Alex's hand.

"No, I should go, so you can get some sleep. We've got to be in early in the morning." Alex rubbed her back, enjoying the pressure of Regina's body against hers.

Regina picked her head up. "Alex, it's late. Just stay. Please?"

Alex regarded her quietly, then smiled, hanging her head. "I don't have any defense for you."

"You don't need one," Regina whispered and tugged her hand as she led her into the bedroom. She rummaged through one of her drawers and tossed a T-shirt to the doctor. "Here. You look good in them." She folded her arms over her chest and pursed her lips watching Alex's reaction. "Hmm, it was especially nice seeing you stand there by the sliding door."

"Y-You were awake?" She buried her face in the T-shirt and groaned audibly, remembering that morning in Provincetown. "Let me go get changed before I get into any more trouble."

When she returned from the bathroom, Regina was already curled up on the mattress, smiling as Alex approached the bed. She crawled into the bed and stretched out beside the blonde. "I can't believe you were awake," she whispered into Regina's ear.

Regina snickered and snuggled closer to her friend. "You're blushing."

"I am not," Alex growled, covering her eyes with her arm.

"You are too," Regina teased and pulled the blankets up over the both of them.

Alex smiled at the gentle banter and whispered back, "I am not."

"Give it up. You're busted and you know it." The blonde rubbed her hand over Alex's stomach. Alex covered her hand with her own and then closed her eyes. Regina watched Alex's breath deepen as she relaxed. "Alex?"

"What?" The doctor slowly opened her eyes and looked at the younger woman.

"Thanks for trusting me tonight. It means a lot to me that you do," Regina said, her eyes twinkling gently.

Alex stared at Regina incredulously. "I...um, you're welcome," she whispered, then reached up and turned off the light.

# Chapter 18

Regina finished changing into her scrubs and shut her locker. She slipped an elastic band from her wrist and pulled her damp hair back into a braid. She wasn't sure how she managed to wake up on time. Last night, she had lain awake in bed thinking for a long time after Alex had drifted off to sleep, emotionally exhausted from her confession.

Alex had held her firmly at arms' length for so long despite the attraction that they both felt. Regina smiled, knowing that last night had been a crossroads of sorts for them because the older woman had finally let her inside. She knew that, for Alex, there were few people who she trusted enough to let them get that close. It made her feel special.

The door swung open and Sandy bustled in, interrupting her thoughts.

"Hey, Regina." Sandy walked over to her locker and opened it. "What did you and Alex end up doing last night?"

Regina stared at Sandy's back for a few seconds before her brain finally kicked her mouth into gear. "Uh, we went for a walk."

"Yeah? Where'd you go?" Sandy asked, as she tugged her scrub top over her head.

Alarm bells sounded in Regina's head as she tried not to stammer.

"By the reservoir," Regina said, certain that her face was now three shades darker than when the conversation started. She turned around, opened her locker, and fished needlessly inside for an extra pen. "How's it look out there today? Busy?" she asked, hoping to change the conversation.

"Well, if it was going to be quiet, you just jinxed us for sure." Sandy winked at her and opened the door. "Oh, hi Alex. Have a nice walk last night?" She smiled impishly up at the attending and walked out into the department.

Alex looked at the closing door, then back at Regina's face. "Hi. You okay?"

"Yeah, I'm fine. I just need some coffee." Regina stifled a yawn. She wasn't sure what made her so uncomfortable about Sandy asking her about last night. Maybe it was just the fact that Sandy knew Tina and well, that's how stories got started around here.

The taller woman nodded at the white bag she set on the bench. She had extricated herself from Regina's embrace around five a.m. and kissed the blonde, telling her she would meet her at work. "I picked up a couple of cups at the diner. Milk and sugar."

Regina watched as Alex slipped out of her shirt, leaving well-toned upper body clad only in a sports bra. "Thanks, you didn't have to do that."

"I know." Alex pulled a set of scrubs from the pile on the cart. Quickly stripping out of the rest of her clothes she pulled on her scrub top. A wave of heat rushed through Regina's body as she watched from the bench.

Alex turned around as she pulled on the bottoms. Noticing the slightly unfocused look on Regina's face, she raised an eyebrow in question. "What's wrong?"

Regina shook her head. "Nothing, I, uh, oh boy." She quickly stood up and walked to the door feeling flustered by her reaction to seeing Alex undressing in front of her. "I need to go. I'm going to go check and see if we, uh, have any patients."

"What about your coffee?"

Regina turned, opened the door, and slipped out of the locker room, leaving Alex standing there wondering what she had just missed.

The resident didn't see Dr. Jameson bearing down on her until it was too late and she collided into him. The stack of folders he carried flew into the air and scattered across the floor in disarray.

"Oh, I'm sorry." Regina dropped quickly to her knee and scrambled to pick up the papers that dropped to the floor.

"Son of a bitch! Why don't you watch where the hell you're going next time?" he said as he rushed to pick everything up. He glared at her and yanked the papers quickly out of her hand.

Regina stood up and took a breath, watching him walk down the corridor and disappear around the corner. "Prick," she said under her breath and headed over to the nurse's station. Sandy looked up as Regina appeared in front of her. "God, is he always such a jerk?" Regina still felt stung by his obnoxious remark.

Sandy nodded her head. "He's got absolutely no social skills whatsoever. Don't waste your time on it. Hey, Marcus is down in room five. I think he could use a hand in there."

"What's he got?" Regina asked.

"A shoulder dislocation that he can't reduce," Sandy said. "The guy was screaming before Marcus even touched him."

Regina switched directions and headed down the hallway, grateful for the chance to be busy with a patient. Marcus looked up at Regina as she walked into the room and gave her a pathetically relieved smile. "Regina, I can't reduce his shoulder. He fell off a ladder and popped it out when he landed on the ground."

Regina walked up to the stretcher and peered down at the man. "Hi, I'm Dr. Kingston. What's your name?"

"Thomas." He looked Regina up and down, his eyes widening. "You said you were getting help, Doc." He looked at Marcus, a worried look on his face. "She's half your size. What's she going to be able to do if you can't yank it back into place?"

Regina gave him a wry smile. She pulled on a pair of gloves. "You look like you play football."

"Yeah," he said, watching her warily as she filled a needle with medication.

"What position?" Regina asked.

"Linebacker."

"Hold still. I'm giving you some more muscle relaxant." He winced as the needle pierced his skin. "So what were you doing up on a ladder so early today?" Regina asked, glancing up at Marcus giving him a knowing look, as she threw the needle in the sharps container. "Thomas, I want you to roll over and hang your arm off the edge of the table. Marcus, get me a sandbag so I can weight his arm down."

"Is it going to hurt a lot?" he asked.

Regina sat on the floor and crossed her legs. "Probably when the joint slips back in place. Okay, Thomas, I'm going to strap this weight around your wrist." She took the sandbag that Marcus handed to her.

"Now what?" Thomas said, looking down at Regina.

Regina smiled up at him. "Tom, this will go a lot easier if you trust me." Regina took hold of his arm after a few minutes and turned it slowly back and forth. She felt a subtle pop as the joint slid back into place. "Okay, that should do it. Marcus, let me know what the post-reduction film looks like."

❖ ⌘ ❖ ⌘ ❖ ⌘ ❖

Alex walked into the conference room and spotted Jon sitting at the other end of the table. She walked over and slipped into the chair next to him. "Hi. How's Chris doing?"

"Tired and she's pulling a double shift today," he said, reaching across the table for a donut.

Alex surveyed the table. "Oh great, Jameson calls us in here so we can listen to another drug rep. Wonderful. Like we don't have better things to do with our time."

"How do you know it's a drug rep?" Jon asked, wiping the white powder from his lips.

"Who else comes in here and plies us with this crap?" She pointed at the pile of donuts on the table, then crossed her arms and tilted her head so she could peer under the table. She spied a brown box and reached out with her foot, tilting it toward her. "Uh, huh. A whole box of samples to give out."

Jon shook his head. "Alex, you are getting too cynical in your old age."

Alex sat back in her chair, her eyes narrowing as Dr. Jameson walked into the room smiling and laughing with the woman beside him.

"Thanks for inviting me, Dr. Jameson." She smiled and looked around the room as he took his seat. "Hi everyone. My name is Donna Sanders."

Jon turned his head and rolled his eyes at Alex as the bubbly personality standing in front of them, dressed in a snug-fitting pant suit, launched into her monologue. Across the room, a beeper shrilled noisily and the medical director fumbled with the one on his belt in irritation, finally silencing it after several seconds.

"I know you're all really busy so I won't keep you long." The rep breezed through several minutes of research about a new drug she wanted the doctors to try for their trauma patients.

Alex settled back in her chair and crossed her arms, her mind wandering far from the meeting. A smile played at her lips as her mind conjured up an image of one blonde-haired petite woman smiling at her. Jon leaned over and discreetly nudged her elbow.

"Care to let me in on what's so amusing?" he whispered.

The dark-haired woman turned her head slowly and raised an eyebrow.

"Okay, I'll take that as a no," he said quietly and went back to listening to the woman at the head of the table.

The woman dug through her leather briefcase and pulled out a thick file that she set on the table.

"Dr. Margulies, I was wondering if you could look at something for me?"

Alex lifted her head and met challenging brown eyes staring back at her. "I'm sorry, I didn't get your name." She leaned forward in her chair, folding her hands loosely on the table.

"Donna. Donna Sanders," the woman replied impatiently.

Alex nodded her head. The tension in the room rose palpably as Dr. Jameson shot her a warning look from across the table. *What are you up to now, Jim?*

"What's your question, Ms. Sanders?"

The drug representative opened the file and pulled out several packets of paper. "I was wondering why your team of doctors haven't been using this medication on your trauma patients who are at risk for cardiac complications in this emergency department."

Alex raised an eyebrow and reached her arm out across the table. "May I?" She smiled easily up at the woman and took the file from her. She scanned down a list of names. Most of them were patients that had been treated over the second and third quarters of the year in the emergency department. She recognized several by the primary diagnosis and detailed medical history printed on the sheets. Her irritation growing at the presumptuous attitude, Alex shoved the papers over to Jon and picked up the file containing the research.

"Dr. Margulies?" The drug rep leaned forward on the table, watching with interest.

Alex scanned the data quickly, set the file down on the table

and closed it. She looked up, her eyes narrowing as she focused
on the adversary standing across from her.

"Ms. Sanders, this..." Alex looked down at the folder in disgust and shoved it back across the table to her, "...research isn't
worth the paper it's written on. For one thing, there aren't
enough subjects for it to be statistically relevant *and* a first-year
med student could put together a better research model than your
staff did."

"That research has been backed up by the AMA," the rep
defended testily.

Alex laughed. "Really? In what journal? Oh, and let me
guess, T&M funded the research trials? From what I've read,
that medication is useful on a very small population and there
are no independent trials that have proven that its benefits out-
weigh the complications of prolonged use, which the FDA
reports is longer than twenty-four hours." She stood up and ran
her fingers along the surface of the table as she stepped closer to
the woman. "Tell me, Ms. Sanders, who's paying who for the list
of patient names from our ER?" Alex glared at Dr. Jameson as
she said this.

The woman's face reddened and her body stiffened at the
accusation. "That is perfectly legal. You know that pharmaceutical benefit management firms approve every drug a patient
takes. It's in our database."

"Legal or not," Alex was face to face with the woman now,
"I think these patients would find it rather embarrassing to know
that some stranger knows the intimate details of their medical
history, all for the sake of making a profit. I find that offensive.
Why don't you come back when you have something of rele-
vance to discuss?" She stalked out, leaving the rest of the room
in stunned silence.

She was halfway down the hall when Jon jogged up beside
her. "Jesus, Alex, are you trying to make enemies in there?"

She turned to him, still bristling at the brazenness of the
drug rep. "Do yourself a favor, Jon. Stay out of whatever scheme
Jameson has going on."

"I'm with you, Alex, but be careful. Jameson is already gunning for you. All you did was just piss him off more."

"So let him." She took a breath and shook her head, letting
go of some of her anger.

The door from the conference room banged open behind
them and Dr. Jameson stormed past the two doctors. He stopped

mid-stride and whirled around, glaring up at Alex. "This isn't over by a long shot, Alex. I'm still the medical director here."

"Then act like it." She pushed open the stairwell door and looked back at Jon. "I'll catch up to you later. I'm covering the clinic this afternoon."

❖ ⌘ ❖ ⌘ ❖ ⌘ ❖

Aside from the normal minor accidents, mostly bumps and bruises, the day had been relatively quiet so far. Regina finished the paperwork for the man she treated earlier. He was in surgery now, having his index finger reattached after a run in with a lawn mower and a stick that was stuck in the blades. The resident looked up at the clock and realized that it was late in the afternoon. She had yet to see Alex since their meeting in the locker room. She walked down the hallway toward the nurse's station, hoping to find her.

Sandy was busy talking to a doctor at the other end of the room. Regina turned around and noticed a man standing at the desk holding a clipboard, looking lost and definitely out of place in his suit and tie.

He smiled, obviously relieved when he saw Regina approaching him. She groaned inwardly, hoping that this wasn't another drug rep peddling their newest, latest concoction.

"Hi, my name's Dean. Is Dr. Jameson around?"

"I don't know. I can have him paged, if you want," Regina said, more than happy to pawn him off on someone else.

"That would be great. I have some new IV pumps he wanted to use in the department. I just need his signature to release them to him."

The unit clerk looked up at Regina. "I got it, Dr. Kingston." She picked up the phone and dialed the number. "Hi. I need Dr. Jameson paged to the ER. Thanks." She hung up the phone and looked at the man. "If he's in he'll call back."

Regina returned to her work, pulling up some lab reports on the computer, writing out discharge orders for two of her patients, and calling radiology to check on another she sent down earlier for tests. She was aware of Dean fidgeting as he stood by the desk, looking nervous and checking his watch periodically.

"Excuse me." He leaned over the desk. "Do you think you could page him again? I have another client I have to meet with and I don't want to be late."

Regina looked up from the computer and glanced over at the clock. This was sure to piss their medical director off, paging him twice in less than fifteen minutes. "I'd give him some more time."

Two minutes later the ER doors banged open at the other end of the hallway. Dr. Jameson stormed toward the desk. "Who the hell paged me out of my meeting?" He ignored the startled glances he got from the staff and patients alike as he marched past the crowded waiting room.

Regina watched as his nostrils flared and the pupils dilated as he shifted into overdrive. *Oh shit.* "He needs a signature to release these pumps to you." She pointed at the rep standing across from the desk.

"Dr. Kingston, don't you know anybody could have signed for these goddamn pumps. What are you, stupid?" he shouted at the resident, leaning over the desk at her.

Regina stepped back, staring in shock at the doctor's outburst.

"Damn residents," he cursed. "None of you can make a decision without someone holding your hand."

Sandy leaned across the desk. "Why don't you shut your mouth before you have every patient in the waiting room out here watching your performance."

"Stay out of it," he snapped at her.

"Uh, Dr. Jameson." The rep tried desperately to intervene. "You probably just don't remember. You said you were the only one who could sign for these."

"That's ridiculous. I can't believe you people would pull me out of a meeting to come down here and sign for this crap." He grabbed the clipboard out of the rep's hands and hastily scrawled his signature on the sheet, ripping the edge of the paper with the force of his pen.

Slamming his hand down on the counter, he glared at Regina. "Next time, sign for the pumps your—" He never finished his sentence as a look of utter shock came over his face. His jaw worked and his hand gripped the chest-high counter, his knuckles whitening as he held on for support. His eyelids fluttered closed and Regina could see the whites of his eyes as they rolled back up into his head.

"What the...? Ah, shit." Sandy jumped to her feet and darted past the desk.

"Get out of the way." Regina scrambled around a chair, pushing the drug rep out of the way. She grabbed Dr. Jameson around his waist, as he started an awkward slide down to the cold tile floor. Regina staggered back under his weight, trying unsuccessfully to let him down slowly. She scooted around to his shoulders and shook him roughly. "Dr. Jameson?" His eyes fluttered open and for a moment he focused on her. Then the light faded out of brown eyes, leaving them flat and lifeless. Regina felt for his carotid pulse in his neck. She closed her eyes, willing her own heart to stop racing so she could concentrate on feeling for his heart beat. She shook her head and bent closer over his mouth, listening and feeling for air. *Damn.* "Sandy! Get the crash cart, now!"

"Do you have a pulse?" The nurse started backpedaling down the hall.

"No. No pulse, no respirations," Regina called out to her. *Son of a bitch, I can't believe this is happening.* She tilted his head back and pressed her mouth over his, pinching off his nose and giving him two breaths. She slid down to his chest and pumped on his chest.

"C-can I do anything?" the rep asked, bending over her.

Regina glanced up at his face, as she kept pressing down on the medical director's sternum. "Yeah, go sit down and put your head between your knees." *I don't need you passing out, too.* She scooted back up to Dr. Jameson's head and blew air twice more into his lungs.

Sandy pulled the cart up beside them. "I'll get a twelve lead on him." She ripped open his shirt, popping the buttons off and scattering them across the floor. The nurse slapped the leads and wires onto his chest, then flipped the portable monitor on and waited for it to pick up the rhythm of his heart. "Stop compressions."

Regina sat back on her heels and grabbed the bag mask resuscitator off the top of the cart. She looked at the nurse's station and found the unit clerk staring down at them in shock.

"Call a code. We need help down here." She looked back up at the monitor. "Shit, he's in V-fib." Regina watched the rhythm on the monitor that told her the chambers of his heart were contracting ineffectively, his blood pooling uselessly there. "Give me the paddles and charge to 200 joules." Sandy squirted the gel on and rubbed them together, handing them to Regina. She waited until the machine charged. "Clear!"

Regina leaned over and depressed the buttons. The high-pitched whine of electricity powered through the cables and the medical director's body convulsed on the floor as the counter shock tried to get the heart to start beating normally. A door slammed open and she heard footsteps running down the hallway from behind her.

Alex crouched down on the floor beside her. "What happened?" she asked looking up at the monitor and studying the rhythm.

"He was yelling and then he just went down," Sandy explained.

"Sandy, we need an IV line hook-up and a blood gas."

"Got it." She handed Alex the setup from the cart.

Alex bent over the doctor and snapped rubber tubing around his upper arm. "Someone, get these people out of here. We don't need an audience," Alex ordered as she saw several family members walking hesitantly toward the commotion on the floor. She jabbed the vessel with the needle, and took the line from Sandy and piggybacked it to the IV catheter.

Regina watched as the rhythm of the heart on the monitor fluctuated and then fell back into ventricular fibrillation. She turned the knob to 260 joules. "Clear."

Alex sat back on her heels and lifted her hands away from the body.

Placing the paddles on the already reddened areas of his chest, Regina depressed the buttons and watched as the electricity shocked the heart briefly out of its near-fatal rhythm. "Shit, come on, don't you do this." Regina charged the machine to 300 joules and shocked him again.

Setting the paddles down, the resident yanked open the drawers on the code cart and pulled out an ET tube. "I've shocked him three times and he's still in V-fib."

"Give me one milligram of epinephrine." Alex held her hand out for the syringe.

Regina tilted his head back and opened his mouth. Inserting the scope, she slid the ET tube down into the trachea. "It's in. Bag him."

"I've got it," Dr. Torres said breathlessly as he knelt down next to Regina. He heard the code being called just as he sat down to eat in the cafeteria. The doctor took the bag and rhythmically squeezed it. More footsteps came running down the corridor as the rest of the code team arrived.

"Charging at 360." Regina leaned over Dr. Jameson's chest. "Clear!" She depressed the buttons and shocked him again. Over the clamor of voices and the chaos around them as other patients were brought into the ER, they went through the same sequence three more times. After the third defibrillation and an injection of lidocaine, they finally managed to get a normal rhythm on the monitor.

Alex looked up at the crowd of faces, mostly junior residents and interns that always responded in code situations. She pointed at one of them. "You, go get a stretcher and make yourself useful. Somebody call the cardiac unit. Tell them we need a bed now."

No one moved. They stared in shock at the medical director lying splayed out on the floor, covered in wires and IV tubing. Alex pulled herself up to her full height. "I said move. Now!"

They scattered hurriedly. Alex stared back down at the floor littered with bloody gauze, ampoules of medication, and packages of medical instruments. "Sandy, find out what attending is covering the cardiac service tonight and tell them to get them in here now."

Several of the junior residents lifted the limp body of Dr. Jameson up onto the stretcher.

"Let's get him up to the CCU now," Alex said, as she slipped a portable cardiac monitor onto the stretcher and hooked the leads to it. "We've got it." She looked at Dr. Torres.

He turned the bag mask resuscitator over to Regina, who took over squeezing the bag as she pulled the stretcher and Alex pushed from behind. They stopped at the elevator and waited, neither saying anything as the shock of the whole situation settled on them. The doors opened and several staff members turned around laughing and joking amongst themselves.

"Off, now. We need the elevator," Alex said, motioning with her head. The laughter ended abruptly and they filed quickly out to either side of the stretcher.

"Thanks," Regina said quietly, as one of the nurses looked up at her. The doors slid closed behind them and Alex punched the button for the third floor.

She looked down at the monitor, checking the rhythm, and then back up at Regina. "You okay?" she asked, seeing the haggard look on Regina's face.

Regina nodded her head and went to move her hair back off her face until she saw the blood on her hands. She made a face

and wiped them off on her scrubs. "One minute he's standing
there screaming at us because of some stupid IV pumps and the
next," she spread her hands out in a helpless gesture, "he just
gets this weird look on his face and goes down."

Alex looked up as the door opened. She leaned back and
pulled the stretcher out of the elevator. It was a short walk down
the corridor and through the glass doors, onto the critical care
unit. Alex waited at the desk as Regina wrote a note in the medical record. She hesitated before she leaned over and touched her
shoulder. "I'll meet you downstairs while you finish up here.
I've got to make some phone calls."

❖ ⌘ ❖ ⌘ ❖ ⌘ ❖

An hour later, Regina still felt numb as she pushed the door
open and walked into the ER department. The evidence of the
chaos that took place earlier was gone except for a small group
of staff standing at the back of the department talking in hushed
tones.

Sandy walked up to Regina as she neared the desk. "How is
he?"

"Alive. He's got an eighty percent blockage in three of his
arteries. They're going to take him down to the OR and do a tri-
ple bypass."

Sandy stood beside the resident. "You okay?"

"Yeah, just great. I guess I need to finish seeing my
patients." Regina looked up at the board and noticed that most of
the patients she had been treating before were gone. "Hey, who
took my patients?"

"Jon and Alex."

Regina walked down the hall and stuck her head into one of
the rooms. "Hey, you didn't have to finish all my patients,
Alex."

"I didn't. Jon and I split them. We needed the beds." She
finished tying off a knot on the leg wound she stitched closed.
"Don't worry, you didn't miss much. Two head lacerations and
this one," she nodded at the man lying passed out on the
stretcher, "kicked in a plate glass window." She took the scissors
and cut the silk thread. Alex looked up at Regina. "How is he?"

Regina shrugged her shoulders and repeated what she told
Sandy earlier.

Alex nodded her head impassively. "Our shift's over. You

want to get something to eat? I'm almost done here."

"That's the best offer I've heard all day," Regina said. A warm thrill passed through her as the tired blue eyes lit up and a radiant smile flashed back at her.

❖ ⌘ ❖ ⌘ ❖ ⌘ ❖

The diner was crowded and noisy, so they ordered Chinese take-out instead. They were both off tomorrow, the first time all week, and neither cared about staying up late.

"Hey, I know a great spot where you can see the New York City skyline. You interested?"

"Let's go." Regina chuckled, knowing that Alex couldn't stand being around crowds of people for long, especially after a hectic day in the hospital.

True to form, Alex drove on a winding, narrow one-way road that led up to a vacant parking lot. They walked over to a couple of benches and settled down next to each other to eat. It was a clear night and they could see the skyline lit up from across the river.

Alex leaned back, stretching her long legs out in front of her and crossed her ankles. "You did good in there, today."

Regina finished chewing her egg roll and swallowed. "Thanks. I don't think I'd want to be in that position too often. It's very surreal working on someone you know."

"Mm." Alex turned her head and regarded the blonde. "Have you heard anything from your parents?"

Regina shook her head. "I talked to Jeff yesterday. He wants to come out here for the holidays and bring Darryl with him."

"So you could spend the holiday with part of your family." Alex glanced at the blonde, who was chuckling. "What's so funny?"

"I was just thinking about you, meeting my brother."

"Is that a problem?"

"No, except that I think he thinks you're a guy."

"What? You told him about me?"

"Kind of. I called him when we got suspended to ask his advice and he just made the assumption. I didn't correct him and at the time it didn't seem that important."

Alex snorted and slumped lower on the bench. "Didn't seem important, humph."

"At the time, it didn't seem important," Regina corrected

and poked her playfully in the side, trying to keep the conversation from getting too serious.

Alex grabbed her hand and kept Regina from trying to tickle her again. "Is it important, now?"

"You mean telling my brother about us? I think it is," Regina replied softly.

"Why's that?" Alex leaned closer, and her lips grazed Regina's ear.

The blonde closed her eyes and gasped softly as Alex slipped her arm under her jacket and pulled her closer. "I can't concentrate with you doing that," Regina protested weakly.

"Do you want me to stop?" Alex stopped nibbling on her earlobe and pulled back to look at her.

"No," came the breathless reply.

"So, why is it important now?" She asked as her lips moved softly over the exposed skin on Regina's neck.

"Oh, I...God, I can't believe we're doing this on a park bench."

"There's no one around besides us and a few animals." Alex chuckled and rubbed her cheek against Regina's. "You haven't answered my question, yet." Her hands started a gentle rhythmic stroking of her back.

"I-I care about you, Alex." Her hands slid around Alex's neck as she pulled her closer. "I don't know where this is going, but I know how I feel inside."

Alex backed off and rested her forehead against Regina's. "I care about you, too, but I...I'm scared," she admitted.

"Don't be scared, Alex. This feels incredible." Regina lifted the dark woman's face and smiled before she leaned up and placed a slow, lingering kiss on her lips.

They sat there quietly absorbing the warmth from each other's body as their heart rates and ragged breathing returned to normal. Alex broke the companionable silence.

"So, what are you doing tomorrow?"

Regina hugged her gently, burying her head in Alex's black leather jacket. She inhaled the rich smell of the leather and smiled at the vague sense of familiarity. "Try to do everything that I should have done this week but haven't. How about you?"

"The same and then I have to head over to the hospital and do some things in Dr. Jameson's office that he hadn't gotten to today."

"Want some company?" Regina glanced up at the pale blue

eyes looking back at her.

❖ ⌘ ❖ ⌘ ❖ ⌘ ❖

Later the next day, the doctor sat behind the medical director's desk, her dark hair hanging loosely around her shoulders. She looked forlornly at the scattered piles of medical journals, discharged patient records, and stacks of paper littering the small office. *Great. How the hell am I supposed to find anything in this disaster area?* With a resigned sigh, she set to work on organizing the office. She found the partially completed budget for the emergency department that was already long overdue, and finished it. As she completed her work, she glanced out the window, her thoughts drifting easily to a more pleasant subject.

It had been a long time since Alex had someone that she shared similar views with, not just about treating patients, although through their work they did have a lot in common. There was a connection that she felt with Regina, something intangible, but nevertheless there, and she liked the way it made her feel.

A knock came at the door and Alex pulled herself out of her daydream. A now familiar face peered back at her from the doorway.

"Hi." Alex's face brightened and she stood up from the chair, stretching the kinks out of her tall frame.

Regina pushed off the doorframe and held out a bag. "Here, I figured you could use some food by now. You probably haven't stopped to eat anything all day."

"You didn't have to do this, Regina." Alex leaned against the desk, peering inside the bag. "Thanks," she added softly.

She'd never been comfortable with anyone doing things for her; usually it meant they were looking for something in return. Alex was slowly learning that this was not the case with Regina, it was just who she was. Alex pulled out the container and opened it. She looked at Regina in surprise. "You cooked this?"

A blush spread over Regina's face and she turned away to hide it. "Yeah. When was the last time you ate something other than cafeteria or take-out food?"

Alex chuckled. "Good point. Wow, this is really good," she said, in between bites of the pasta.

"God, this office is a mess." Regina leaned on the desk, looking around in disgust.

Alex nodded as she swallowed another mouthful of food. "I already spent two hours sorting through junk. Do you know anyplace where I can rent a fork lift?"

Covering her face with her hand, Regina snickered. "You want some help going through the rest of this stuff?" She motioned with her hand at the waist-high stacks of dust-covered journals.

"Sure. Why don't you start over there?" Alex pointed to a pile of journals in the corner of the office. "Anything over two years, just throw it out. The medical library has copies anyway."

They worked side by side for several hours, sorting through outdated journals and filling several garbage cans with trash. At one point, Regina looked up to see Alex folding up a piece of paper into an airplane. Sitting back, she watched quietly as Alex, totally engrossed in what she was doing, creased the folds into the paper, inspected her work carefully and then raised her arm up for a test flight. Their eyes met and the look of surprise on Alex's face made Regina think of a little kid getting caught with her hand in the proverbial cookie jar.

"I...uh." Alex cleared her throat and looked down at the paper plane. "Just some stupid game my brother and I used to play when we were kids." She shrugged her shoulders and tossed the plane into the air. It arced lazily upward, looped once and then spiraled toward the floor, coasting out into the hallway.

Regina's eyes lit up as she watched it then she scrambled quickly to her feet and retrieved it from the floor. Standing in the empty hallway, she tossed the airplane into the air. It flew upward and then spiraled down to the floor, hitting nose first.

Alex followed her out, watching as the plane hit the ground, crumpling its nose. "Hey, you busted my plane," she protested, pushing out her lower lip into a pout. She bent over and picked up the paper plane.

Regina looked up, her eyes widening and then she burst into laughter at the comical expression on Alex's face. "I think we can fix it," she assured the older woman. Regina took the plane from Alex, smoothed the nose out with her fingers, and handed it back to her. "How's that?"

Alex took the plane, looking quickly down the empty hallway in both directions. With a glint of mischief in her eyes, she turned Regina around, put the plane in her hand and stood behind her. Regina's body reacted instantly to the sensation of Alex's strong hands on her hips as she leaned back into Alex's body.

"Like this," Alex said, as she pulled Regina's arm back. "Let go when I tell you. Now." Regina released the plane and watched as it looped twice and spiraled halfway down the corridor before it glided silently to the floor.

"Wow," Regina whispered, referring more to her sensations than the plane's graceful flight.

The more rational and logical side of Alex's brain tapped her soundly on the shoulder. *What the hell is wrong with you? Christ, all you need is one of those ultra-conservative, highly starched executives to walk down the hall and you'll both be history.* "Uh, yeah. I think I should get back to this stuff. I still have a lot to get through." Alex quickly turned away and ducked back into the office, still berating herself for acting so silly around Regina.

Regina let the erotic sensation fade before she finally moved and trotted down the hallway. Retrieving the plane, she smiled as she held it in her hands, wondering if Alex realized how much of herself she revealed when she let her guard down like this. She walked back into the office and set the plane on the desk.

"You didn't tell me you had a brother, Alex." Regina went back to sorting through journals, noticing that Alex tensed briefly before she answered.

"I guess it just never came up before."

"What's his name?" Regina asked, trying not to sound like she was prying. She wanted to know more about Alex's family but it was like pulling teeth to get her talk about herself.

"John."

Regina considered asking Alex another question but decided she would leave it for another time. "So how long do you think Dr. Jameson is going to be out?" Alex relaxed visibly in her chair. Regina smiled, congratulating herself for backing off when she did.

"If all goes well, I imagine somewhere between six weeks and three months."

"Mm. Housekeeping is going to love this," Regina commented as she stood up and dragged another overflowing container into the hallway.

Alex grinned and crumpled a piece of paper in her hand and tossed it at Regina.

"There's more for your collection," she teased, as Regina caught it and flipped it into the can. Alex set to work on another pile on the floor, sorting through papers. Her hands stilled and she stared down at the documents.

"Aw, shit."

"What's wrong?" Regina wiped her hands on her jeans, leaving two dusty handprints on her thighs. She walked over and knelt down beside Alex, peering over her shoulder.

Alex threw them down on the floor and cursed again. She stood up and paced the office.

Regina picked the papers up and read them, a frown creasing her brow. "Alex, I don't understand. I thought all the research projects going on in the hospital had to be approved by the research committee."

Alex stopped pacing and stood with her hands on her hips. "You're right." She pointed at the papers Regina held. "Apparently, he's got a deal going with this drug company. Every time he dispenses this medication to a patient, he writes a note about the effectiveness of the treatment, even if it isn't." She snorted derisively. "If that's what you want to call it. And then they pay him."

"Didn't you tell me he did this before?" Regina sat back on her heels still looking up at Alex.

Alex nodded her head, staring down at the floor. *Talk about stepping in shit.* She turned to Regina, her eyes darkening with anger. "That son of a bitch. No wonder he was so hot to get me out of here. He knew if I found this, I could bury him this time."

Regina watched as Alex paced back and forth across the office. "Alex, what are you going to do?"

"Well, that depends. I could report him to Office of Investigations for medical malpractice and fraud or I could let the hospital handle it. Either way, he's screwed."

"Alex, couldn't you go to him and tell him what you found?"

"What for? So he could try and weasel his way out of what he's been doing?"

Regina stood up and held the papers out to Alex. "No, so he has the opportunity to come clean about it and let the hospital handle it how it sees fit."

Her mind raced through everything that Jameson had put her through over the past year. *You don't owe that bastard anything. You know he would fry anyone in the emergency department for much less than this.* Alex stared back at Regina, her jaw clenching and unclenching as she considered her options. "Why would you want to go easy on him? He tried to suspend your privileges as well."

"Who says it's going easy on him? If he won't admit to what he's done, then go to the medical committee. He's going to end up losing either way. Let the committee be judge and jury, not you."

Alex contemplated Regina's words. It would be sweet to even the score with Jameson, with a very public humiliation. The bastard certainly deserved it for what he had put her through. Then again, Regina had a point. She could still make sure Jameson was punished for getting monetary kickbacks from a drug company. She'd just let him hang himself in his own good time.

Alex hastily retrieved the papers from Regina and locked them in one of the file cabinets. "I'll talk with him when he's out of the hospital."

# Chapter
# 19

It took several weeks of wading through old medical records and reviewing the files in Dr. Jameson's office for Alex to learn how long he had been involved in this scam. She had known something was wrong when the drug representative handed her the list of patient names at the meeting several months ago. The attending slowed to a halt as she approached the medical director's office, noticing that the door was ajar and the light was on.

"I didn't expect to see you back here so soon." She leaned against the doorframe and crossed her arms, holding the large envelope against her chest. She looked at the pale and gaunt visage of the doctor whose post she temporarily occupied.

"Did you think I'd let you run this department for one minute longer than I needed to?" Dr. Jameson asked coldly from behind his desk.

For a long tense moment their eyes locked, then the medical director returned to rummaging through the piles of paper that were stacked on his desk. "At least you did a half decent job of cleaning up in here."

"Really? You look like you're having trouble finding something." Alex stepped inside the office and shut the door. *Good thing I made copies of everything I found last week.*

The medical director sat back in his chair and regarded the dark-haired woman. "What do you want, Margulies?"

Alex lowered herself into a chair and crossed her long, mus-

cular legs. "I thought I might give you an opportunity to explain
this to me." She handed him a three-inch thick folder that she
pulled out of the envelope. "These are all patients you gave that
new cardiac drug to in the emergency department. There're at
least twenty that should have never received it. They simply just
don't fit the protocol for it." She waited as the doctor flipped
through the medical records.

"It's experimental. What's your point?" He threw the file on
his desk in irritation.

"It's a pretty simple concept, actually. You prescribed medication that wasn't appropriate, simply because this drug company was willing to pay you for using its products."

"You don't have any proof." The medical director shifted
uncomfortably in his seat, his eyes darting nervously from
Alex's face.

"Actually, I have enough proof to bury you and that woman
you brought in here peddling those drugs. Here, why don't you
take a look?" Alex stood up and upended the envelope onto his
desk, showering it with checks and vouchers for free airline
miles that had been in the top drawer of the doctor's desk. She
smirked at the look of panic on Jameson face. *This is bad; I'm
enjoying this way too much.*

"What the hell do you want?" Dr. Jameson asked, wiping a
hand nervously across his mouth.

Leaning on her hands, she towered over the doctor. "Funny
you should ask. I want you to go to Dr. Mitchard and the medical
review committee and tell them exactly what you did. You jeop-
ardized patients' health for the sake of making money, you bastard."

"What, are you nuts? I-I'll lose my license," he stammered.

Alex shrugged indifferently. "You should have thought
about that before you got involved with this crap again. At the
least, they'll probably turn it over to the Office of Investigations. From there, who knows?"

"What makes you think I'm going to tell them anything?"

"Because if you don't, I will, Jim. It's your choice. Your
chances of getting leniency are a hell of a lot better if you report
yourself than if I do it."

The medical director sat back in his chair and looked at the
pile of papers littering his desk. "You know I could make this
worth your while, Alex. There's a bank account I have here." He
fumbled through his desk and pulled out a folder. "You could

take everything that's in it and we could just forget about all this." He waved his arms over the desk.

Alex shook her head. "Not interested. You've got a day to make up your mind, Jim. After that, I'll go to Dr. Mitchard myself." Alex leaned over and picked up the folder containing the bank account. "I'll just hold onto this along with everything else I have. Remember, you've got one day." Alex walked to the door. "Oh, by the way, if you're interested, you can thank Dr. Kingston for saving your life."

Not waiting for an answer, Alex walked out into the hallway and bypassed the elevator. She ran down the stairs and burst into the ER.

She spotted Sandy coming out of one of the trauma rooms and fell into step alongside the nurse. "Have you seen Regina?"

"Yeah, she's in room four." Sandy looked up at Alex suspiciously. "What's up with you, that you're in such a hurry?"

"I promised to do something for her and I'm late." Alex slipped quietly into the room, leaving Sandy standing in the hallway with a perplexed look on her face. Peering around the curtain, she saw Regina sitting on a stool, leaning over the counter. "Regina?"

She heard the muffled curse, as the resident set the syringe down and glared back at her. "Alex, I wish you wouldn't sneak up on me like that."

"I wasn't sneaking," Alex protested, then walked up beside her and rested a hand on her shoulder.

"If I don't hear you, then yes, you are sneaking."

The attending chuckled softly as she looked down into the fiery green eyes. "Why didn't you wait for me? I told you I'd do this." Alex took the band from around Regina's arm.

"I didn't want to bother you."

Alex sighed and looked down at Regina fondly. "You are not bothering me. Don't you know that by now?" She took the syringe from the Regina and looked for another vein in her arm.

Regina's smile reached her eyes, making them shine brighter than they normally did. "Did you talk to Dr. Jameson?

"Yeah, I told him he could tell the board himself or I would do it for him."

"So, what did he say?" Regina winced as the needle pierced her skin.

"Sorry," Alex said, glancing up at her quickly. "He offered me his bank account to keep quiet."

"He what?"

"It's in that folder. Ah, ah, hold still or you're going to have one heck of a bruise. There." She slipped the vial on and watched as it filled with blood. "Okay, all done."

Regina picked up the folder and opened it, her eyes widening as she read what was inside. "Holy shit. That's a lot of money."

Alex looked down at the tube of blood she held. "Yeah, can you imagine how many people he gave these drugs to make that amount? I think what we found was just the tip of the iceberg." Alex took a breath. "Let me get started running the tests for you." She looked at Regina's face, her heart skipping a beat at the eyes brimming with tears. "Hey, are you okay?"

Regina lowered her eyes. "I'm sorry. I can't believe how nervous I am."

"Hey, none of that, now. You've made it this far." Alex moved closer and wrapped her arms tightly around the smaller woman. "Whatever happens, I'll be here. You know that, right?"

Regina leaned into Alex, resting her head against her side. "I know."

Alex slipped her hand under Regina's chin, lifting her face up to hers. "As soon as I know anything, I'll find you." She pulled Regina into a quick hug, let her go, and disappeared out of the exam room.

❖ ⌘ ❖ ⌘ ❖ ⌘ ❖

Regina walked into the staff lounge and slumped down onto the creaky, old, vinyl-covered couch. She was exhausted after being at the hospital for forty-eight hours straight. Her shift was long over and she should have been home sleeping in her bed many hours ago. Instead, Mother Nature had alternate plans, engulfing the whole east coast in a major winter storm, dumping close to three feet of snow from North Carolina to Massachusetts overnight. All the medical and ancillary staff that were on duty at the medical center the day before had been mandated to stay until the state of emergency was lifted and the rest of the employees could get to work. Curling up on the couch, Regina settled down for a quick nap. The door opened and she cracked one eye open, watching as Sandy walked in and collapsed unceremoniously into an old, orange, vinyl chair.

"I don't think I've ever seen this much snow before."

Regina tilted her head back and yawned. "I looked out a couple of hours ago. I couldn't see the tops of the steps down to the parking lot."

Overtired from lack of sleep and too much caffeine, Sandy giggled. "Forget about getting your car out, it'll be plowed in for days."

"You haven't heard from Alex, have you?" Regina asked, pulling her lab coat around her.

"No, she was scheduled off today and tomorrow." Sandy sat up straighter suddenly more alert. "What is up with you two, anyway?"

Regina scrunched down against the back of the couch, folding her arms across her chest. "We're friends, Sandy."

"Oh please, spare me." Sandy waved a dismissive hand in the air. "I've been there, Regina, ten years. I tell you, I know the signs." Sandy turned the chair around and propped her feet up on the couch, cutting off any chance for escape that Regina might have been considering.

"What do you mean, you know?" Regina resorted to closing her eyes against the probing look she was getting from Sandy.

"Listen, I know what Alex has been through in the past year and I'll tell you I haven't seen her look as happy as she does than when she's around you, my friend."

Regina hung her head, hiding the heated blush she felt on her face. "Come on, Sandy."

"You don't believe me? I swear, I'm going to throttle you both. Let me tell you something. Alex does not, I repeat, does not allow herself to take a personal interest in any of the residents she works with. So you tell me then why she's taken you home when you were sick, personally taken care of your lab tests, and resigned her position three months ago so that Jameson wouldn't go after you?"

Sandy dropped her feet onto the floor and leaned forward, looking into stunned green eyes. "Didn't know that, did you? Well, don't tell Alex I ever told you that because she'd kill me if she knew." Sandy stood up and stretched. "I'll see you later, Doc. Get some sleep." She left the young resident sitting in the lounge alone with her thoughts.

Sandy walked out into the hallway and spotted Alex coming through the door. *Next...*

"Hey boss, what are you doing here today?" Sandy smirked, knowing Alex hated when she called her that. She coined her

new title the day after she found out the doctor was appointed
acting medical director of the emergency department and had
taken every opportunity to tease her about it.

Alex stomped her boots off inside the door and shook the
snow from her hair, pointedly ignoring Sandy's comment. "Figured I come in and help out. They held over the staff from last
night. Right?"

Sandy nodded her head. "Yeah, we're all pulling double
shifts until they lift the snow emergency. It's been dead here
anyway. No patients are coming in and none are going home.
Speaking of which, how the hell did you manage to get in here,
anyway?" She crossed her arms and regarded Alex coolly.

"I have my ways." Alex brushed past her.

Sandy made a face. "Uh huh. It wouldn't have anything to
do with the fact that a particular resident has been stuck here for
the past day now, would it?"

"Give me a break, Sandy." Alex slipped out of her coat, trying her best to avoid looking at Sandy's face. "Actually, I came
in to check and see if her blood tests were ready. How's everyone
else holding up?"

"Exhausted. Most of yesterday's day shift is passed out on
anything that resembles a bed."

Alex turned around. "Where is Regina anyway?"

"In the lounge, asleep." Sandy tried hard not to let the
knowing smile creep across her face.

"When she wakes up, let me know," Alex said, as she
walked into the locker room to change.

Alex spent the next several hours checking on patients, giving the already exhausted staff a chance to rest. When she was
done with her rounds, the doctor trotted down the stairs and
walked into the emergency department. "Hey Sandy, is Regina
awake?"

"She just went looking for you."

Alex rolled her eyes. "Damn. She went up to Jameson's
office?"

"Yeah."

Alex leaned on the desk, raising an eyebrow at Sandy's ear-
to-ear grin. "What are you smiling at?"

"Nothing," Sandy said, as she quickly found something else
to do.

Alex sighed, talking more to herself than to Sandy. "Might
as well stay here. She'll be back down as soon as she sees I'm

not there." She tapped her hands on the desk restlessly and looked down the hall.

Moments later, the door swung open and Regina walked through them looking rumpled and still half-asleep. Alex met her half way down the hall.

"What are you doing here?" Regina stifled a yawn.

Alex took hold of her arm and pulled her over to a room. "I just got your blood tests back."

"Oh God." Regina's eyes widened. "Did you read them?"

Alex handed her the paper and smiled down at her friend. "You're home free, kiddo."

Regina let out a scream and threw her arms around Alex, pulling her into a bear hug. "Oh God, I can't believe it's over." Tears ran down Regina's face as she held onto Alex. "It's really over. Oh this is so awesome." She squeezed Alex again. "Thank you, thank you, thank you."

Alex gave her a crooked smile and extricated herself from Regina's arms. "Easy, I need those ribs." Alex found herself the recipient of another bear hug. "Um, Regina, I think maybe you should let me go. We're going to have an audience out here in a minute."

They heard the nurse's voice from down the hall. "What are you carrying on about down there?"

"Sorry." The resident quickly released Alex from her grip, immediately self-conscious of the attention she was drawing to them. Stepping back, Regina saw Sandy leaning over the desk, looking down the hallway at them.

She laughed at the expression on Alex's face and ran down the hall toward Sandy, briefly turning around and looking back at the doctor. "Don't go anywhere."

Alex rolled her eyes and shook her head. She could tell this celebration was going to take a while. Marcus staggered out from one of the rooms, still half asleep, to see what all the commotion was about. She watched the brief hesitation of emotion as Regina showed him the piece of paper and then he pulled her into a bear hug, lifting her off the ground and spinning her around in the air.

Alex walked over to the nurse and tapped her on the shoulder. "When she's done celebrating, tell her there's something in the refrigerator for her."

"Where are you going?" Sandy eyed the doctor suspiciously.

"I'll be outside. I'm going to help Jon try and shovel his car out, so he can get the hell out of here and go home." After slipping away quietly, she got dressed and headed outside into the snow.

A while later, Regina walked back to the desk and flopped down into the chair besides Sandy. "I think I know what it's like to be floating on a cloud right now."

Sandy cuffed her across the shoulder. "Now there's a reason to celebrate. We should go out Friday night."

"Yeah, that's a great idea." Regina sat up straighter and looked around the department. "Hey, where is Alex?"

Sandy rocked back in her chair and feigned boredom. "Outside, shoveling snow. She said to tell you there's something in the refrigerator for you."

"Oh." Regina tilted her head and frowned. "I guess I should go see what it is." She jogged into the staff lounge and opened the refrigerator door. A smile spread across her face and she closed her eyes. "Oh wow, she remembered." Regina shook her head, pulled the box out and opened it.

The resident laughed, remembering the hopeful words she had uttered several long months ago. She pulled the bottle out of the box and noticed a card attached to it. She opened it and sat down to read it.

> Regina,
>  Here's that bottle of chilled champagne.
>  Have fun celebrating.
> Alex

Regina tucked the note in her pocket and headed to the locker room. Changing quickly out of her scrubs, she headed down the hallway towards the ambulance bay, carrying her backpack with her.

"I guess they gave up trying to shovel snow." The resident stood next to Sandy, their breath fogging the glass door as they peered outside at the falling snow.

Sandy glanced at her and chuckled. "Be careful out there, I don't think Alex is taking any prisoners."

Regina snorted at several of the staff engaged in a snowball fight. Alex was perched menacingly on the hood of one of the snow-covered ambulances, gamely picking off anyone who came too close to her. Unable to resist the opportunity, Regina scooted out the door and packed a ball of snow in her hands. *Oh, this is way too easy.* Wading through the drifts of hip-deep snow she crept closer and took aim. The attending was busy nailing Jon with a flurry of snowballs and never saw the one that Regina threw at her with unerring accuracy until it was too late and the wet, hard-packed snow struck her in the side of the head.

"Hey!" Alex whirled around, her eyes seeking her attacker. She brushed the snow from her hair and cackled wickedly, jumping down into the snow. "You are in serious trouble, Dr. Kingston." She shook a finger at Regina, her eyes gleaming as she advanced on the wide-eyed resident.

Regina backtracked, laughing at the same time, knowing it was futile to try and get away. She tried anyway and was quickly caught by two strong arms curling around her waist. The blonde-haired woman screamed, flailing her arms, and got pummeled with snowballs as Jon and Marcus converged on the two of them. Regina was lifted out of the drift and carried over Alex's shoulder as the woman tramped through the white stuff toward a large pile of snow.

"Alex, don't you dare." Regina struggled in vain, trying to get loose from the two powerful arms wrapped around her legs.

Alex laughed. "Too late. Whoops." She dumped Regina off her shoulder and into the drift of powdery snow.

Regina struggled to sit up, only managing to sink deeper into the pile of snow. Alex reached down and pulled her up, grinning at her. Another volley of snowballs descended, pummeling Alex in the back. She turned around and she arched an eyebrow as Marcus prepared to throw another one.

"Don't even think about it, Marcus," Alex warned.

"Ah come on, Alex, you're no fun."

"Oh, I'm lot's of fun. Just remember I have keys to the on call room." Alex looked at Jon. "What was that we did to that resident a couple of years ago? You remember, don't you? We rolled him down to the morgue one night. Toe tagged him and all. Should've heard him screaming when he woke up between two cases."

"You didn't?" Marcus asked, his face notably paler than a moment ago.

"Oh, yes she did, Marcus." Jon swatted the packed ball of snow out of his hand. "I'm cold, how about you?" He winked at Alex before he walked away.

Alex turned back around, green eyes regarding her curiously.

"You didn't?" Regina asked, staring up at her.

"No, but I would've liked to. Ooh, you are going to be cold." Alex brushed the snow off Regina's coat.

"Yeah, no thanks to you." Regina threw a handful of snow up at Alex who ducked away from most of the powdery cloud. "You remembered what I said that day it happened."

Alex looked down at her hands and then glanced up almost shyly at Regina. "How could I forget?"

Shaking her head, Regina looked up at Alex and ran her hand down the front of her jacket. "I just came out to say thanks...for everything."

"Really? Heck of a way to say it, nailing me in the head with a snowball." Alex smiled at Regina, her eyes sparkling a pale blue in the brilliance reflected off the white snow. "Here, I wanted to wait until you got your results back to give this to you."

"What's this?" Regina frowned and took the envelope that Alex handed to her.

"Just open it." Alex stomped her feet, shaking the white flakes from her boots and pants. She then walked over to her Jeep and started brushing the snow off the windshield.

"Alex." Regina looked up from reading the lab results and walked over to the doctor. "You didn't have to do this."

"Yes, I did." Alex crossed her arms over her chest, peered down at her boots, and rocked back on her heels. "Six months ago, I would have never considered it important. You changed that. You changed everything in my life."

A smile spread over Regina's face and she tugged on Alex's jacket. "Feel like celebrating with me? I've got this great bottle of champagne we can open."

❖ ⌘ ❖ ⌘ ❖ ⌘ ❖

Alex slipped off her coat and boots and followed Regina into the kitchen. She watched with amusement as Regina climbed up onto the counter and retrieved two wine glasses from the top shelf of the cabinet. "Need help?"

"No." Regina slid back down to the floor and turned around. "Can you open this for me?" She held the bottle out to Alex.

"Sure." Alex popped the cork and poured the champagne into the glasses Regina held. "We should make a toast." Alex set the bottle down and met Regina's gaze.

Leaning back against the counter, Regina ran her fingertips over the rim of the glass, trying to collect her thoughts. "You know, something occurred to me the other day, Alex."

"Mm, what's that?" Alex asked, her heart beating a little faster as she waited for Regina to finish.

"You're the only person who's been there with me through everything the past few months." Regina exhaled nervously. "You've been my best friend, my confidante—"

Alex looked down at her glass. "Regina, you don't have to say anything."

Regina took Alex's glass and put it on the counter next to her own. She slid her hand around Alex's neck, pulling her closer and kissing her thoroughly, leaving no doubt in Alex's mind as to what she wanted. Pulling away, Regina looked up into half-closed eyes and smiled. "You didn't let me finish," she whispered.

"I guess I didn't." Alex leaned forward and touched her lips to Regina's again. Slowly she increased the pressure, her tongue gently probing and teasing the blonde's lips apart, slipping inside to caress and explore the smaller woman's mouth. She pulled away, then dipped further, exploring the curve of her neck.

Alex reached behind Regina and picked up one of the glasses. She held it up to Regina's lips so she could drink the champagne and then did the same for herself.

"To my best friend," Alex offered and kissed Regina deeply again, tasting the champagne they had just shared. Regina pressed her body against Alex's in response, so Alex continued her nibbling, as her hands roamed gently over Regina's back. She pulled the smaller woman against her. "Mm, you feel good."

"So do you." Regina's head fell back, giving into the intense sensations already stirring in her body. Alex's touch was quickly driving coherent thought from her head and her legs felt weak. "Oh, ah, legs, um, I don't think I can stand."

Alex chuckled and slid her hands around Regina's waist. She boosted her up onto the counter and leaned forward. "Better?" she asked, blue eyes twinkling as she looked into Regina's.

"Oh, yeah, I think I like this vantage point." Regina wrapped her legs around Alex's waist and pulled the taller woman closer between her thighs. Her hands ran up the front of Alex's shirt, exploring the curves and valleys, before undoing several buttons to reveal the soft skin she was seeking. "Mm. I definitely like this."

Taking full advantage of her newfound height, Regina ran her lips over the sensitive skin at the base of Alex's neck, then worked her way lower to the swell of her breasts. The dark-haired woman gasped and leaned forward, steadying herself on the counter with her hands, as Regina continued to nip gently at her neck with her teeth. "Having a problem standing?"

Alex growled in her ear and found Regina's earlobe, tugging playfully on it with her teeth. "Just you wait."

"I've been waiting." Regina undid several more buttons, slid her arms underneath Alex's shirt and ran her hands over the smooth skin of her stomach.

Alex found Regina's mouth again, quieting the gentle banter and eliciting a moan from her as she tugged gently on her lower lip, pulling it into her mouth. Regina responded, deepening their kiss until they were breathless.

Alex looked at Regina. "Um, I think maybe we should find somewhere else to continue this. What do you think?"

In answer, Regina hooked her legs tighter around the taller woman's waist, pressing her pelvis against her and kissed her again.

"Do that again and we'll both end up on the floor," Alex gasped. Regina held on and giggled as Alex slipped her hands under her thighs, lifting her off the counter. Regina's hands roamed over Alex's full breasts and taut nipples. "You better stop that or I'm going to drop you," Alex growled playfully.

Regina looked at her and grinned sheepishly as she stilled her hands. The dark-haired doctor carried her into the bedroom and sat back on the edge of the bed with Regina kneeling astride her legs. Regina's eyes widened and she yelped as Alex leaned backwards, falling onto the bed taking Regina with her.

"I-I've never done this before," Regina admitted, a sudden surge of uncertainty plaguing her as she leaned over Alex, inches from her face.

Alex brushed Regina's hair back over her shoulder. "Shh. It's all right. Just lie here with me." She shifted on the bed, pulling Regina up alongside her.

Snuggling against the taller woman, Regina settled her head against her shoulder. Her arm draped over Alex's waist, and she ran her fingers idly over the soft cotton shirt. It was so easy for her to get lost in the sensations, as Alex rubbed her hand lightly over her side, lightly grazing the curve of her breast.

She basked in the warmth radiating between their bodies as they touched along their length. Closing her eyes, Regina felt soft lips press gently against her forehead. She propped herself up on her elbows and studied Alex's face. Alex leaned in and gently touched Regina's lips with her own.

Regina let out a small whimper at the intimate touch and pressed into it, feeling Alex's fingertips tracing the sensitive skin over her face and neck. Rolling over onto the dark woman, their bodies molding perfectly together, Regina felt a surge of heat flow through her as Alex rubbed her hips slowly against her. Regina brushed her lips against Alex's chin, then nibbled the corners of her mouth. She could feel Alex's mouth curve into a smile as their lips pressed together and then she pulled back to look at her.

Shaking her head, Alex tried to get a handle on the giddy feeling that swirled around inside her gut. She ran her hand down Regina's arm, grinning at the gooseflesh that followed her touch. Alex intertwined her fingers with Regina's and brought her hand up to her lips.

"Are you sure you want to do this?" She kissed the back of Regina's hand, looking up at the woman who had stolen her heart. She was pretty sure she knew the answer but she wanted to ask Regina anyway.

Regina looked down at their clasped hands, feeling helplessly drawn toward Alex. "God...yes," she answered, feeling an ache deep inside her. A mischievous grin broke out on Alex's face. "Alex, what are you...oh, ah." Alex took Regina's thumb into her mouth pulling, and sucking seductively on it with her lips and her tongue.

"This...mmm...is what I want to do to you, all over," Alex whispered hoarsely.

Regina opened her eyes and focused on Alex's lips as she slowly took each of her fingers into her mouth, sucking gently and teasing her mercilessly with her tongue. Each stroke sent shivers up her spine and her head lolled forward as she gave into the exquisite sensation.

Alex ran her fingers through her hair, resting them lightly on the nape of her neck. Alex relinquished her attack on her fingers and instead nuzzled her lips against the soft skin below Regina's ear. The blonde closed her eyes, as her head fell forward onto Alex's shoulder. Alex...please hold me," she gasped, her senses reeling.

"It's okay." Alex rubbed her hands over Regina's back. "I won't do anything you don't want."

The blonde nibbled the sensitive skin at the base of the dark woman's throat. "No, I want you," Regina whispered as she ran her hands through Alex's silky, soft hair.

She knelt over Alex and quickly undid the rest of the buttons on the taller woman's shirt, tugging it impatiently from her jeans. Briefly, she met pale blue eyes darkened with desire and she pressed her palms against the warmth of Alex's skin and ran them lightly over the well-toned stomach. Her own body shuddered as the muscles quivered involuntarily at her touch.

Alex sat up and pulled her lover with her so they sat facing each other, the blonde's legs draped over her hips. Their eyes met and Alex took Regina's face in her hands pulling her mouth to hers, kissing her gently, then, more intensely as Regina responded to her.

Hands trembling slightly, Alex reached up between their bodies and started unbuttoning Regina's shirt. Regina stopped the gentle kisses to her neck and grinned against her skin. The blonde pulled back to quickly unbutton the last few for Alex.

Regina shrugged out of her shirt as Alex slipped it from her shoulders. The brunette slid her warm hands across Regina's back and dexterously unclasped her bra, sliding it off her body. Her caress sent tremors through the younger woman's body. Alex pressed her lips to the skin at the base of the Regina's neck then trailed her mouth lower, cupping her breasts and teasing her nipples into erect peaks with her fingers.

"You're beautiful." Alex raised her head and looked into Regina's slightly unfocused eyes, before she kissed her again.

Regina helped Alex remove her own shirt. She ran her fingertips over the dark woman's face, trailing them over her neck and exploring the strong muscles in her shoulders. Tracing her fingers over the taller woman's ribs, Regina slipped them down inside the waistband of Alex's jeans, feeling the shallow, rapid breaths of pleasure. Alex closed her eyes and her head fell back on her shoulders. She undid the button on the dark-haired woman's pants, eased the zipper open, and slid her fingers down inside through the curly hair.

"Oh, Regina, ahh—"

She heard the sharp intake of breath as her fingers cupped, then brushed against the silky wetness as she parted Alex's lips. Her own desire skyrocketed as she realized the effect she was having on this woman.

Alex jerked her head forward, and clamped her hand over Regina's wrist, stopping her hands from their gentle exploration.

"Come here," Alex growled. She pulled the smaller woman to her, claiming her mouth. The blonde's world rotated and she found herself pinned underneath Alex's weight. Her breathing became ragged as the dark-haired woman resumed her intimate exploration, leaving a fiery trail down Regina's neck and belly, tasting her skin with her tongue. The blonde shifted her hips as Alex undid the smaller woman's jeans and pulled them off her legs.

Alex leaned over her and let her hair brush over Regina's body as she slowly kissed her way back up to her face.

She felt Regina's hands on her hips pushing her back, and she protested the interruption. "W-What?"

"Uh, uh. These go too." Alex caught her breath as Regina's hands roughly tugged her jeans down over her hips. The blonde smiled up at her, pushed her over onto her back and pulled the jeans off to land in a heap on the floor. "I want you naked against me."

Regina ran her hands up over Alex's ribs, and her palms gently circled her breasts, teasing her already taut nipples. She leaned closer and captured one hardened nipple between her lips and tenderly caressed it with her tongue.

Alex arched her back and threw her head back, closing her eyes, willing her body to slow its eager response. She lifted Regina away from her and deposited the smaller woman on her back, shaking her head as Regina protested weakly.

"Not so fast. I get to lead first," Alex teased, lowering herself. She touched her lips to Regina's in a long, slow kiss as their bodies came together.

Regina trembled, only aware of her lover's gentle touch and the contact of their bodies. Her body turned and arched under Alex's capable hands as they moved over her, stroking and caressing her flesh. A soft cry escaped the blonde's lips as Alex's hand slid up the inside of her thigh, gently exploring, and increasing Regina's desire with her feather light touch.

"Do you like that?" Alex whispered, as her fingers swirled and dipped along the edge of Regina's wet opening.

"Alex, oh God...need you inside, please." Regina arched her back, her hips shamelessly rocking, moaning softly as Alex's mouth hungrily claimed her breasts. Alex's fingers slid deep

inside the blonde, filling her completely, and then withdrew
slowly to her lips. Again and again, she entered her, the rhythm
of their bodies bringing a ragged cry from Regina's lips. As her
body became taut, Regina wrapped her arms tightly around
Alex's back, holding her desperately. Wave after wave crashed
through her, leaving her struggling for breath, her heart hammering wildly in her chest.

The sensations were overpowering. Regina's release came
in a rush of warm, incredible feelings that suffused through her
core. It was as if Alex's touch had reached deep inside her soul.
The blonde opened her eyes to look up into smiling blue ones.

Alex lowered her head against Regina's shoulder, still
amazed at Regina's response to her and no less surprised at her
own climax that came seconds later. *Jesus, since when does that
happen to me?* Slowly, she pulled the young woman against her
and held her tightly, wondering what she had done to deserve
someone this precious in her life.

Afterwards, Regina lay curled tightly against Alex's body,
wrapped securely in her arms, listening to the slow steady beating of Alex's heart, feeling content and peaceful. She didn't
know why but tears came to her eyes and she tightened her grip
on Alex. Her lover lifted her head and peered down at her, feeling the change in her breathing. Alex wiped the wetness away
with her fingers. "What's wrong?"

Regina shook her head, embarrassed. "Nothing. I just...no
one ever made me feel that way before."

Alex ducked her head and captured Regina's lips, gently
exploring her mouth with her tongue. Clasping Regina's hands in
hers, she pressed them into the bed over her head as their kiss
deepened. After some moments, they finally broke away, breathless. Slowly, sliding down Regina's body, Alex caressed her
belly with her lips.

"Let me do this for you," she whispered and tugged Regina
to the edge of the bed. Alex knelt on the floor and put her hands
on Regina's hips. Slowly, she brushed her tongue along the
inside of Regina's thigh.

"Alex, mm, oh God," Regina gasped and arched her back in
response to Alex's warm breath, followed seconds later by the
warm, delicate touch of her lips.

Alex watched as Regina closed her eyes and opened her
mouth slightly in an "oh" of pleasure. Listening to Regina's
breathing coming in ragged gasps, the dark-haired woman

touched her lips to the engorged flesh, tasting now what her fingers had possessed earlier. Feeling her own desire burning on the edge of control, Alex slowly explored Regina with her mouth.

The smaller woman clasped the dark-haired woman's hands, holding tightly. Her body shook as Alex's mouth claimed all of her.

Wrapping her arms around the blonde's hips, Alex felt Regina's shuddering orgasm as she collapsed against her. Regina called her name. She slipped up beside her and cradled Regina in her arms. Alex lay on her side, rocking the smaller woman in her arms. "I'm right here, baby. I'm right here," she whispered in her ear. Afterwards, they curled around each other, slowly drifting off to sleep.

When Regina woke up it was dark outside and the clock on the nightstand read two o'clock. It took her a couple of seconds to shake the cobwebs out of her brain and realize that it was two o'clock in the morning. She lifted her head from Alex's shoulder and looked up at her face. For once, it was relaxed and peaceful. She was still sleeping so Regina lay quietly next to her, soaking up the warmth of their bodies tangled together beneath the covers. Regina shivered in delight remembering what they had shared earlier. She pulled herself up onto her elbows and brushed an errant lock of hair out of Alex's face. The moonlight was just shining through the window, its soft light reflecting off of Alex's face, and Regina's breath caught in her throat.

In that instant, it was like pieces of her heart and soul, pieces she didn't even realize were missing, fell into place. Regina bent forward and gently kissed Alex on her lips. She settled back, watching the eyelids flutter open and sleepy blue eyes look back at her. Alex smiled and brushed Regina's face with her hand.

"Hi there," Alex said, her voice deep and husky from having just woken.

"Mm. Sorry I fell asleep before," Regina said. She smiled and nibbled at Alex's earlobe, eliciting a soft moan from the woman.

"Don't be." Alex slipped an arm underneath Regina and pulled her closer.

Regina moved her lips to Alex's neck, kissing the sensitive skin over her collarbone. She stretched her body out along Alex's taller frame, rubbing against her, enjoying the simple pleasure of lying pressed up against her solid length.

"Oh, I want to make love to you." Moving back up to Alex's mouth, she kissed her lips with the increasing intensity of her own desire. Slowly, she caressed Alex with her hands, feeling the sharp intake of breath as she lowered her head and kissed the softness of her breasts, remembering what Alex had done to her and wanting to give that same feeling back in return.

Regina slid her hands over Alex's stomach, gently exploring the planes of the woman's body, and shifted her own body so she could reach down the long muscular lines of her legs. Her stroke moved lightly up Alex's calves, behind the sensitive skin of her knees, and finally back up between her thighs.

Alex's hands tightened on Regina's shoulders, her hips moving, responding to Regina's gentle touch. "Oh God, Regina, can you be inside me...please?"

"Anything," Regina whispered.

"Regina." Alex's finger's dug into her lover's shoulders. Her breathing quickened to ragged gasps and she trembled as Regina moved inside her. Alex's voice trailed off as she gave herself over to the overwhelming sensations cascading through her body.

As her body relaxed, Alex looked down at Regina's gentle face. Regina's head was nestled in against Alex's chin, eyes closed, her breathing slow and even. It was like the whole world had disappeared around them, leaving just the two of them. All Alex felt was a quiet sense of peace. With one arm wrapped around Regina's shoulder and her other hand holding Regina's own on her chest, Alex rubbed her thumb over the soft skin of Regina's wrist.

They had been lying quietly together, absorbing the gentle contact of their bodies, when Regina stirred and looked up at Alex. "What are you thinking about?"

"Do you have to ask?" Alex asked, smiling seductively and rolling over on to her.

# Chapter
# 20

The tall, dark-haired woman lay awake, her head resting on one hand, watching her new lover snuggled next to her, breathing deeply as she still slept. Life seemed so simple and uncomplicated lying there, under the nest of warm blankets, with this sweet, gentle soul. *What did I ever do to deserve this?* The older doctor lightly ran her fingers through the blonde locks, smoothing them away from Regina's face. *So, where do we go from here, Regina? What do you want out of this and am I even capable of giving it to you?*

Alex closed her eyes trying to imagine what her life would be like without Regina in it; the future she envisioned faded to a murky black void and a terrifying feeling of desolation overwhelmed her. To lose Regina would be more painful than death itself.

Swallowing the lump forming in her throat, the doctor forced the foreboding thoughts into the far recesses of her mind. The taller woman leaned forward and woke Regina, calling her name softly and kissing her forehead.

The younger woman squirmed, hearing her name called from very far away. Slowly, she awoke, relishing the warmth of her bed and the softness of Alex's body nestled against hers. Blinking, Regina lifted her head and peered up, finding a pair of blue eyes curiously looking back at her. She snuggled back down against Alex's shoulder and wrapped her arm snugly around her waist, an impish grin forming on her lips.

"Morning." Regina kissed the smooth skin beneath her lips, content just to listen to the beating of the woman's heart beneath her ear.

"Good morning yourself, sleepyhead." Alex playfully ruffled Regina's hair. Lifting her head, Alex smiled at the way Regina wound herself in a tight embrace over her body. "You look cute lying here all snuggled up."

"I'm glad you think so." Regina glanced up at her. "This is what I look like in the mornings."

Pulling Regina on top of her, Alex wrapped her in a hug. "Mm, I think I can live with it."

Regina laughed and rolled off of Alex. "Yeah, well I hear the shower calling my name." Sitting up, the young doctor stretched her arms overhead.

"Nice view." A hand reached out and touched her, fingers gliding seductively down her sensitive flesh and wrapping around her waist, pulling her into a warm embrace.

"Hey, no fair." Regina squirmed and laughed as Alex nibbled at the exposed skin.

"Who said anything about fair?" Alex arched an eyebrow as her lips meandered lower.

"Take a shower with me?" Regina offered as she slid out of the caress and walked toward the bedroom door.

"Well, now that's an offer I can't refuse." Alex winked at Regina. She chuckled at the pink flush rising in the blonde's cheeks before she disappeared out of the room. *Oh, I am in deep here,* the brunette mused as she got up.

Regina stood under the hot water with her eyes closed, letting it pound on her back, wondering how she could have ever been afraid of following her heart in the first place. She'd fallen in love with this woman and she couldn't alter her course now even if she desired to. *You're all I want, Alex—having you here, holding you, loving you—is all I want.*

After last night, just the thought of being with this raven-haired, blue-eyed beauty left her breathless and wanting. She loved to bury her head against the doctor's shoulder, pressing her face against the exquisite softness of her breasts, melting in the warm embrace of Alex's arms, breathing in her intoxicating scent. Even her orgasms with Alex had been overwhelming and all encompassing, like a bright light exploding deep inside and speeding out from her core, warming her all over.

She opened her eyes when Alex slipped in beside her, and once again Regina felt a firestorm of desire building inside. She ran her fingers down Alex's stomach, teasing as she feathered them through the curls below.

Alex bit her lower lip and closed her eyes, letting out a low growl as Regina continued her playful exploration.

"You're going to kill me." Alex captured her hand and brought it up, sucking on moist fingers and stepping closer so their bodies were pressed together. "Let me wash your hair."

A sensuous wave coursed through the blonde as sure hands ran through her long hair, lathering it thoroughly. Regina let out a small moan and leaned against Alex, resting her head against her chest.

"Oh, what are you doing to me?" Regina gasped, sliding her hands around and caressing Alex's buttocks.

"The same thing you're doing to me, I think." The brunette walked her back under the spray and rinsed her hair. Watching Regina stand naked under the stream of water with her eyes closed and her head tilted back made Alex want to make love to her all over again.

She turned the shorter woman around so the spray was out of her face and gently captured Regina's lower lip between her teeth and sucked, slowly pulling it inside her mouth.

Hands slid around her waist, pulling her close as Regina steadied herself against Alex's body. "Mm, oh—" Regina's words were cut off as Alex let the soap drop. One arm curled securely around Regina's waist as another hand slipped down her stomach. Alex's fingers slid between Regina's thighs, teasing and promising more.

Regina gasped at the touch and pressed her hips into Alex's hand, wanting the contact and needing her inside. Alex yelped as her back pressed against the cold tiles. She stared down into sultry green eyes. "I think we should get out of here before one of us falls."

"I thought this was supposed to be the obligatory let's-make-love-in-the-shower scene." Regina smirked up at her.

Alex rolled her eyes. "Maybe in the movies, but I'm not that acrobatic. Here." She gave her a lopsided grin and handed the bar of soap back to the blonde. Leisurely, they finished washing each other and climbed out of the shower.

Alex left Regina in the bathroom and put on an oversized T-shirt. She walked to the bedroom window, and looked out at the snow-covered landscape. When she heard Regina approach her, she turned and smiled as the blonde wrapped her arms around her waist, snuggling close.

"I can't stop touching you." Regina nipped gently at Alex's breast through her shirt and watched with pleasure the reaction her touch had on the taller woman.

"I guess you feel more awake now?" Alex glanced down at her, the slightest hint of a smile playing at the corners of her mouth.

Regina poked her in the side. "Hey, it's not my fault. I was at the hospital for twenty-four hours straight and then was up most of last night."

"Uh huh, and whose fault was that?" Alex nudged her back, playfully reminding Regina of just who had ambushed whom several hours before dawn. "You just couldn't let me sleep, could you?"

Regina groaned and buried her head in her hand, knowing that further discussion along this topic was only going to get her deeper in trouble than she already was.

Alex took mercy on her and nuzzled her face in Regina's hair. "Sorry, you're just fun to tease, that's all." Regina's hair was still wet from the shower and Alex could smell the fresh scent of the herbal shampoo and soap on her body.

It was nice and somewhere inside stirred a memory, just beyond the reaches of her consciousness. *Weird, kind of like hearing an old song and having all those emotions wash over you, bringing you back to that one moment in time.* Alex blinked and shook her head discarding the thought as being disgustingly romantic.

"You must be hungry. I know I am." Regina patted Alex's stomach.

"I'm starved."

Regina felt the subtle change in Alex's breathing as she looked back out the window. "What's on your mind?"

Alex glanced down at the green eyes peering up at her from underneath the blonde, wet, tousled hair. "Mm. You." She tilted Regina's face up to hers and kissed her, feeling a stirring of desire course through her again. The tall woman tightened her arm around Regina as she leaned heavily against her.

"Oh." Regina breathed out, blinking to clear her vision and focus her thoughts. "I, um, Alex?"

Regina caught her breath as warm lips trailed down her neck, and the terry cloth towel that was wrapped around her torso loosened and fell away.

"Um, I thought you were hungry." Regina's hands, trembled slightly as she slipped them around Alex's neck. Alex walked her back to the bed, and laid her down on her back across it. The T-shirt grazed the blonde's naked skin and she gasped at the contact.

"I am." Alex's eyes twinkled as she pulled Regina's arms up over her head, and started kissing her.

❖ ⌘ ❖ ⌘ ❖ ⌘ ❖

Regina lifted her head and looked at the clock next to her bedside table. "You know, we're not getting very far today."

Alex rolled toward the smaller woman and cocked an eyebrow upwards. "Really? I thought we were."

A pillow shot across the bed and smacked Alex in the head.

"Hey!" Alex grabbed it from Regina and pounced on top of her. "Careful, you're going to get yourself in trouble here."

"Promises, promises," Regina challenged her playfully as she lay pinned beneath Alex's body.

"Don't push your luck." Alex rocked her hips against the woman lying beneath her and let out a low, guttural growl.

"We'll just have to see about that." The young doctor smirked as she sneaked a hand out, caught Alex off guard, and tickled her just below her ribs. This was rewarded with a frenzied wrestling match with both of them almost falling out of the bed—except that Alex grabbed the head board, catching them before they tumbled over the edge of the mattress. They took a few minutes to catch their breath, and then laid quietly beside each other.

Regina looked into Alex's eyes and saw something in them that raced through her like electricity and then it was gone. "Alex."

"Regina." They laughed as they spoke at the same time.

"You go first," Alex said, rolling onto her side and touching Regina's face. *God, you take my breath away.*

Regina turned her face and kissed the palm of Alex's hand. "Can I ask you a question?"

"Yeah." The taller doctor shifted uncomfortably as she anticipated the question that was forming in Regina's mind.

"What are we going to do about this?" Regina motioned between them with her hand.

Alex tilted her head and smiled, a relieved chuckle escaping her lips. *Okay, well at least we're not onto a more serious topic.* "You mean, what are we going to do about us and work?"

Regina looked up at her and nodded her head, suddenly feeling like the entire world would know about them the minute they walked out of the condo.

Alex hadn't given much thought about how it would be for Regina at work after last night. She had walked down this road before and, frankly, she really didn't give a damn what other people thought about her. There was certainly a significant contingent of gay and lesbian employees at the hospital, but she kept to herself over the years and chose not to socialize with them except for the rare occasion that she went out with Sandy and Tina.

"People see what they want to see, Regina. Some people might think we're just friends, and others," Alex shrugged, "who knows? Let them think what they will. As long as we don't bring our relationship to work, nobody can say anything."

"What about Sandy? She asked me about us yesterday." Regina stared down at the rumpled sheets and nervously toyed with them.

"What did you tell her?"

"That we were friends."

"Well, we are friends. Right?" Alex replied, leaning in and gently caressing Regina's lips with her own.

"I don't think she believed me. She said she wanted to throttle the both of us."

"She did, did she? I'm going to have to a word with that woman." Alex chuckled. "I don't think we have to worry about Sandy saying anything. She's known about me for as long as we've worked together. The mystery was over the night we spotted each other in one of the local gay bars. We just looked at each other and then laughed because there was no sense trying to pretend we didn't notice the other."

Regina leaned into the caress and sighed quietly. Rationally, she knew Alex was right. The young doctor was still reveling in the dizzying heights of passion that Alex brought her to, and she wondered if, by just looking at her, people would be able to see what she felt inside for this woman when they went to work in a few hours.

Later in the morning, as they readied for their shifts, Regina stood in front of the mirror, pulling her hair back into a braid and watching as Alex slipped into her clothes. Sensing the resident watching her, Alex looked up from tying her bootlaces and returned the gaze into the mirror.

"What's on your mind?" She stood and stomped her feet, shaking her jeans down over the boot tops as she looked at her lover.

A blush crept up her cheeks, as Regina realized that Alex had caught her pensive stare. "Nothing."

"Uh huh, and I'm Queen Elizabeth. I know that look, Dr. Kingston. Don't lie to me." Alex set her hands on the shorter woman's shoulders as she looked at their reflection in the mirror. "Well?"

Regina turned, wrapped her arms around Alex's waist and buried her head against the doctor's shoulder. "It's nothing. Come on, we have to get to the hospital." *Nothing, except I'm head over heels in love with you.*

❖ ⌘ ❖ ⌘ ❖ ⌘ ❖

Alex propped her elbow on the desk of the nurse's station as she regarded the new residents milling uncertainly about her. Today the rotations changed; it was out with the now well-trained, experienced residents and in with the new ones. *God help me,* she thought.

Marcus stayed on to give the report on the current patients and to help get the new residents settled before he left in two days for a short vacation. Regina, having missed a week with her suspension, although nullified by the board, stayed on to finish her time out before deciding what she was going to do after this rotation. Alex knew she had several offers on the table from various hospitals and clinics, including Xavier's pediatric department. She hadn't pressed Regina about what she wanted to do, deciding that despite her own personal feelings for the doctor, Regina needed to do what was best for her without any outside pressure. *Besides,* Alex thought, *you have no claim on her.*

"Okay people, can someone please start rounds? We don't have all day and I know Marcus would like to start his vacation as soon as possible."

She listened as Marcus stepped closer and rattled off the vital statistics for each of the patients in the emergency department. Alex frowned at one point and shook her head. "Wait, back up. I want you to run a set of complete lab values on this guy in bed seven."

Out of the corner of her eye, she caught a flash of blonde hair as Regina emerged from one of the exam rooms. Her throat went dry and she swallowed hard as the resident turned and saw her. Regina's eyes softened and a shy smile appeared before she walked to the sink and washed her hands.

Alex pulled her attention back to Marcus, nodding in agreement with his diagnosis. "So you're getting a CT scan to confirm that, right?"

Marcus nodded. "Yes, he's on his way as we speak."

"Good, good. Surgery won't touch him without it." Alex glanced back to the space where Regina had been moments before, finding it vacant. She sighed and then realized Marcus' pupils were dilating, a look of panic setting in as he thought she was about to rip into him. "All right, we've got an MRI in two, wound cultures pending in four, a CT scan in seven, and an ultrasound in eight. Any questions?" She stared hard at the group. "If you're not sure about something, find Dr. Kingston. She's your senior resident until the end of the week. Marcus, enjoy your vacation."

As the residents scattered to their various duties, Alex scanned the assignment board. She turned toward the sound of heels striking the linoleum floor and the Vice President came up beside her.

"Alex, I need to speak with you, now. Where can we go?"

"The lounge, if it's empty," Alex offered.

Alex held the door for Cassandra as they stepped into the staff lounge. "Sandy, would you give us a moment?"

The blonde looked up, surprised to see the Vice President standing next Alex. "No problem." Quickly she gathered her clipboard and coffee before she slipped through the open door.

Cassandra turned to Alex as the door closed and crossed her arms. "There's a rumor going around and I hope you can shed some light on it."

"If I know anything."

"Apparently, Dr. Jameson has been working very closely with a drug representative for the past several years." Cassandra paced back and forth across the room. "It turns out that the Office of Investigations is looking into this company's practices and is filing a suit against them for fraud and malpractice. The trail has unfortunately led to our back door."

"Why aren't you talking to Dr. Jameson about this?" Alex leaned back against the counter and folded her arms.

"He's refusing to cooperate and now he's got an attorney. Alex, I need to know if there are any more surprises before OIG ends up on our doorstep."

Alex met Cassandra's gaze. "While he was on medical leave I found some things in his office that were suspicious. I confronted him three days ago when I finally put everything together. I gave him a day to make up his mind about how he wanted to handle it. I guess he made his decision."

"I'm surprised you didn't call OIG yourself." Cassandra cocked her head and stepped in front of the taller woman. "Why didn't you, Alex?"

"I probably would have, except someone gave me a different perspective on how to handle it."

The VP regarded Alex thoughtfully. "Well, I'm in meetings all day and tomorrow I'm off site until the evening. Bring what you have to my office and we'll go through it together."

"As soon as I'm done with my shift, I'll bring it up." Alex walked over to the sink and ran some water before filling a cup with it.

"Good."

The attending took a deep breath as she walked out of the lounge behind the Vice President. She guessed that the medical director was running scared now that his carefully devised plan was falling down around him. She looked up as she heard her name and couldn't help the grin that spread over her face. "Hey, are you doing okay?"

Alex had purposely kept her interactions with the young resident to a minimum during their first shift back to work, sensing Regina's awkwardness with this new facet to their relationship and how it might affect them.

"Yeah, fine." Regina pulled her eyes away from Alex's piercing gaze. *Okay, breathe, Regina. Yeah right, you're only standing inches from the woman you spent half the night making love to.*

Sandy looked up from her work, as the two doctors approached. "God, I'm glad this day is almost over. They must've had a two for one sale today. I don't think I've seen this many people come through here with the flu at one time."

"I didn't see any signs posted out at the road. How about

you, Regina?" Alex leaned on the counter and plucked a potato chip out of the bag that Sandy held and popped it into her mouth.

Regina, still light-headed from her body's visceral reaction, just stared at Alex.

Sandy waved a hand in front of her face. "Earth to Dr. Kingston. You all right, Regina?"

"Yeah, I'm fine," she responded, looking up at the nurse, a perplexed expression on her face. "Why?"

Sandy's eyes flicked slowly over the two of them and rested on Regina. "You looked, uh, flushed."

Regina dropped her head into her hands and groaned, as the warmth from the heated blush crept up her face. "Great, this one's making jokes. Maybe I'm getting hot flashes."

Alex choked on the water she was swallowing and laughed. Seeing the incensed look she got from Regina, she stepped back and held up a hand. "Sorry," she gasped in between coughing fitfully.

Sensing something else going on, Sandy looked back and forth between the two doctors and rolled her eyes. "Hey, we're all going out Friday night, right?"

"Yeah, I thought we already decided that." Alex glanced down as the beeper on her waistband vibrated. She frowned, wondering who would be paging her to an outside line.

The brunette reached over the desk, grabbed the phone and quickly punched in the numbers, waiting for the operator to connect her. "This is Dr. Margulies."

The voice that came over the line sent a chill down her back.

"Well, well. If it isn't the illustrious doctor, herself. You should feel quite honored, Alex. You're the first person I've called since I posted bail." There was long pause as the doctor held onto the phone. "What's wrong, Alex? Cat got your tongue?"

"What do you want?" Alex shifted her feet and leaned on the desk, holding her head in one hand and wishing desperately she had taken the call elsewhere. Now, whether she liked it or not, she was going to have an audience with Sandy and Regina standing on either side of her.

"How nice of you to ask. Tell me, how's your girlfriend? You know the cute blonde. The one that was following you around like a puppy last time I saw you." Dana laughed.

Alex turned away from Regina and lowered her voice. "Get

to the point, Dana."

"The point, hmm, oh yes, I remember now," the voice on the other end of the line taunted.

"Are you drunk?"

"Nope, I'm drunk and high. Get it right, Doc." Dana's voice suddenly turned menacing. "You bitch. You set me up, Alex. I know you did."

"You got sloppy, Dana. It was just a matter of time before you got caught."

"Bullshit! I hate you, Alex. I hope you die and rot in hell."

"Dana, where are you?"

"What do you care where I am?"

"You're Lana's sister; I care. I don't want you ending up in the morgue with a toe tag on you."

"I don't need your help."

"Where are you?" There was silence on the other end of the phone as Dana stubbornly refused to answer Alex. "Damn it, Dana. You're in enough trouble already."

"I'll be seeing you, Alex, real soon, love." The line went dead and Alex held the receiver in her hand for a moment, staring at it numbly before she placed it back in the cradle.

"Alex?" Regina asked, looking up at the dark-haired woman with a worried expression on her face.

"Alex, I don't know why you waste your time," Sandy hissed at her from across the desk.

"Don't go there, Sandy. I...I have to find her." Alex backed up a step, her eyes darkening at Sandy's remark.

"When will you learn? Nothing you say or do is going to change what Dana does with her life. She is not going to give up using drugs for anything or anybody. Least of all, you."

"Alex, wait." Regina hurried after the attending as she disappeared around the corner and banged through the ER doors. Regina caught the door as it slammed back off the wall into her and pushed it open, calling out the doctor's name as she rounded the corner.

Alex hesitated and slowly turned around, waiting as Regina came up next to her.

"Can I walk with you?" the resident asked.

The doctor nodded her head and continued down the empty corridor. She pushed open the glass door and a blast of frigid air met them as they walked outside. Alex stuffed her hands into her pockets, ducked her head against the wind, and strode silently up the hill that led past the loading docks. She changed directions as an eighteen-wheeler beeped as it backed up the drive. The taller woman didn't have to look back to know that Regina was trying to keep up with her.

The resident crossed her arms over her chest, tucking her hands under her arms. Her scrubs and cotton lab coat were little comfort against the cold wind and the snow that blew around them.

"Alex, slow down."

Regina jogged along as the taller woman slowed her gait, allowing the blonde to catch up with her.

"You know you are incredibly bull-headed, Alex. You don't even know where Dana is, do you?" Regina stood in front of Alex defiantly blocking her path. "Sandy's right; whether you like it or not, it's Dana's choice to do what she wants with her life." Regina shivered and looked down at the ground, studying her sneakers. "Listen, I know you feel like...you have to make things right, because of what happened with Lana, but ultimately it's Dana's decision, not yours, Alex."

The doctor looked out off in the distance, her jaw muscles contracting as she clenched her teeth together. "I promised Lana I'd take care of her. Hell of a job I'm doing, huh? She's like a bad penny that just keeps coming back. I don't know what to do anymore."

Regina stepped closer to the woman and took hold of her arm. "Alex, look at me." Alex pivoted slowly. Her blue eyes looked briefly at the blonde and then stared down at the ground. "She's going to keep coming back as long as she knows she can manipulate you. Don't you see, Alex? You've got to just let her go. Whatever happens, no matter how bad it is, you can't be there to keep picking her up." Regina let go of Alex's arm, afraid she had pushed too far. "Just...just think about it." The blonde shivered, her teeth chattered from the cold. "I'm going back inside."

The wind whipped Alex's hair off her shoulders as she stood watching Regina's retreating form. As the door closed behind the resident, the doctor turned and continued walking up the hill.

Regina didn't see Alex for the rest of her shift and she worried that the doctor had gone out looking for Dana anyway. The young woman, resolving to let doctor do what she felt she needed to, quietly finished her work. Later, in the locker room, she carefully taped a note to Alex's locker and then returned home alone.

❖ ⌘ ❖ ⌘ ❖ ⌘ ❖

Regina hurried to turn the key in the lock as she heard the phone ringing inside. She ran across the living room in her wet boots, almost falling on the hardwood floor in her effort to get to the phone.

"Hello?"

"Regina, it's Dad."

"Dad? Is everything all right?" Regina sat down heavily on the couch, catching her breath as she listened. This was the last person she expected to hear from, considering the blow out she had with her mother over a month ago.

"Yes, everything is fine. Well no, it's not. It's your mother."

"Oh, Jesus, what's wrong? Is she sick?"

"No, no. I know you tried to call and even though she won't admit it, this whole thing is killing her."

Regina hesitated. "She told you about me?"

"She didn't have to. I heard the whole thing from the living room."

"Oh."

"Regina, I wanted to know if you would come up this weekend and talk with her."

Regina groaned and buried her head in her hand. "Dad, you know I want to but I'm working all weekend."

"Oh." His voice became muffled as he turned and talked away from the phone. "Mom doesn't know you're calling me, does she?"

"No, she doesn't. It doesn't matter." He sighed. "If I find a way to bring her down there, will you talk to her?"

"Do you think she's even going to want to see me?" She was surprised to hear his voice choke when he spoke again.

"Regina, I already lost one son, I'm not losing my daughter as well. I want you back. I want you both back."

Regina wiped tears away and leaned back on the couch. "I'll talk to her, Dad. Have you talked to Jeff, yet?"

"No, that's going to be a lot tougher. Your mother and I did a lot of damage to that relationship. It's going to take a long time to repair all that."

"I think the sooner you start, the better. You've lost so much time already."

"I know, little one."

Regina laughed softly. "You haven't called me that in years."

"Eh, your old man's getting sentimental. Let me get off this phone before I make a fool of myself."

"You're really going to bring her down here?"

"Kicking and screaming if I have to."

"I get off at nine tomorrow night."

"We'll be there."

"Goodnight, Dad."

Regina pressed her head against the wall and sighed heavily before she hung up the phone. Over the next couple of hours, she tried unsuccessfully to distract herself by watching television and reading, but her thoughts continued to revolve around the fact that her parents' impending arrival was coinciding with her newfound relationship with Alex.

She wasn't even sure she wanted to tell Alex that her parents were coming down. Things were complicated enough already without adding them to the mix. *Oh boy, this is going to be interesting.* Finally, unable to resist her body's need any longer, Regina drifted off to sleep as she lay on the couch.

It was shortly after midnight when the shrill ringing of the phone jerked her awake. She fumbled for the phone and mumbled a barely intelligible hello.

"Hi, I just read your note. I woke you up. I-I'm sorry."

Regina smiled. The familiar voice was deep and sensuous as it came over the phone line and her ears reddened as the heat stirred in her guts. "No, it's...it's okay. I fell asleep on the couch. Are you still at the hospital?"

"Yeah. We had a couple of admissions come in, so I stayed and helped out."

"Do you want to come over, Alex?" Regina inquired hopefully, staring into space and thinking about her lover.

"Aren't you getting tired of having me camped out at your place?" Alex joked to hide her nervousness. Throughout the day, she thought about the blonde, wondering what she was doing.

Regina blushed. "I hardly call one night camping out, Alex, and, no, I miss you."

"Give me ten minutes." Alex chuckled softly into the phone. "I'll be right over."

A short while later, Regina heard the Jeep pull into the driveway. Regina opened the door before the taller woman made it to the steps, and let Alex inside. The doctor looked tired and the dark circles shadowing her pale blue eyes revealed the stress she had been under. After she shed her coat, scarf, and gloves, Alex pulled Regina into a tight hug.

"God, I've wanted to do that all day." She buried her face in the smaller woman's neck, inhaling the fragrance of her perfume.

Regina removed the leather band that held Alex's braid in place. She ran her hands through the woman's thick hair, settling it around her shoulders.

"Are you okay?" Regina rubbed her hands over the bulky sweater that Alex wore.

Alex tightened her arms around Regina, gathering strength from the contact. "Yeah," she breathed out. "I...thanks for being there and talking some sense into me. I'm not sure what the hell I was planning on doing." She knew it was an automatic reaction for her to try and help Dana.

"She scares me. I don't want her to hurt you, Alex." Regina buried her head against the taller woman's shoulder.

"Don't worry, nothing is going to happen. I won't let it," Alex reassured the young woman. The brunette lowered her head and gently kissed the soft lips. A sensation stirred deep down in her belly as they slowly reacquainted themselves; their caresses becoming more fervent as memories of their recent lovemaking ignited the passion that had been dampened by the long day at work.

After several more minutes, they slowly broke off their embrace and gazed quietly into each other's eyes.

"Wow." Regina was very aware of her racing heartbeat and the pulsing between her legs. "That was some kiss."

The taller woman slid her arms around Regina's waist, pulled her close and nibbled an earlobe. "Mm, let's see what else you like."

"Oh, that's not fair, Alex." Regina tilted her head back and groaned as her body trembled under her lover's touch.

Still holding onto Regina, Alex walked her backwards until the smaller woman was pressed firmly up against a wall in the bedroom. She ran her hands against the blonde's skin, running lightly over the swell of her breasts, smiling as she felt the nipples harden at her lingering touch.

Regina pulled Alex's head down and kissed her hungrily, their tongues and lips teasing each other. The blonde lowered her hands to Alex's hips, pulled her close, and rubbed her body against the taller woman. "Oh, I want you so much."

Alex obliged her need by slipping a thigh up between the blonde's legs. "That's it, just let go," she coaxed. The taller woman slipped Regina's shirt off and ducked her head, first drawing one nipple and then the other into her mouth.

"Oh, your lips, they're so soft." Regina gasped, feeling the dampness from her arousal as she rocked her hips over Alex's muscular thigh. "Don't let me go. I'll fall."

"I've got you." Alex worked the button free on the blonde's pants and tugged the zipper down. She slipped her hand down through the blonde curls and caressed her, tightening her grip around Regina's waist with her other arm as the younger woman tensed against her.

"Alex, I...don't think I can come like this."

"Yes, you can. Just relax." Alex lowered her head and captured Regina's lips in a heated kiss. She nibbled at her lips and tongue, as her hand caressed and stroked the younger woman's hot and swollen flesh. "Ah, Regina, you're so wet. I want you right here."

The blonde closed her eyes and tilted her head back, her breaths quickening in response to Alex's touch. Her lover's tongue and lips played along her neck, slowly gliding lower over her breasts. Alex moved against her, and knelt in front of her as she removed Regina's pants.

Alex rubbed her face over the silky skin of Regina's belly, inhaling the scent of her arousal as she sank back on her heels and brushed her lips against the damp curls. Regina moaned softly as Alex pressed up against her, tasting the moistness on her lips.

The blonde's hands clenched and unclenched at her side, her hips undulating against the exquisite sensations coursing through her center. She clutched at Alex's shoulders, steadying herself against the tremors that threatened her legs to give out on her. "Alex, oh...oh God. What are you doing...to me?"

The dark haired woman pulled away, her fingers replacing her lips and tongue. "Making love to you, baby. Making love to you."

Regina's head lolled forward and she held tightly to the shoulders in front of her. She gasped as Alex's fingers slid inside. Her hips moved in rhythm with the slow stroking movements that sent a fire speeding out from her center. "Alex...I, oh right there," she whispered, her hands clutching Alex's arms.

She cried out as Alex's tongue covered the engorged head of her clitoris and stroked over its length.

Regina's words caught in her throat and she sobbed, her body and soul overcome by the intensity of her climax as Alex claimed her. She collapsed against the woman, holding onto her, panting from her release. "Oh, God. Don't move, just hold me."

"I'm right here." Alex held onto Regina as her body shuddered several more times.

"I can't move," Regina responded drowsily, her body limp and spent. She gasped again softly as Alex removed her hand, stood up, and gathered her into her arms. The blonde brushed the dark hair back, lifted Alex's head and kissed her mouth, tasting the evidence of her own passion.

Alex pulled back and searched her eyes, before she ducked her head and kissed the blonde thoroughly. *Ah, Regina, never in my dreams did I imagine it could be like this.* After a few minutes, Alex felt the blonde's body relax against hers. "Hey, are you falling asleep on me?" she teased, wrapping her arms tighter around the woman.

Regina lifted her head off Alex's shoulder and smiled crookedly, stifling a yawn. "Mm, you make a nice pillow."

Alex looked down at the smaller woman and patted her side affectionately. "Right now, you look like you could fall asleep standing up. Come on."

The resident didn't resist when Alex tugged her toward the bed and crawled into it beside her.

"I think I could fall asleep on a bed of nails," Regina said, as she leaned into Alex's body.

"I think the bed is a much safer option, don't you?" Alex whispered as she nuzzled Regina's neck with her lips. Her fingers drew a lazy pattern over the firm muscles of the smaller woman's stomach, dipping lower between her thighs.

Regina curled against Alex's body, sighing in contentment. "You're incorrigible," she whispered, her mouth closing softly on the earlobe in front of her.

Alex shivered at the touch. She slid her arm back up around Regina's waist and pulled her close. "I can't help it. You drive me crazy."

Regina rested her head on her hand as she watched the doctor's eyes drift shut. *I never dreamed I could feel this way, want someone the way I do you. I love you, Alex Margulies.* Alex felt Regina watching and turned her head, looking at the blonde.

"I thought you were sleepy. Now, what's going on inside that head of yours?"

The blonde closed her eyes and shook her head. "My father called before you came over."

Alex propped her head up on her hand and raised an eyebrow. *So, your father's the one that breaks the ice.* She remembered what Regina told her about her fight with her parents. "I guess that was a surprise."

Regina blew out a breath and ran her finger over the sheets between them. "Yeah, he wants to bring my mother down here, tomorrow...to talk."

The brunette noticed the pensive look on her lover's face, slid her hand under Regina's chin, and lifted her face. "How do you feel about that?"

Regina shrugged her shoulders. "I don't know what I'll say to her that will change how she feels."

Alex caressed Regina's cheek as she studied her face. "You're not going to change how she feels, Regina. She's the only one that can do that. Just be yourself."

Regina smiled, slid her hand into Alex's larger one and entwined their fingers. She brought the woman's palm to her lips and kissed it gently, then slid it down so it covered her heart. "I want to spend more time with you. I don't care what we do. Just being together. It makes me feel...whole." When she looked back up she saw the startled expression on her companion's face.

Alex swallowed nervously as her mind registered what Regina said to her. "I make you feel that way?"

The blonde let go of Alex's hand and ran her fingers through her lover's hair. Her hand rested lightly on the nape of her neck and she rubbed the soft skin, eliciting a low growl from her companion. "Yes, you do. You have no idea how amazing you are to me. You make me feel alive, Alex." She smiled at the wide-eyed look of shock on Alex's face.

Alex shook her head. "How can you say that, after everything I've told you? I see things in you I wish I could be, your strength, your courage—"

"Alex, I think I lost track of how many times you've taken care of me or protected me from Derrick."

"I'm not talking about that kind of strength, Regina. What you have inside, that's what makes you strong." The taller woman touched the blonde's chest. "I don't have that kind of strength."

"Yes, you do. You're alive and here, and talking to me. If you didn't have that strength, you wouldn't be here right now." Regina pulled her into a tight embrace.

Alex wrapped her arms around the smaller woman as if her life depended on it. "I wouldn't have made it through the past few months if it hadn't been for you," she whispered hoarsely.

"You would have found a way, Alex," Regina reassured her, keeping up the gentle rhythmic pressure of her hand on her neck.

"I did find my way. You."

Regina lifted her head and looked quietly into blue eyes that reflected back to her an understanding that extended beyond words. Wrapped securely in each other's arms they held each other, content to drift peacefully off to sleep comforted by each other's presence.

# Chapter
# 21

The next day brought more snow and foul weather and the ER was busy again as people fell victim to their own carelessness or various other afflictions. Regina walked out of one of the exam rooms and washed her hands for what seemed like the twentieth time today. She had seen her tenth flu patient already and from the way things looked in the waiting room, nothing was going to change anytime soon.

Down the hallway, she saw Alex leaning over a man, listening to his chest with her stethoscope. Alex brushed her braid off her left shoulder as she straightened up. She wrote something in the chart that she then handed to one of the medical students standing next to her.

Their eyes met as they walked back toward the nurse's station and the resident swore Alex winked, as she got closer. "Crazy day, huh?"

"You love it when it's like this." Regina smiled up at the doctor, knowing how much Alex thrived on the chaos. She'd seen it time and again over the past few months; it was when things fell apart and life hung tenuously in the balance that the doctor was at her best.

In those moments, Regina had seen a side to Alex that was devoid of all the emotional turmoil that haunted her subconscious. The blonde stole a glance at her taller companion and wondered if what they had discovered in each other would be enough for Alex to let go of the past and allow them a chance at a future together.

The young resident's attention was drawn to Sandy as she spoke sharply into the phone. "Well, tell them we need the beds. Community Medical Center is already diverting major traumas so we have to take them." She slammed the phone down in aggravation and muttered under her breath.

"That bad?" Regina asked.

"Can that patient be discharged?" Sandy pointed to the chart Regina was holding.

"As soon as the IV is finished. The orders are already written."

"Good." She grabbed the chart from her and glanced up at Alex. "Dr. Mitchard was looking for you earlier and we have another patient the paramedics just brought in."

"What did she want?" Alex asked.

"She said she'd find you later."

Regina glanced down the hallway toward the entrance of the emergency room and gasped. "Oh my God."

"What?" Alex turned to follow her partner's gaze and saw a man standing just inside the door. She recognized the family resemblance and leaned closer to the blonde. "I take it that's your father."

Regina nodded mutely. "Oh, shit. I can't believe he's here. I-I told him I got off at nine."

"Well, you better go get him away from the ambulance bay doors before he gets run over by an overzealous paramedic," Alex advised her quietly.

Regina stepped hesitantly away from the desk and walked awkwardly down the hall toward her father.

Regina's heart hammered rapidly in her chest as her father turned and focused on her. *Oh this is not good. How is it that parents can reduce you to feeling like a little kid again just by the look they give you?*

"Dad?" Regina stopped, standing awkwardly in front of him. "I-I still have an hour to go. I wasn't expecting you for a while yet."

He gave her an apologetic grin. "I know." He turned towards her and tucked one of her hands into his larger one.

Regina started at the unfamiliar gesture. "Dad, what's wrong?"

"She wouldn't come with me. I'm sorry, Regina."

The blonde swallowed and averted her eyes to hide the pain from her father. *Why did I think that she would?* "It was a lot to expect that she would, Dad. She's upset."

"You're her daughter." His voice was filled with hurt and anger.

Regina mustered her own reassuring smile when she met his gaze again. "It'll be all right, Dad. She needs time." She turned back towards the desk. "Come on, at least you can get some coffee while you wait."

"So, this is where you work," he commented as he walked past several stretchers lined up against the wall.

"This is what I do, Dad," she replied and guided him past the exam and trauma rooms that were mostly filled with sick and injured in various stages of triage. The resident winced inwardly as she saw his eyes react to the pain and suffering that was part of a daily routine to her now. It wasn't that she was immune to it, not by a long shot. In the months she had been here, she had developed her own defenses and learned to hang onto the successes, so the memories carried her along during the really bad traumas.

Regina had been trying to decide since last night if she was going to introduce her parents to Alex and, if she did, what she would say. Now, as she neared the desk and saw the statuesque woman crouched in front of a woman in a wheelchair, she knew her answer. *I don't care what he thinks. He's down here. This is who I am and that is the woman I love.*

The resident waited as Alex stood up and motioned to one of the medical students to come over. She handed him the chart and gave him instructions before she turned the patient over to a tall, lanky man. The doctor stood with her hands on her hips watching the medical student disappear into one of the exam rooms. Her dark head turned and her chin lifted slightly as she met Regina's gaze.

"Alex, this is my father." She saw the imperceptible softening in the blue eyes as Alex stared at her for a second then turned and offered her hand to the man.

"Mr. Kingston." She grasped his hand, her demeanor still guarded as they sized each other up. *Next time, we're going to have to discuss strategy before we do one of these impromptu introductions, my friend.* "Your daughter's an excellent doctor."

"It's Roger and I know she is."

Regina let out a breath as both of them relaxed slightly. She heard an exaggerated cough behind her and turned to see Sandy standing behind the desk, arms crossed and a comical expression on her face. "Well, I know where I rate now. Huh, Dr. Kingston? Good enough to work by your side in the trenches, but..."

"Sandy," Regina objected but the nurse winked at her and reached over the desk to take her father's hand.

"Hello, Mr. Kingston. I'm Sandy. Don't let that tall dark-haired one fool you. She thinks she runs the emergency department. I just haven't let her in on the joke yet. How about I show you where we have drinkable coffee in this joint while they go save the world?"

Roger smiled disarmingly as the nurse walked around the desk and took his arm. "Thanks, I think I could use some. It's cold out there tonight."

Regina turned and glanced at the taller woman standing behind her. "Breathe, Alex."

Alex snorted from behind her. "I am." She watched Sandy walk down the hall leading Regina's father into the lounge then grumbled something about checking on a medical student.

Regina scratched her temple and blew out a breath as Alex brushed by her and headed down the hall. Sandy came up beside her a few minutes later and poked her in the back. "Thanks," Regina said, smiling.

"Don't mention it. I really wasn't relishing the prospect of having to do CPR on the two of them right here in the middle hallway. Too much paperwork to fill out."

They snickered and then laughed as they looked at each other.

A moment later the radio crackled and came to life on the desk. "Aw shit. This can't be good." The blonde nurse turned and quickly picked up the microphone. Alex reappeared from the exam room and stepped forward, listening to the garbled voice coming through over the receiver.

Sandy glanced up as she wrote down a few quick notes. "Motor vehicle accident. One critically injured. They're five minutes out."

Alex stepped away from the desk, grabbed an isolation gown from one of the bins, and slipped it on, her mind already running through all the clinical scenarios they might be up against. "I'm going to need your help, Regina."

Regina quickly followed, grabbing a pair of gloves from one

of the wall boxes. She stopped one of the medical students as he walked out of the lounge.

"Michael, we've got a trauma coming in. You need to be there to work on your procedures."

"I just have to run something down to the lab."

"Well, hurry up and get back here," Regina said as she pulled her protective goggles on and ran toward the ambulance bay just as the paramedics banged through the emergency room doors.

"We've got a twenty-one-year-old male, ejected from his vehicle, and thrown approximately fifteen feet. We intubated him in the field. His pulse is thready, blood pressure is ninety." The litany continued as the doctors and paramedics rushed the patient down the hallway and into the trauma room. They wheeled the stretcher up alongside the table and efficiently transferred the young man over.

"What's his name?" Alex asked.

"Tim, Tim Johnson." The paramedic glanced down at his clipboard. He collected the backboard from the technicians and walked slowly out of the room. He bumped into one of the medical students who barged through the door, tying his mask behind his head.

"Sorry," Michael mumbled.

"Tim, can you hear me?" Alex called out. She bent over, flashing her penlight over his pupils. "His right pupil is fixed and not reactive."

Regina rubbed the knuckles of her fist over his sternum. "He's unresponsive to pain."

"Let's get a CBC, type and cross match for four units of blood. Do a drug and alcohol screen. I need two more IV lines, sixteen-gauge with normal saline. Hang a Dopamine drip and get a catheter in him, now. Let's move people! Get his clothes off," Alex barked, as she ran skilled fingers over his skull and face. Probing gently, she felt a depression in the back of his head. "He's got a depressed skull fracture."

As Sandy reached around Alex hooking the tube coming from his mouth to the ventilator, one of the ER techs was already on the phone calling the OR and another was quickly cutting away the young man's clothes.

Regina listened for breath sounds, moving the stethoscope deliberately over his chest. "I've got decreased breath sounds on both sides. Check the position of the tube."

Alex bent over and pulled the endotracheal tube out a couple of inches. "Anything?"

Regina shook her head, still listening with the stethoscope. "Decreased breath sounds, both sides. I need two chest tube kits."

"I got it." Sandy grabbed the kits out of the cabinets. After ripping the covering off of them, she dropped the kits on the instrument tables then handed Regina a scalpel.

Regina grabbed the instrument from the nurse and quickly made a six-centimeter long incision between the young man's ribs. Using her fingers, she spread the hole and inserted the tube until she felt it break through the outer lining of the lung. Working quickly, she sutured the wound closed.

"I got the lines in," Michael announced moments later, as he hung the bags up on the IV pole. He backed up and bumped into the instrument tray, knocking it over with a loud crash.

"God damn it, watch what you're doing," Alex growled as she made a quick incision and pushed her fingers inside, making the hole wider. "Sandy, get me another kit, now."

Embarrassed at his clumsiness, Michael skulked behind the attending and picked up the tray stand, setting it upright. He stood at the foot of the stretcher watching awkwardly as the two doctors worked feverishly over the patient. Sandy shoved a plastic kit in his hands. "Make yourself useful and catheterize him."

"Thomas," Regina called to the technician. "Dress this wound for me." Moving around him, she grabbed the portable ultrasound unit and performed a scan of the patient's abdomen. "He's got blood in his abdominal cavity. The aorta is torn."

One of the technicians watched the automatic cuff around the patient's arm inflate and measure his blood pressure. "His pressure's ninety and dropping."

The door to the trauma room swung open and one of the nurses stuck her head in. "Dr. Margulies, we've got another trauma on its way."

"Page Dr. Washington and Dr. Jack. We're busy," Alex snapped, without looking up from the patient as she inserted the tube into the chest wall. "Give him point five of atropine and open up the IV's all the way." Alex looked up at the monitor. *Shit, we're losing him.*

"They are," the medical student said.

"Then squeeze the bag in," Alex ordered. "He's losing volume as fast as we're putting it in."

One of the nurses ran into the room and handed Sandy the four units of blood. "Here, check it with me," Sandy said, pulling her back. Quickly, they compared the labels with the patient's blood type, and then Sandy hung the bags and piggybacked them to the IV lines.

"There's a hundred cc's of blood in the bag," Regina said, as she held up the catheter bag.

"He's bleeding out. Do we have the O-neg yet?" Alex demanded

"It's already going in," Sandy said.

One of the surgeons, still in his bloodied surgical scrubs from his last case, ran into the room pulling on a mask. "What've we got?"

"Blunt abdominal trauma, closed head injury, internal bleeding, blown pupil, his blood pressure is ninety over palp," Sandy quickly reported.

Moments later, outside in the hallway, they heard a frantic voice calling the young man's name. Alex glanced up as the man's voice drew closer. "If those are the parents, keep them the hell out of here. They don't need to see this."

One of the other nurses stepped out of the room and looked down the hallway. She cursed under her breath and jogged in the direction of the police officer and the two people she guessed were the man's parents. She heard the father's question as she came up alongside them.

"What happened? The hospital called and said my son was in an accident."

Derrick pulled his cap off and scratched his head. "Sir, a drunk driver hit your son's car."

"He's all right, isn't he?" The woman's voice trembled and she clutched her husband's arm.

"Sir, please come with me." The nurse glared up at the officer, angry that he had told them about the drunk driver. "The doctors are taking care of him right now."

The father turned and stared down at the nurse. "Where's my son?" he demanded, pushing abruptly past her. "The officer just told me a drunk driver hit my son. I want to see him now, dammit!"

"Sir, please, the doctors will be out to speak to you when they can." The nurse dressed in blue scrubs tried to guide him toward the waiting area but he shrugged her hand off his arm.

"Where is he?" he demanded, wrapping an arm around his

wife's shoulders as she stood beside him.

The nurse had the couple almost past the trauma room when the doors behind them crashed open and the paramedics, followed by two more police officers, rushed the driver of the other car into the emergency department.

Dr. Washington ran past the nurse in the direction of the paramedics. "Let's go," he said, pointing with his finger. "Room three is open."

The man turned, watching the stretcher disappear through the doors and then his eyes were drawn to the movement in the room adjacent to him.

Inside the chaotic trauma room, Alex looked up at the monitor and watched the short bursts of abnormal heartbeats. "He's throwing PVC's. Give him a loading dose of Lidocaine."

Regina reached behind Sandy and grabbed the vial of medication from the med cart. After quickly drawing the medication into the syringe, she grabbed the IV and jabbed the needle into the port, depressing the plunger.

Everyone watched the monitor as the medication, at first, controlled his heart's wild contractions, and then gave way to the failing muscle. The monitor alarmed shrilly as the man's heart rate suddenly flat-lined on the monitor.

"Asystole. Give him one milligram of epinephrine, now." Alex leaned over him and compressed his chest. Regina grabbed the defibrillator paddles from the code cart, charging them to two hundred-seventy joules, and brought the paddles down onto his chest.

"Clear," she said, and Alex backed away, raising her hands from the body. She pressed the buttons and watched as the body convulsed on the stretcher.

Alex met Regina's eyes briefly in a knowing glance. They were in a battle against time and it was quickly running out on the patient lying beneath them on the stretcher. They repeated the sequence two more times, increasing the drugs and charging the paddles higher each time in an attempt to restart his heart.

"What about a thoracotomy and cross-clamping the aorta?" Regina asked, as she stood by with paddles charged and ready, and Alex pumped on his chest. She wasn't ready to give up just yet.

The surgeon shook his head as he watched with growing detachment what was going on at the table. "The mortality rate is ninety percent with a blunt abdominal trauma. There's too much damage; nothing we can do."

They worked on the young man for several more minutes, desperately trying to bring him back from death's door, but to no avail. Finally, Alex straightened up, looking up at the flat line on the monitor. She hated admitting defeat. "Time of death: eighteen forty-five." She ripped her gloves off and threw them on the floor in disgust.

The surgeon shook his head and walked outside the room. "What a waste. The guy never had a chance."

Outside, the father shoved the nurse away from him and grabbed the door as it started to swing closed. "No! Why are you giving up? You can't stop."

Everyone in the room stood rooted in place, shocked at the sudden, unexpected appearance of the man and woman, both obviously the young man's parents.

Regina who was the closest to the distraught father, hesitantly stepped closer, and put a hand on his arm. "Mr. Johnson, I'm sorry. Your son sustained a severe head injury and massive internal damage to his organs. We used all our resources."

The woman who had been standing mutely, clinging to her husband's arm, buried her head against his chest and let out a low, keening wail.

Regina looked into the man's face wishing desperately that she didn't have to say the next part. "I'm sorry, Mr. Johnson, but we couldn't save him." Regina clenched her jaw nervously at the anguished expression on the man's face.

Sandy grabbed Alex's arm and directed her to the adjacent door. "Jon needs you next door. I'll help Regina with the parents. Go."

Alex could hear the commotion coming from the trauma room as soon as she stepped through the adjoining doors. Her gut clenched when she observed the struggle that was going on with the patient on the table.

"Let me go, damn it. You're not taking my clothes off."

"Thomas, hold her down." The woman on the stretcher flailed her arms violently against the doctor.

Two quick steps brought Alex up beside the stretcher and she grabbed the woman's arms and pinned her down to the stretcher. Her eyes widened as she recognized the woman.

"Dana, shut up and stop fighting with them."

"Let go of me, you bitch." She spat in Alex's face. Dana reached inside her coat.

"Whoa, Jesus Christ, get that!" Jon yelled, as he grabbed Dana's arm. Alex's ears picked up the clatter of metal on the tile and her brain slowly registered the fact that Dana had pulled out a gun. Alex quickly retrieved it from the floor.

"Make sure this gets into the lock box and call security," she growled as she shoved the butt of the gun into a technician's hands. His eyes bulged as he gingerly took hold of the shiny, black handled weapon and ran out of the room.

Jon grabbed Dana's hand, pinned it to her side, and quickly tied it in a restraint. "She's got a tender abdomen and she needs to go to the OR for an exploratory laparotomy."

"Fuck you! Let go of me," Dana growled.

"Shut up, Dana." Alex leaned over the struggling woman, as she tied Dana's other arm down. "What happened?"

"She broad-sided the kid you were working on."

"Shit." A wave of revulsion swept through Alex as she stared at Dana in disbelief. She yanked the restraint tight around her wrist and glared at the wild-eyed blonde, struggling to contain her anger at the senseless loss of life that Dana had caused. "Let's get her to CT scan, now." Alex jerked the rails up on her side of the stretcher.

There was a loud crash just outside the door, followed by several cries of alarm as a supply cart slammed into the wall and tipped over, sending boxes and plastic bins scattering across the floor.

"What the hell is going on out there?" Alex heard angry shouts and then the door to the trauma room slammed open behind her.

"Let her die."

The hair on the back of Alex's neck stood up at the sound of the voice.

The two doctors looked up at the same time and stared at the man pointing Dana's gun at her as she lay on the stretcher. Outside the door, they caught a glimpse of Sandy leaning over the technician who was sprawled on the floor.

"She didn't give my son a chance. She doesn't deserve one."

Alex straightened up slowly, aware that Jon was now moving the stretcher toward the side door away from the man with the gun. "It's not our decision to make, Mr. Johnson. Give me the gun. No one wants anyone else hurt tonight." Alex slowly reached her hand out.

The man stepped closer, his hands trembling as he held the

gun in front of him. "You're not taking her anywhere."

"Mr. Johnson." Regina stepped through the door behind him, holding her hands up in front of her as he whirled around pointing the gun at her.

"Regina, get out of here," Alex hissed at her.

The resident shook her head and held the man's gaze as she stepped closer. "Please, Mr. Johnson, your wife just lost her son. She doesn't need to lose her husband, too."

"Alex, we've got to move her. Her pressure is dropping." Jon set the portable monitor on the end of the stretcher and hooked the EKG wire to it along with the pulse oximeter.

"No!" The man spun around now holding the gun on Jon as he worked on the injured woman.

"Get a dopamine drip started and push another liter of fluid, Jon." Alex didn't take her eyes off the distraught father.

"That bitch killed my son!" He stepped closer to the stretcher, his whole body shaking as he started to squeeze the trigger.

"I know." Regina stepped up beside him and held her hand out. "Give me the gun, Mr. Johnson. You don't want to do this."

He turned and stared down at the blonde pleading with him.

There was the sound of footsteps running down the hallway and more shouts of alarm. Alex edged closer, thinking she had the best chance to grab the gun away while he was focused on Regina. She could sense the man's resolve crumbling as he stared at Regina, the hand holding the gun slowly lowering to the floor.

Out of the corner of her eye, she picked out the blur of blue fabric as two police officers filled the doorway to the trauma room.

"No!" Alex waved them back.

Startled by the officers' appearance, the man cried out and spun back around, pulled the gun up and aimed it at Dana. At the same time, Alex darted forward, her outstretched hand grabbing for his wrist. For one instant, Regina met Alex's eyes as the doctor struggled to wrestle the gun from the father's hands. The sharp staccato report of a gun firing drowned the younger woman's cry.

A look of surprise registered on Alex's face as something punched her in the chest and stole her breath away. She stumbled, her legs collapsing underneath her, and she fell to her knees. Far away, she heard voices shouting as pandemonium broke out around her.

She dropped face down on the floor, feeling the cold tile on her face and her hands. The two police officers barreled through the door, pushed Regina aside, and knocked the man into a code cart, spilling its contents across the floor.

Jon pulled the stretcher with Dana on it out of the room and into the hallway as Regina scrambled forward, dropped to her knees, and grabbed Alex by the shoulders. She rolled the injured doctor over and saw a dark red stain blossoming over the front of doctor's scrub top.

"Regina." Alex's voice was little more than a whisper as she slowly focused on her lover.

"D-Don't say anything, Alex. Just hold on." Regina's hands trembled as she grabbed a package lying on the floor and ripped it open, slapping the pressure bandage over the ragged hole in Alex's chest. She pressed her hand over it, slowing the flow of blood, and looked around frantically. "I need help in here!"

She could hear Jon in the hallway barking out commands as he turned Dana's care over to a surgical resident and a nurse. In front of her, the officers were dragging the man to his feet, stumbling and tripping over contents of the code cart as they hauled him out of the room.

"Sandy! I need help."

The nurse bumped into the officers as she ran into the room, followed by one of the techs. "Oh my God!"

"Help me," Regina pleaded, still pressing her hand down over the bloody wound in Alex's chest. "We've got to get her on a stretcher."

"On three...one, two, three," Regina directed and together they quickly lifted the attending off the floor and onto a stretcher. Alex groaned and passed out as a wave of intense pain exploded inside her chest.

Meanwhile, Jon raced back down the hallway and caught Maggie's attention, as she talked frantically into the phone.

"No, I can't hold on, just tell them to be ready. I don't care who they have to bump. Tell them it's one of their own doctors, dammit!" She slammed the phone down and caught up with Jon as they got to the trauma room. "The OR's on standby."

"Good. Thomas," Jon called to the technician as he ran out of the trauma room across from them. "I need four units of O-negative blood."

"I gotta get something for one of the residents."

"Just get me the damn blood," Jon snapped, as they turned the corner into the room.

"I need a blood pressure on her." Regina turned around to grab a pair of gloves and bumped into one of the police officers coming back into the room. Shock registered on her face as she recognized who it was.

"Move, Derrick." She shoved him out of the way.

"I have to get the gun and the shells," he said, shoving her back. Jon appeared and grabbed Derrick by the shoulders with both hands.

"Get the hell out of here," he ordered, shoving Derrick out of the room. "Move!"

Regina looked up as Marcus ran breathless into the room, from having been stat paged overhead. "Marcus, get over here and help us."

"Son of a bitch." His voice cracked when he saw Alex lying covered in blood on the stretcher. "What happened?"

"Blood pressure is one-hundred over fifty," Sandy reported.

"Good breath sounds bilaterally," Regina said, as she listened to Alex's chest with the stethoscope.

"She's losing volume. Get two 16-gauge lines in now and start a Dopamine drip," Jon ordered.

Alex blinked her eyes. It was dark and eerily quiet around her. She heard a rushing noise in her ears, and then a searing pain exploded in her chest. Above her, she could hear disconnected voices shouting frantically.

"I need a larger needle." She heard Regina's strained voice and she stared up at the blonde through the oxygen mask that covered her face. From a distance, someone shouted at Regina and she pulled away out of Alex's line of sight.

"I don't care what size. Just give me a larger needle."

Cool air hit her skin as scissors ripped away her scrub top to expose her chest. Something cold and wet swabbed her neck and Alex felt a prick in her arm and then a burning pain in the base of her neck as another line was inserted.

"Alex." Regina was staring down at her now. Setting her hands on either side of her head, she leaned over her.

"R-Regina?" Alex asked hesitantly, trying to focus through the pain and the confusion. It hurt to breathe; everything was jumbled in her mind and she couldn't remember what happened, only knew that something went terribly wrong.

"Alex, look at me." Blue eyes drifted away, then slowly

tracked back to meet Regina's. "Do you know where you are?"

The doctor nodded her head slowly. "Hospital. I-I'm sorry."

"Don't say that." Regina shook her head fighting back tears. "You stay with me. You're going to be okay. I promise."

"C-cold," she said through chattering teeth. Everything seemed to be fading, getting farther away and harder to hold onto, as she tried desperately to stay focused on Regina's face. A swirl of red, blue, and green lights danced in her peripheral vision and then everything started to go a fuzzy white. *Oh God, please not here. Not like this.* Mercifully, the drugs injected into the IV pulled her down into a blissful indifference as the opiates coursed through her veins.

"Pulse is one-twenty."

"Where's the blood?" Regina demanded.

"It just came in." Sandy grabbed the units of blood from Thomas and pushed him over to the table. Jon helped Sandy hang the blood, piggybacking the lines and slipping the pressure sleeves over the IV bags to force the fluid in faster.

"We need to move her, now," Dr. Washington said, as he watched the monitor. The doors to the room banged open and Dr. Kelly, one of the surgeons, ran in pulling on a gown and gloves. "What the hell happened?"

"Gunshot wound to the chest. We've pumped in two liters of fluid and she's on her first unit of O-neg blood," Jon said.

Sandy pointed to the catheter bag. "She's bleeding out. There's another one hundred cc's in the bag. Her systolic pressure is dropping."

"It could've hit one of the kidneys," Regina said, as she searched for another vein in Alex's arm. "She needs volume. Squeeze in another bag of fluid." Regina jabbed another needle into a vein and set up another line.

"Let's go, let's go," Dr. Washington ordered, pulling up the rails of the stretcher. The surgeon stopped the stretcher. "No, she won't make it to the OR." He turned and grabbed a clear plastic package from the shelves behind him. "We have to stop the bleeding. Intubate her and prep for a thoracotomy, now," he ordered, as he tore open the plastic wrapping and pulled out the sternal saw.

There was a split second hesitation as everyone realized what they were about to do. Sandy grabbed a large sterile bundle off one of the shelves and broke the seal, setting the instruments on a tray that was next to the surgeon.

"Give me an amp of epinephrine and a number eight endotracheal tube," Jon barked as he slipped up to the head of the stretcher. He ripped open the package of tubing and tilted Alex's head back. Seconds later the tube was hooked up to the ventilator, pumping oxygen into Alex's lungs.

Regina quickly moved to the side of the table, shrugging into the sterile gown that one of the techs shook open. She glanced up at the monitor and saw the rapid heartbeat displayed on the monitor. "She's tachycardic."

One of the nurses squirted Betadine down the center of Alex's chest, lengthways between her breasts, and then hastily laid the sterile drapes around the site. By the door, Thomas slammed the phone down. "The OR's waiting for us."

Jon made the incision down the length of Alex's sternum with the scalpel. The moment he lifted the scalpel away, Dr. Kelly leaned over Alex and pressed the blade of the reciprocating saw against the bone, then pressed the trigger. Regina physically recoiled at the high-pitched buzzing sound and the sight of the serrated blade ripping through the length of the glistening white bone, spraying a mist of bone dust and blood into the air.

The resident grabbed hold of the stretcher to steady herself, fighting back a wave of nausea, as she looked at the ashen face lying swathed under blankets and medical equipment.

Jon grabbed the rib spreader from the tray. He inserted the tool between the space in the breastbone, rapidly turned the crank, and locked it in place. He held it steady and moved back a step to give the surgeon room.

Dr. Kelly bent over the open cavity of Alex's chest. "Dammit, give me more suction. I can't see a goddamn thing with all this blood."

Marcus reached over and the sound of the suction gurgled loudly, almost drowning out the sounds of the ventilator as it whooshed and beeped at the head of the table. As he was doing that, Sandy ripped open the sterile packaging around a stack of sterile gauze towels and shoved them inside. She quickly pulled out the blood-soaked towels and threw them on the floor, then repeated the process several more times.

Regina watched as the surgeon groped inside, desperately trying to find the source of the bleeding. They were losing her. Regina could feel it happening. A strong sense of dread filled her and she fought to control her fear. *Oh God, no, please don't let this happen. Hang on, Alex, please, just hang on a few min-*

*utes more.*

The resident stepped forward. "You're taking too long," she said, through clenched teeth. She grabbed a pair of sterile gloves from the box behind her, tore open the package and quickly shoved her hands into them.

The surgeon glanced up at her. "You're not a surgeon, Dr. Kingston," he grunted, as he continued to search futilely with his hands.

"We're losing her. Let me at least try." Regina didn't hesitate as she stepped forward and leaned over Alex's body. She grabbed a sterile towel from Sandy and reached inside, stopping the flow of blood with the pressure, then watched for the split second when the damaged vessel uncompressed and started to pump out the crimson colored blood again.

"There it is." The surgeon moved his hands, exposing the torn vessel.

"I see it," Regina said, as she searched around with her hands. "Give me a clamp." She grabbed the instrument from Sandy's hand and clamped the large vessel. "I need three-o silk. Hurry up, dammit. Jon, I need more resection," Regina ordered, and waited a moment as the doctor cranked the rib spreader, allowing her more room. "That's it, good. Hold it there." Regina worked quickly, sewing the hole in the vessel closed.

"Good, good," Dr. Kelly said, as Jon applied more pressure to the rib spreader and held it in place.

Sandy glanced up at the monitor. "Her pressure is stable: one hundred over fifty and holding."

"Okay, let's move, now."

"Here." Dr. Washington threw several layers of sterile gauze over the open wound in the doctor's chest and poured sterile water over it to keep the exposed tissues from drying out on the short trip to the OR.

"Come on, let's move." There was a flurry of activity as the team unhooked the myriad of lines and tubes.

"Don't forget the drug box," Sandy called out, as she back-pedaled, pulling the stretcher with her towards the door.

"I got it. Watch the lines!" Thomas rescued one of the IV's from snagging on a med cart.

Jon grabbed the supply cart and hauled it upright. With Marcus at the head of the stretcher, squeezing the bag mask resuscitator, Regina and Sandy pulled the stretcher into the hallway. At a dead run down the hallway, the surgical team met the stretcher half way to the OR.

"We got her from here, guys."

Regina stared after the stretcher as the doors swung closed behind her. The silence in the hallway was deafening as they stood there. There was nothing to do now but wait. Regina's breath went ragged as she collapsed back against the wall. She slid to the floor as she finally let go of the rigid control she had been holding during the whole ordeal. Her vision narrowed as two pairs of hands took hold of her arms and lifted her. Then suddenly, she knew only darkness.

# Chapter
## 22

Still dressed in her bloodied scrubs, Regina sat outside the operating room suites in the waiting room, oblivious to the noises and activity going on around her. All that she could think of was that she had told Alex not to go after Dana and now a day later an innocent boy was dead and Alex was in critical condition with a bullet in her chest.

*Whatever happens, no matter how bad it is, you can't be there to keep picking her up.* The words kept running through her head and she couldn't help but feel somewhat responsible for what happened tonight.

The blonde resident tilted her head back against the wall and closed her eyes, seeking a respite from her clamoring thoughts. It had been two hours and Alex was still in the OR. There was damage to her spleen and her lumbar vertebrae had barely been spared the damage that the bullet did as it penetrated her body.

"Here, Regina, take this." Sandy sat down next to her and handed her a cup of soup and some tea from the cafeteria.

"I can't eat this, Sandy." The resident shoved her friend's hand away and lifted her head, a forlorn look in her tear-stained eyes.

"You've got to try and eat something, Regina." Sandy squeezed her arm. "Jon is getting her personnel folder for an emergency contact. Is there anybody I can call? Any family that could be here for her?"

Regina stared at the opposite wall, fighting back another wave of intense emotion that threatened to overwhelm her. "I don't know. Her mother...she hasn't spoken to in a long time. I-I think she's in Arizona. I really don't know. Oh God, Sandy, I told her not to go after Dana. What if she had found her?" She dropped her head down into her hands and stifled a sob. "None of this might have happened."

Sandy shook her head vehemently. "Don't even think that. No one is responsible for that boy's death except Dana. Besides, if Alex did find her, who knows what might have happened. Dana might have been crazy enough to shoot her in some back alley and leave her for dead. At least it happened here, and thank God we were here for her."

Regina shuddered at the thought. "Sandy, you know she was coming after Alex."

The nurse nodded her head grimly. "I know."

"Oh God, this is such a mess." Regina jumped to her feet and paced anxiously back and forth across the crowded waiting room.

Sandy sat quietly watching her distressed friend. "Regina, there's not a whole lot you can do right now. Why don't you get some rest? I'll wake you as soon as I hear anything."

Regina stopped pacing and turned around to face Sandy. "I'm not leaving her. I want to be here when she wakes up."

The nurse pushed herself up to her feet and caught Regina's arm. "Hey, you need to take care of yourself right now so you *can* be there for Alex when she does wake up." She held up a hand to forestall the protest on Regina's lips. "I don't want to hear it. Sleep in one of the on call rooms."

Regina hesitated as her green eyes searched the nurse's. "You promise you'll call me as soon as she's out of surgery?"

"I swear you'll be the first to know." Sandy wrapped her arm over Regina's shoulder and led her out of the waiting room.

They walked down the quiet corridor passing the doors that led into the surgical suites. As they turned the corner into the hallway that led to the ER, Regina stiffened and clutched Sandy's arm.

"Shit, what is he still doing here?" Sandy growled under her breath. "Didn't you get a restraining order?"

"Yes, but he can still be here if it's work related. Oh God, I can't deal with this now."

Derrick walked toward the two women. "Regina, I was looking for you."

"What do you want, Derrick?" Regina asked warily.

He spread his hands apart as he got closer. "I just wanted to make sure you were okay."

Sandy gave him an incredulous look as she strategically guided Regina around the officer. "You want to make sure she's okay? That's a laugh. You were there, you asshole. What do you think?"

Derrick persisted, following them down the hallway. "You know, Regina, none of this had to happen. All you have to do is just walk away from that doctor and everything would be back the way it was...your family...us."

"Us?" Regina whirled around and glared back at Derrick defiantly. "You self-serving son of a bitch! Don't you dare walk in here and tell me that what we had was something special. It was a lie, every last bit of it was a lie." She was so angry she shook as she stepped closer to him. "If you hadn't run into the room and scared the crap out of that man he would have never pulled the trigger on that gun. We almost had him talked out of it. You might as well have shot the gun yourself."

The door burst open at the end of the hallway and Dr. Washington stormed toward them. "Hey! What the hell is going on out here? I can hear the noise all the way down at the desk." His eyes narrowed as he recognized the police officer standing in front of Regina.

He stepped in between Regina and Derrick and went nose to nose with the man.

"You! Haven't you caused enough trouble around here for one day? If you had kept your mouth shut about that drunk driver, that man would have never reacted the way he did."

"The father had a right to know what happened to his son."

Dr. Washington grabbed Derrick's shirt and shoved him back against the wall. "It was bad enough they had to deal with losing their son today, but you had to go and dump that piece of news on them as well. There was a time and a place for it. It was *not* outside the trauma room as their son was dying." His eyes flashed angrily and he balled his right hand into a meaty fist.

"Jon, no!" Sandy grabbed the doctor's arm to keep him from hitting Derrick. "Let it go. He's not worth it."

The doctor's nostrils flared as he let some of the anger fade. Slowly he released his grip on Derrick's shirt and stepped back from him. "You get your ass out of this hospital, now," he growled. He turned to Regina and Sandy. "Come on, let's go, ladies."

Derrick grabbed Regina's arm as she walked by. "Regina," he sneered, "maybe you ought to wake up and realize your real family is more important than whatever that woman can offer you."

Without even thinking, Regina backhanded him hard across his face, snapping his head back. "Get out, Derrick. Just get out, you bastard!"

Stunned by her reaction, Derrick rubbed his jaw and blinked, clearing his vision. He watched in a daze as Regina and her two colleagues walked toward the ER, leaving him standing alone in the hallway.

Most of the staff was quiet, talking in hushed whispers as the three of them entered the ER. It was always difficult losing someone so young. This, coupled with the additional strain of having one of their own critically injured in the melee that followed the young man's death taxed the staff to their emotional and physical limits.

Jon quietly disengaged himself from the two women and walked over to a small cluster of medical staff. "Come on, people, I know this has been a shitty day for us, but we still have patients to take care of." Reluctantly, the small group dispersed quickly, the routine of their work a balm to the chaos that had reigned earlier.

He turned to Marcus who had stayed on beyond his shift to help out. "Everyone has their assignments?"

"It's all taken care of, Jon. I called Dr. Ortiz and let him know what happened. He's going to help cover Dr. Margulies' shifts in the meantime. I'll stay and help too."

Jon nodded, knowing that Marcus was voluntarily giving up his vacation to help out with everything. "Thanks, man. I owe you one."

Across the hallway, Sandy guided Regina into one of the exam rooms and ushered the resident up onto the treatment table.

"Sit. Let me see your hand." She shook her head as she inspected the growing purplish discoloration on the back of the resident's hand. "Nice job, slugger."

Regina slumped forward as her body acknowledged the pain shooting up her forearm. "I broke it, didn't I?"

"Looks like it. Hold still," the nurse admonished gently,

inspecting the resident's swollen hand.

"Great, a perfect end to the day." Regina winced as Sandy wrapped a bag of ice around her hand with an Ace bandage. "Is my father still here?"

"One of the nurses sent him down to the cafeteria when all hell broke loose up here. He's around here somewhere. Things are still pretty wild around this place. I'm going to get one of the docs to X-ray this and then cast it for you. Just rest for awhile." Sandy saw the look of worry in her friend's face and squeezed Regina's shoulder. "She's got the best people taking care of her."

Sandy left the room and returned several minutes later with one of the new residents in tow. "Regina, this is Tom. He'll take care of you."

Regina looked at the exhausted looking doctor and sighed. "All right, let's get this done with."

Tom gingerly held the woman's arm. "Dr. Kingston, this will go a lot faster if you sit down," the dark-skinned man advised her as he wrapped strips of fiberglass around her hand and wrist.

Green eyes flashed angrily and then she relented, sitting down on the stretcher. "Sorry," she muttered, trying to contain her nervousness.

"Regina." Her father walked into the exam room as the resident finished wrapping the fiberglass strips around her arm to cast the fracture. His eyes widened when he saw the cast being applied to her arm. "What happened to you?" He laid a hand on his daughter's shoulder as he came up beside her.

"It's a long story, Dad." Regina looked up at him miserably.

He sat down beside her on the stretcher, waiting in silence until the resident finished his job and hastily left the room.

"How's the doctor who got hurt?" he asked softly. There was no need for him to ask about the young man. He overheard some of the staff talking as he walked back into the ER minutes before.

Regina's body sagged and she shrugged her shoulders in response to the question. "She's in bad shape. They don't know if she's going to make it," she whispered, fresh tears falling anew and staining her scrub top.

Gently brushing the blonde hair back behind his daughter's ear, Roger pulled her against him. "You're good friends with her?"

Regina remained silent, watching her father's eyes as they

looked into hers. She hesitated, moving her hand idly over her cast as she studied him anxiously.

He dug inside one of his pockets and pulled out a hard candy, offering it to her. She shook her head and smiled at the familiar gesture from her childhood. *I wish it were still that easy to make everything all better, Dad.* "No thanks."

"You're my only daughter, Regina. There was a time when you could tell me anything."

She laughed suddenly. "I was a kid then."

"You're still my kid, no matter what."

She swallowed nervously and gathered her courage as she gazed up at the anxious brown eyes. "Dad, what would you say if I told you I'm in love with her?"

A startled expression came over his face and he looked down at his hands while he fiddled with the plastic wrapping around the hard candy. "H-how long have you known her?"

"Six months." Regina stared down at her hands. *Six of the best months of my life.* Everyday was an adventure. She looked forward to each shift they worked together, and felt a soul deep loneliness each time they parted company.

"How can you be sure?"

*I've never been surer of anything in my life.* "How did you know you loved Mom?"

Her father's breath caught and his eyes widened in surprise and anger. "You'd compare this to your mother and I?" His voice was tinged with disbelief as he stared at his daughter.

Regina sat up straighter and squared her shoulders. "I've never felt more complete than I do when I'm with her." *Why didn't I tell her that when I had the chance to?*

The door opened and Regina looked up as Sandy poked her head in and motioned her over.

"Tina called. They're just bringing her up to recovery now."

"Dad, I'm sorry. I've got to go."

He held her arm for a second, his eyes filling with tears when he let her go. "I'll be at the hotel until tomorrow night if you need me."

Regina jumped off the stretcher, ran out of the room, dogged a stretcher being wheeled down the hallway by an orderly, and barely missed plowing into one of the housekeepers who was mopping the floor.

❖ ⌘ ❖ ⌘ ❖ ⌘ ❖

The surgeon's words echoed hauntingly in her head long after he had left the recovery room.

She lost four units of blood. There was damage to her spleen...swelling in her back from the bullet compressing the spinal cord...the next seventy-two hours are critical for her.

She lost track of the hours while she sat in the uncomfortable chair, facing the hospital bed in the recovery room and then later in the Intensive Care Unit after they transferred Alex. She watched the steady rise and fall of the dark-haired woman's chest as oxygen was pumped in and out of her lungs by the ventilator.

"Regina," Tina said, as she walked into the dimly lit room.

The blonde looked over her shoulder and gave her a tired half smile. "Thanks for letting me stay with her."

The nurse rested a hand on the resident's shoulder. "It's good that you're here for her, but you need to get some rest, too."

"I will," the resident answered absently. She stared at the steady green fluorescent blips on the monitor recording Alex's heartbeat and respirations.

Tina stood next to Regina for a moment before she spoke. "Alex is strong, Regina. She's going to pull through."

Regina nodded her head and said a silent prayer hoping that Tina was right. Right now all she wanted in the world was her best friend and her lover back.

"If you need anything, let me know." The nurse squeezed her shoulder and then left her alone in the room.

The blonde moved to the edge of the hospital bed. Careful to avoid the tubes and IV lines that snaked over Alex's body, Regina slipped her hand under Alex's and squeezed it gently.

"Alex." She brought her lips close to her ear. "I'm right here." The blonde brought the back of the woman's hand up to her face and held it against her cheek. "You hold on, you hear me?" She stroked Alex's face with her other hand. "I can't lose you." *Not after I just found you.*

The rhythmic whoosh and click of the ventilator at the bedside penetrated the drug-induced fog. Alex blinked and opened her eyes. Her eyes focused briefly and she saw the white speckled surface of the ceiling tiles above her bed. She didn't know how long she had been out. She was only aware that time had passed by the amount of light reflecting through the window on her left.

Her first clear realization was the bone-deep throbbing pain in her chest, followed by the strong perception of someone sitting by the bedside, watching over her. Echoes of frantic voices replayed in her head as vague memories slowly surfaced and then disappeared. She remembered seeing the flash of metal and feeling the sudden, intense, crushing sensation in her chest as she fell to the ground.

A surge of pain rolled through her and she thrashed her head against the pillow, briefly fighting the ventilator. A soft voice whispered reassurances in her ear and a gentle hand brushed her bangs off of her face before she slipped back into the opiate-induced stupor.

Regina closed her eyes, as the tears came again. "You've got more courage than anyone I know. I need you to be strong and fight. Promise me you'll fight. I'm going to be here when you wake up." Regina bent over and kissed the brunette's forehead. *Please don't leave me.*

❖ ⌘ ❖ ⌘ ❖ ⌘ ❖

She was dressed in scrubs, standing alone in an empty room devoid of light. Her hair hung loosely around her shoulders and was pulled back on the sides by two small braids that were bound in the back by a leather barrette. *Am I dreaming?* She turned around, rubbing her hands over her arms as a chill settled over her. *Why am I so cold?*

Behind her she felt a faint breeze and looked over her shoulder to see a door cracked open with a soft, white light filtering into the room, casting a bluish hue along the wooden floor. She could feel it gently beckoning to her and she moved toward it.

There was no fear, just a sense of restfulness and peace. Her hand was on the door, pulling it open when she felt a momentary heart-wrenching wave of emotion that left her breathless and doubled over.

Alex turned and found herself standing face to face with Regina, close enough to touch the smooth skin of her face, to whisper in her ear, to feel her heartbeat, only she couldn't. Something separated them. The pain of their separation broke her heart and then suddenly the room, Regina, and the light were gone.

❖ ⌘ ❖ ⌘ ❖ ⌘ ❖

Someone cleared her throat from behind her and Regina turned around to focus on the tall, blonde woman standing outside the door.

"Dr. Kingston, I know this isn't a good time but I need to talk to you." Dr. Mitchard's eyes flicked once to the bed where her chief attending laid hooked up to a myriad of lines and tubes and then returned to Regina.

The resident straightened slowly and walked toward the Vice President. Reluctantly, she followed the stern looking woman down the hallway and into an empty ICU room.

"I'm asking you this in strictest confidence, Dr. Kingston," the doctor said as she turned around and made eye contact.

The resident felt her heart constrict at the words. A thousand confused thoughts whirled in her head, closing her eyes she willed her heart to stop racing and think clearly. "I understand, Dr. Mitchard."

"Yesterday morning, I asked Dr. Margulies about Dr. Jameson's interactions with a specific drug company. I need to know if she discussed anything with you."

It angered Regina that the VP didn't even bother to ask how Alex was. She let it pass, however, knowing that she needed to proceed cautiously. She remembered that Alex had asked her to stay out of the whole mess. *I'm sorry, Alex. I know you didn't want me involved but I don't have a choice anymore.*

"She didn't tell me anything specific," Regina answered carefully.

The doctor studied her closely and Regina had a strong sense that the woman didn't believe her. "Dr. Kingston, I know you're good friends with her and I understand your concern over what happened tonight, but I need to know if she has any documents that might help with the investigation. Without them, things look very bad for the whole ER department, your attending included."

"Why? I don't understand."

The executive's eyes narrowed as she studied the young doctor. "Dr. Kingston, the drug company is under suspicion of fraud and the hospital is linked to them. We need to disassociate ourselves from whomever, or whatever happened, as quickly as possible."

It suddenly became very clear to Regina what the Vice Pres-

ident was trying to do. She guessed from the urgency in Dr. Mitchard's voice their illustrious VP had either tacitly approved of
kickbacks by not intervening or had been a willing party to it all
along. Dr. Mitchard had to find out how many people knew about
this. Regina seethed as she stood in front of the woman.

Disassociate, my butt. You're looking for a fall guy and you
think with Alex out of commission she makes an easy target.
Well, think again, Dr. Mitchard.

"Dr. Mitchard, I'm afraid I can't help you. I don't know
anything about any documents." Regina turned and walked
quickly out of the room. The landscape had shifted dramatically
in one short meeting and the person she once trusted was no
longer the ally Regina thought she was.

She slipped back into Alex's room and stood at the bedside.
A few minutes later, one of the nurses came in and asked her to
leave so she could change the bandages. The blonde leaned over
and kissed Alex on the forehead, ignoring the curious stare she
got from the woman.

Regina wasted little time returning to the ER and immediately went in search of Dr. Washington. She found him tucked
away in one of the exam rooms pouring over a pile of charts.

He looked up and sat back in his chair when she walked in
the room. "How is she?"

"They gave her four units of blood and repaired the damage
to her spleen. They're worried about what damage there might be
in her back from all the swelling."

His eyes narrowed, sensing the conflict within. "What else
is bothering you?"

Regina looked up at the ceiling and blew out a breath. "Dr.
Mitchard just paid me a visit. She wants to know if Alex told me
anything about Dr. Jameson."

Jon set his pen down and crossed his legs. "At this point I
think everyone knows he was getting kickbacks from the drug
company."

Regina shook her head. "They're looking for someone to
take the fall. I think they're going to point the finger at Alex."

"How can they? She didn't do anything wrong."

"No, but she's looking to do damage control before the
investigation shows that this was going on right under her nose
and she didn't know about it."

The doctor sat back in his chair and blew out a breath.
"Shit! All right, let me think about this, Regina. In the mean-

time, go home. You need to sleep."

❖ ⌘ ❖ ⌘ ❖ ⌘ ❖

Regina didn't go home. She collapsed on a stretcher in an empty exam room and got little sleep that night. The sleep she did get was fitful. Her mind played tricks on her and she kept suffering through the same dream.

She kept seeing herself reaching out and holding Alex's face between her hands. Her friend, her lover, was dying, and she could feel her slipping away. She couldn't do anything to stop it from happening. Finally, after waking with a cry, Regina hauled herself off the stretcher and stumbled up to ICU.

The blonde walked up to the nursing night shift on the unit and asked for Alex's chart. She knew she shouldn't be doing this; she was using her privilege as a doctor to read the medical record but she had to know how Alex was doing. She flipped the pages to the last entry and felt a weight lift when she read that they had taken her off the ventilator. She headed directly to Alex's room, drew the curtain and pulled the chair up beside the bed. No one contested her being there. Dressed in her scrubs and lab coat they didn't question her presence, at least for now.

Regina sat next to the bed. She rested her head on the bed rail and watched as Alex slept unaware of what was going on around her. Scooting closer she traced her fingers over the woman's face.

"Alex, it's me." She glanced up as a nurse entered the room, but continued to talk to her softly. She knew that, despite her heavy sedation, Alex could still hear what was going on around her. "Everyone in the ER is asking about you. Jon said he was going to come up later today and see you. I miss you, Alex, please come back. We need you." Bending forward, she kissed her forehead.

❖ ⌘ ❖ ⌘ ❖ ⌘ ❖

The room was dark again when Alex blinked and opened her eyes. There was the deep, throbbing pain in her chest but, thankfully, the tubes in her throat and chest were gone. She heard the whirring and clicking of the IV pumps as their motors pumped the fluids into her veins. Slowly she turned her head and saw someone sitting slumped forward onto her hospital bed, a blonde head resting on crossed arms.

She turned her head slowly to the right and saw a bed rail, beyond it was a sink and a cabinet. A window to the outside world told her it was dark out. She turned her head back to the left and looked at the sleeping form.

Tentatively, she moved her hand, touching the soft blonde hair splayed out over the mattress. A sense of utter relief flowed through her when she felt the soft strands of hair run through her fingers. *You're real; it's not a dream.*

"Regina?" It came out in a hoarse whisper.

The blonde head lifted, eyes blinking in slow comprehension. "Y-You're awake." Regina slipped up beside the doctor and caressed her face with her good hand.

"I...love you," Alex whispered, leaning into Regina's hand.

"I love you, too, sweetheart."

Alex swallowed painfully, her throat still sore from the breathing tube. "Dana?"

Regina swallowed and slowly nodded her head. "She's alive."

"I'm sorry."

"Shh, get some rest."

"You saved me." Alex moved her arm and took hold of Regina's hand.

The resident shook her head. "It was a group effort, believe me."

Alex winced and swallowed painfully. "My chest hurts."

Regina leaned over and kissed her lips. "It should after what you went through. Go to sleep."

Alex shook her head. "Don't want to miss you."

"I'm not leaving," Regina whispered.

"No?"

"Not ever."

Alex reached up weakly with one hand and pulled Regina to her. "I love you."

# Chapter
# 23

Regina stayed with Alex, talking softly to her until the injured woman slipped back to sleep. She knew that the doctor had a long road ahead of her, but that was later; right now, she was just happy to have her alive. They would deal with whatever lay ahead as it happened.

Alex struggled in her sleep, crying out briefly. "Shh, you're going to be all right, Alex," the blonde reassured her.

Later, Regina dragged herself down to the ER for the start of her next shift, having gotten little more than a few hours of sleep in the past forty-eight hours. It was hard to believe what had happened as she looked around the department, now relatively quiet compared to the bloody chaos that had reigned just a day before.

Sandy and Marcus were standing together at the desk talking quietly to each other as Regina approached. The rosy-cheeked nurse pulled away from the conversation when she saw Regina. "How's she doing?"

The resident swayed slightly on her feet as she struggled to focus her sleep-deprived mind. "They took her off the ventilator a few hours ago and she woke up briefly. She's in a lot of pain and pretty confused about what happened."

Sandy wound her arm over the resident's shoulders and squeezed her. "You know, Alex has the constitution of an old war

horse. Just wait, she'll be full of piss and vinegar soon and then
God help us all, she'll be throwing the nurses and medical students out of her room in a few days."

Marcus patted Regina's shoulder. "They have no idea what
they're in for when she feels better."

Regina allowed herself a small grin at the description,
knowing full well the wrath that her lover could muster when she
was good and riled up about something. Her expression turned
more serious as another thought invaded her mind.

"Do you know that Dr. Mitchard paid me a visit when I was
up in the ICU earlier?"

"Really?" the nurse asked.

The resident snorted. "Sandy, she didn't even bother to ask
how Alex was doing. All she wanted to know was if Alex had
told me about any documents that might point the finger at Dr.
Jameson. She had the audacity to say that the hospital needed to
disassociate itself from the whole mess."

Sandy unleashed a string of curses. "Nice of them to care so
much."

"You know, Alex wasn't my favorite doctor, Regina, but
what Dr. Jameson did was disgusting. Now that he's got a big
time attorney making noises for him they're looking for the easi-
est target," Marcus grumbled.

"We need to get everything that Alex copied and go to the
Executive Committee with it before this gets any more out of
hand," Regina stated, her voice furious at the implications.

"Do you know what she did with the files?"

"No, she didn't tell me what she did with them. She didn't
want me getting involved," Regina replied.

"Well, she doesn't really have much of a choice at this
point. If she's up to it, maybe Jon can ask her when he goes up to
see her at the end of his shift today," Sandy offered.

"Maybe. She's really out of it for the most part," Regina
told her, still very much worried about Alex. A second later, her
attention was drawn to the ambulance bay doors as they banged
open and two paramedics wheeled a stretcher down the hall. She
turned to the nurse. "Sandy, who else is on with me today?"

Marcus stepped up beside her. "No, Regina, go home. I'll
cover your shift."

Regina turned around and stared at him in shock. "Are you
serious? What about your vacation?"

"It's three days, I can go any time. Besides, you're dead on your feet, Regina. Go on." He turned her around and gently pushed the exhausted resident toward the locker room.

A sense of profound relief flooded through her and she leaned against the counter as she let her guard down for the first time in many hours. "Thank you. You have no idea how much I appreciate it."

He waved her off. "Get out of here and get some sleep will you?"

Relieved from her shift, Regina hastily gathered her belongings and headed home for a few hours of desperately needed slumber.

❖ ⌘ ❖ ⌘ ❖ ⌘ ❖

Later that day after finishing his shift, Jon stepped quietly inside the cramped room in the intensive care unit. For a moment, he scanned the room before coming to rest on his injured colleague. Every bit of information about the woman's vital functions was displayed on the monitor over the bed via the wires and tubes hooked to her body.

He tried, in his mind, to reconcile the sight of the woman he had worked with over the years, and the one that was lying so vulnerable in the bed. She had always been somewhat of a loner, but her tireless dedication and loyalty to the patients had made him believe there was a whole other person hidden inside the armor she wore.

He realized he had caught more glimpses of that person since the young resident had befriended Alex. Jon wondered briefly about that friendship and what had drawn them together. He set his thoughts aside when pale blue eyes fluttered open and slowly focused on him. He approached the bedside and took hold of the railing.

"Hey there," he said, leaning over and laying a hand lightly on Alex's shoulder. "Regina said you were awake."

The brunette grimaced as a jolt of pain took her breath away. "Ah, I...feel like a truck ran over me."

"You wish it was a truck. I don't recall the oath we took saying anything about taking a bullet for a patient."

"Where is Dana?" Alex rasped through the pain. The small tubes delivering oxygen into her nose were bothering her and she fumbled with them in annoyance.

"Three doors down. They've got a guard outside. As soon as

she's medically stable, she's out of here." Jon studied her face and reached down to adjust the nasal cannula. "You've got to keep that in or you're going to piss off the nurses."

Alex closed her eyes. "I don't...make a good patient."

Jon's face turned serious and he pulled a chair up beside the bed. "Alex, I need to ask you something. Are you with me?"

Alex stared at him, still feeling in a fog from the narcotics. "Yeah," she breathed. "Still here."

"It's about Jameson."

Alex's eyes drifted closed briefly then, opened again. "It's...okay. Mitchard knows."

"That may not be good enough. Alex, I need to talk to the executive board about it. Where are the documents?" She didn't respond. He muttered under his breath when he realized that she had already drifted back to sleep.

❖ ⌘ ❖ ⌘ ❖ ⌘ ❖

Regina stumbled home into her bed and slept for several hours. Later, she showered and threw on clean clothes. She wasted no time returning to the hospital. The resident walked down the stark white corridor that led into the Intensive Care Unit, slipping past the large food cart being pushed by one of the dietary staff. She grimaced at the smell of the warm hospital food and then rolled her eyes when she thought about how Alex would respond to a liquid diet the first day or two after the surgery. It was true, for the most part, that doctors made the worst patients and in this case her lover was probably going to set new standards in the industry.

She chose to dress in jeans and a sweatshirt but still wore her identification badge to limit the hassles she would get from the nursing staff since Alex was still in the ICU and visiting hours were technically limited to family members only. *Family. I wonder if Jon was able to get in touch with anyone?* Regina pushed open the glass doors to the ICU and stepped into the brightly lit unit.

She had been at the doctor's bedside earlier that day, as the darkness had slowly given way to the gray light of dawn, and she hadn't paid much attention to what else was going on around the unit. She had spent the hours, focusing only on the rise and fall of Alex's chest, willing her to fight against the nearly fatal damage the bullet had left in its wake after it ripped violently through her body.

Now, as the resident walked through the unit, she noticed an armed police officer standing at the far end of the horseshoe-shaped row of rooms and realized as she passed him that he was standing outside of Dana's room. It was a somber reminder of the tragic events and what had led up to them.

The blonde pulled her eyes away from the still form lying in the bed and walked up to the nurse's station. She waited as the nurse at the counter finished a phone call and looked up at her.

"Hi. I'm Dr. Kingston. How is Dr. Margulies doing?"

The nurse studied her for a moment and then called over her shoulder for one of her colleagues. "Mary, the doc here wants to know how your patient is doing in room six."

The tall redhead at the other end of the counter looked up and then slowly walked over to Regina. She eyed the young resident dubiously as she stepped up in front of her.

"It's probably not a great time to see her. They just pulled the drain out of the surgical site. It hurt like hell and she's not due for any pain meds for another thirty minutes."

Regina's hand ran over her flank as she shuddered involuntarily at the thought of the plastic tube being yanked out of Alex's body. "I'm going to look in on her."

"I'd let her rest if I were you. She's not exactly in a good mood," the nurse replied flatly and turned away from her.

The resident cocked a blonde eyebrow, annoyed at the woman's attitude. "When did you last check on her?"

"Ten minutes ago." The red head bristled defensively at the question.

"Was she asleep, then?" Regina asked, looking at the curtain blocking the bed from view.

"No."

"If she's in that much pain she's probably not going to sleep until she gets the damn pain meds, so until then I'll be inside with her," Regina announced, ignoring the nurse's indignant response, and turned from the desk.

The blonde walked into the room and pulled the curtain back to look in at her lover. Her chest constricted at the sight of Alex in pain. She was curled into a fetal position on her left side, her head tucked down on the pillow and arms wrapped tightly over her chest.

Regina immediately pulled the chair over, sat down in front of her and lowered the bed rail so she could be closer to her.

Sweat glistened on the older woman's face as her body responded to the pain and the trauma of the surgery she had endured the day before.

"Hey, Alex," she whispered softly. Regina brushed the damp bangs back off her forehead and leaned in to gently kiss her temple.

The dark-haired woman groaned and opened her eyes. "It's you," she whispered in a rasping voice.

"Yeah, it's me." Regina's hand rested on the nape of her neck beneath the tangled locks of her hair. "Is this okay?"

Alex licked her dry lips and nodded her head slightly. "Ah, it hurts."

"I know. Can I do anything?" The blonde scooted the chair closer and lightly massaged the woman's neck.

"Ice?" Alex responded hoarsely, after a moment's hesitation.

"Let me check." Regina disappeared for a few moments and returned with a cup of crushed ice.

"Here." She offered a couple of chips, placing them between Alex's lips.

The doctor sucked them in and then grasped Regina's hand that was resting on the pillow. "Don't go."

"I'm not. I'm right here, love," Regina assured her and leaned in to kiss her damp forehead.

Alex was quiet for a while before she worked up the strength to ask for some more of the frozen chips. She let out a small sigh as fingers brushed over her lips and then slid through her hair, lifting it back over her shoulder. Regina's touch was a welcome balm to the pain and the haze of the narcotics. After she swallowed the ice she looked up at the blonde through glassy eyes. "Thanks...for being here."

"Where else would I be?" Regina asked quietly, brushing her hand lightly through the dark locks of hair.

Alex moved her head closer to Regina's hand and pressed against it, seeking the comfort of her touch. "I dreamed of you."

"Shh, don't talk. You need to rest." Regina continued the gentle stroking at the base of Alex's neck.

The brunette swallowed and moaned softly, then looked up into the greenest eyes she'd ever seen. "W-when I...get out of here." Alex took a breath. "I want to lay under the stars with you. You can point out the constellations."

Regina wiped a tear from her own face. She looked down at

Alex as she struggled to say each word. "Why?"

"That's when I knew. You were...pointing out Orion's Belt to me and I knew."

"Knew what?" Regina tilted her head trying to understand Alex's slightly slurred words.

"I loved you. I always have, right from the beginning."

"I love you too, Alex. I don't remember what it was like not to have you in my life." Regina looked up as one of the nurses walked in and then adjusted the setting on the IV pump.

The blonde watched as the nurse fiddled with the settings and then walked out of the room. She wondered how much the nurse had overheard and then shook her head as she realized how little she cared about whom knew about them. This was the woman she loved and she was done worrying about what other people thought.

Regina looked back down as she heard Alex say something to her. "Jon...was here."

"Sandy told me he was going to come up and see you."

"See me?" Alex blinked, focusing on the blonde sitting before her. "Didn't he see enough earlier?"

Regina blinked, not understanding what Alex meant. She did when the woman weakly lifted a hand and flicked the top of the blue gown draped over her body. Regina caught site of the bulky bandage covering most of her lover's chest and steeled herself against the gruesome image that flashed in her mind. "Sweetheart, don't think about it."

Alex struggled to stay focused and squinted as she looked at Regina. "It was bad, wasn't it?"

Regina closed her eyes, realizing what Alex was asking her. "Later, okay?" *I don't think I can begin to tell you everything that happened.*

Alex stared into Regina's eyes, seeing the tormented look and nodded her head slowly in silent acknowledgment.

Regina lifted her head when she heard a knock on the glass door. "Come in."

A moment later, Sandy peered around her curtain. "Hey. She's awake?"

Regina nodded her head. "They took the drain out."

Sandy winced and stepped quietly toward the bed. Her eyes ran over the form of the tall doctor lying on her side, holding onto Regina's hand. *I think she saved you in more ways than one, my friend.* She stepped to the side of the bed and knelt next to

Regina. "I need to talk to you."

Regina lifted herself slowly out of the chair and walked to the door. She leaned heavily against the doorframe and yawned.

Sandy tilted her head and studied the resident for a moment. "You doing okay?"

Regina blinked several times and rubbed her face in an effort to be more alert. "I feel numb. I know I should be passed out somewhere, but I can't sleep."

"Hang in there. She should be out of the ICU tonight if she keeps doing this well," Sandy reassured the blonde. "Listen, the medical committee called an emergency meeting for later today."

Regina groaned. "What for?"

Sandy shifted her feet uncomfortably, knowing Regina didn't need more stress right now, but being that she was closest to Alex there was no one else to go to. "Dr. Jameson is claiming that Alex harassed him and his attorney is filing a lawsuit against her and the entire department."

Regina tilted her head back against the glass and closed her eyes. "You've got to be kidding me."

Sandy glanced over Regina's shoulder, watching as Alex stirred in the bed. "What better way to deflect the attention away from him than stir up trouble for somebody else?"

Regina took a breath and nodded her head. "He's using all this to his advantage, the bastard."

Alex turned over and opened her eyes, focusing on Regina and Sandy standing just inside the room. "What about Jameson?" she grumbled from the bed.

Sandy looked at Regina who shook her head, silently letting the nurse know not to say anything else.

Alex blinked her eyes and struggled to shift her position in the bed. "What? Regina, tell me." Her hand crept up over her chest as the movement brought more pain.

The resident walked back to the bed and sat down. "Alex, no, don't do this to yourself."

"Tell me." The attending reached out and squeezed Regina's hand, fixing her eyes on her lover.

Regina hung her head and quietly related to Alex what was going on with Dr. Jameson. Her fears about Jameson taking as many people down with him as he could were confirmed with the executive committee meeting on such short notice. When she was done, she looked into weary blue eyes. "Alex, I'm sorry. I know you told me not to get involved with this, but—"

Alex shook her head and slowly lifted her hand up to cover Regina's lips. "Shh, listen to me. I know I can't do this." The doctor groaned softly and dropped her arm down before she continued. "The files are in the back of my Jeep, under a blanket."

"You want me to do this?"

Alex nodded. "No one else can. You were there with me; you know what he did. Just tell them what we found."

"Are you sure this will work?" Regina asked.

Alex nodded her head and touched Regina's face. "Just...stay focused. No matter what he says in there, don't let it shake you."

"Right." The blonde stared down at Alex and smiled nervously.

Alex moved onto her back and closed her eyes. She concentrated on her breathing, focusing on what she needed to tell Regina and pushing the pain to the far recesses of her mind. "Regina." She looked at the blonde. "There's a lot of good people down there...that stand to lose everything they've worked for. Don't let him do that to them."

Regina leaned in and rested her forehead against Alex's. "I won't. I promise."

The curtain pulled back and the redhead glared in at Regina and Sandy. "This is an intensive care unit, if you hadn't noticed."

"I liked her better when I was out of it," Alex growled in Regina's ear.

Sandy leaned over and touched Alex's shoulder. "Hang in there, Alex. This will all be over soon."

"It's time for her pain medication. You should leave, now."

Regina looked up at her without making a move to leave. "Go ahead and give it to her. I'll leave as soon as she falls asleep."

Obviously displeased with Regina's statement, the nurse huffed her agreement and jabbed the syringe into the IV port.

The blonde leaned over Alex's ear and whispered, "I'll be back later. Just rest, baby. I love you."

Alex mumbled something back to her as she slipped under the effect of the injection of morphine and Valium.

❖ ⌘ ❖ ⌘ ❖ ⌘ ❖

"Which lock do you need removed?" The balding engineer

stood at the door scratching his head as he looked at the two women.

"This one." Regina pointed to Alex's locker.

"Uh, I need a work order to be able to do that."

Sandy glared at him and rolled her eyes. "No, you need a bolt cutter, like the one you have in your hands."

"Now listen, I don't need you getting huffy with me. I'm just doing my job," the engineer protested, his already ruddy complexion turning a brighter red.

Regina walked over to him, reading his nametag as she got closer. "Sam, go get a cup of coffee in the lounge, whatever, just let me have the bolt cutter and nobody will be the wiser, right?" She took the tool from his hands and shooed him out of the locker room.

"Pretty soon we're going to need a work order to wipe our butts around here," Sandy complained. She helped Regina position the jaws around the lock.

With a loud metallic snap the lock broke and fell to the floor. Regina quickly retrieved Alex's keys from her jacket.

"Thanks for coming in and helping me with this, Sandy." Regina glanced at the curly-headed blonde as they headed toward the doors leading to the parking lot.

The nurse raised her eyebrows at the resident. "Are you kidding me? When Jon told me what Jameson was up to there was no way I wasn't coming in."

Sandy pushed the door open and let the resident walk past her outside. The bitter, cold wind swirled around them and they held onto each other, trying not to slip on the patches of ice as they carefully worked their way through the partially plowed parking lot towards Alex's Jeep.

"That slimy bastard has been pulling this shit for years and no one has ever been able to pin anything on him. If he wasn't treating the nursing staff like dirt, he was always leaving early and dumping his work on the other docs in the ER to pick up."

Regina disarmed the vehicle and opened the rear hatch door. Just as Alex told her, there were two cardboard boxes underneath the blanket. She flipped quickly through the contents with her good hand as Sandy looked over her shoulder.

"What are those?" The nurse pointed at a stack of papers with a rubber band around them.

Regina looked back at her. "Vouchers for airline miles and checks that the drug company sent him. Nice, little, unbiased

research study the pharmaceutical company and our medical
director was conducting, huh?"

Sandy shook her head in disbelief. "How could he allow
himself to do that?"

Regina shrugged indifferently. "I don't know and I don't
care."

Sandy grabbed Regina's arm. "Are you sure about doing
this, Regina?"

"Sandy, if I don't go in there with this, Jameson's lawyer is
going to spread the blame on every staff member and doctor who
had anything to do with these patients." Regina pulled out a
folder of papers and shoved them at Sandy. "Your signature is on
some of these patient charts. So is mine."

Sandy flipped through the pages, her expression growing
grimmer as she scanned the patient flow sheets and other notes,
looking for signatures. "This is bad, Regina."

The resident nodded in agreement. "You know how the ER
gets: everyone helps out with each other's patients when it gets
crazy. Jameson is going to try and weasel his way out of taking
responsibility for his actions and if he can take Alex down in the
process, all the better."

"B-but none of us did anything wrong. We didn't give the
medication, he did."

"You're right and we can all sit back and do nothing; Jameson will get another slap on the wrist, the hospital will sweep it
under the rug and everyone whose name is associated with these
patients will be on some kind of disciplinary action to satisfy
OIG. Do you want that in your file? Do you want to work with
someone who you wouldn't trust to take care of your dog? I
don't." The blonde took the folder back from Sandy and tossed it
into the box.

Sandy was silent, staring down at the two cartons, weighing
out what Regina said to her. "You're right. It just scares the crap
out of me thinking about what the hospital will do if they take a
hit for this and then come after us."

Regina leaned against the bumper. "Sandy, look, it's your
decision what you want to do. Alex found all this in Jameson's
office. He knows that, so right now she's the one who's most at
risk from him. He'll try and make her take the fall if he can."

"I already know what I want to do." Sandy stacked the two
boxes on top of each other and lifted them out of the back of the
Jeep. "Shut that for me?"

Regina smiled and slammed the door shut.

Together they walked back to the department. Jon met them inside the ambulance bay doors.

"Man, I hope you have something good to tell me."

"As far as he's concerned no one else knows anything. Without Alex to confront him, he thinks he can bury this completely," Sandy growled.

Regina turned to Jon. "We have everything that Alex copied."

Together they walked down the hallway and rode the elevator to the fifth floor. "I know this is a hell of a time to ask, but you *do* have a plan, right?"

"The plan is to go in there, dump this stuff in front of him and let him try and explain his way out of it."

Inside the conference room, Dr. Mitchard sat at one end of the table huddled over a pile of charts. Dr. Timmons, head of the pediatric department, stood against the wall with his arms crossed, glaring back at the Vice President.

"I can't believe the level of incompetence and outright negligence these staff members have displayed," Dr. Jameson's attorney stated, as he looked between the Vice President and Dr. Timmons.

"For Christ's sakes, Cassandra, you expect us to believe that you didn't know any of this was going on. This is bullshit." Dr. Timmons looked up and shoved the file across the table in disgust. "Do you know the kinds of fines the hospital is looking at?" the gray-haired pediatrician asked.

"Peter, I told you, none of this came to my attention until the Office of the Inspector General called three days ago," Dr. Mitchard replied.

"I told you, you would regret keeping Dr. Margulies on board. You should have listened to me," Jameson snarled at Dr. Mitchard.

"The board put it to a vote. There was nothing I could do." The Vice President's voice wavered at doctor's harsh words.

"How do you expect me to run a department when I have the likes of Margulies running around undermining everything that I'm trying to do?" Dr. Jameson slammed his hand down on the table. "She had access to my office when I was out. It's clear to me what happened here."

"Jim, let me handle this," his attorney warned.

Dr. Timmons held up his hand and pushed himself away

from the wall. "That's not what I heard. Your department budget was a month overdue, so it fell in Alex's lap to finish it when you were out on leave."

The lawyer walked over to the doctor. "It's no secret that Dr. Jameson and Dr. Margulies have an adversarial relationship. What better opportunity for her to drive him out than when he is incapacitated."

The pediatrician snorted and walked to the end of the table and looked directly at the medical director. "Jim, who's Donna Sanders?"

The physician's face blanched at the mention of the woman's name and Dr. Mitchard snapped her head up at the end of the table. "How the hell should I know who she is?"

"It seems she worked for T&M up until two days ago. According to the gentleman I spoke to at the Office of the Inspector General, she knows you rather well."

A small cry escaped the Vice President's mouth as she turned her face away.

They all looked up as the door opened and Regina walked in followed by Sandy and Dr. Washington.

"This is a closed meeting. What are they doing here?" Dr. Jameson waved his arm angrily.

Regina dug into one of the boxes and pulled out a sheath of papers. "We know what you did, Dr. Jameson. You're accusing Alex of harassing you because of what she found in your office."

"What the hell are you talking about?" Jameson growled. He looked around the room at his colleagues. "I don't have to stay here and listen to this crap."

"Why? Do you think that you're above it all? The laws don't apply to you? Is that it?" Jon demanded, as he leaned across the table and glared at his medical director.

"You are out of line, Dr. Washington," Dr. Mitchard snapped.

The attorney took a stack of papers from one of the boxes and glanced through them. "We've seen the medical records already. They don't tell us anything," he remarked snidely.

Regina looked at Dr. Timmons. "That only tells half the story. I'd like Dr. Jameson to explain why T&M regularly sent him vouchers for airline miles."

"What airline vouchers?" Dr. Timmons asked as he stepped away from the wall and held his hand out to take them from Sandy.

"Oh for Chrissakes." Dr. Jameson threw his arms up. "Alex can't be here so she sends her bitch instead."

Regina stopped mid-stride and stared at the doctor in shock.

"What?" The medical director leered at her from across the room. "Do you think nobody knows about your fling with that whore?"

The rest of the room fell silent as Regina's face paled. She continued to stare at the medical director as she stepped closer to the table and quietly set the folders down. *Okay Regina, you could leap across the table and bean him in the head with your cast or take him down with what Alex has on him.* Her hands trembled slightly as she took a breath and looked down at the stack of files in front of her, collecting her scattered thoughts.

She raised her head and glanced anxiously at Jon and Sandy, before she met Dr. Jameson's arrogant gaze. "A whore, Dr. Jameson, is someone who compromises their own values for personal gain. Something you've become quite good at over the past year."

"Dr. Kingston, I'd be careful here if I were you. You have your career to consider," Dr. Mitchard snarled.

Dr. Timmons cleared his throat. "Dr. Kingston, I assume you are here because you can contribute something relevant to this meeting."

*There goes any chance at the pediatric position,* Regina thought as she looked at him. "Sandy, can you give me the checks that were written out to Dr. Jameson?"

"Right here," the curly-headed nurse replied and stepped up beside the resident.

"This is ridiculous." The medical director stood up and walked to the door. "I am not listening to this crap."

"What checks?" Dr. Timmons asked, holding a hand out to stop Dr. Jameson from leaving the room.

Regina allowed herself a small smile as she looked at the medical director and then at their department's Vice President, whose face was now several shades paler than when she first walked in the door.

"The checks that Dr. Jameson received after he submitted his *research* to the drug company."

"That's a lie!" Dr. Jameson shouted angrily, backing up to the door.

"Shut up, Jim. Who signed these checks?" Dr. Timmons demanded.

"A woman by the name of Donna Sanders from T&M signed them all." Regina handed the papers across the table to the doctor.

"Cassandra, did you know that Dr. Jameson was getting paid by the drug company to conduct this study?"

The Vice President shook her head and buried her face in her hands. "I swear I had no idea," she moaned.

The gray-haired pediatrician leaned on the table and flipped through the checks that were written out to the medical director. Dr. Timmons turned around and crossed his arms, grimly regarding his colleagues. "Dr. Jameson, you're suspended immediately. I can tell you right now that pending the investigation by the hospital and the OIG, I'll personally move to have your medical license revoked. I'm not sure which disturbs me more: the fact that you actually did this, or that you were willing to discredit your colleagues to save your own hide." He looked around the table and shook his head sadly. "Dr. Kingston's right. You did prostitute yourself, and worse, you're a coward as well."

Quietly, Regina and her two colleagues left the room, listening to angry shouts and accusations being hurled back and forth as Dr. Jameson desperately argued his innocence. Regina turned around as the conference room door slammed shut and watched Dr. Mitchard stalk angrily down the hallway in the opposite direction.

Sandy walked up next to her and whispered in her ear, "You did good, kid. Wait until Alex hears Jameson is gone."

The blonde looked down at her feet as she walked along. "Does everybody really know, Sandy?"

The nurse turned around and stared at the resident. "Regina, I think Jameson was baiting you when he said that. Everyone knows the two of you are close but what difference does it make?"

Jon held the door for them as they approached the elevator. Once the door was closed the normally mild mannered attending tilted his head back and whooped loudly. He laughed at the two women staring at him. "Sorry, but it's probably better than me breaking out into a rendition of 'Ding Dong the Witch is Dead.'"

Sandy doubled over and held her sides as she laughed until she was clutching at the wall to hold herself up. "Oh, I know I shouldn't laugh but no one deserved to get what he got more than Jameson did today."

"Do you think he'll lose his license?" Regina asked quietly

from the corner.

Jon looked at her, noticing the conflicted look on her face. "If that's all that happens, he'll be lucky. Regina, you did the right thing. If you feel badly, just think about all the patients he put at risk by doing what he did."

Regina followed her two friends out of the elevator and reconciled herself as she walked down the hall. Dr. Jameson had chosen his own path and nobody else was responsible for what happened except for him.

As she walked through the ER doors, she saw the familiar profile of her father standing by the nurse's desk. He turned to face her as the unit clerk pointed in Regina's direction.

"There you are," he exclaimed. "I've been trying to call you at home and then I had you paged."

Regina leaned against the desk and smiled wearily. "This hasn't turned out the way either one of us wanted it to, I guess."

"No, I don't suppose it has," her father remarked quietly. He glanced uncomfortably around the department and sighed. "I don't want to talk here. Can I drive you home?"

Regina glanced up at the clock: 8:00 p.m. *Too late to visit, Alex. You're probably sleeping anyway.* "Yeah, that would be fine."

He led the way out of the ER and down the hallway and out to the parking lot. When they stood beside his car, he asked, "Regina, what are your plans now that your residency is done?"

Regina slipped into the passenger seat, leaned back in the seat and folded her arms over her chest. "I don't have to make a decision right away. I have some leeway with that."

Her father started the car and pulled out of the parking space. He glanced at her before he accelerated across the intersection. "What I mean is, there are plenty of jobs up by us if you want to come back home."

Regina stared up at him and tilted her head, trying to comprehend what he was saying. She rubbed her hands together nervously as she realized that what she had said to him several nights ago about her feelings for Alex obviously weren't taken seriously.

"Dad," she looked off into the distance trying to find the words she wanted to say, "if I went back to Massachusetts, I'd be leaving behind the one person in the world I don't ever want to be without."

Her father nodded his head and turned his blinker on, signaling the left turn onto her street. "You know how your mother feels."

"Yeah, I think I have a pretty clear idea on how she feels," Regina said as her condo came into view. She waited for him to turn the engine off, before she stepped out of the car. "Dad, what are you trying to say?"

"Always to the point, aren't you?" He shook his head and glanced sadly at his daughter over the roof of the car. "I don't know if she'll ever change how she feels. She thinks being," he motioned with his hand, "is just wrong."

"How do you feel about," she mimicked her father's hand motion, "my being gay?"

"Christ, Regina, do we have to discuss this here?" he hissed, obviously uncomfortable with their very public surroundings.

"I'm sorry...well no, I'm not." Regina struggled to find the words. "Dad, I almost lost the most important person in my life and I realized that I never told her just how much I love her, and if that bothers you or anybody else, I can't help that."

Her father closed his eyes and rubbed his forehead, trying to stave off the headache coming on. "You can't expect me to be comfortable with it. I need time, Reg, please."

Regina stepped closer and lowered her voice. "Time? Dad, because of this, you've had no relationship with your son for seventeen years. How much more time do you need?"

Her father lowered his eyes and shook his head. "I-I don't know. Are...are you sure about this?"

Regina looked up at him and then glanced at the back seat of the car and saw his suitcase. "Are you leaving today?"

"I have to get back home, Regina."

The blonde pressed her lips together, wondering if all this had been a token attempt after all to draw her away from the woman she loved. "The answer is yes; I'm sure, Dad."

"Well, you know you can come home anytime you want," he said, stepping around the car.

"As long as I come alone, right?" Regina muttered bitterly.

"That's not fair. Your mother and I just want you to be happy." Her father held his hands out, pleading with Regina.

"How do I make you understand? I am happy with Alex."

"It's just hard to believe that she can make you feel..." His eyes left hers and he looked at the ground. "She's a woman, Regina. You need a man to take care of you."

Regina spun around and stared at him. "You would say that.

I don't need someone to take care of me. I just want someone who loves me. Is that so hard to understand?"

Her father looked up at the sky and shook his head. "Please, I don't want to argue, Regina." He stepped forward and wrapped an arm around her shoulder. "I just hope you know what you're getting into." .

"I do, Dad, I do," she whispered and rested her head on his shoulder.

He squeezed her to him and kissed the top of her head. "I've got to go. Take care of yourself." He stepped away and started to walk to the car, then stopped and looked back at her. "I hope Alex is going to be okay."

"She will be." *After all these years, all I ever wanted was for you and Mom to tell me you loved me. Why is that so hard for you? I guess you always sensed that Jeff and I were different. Is that why you pushed me to be with Derrick, because you were afraid to see the truth?* Regina watched as her father pulled out of the driveway and then walked over to the door and let herself inside.

# Chapter
## 24

The next morning Sandy slipped into Alex's room during her break. As she stepped around the curtain, she hesitated. She saw Alex sleeping in the bed and right beside her, lying in the reclining chair, was Regina with her eyes closed and her left hand enclosed in Alex's larger one. Sandy started to back out of the room when a gravelly voice broke the silence.

"Sandy, don't go."

"Oh, hey, I didn't think you were awake." Sandy sheepishly stuck her hands in her lab coat and moved to the end of the bed.

"It's all right. I don't really sleep, just kind of drift in and out." Alex squeezed the smaller hand she held.

"Mm, ah, oh I must have fallen asleep," Regina mumbled softly, as she wiped her eyes and sat up blinking. "Hi, Sandy."

"I thought you went home last night."

Regina ran her hand through her hair. "Just for a little while. I snuck back in after visiting hours."

Sandy peered around to the other side of the room. "No roommate?"

Regina gave Alex a sidelong glance. "Would you believe this one called the woman's attending and reamed him out on the phone at eleven o'clock last night?"

Alex arched an eyebrow and volunteered her reasons. "The woman had peritonitis and he hadn't been in to see her in two days. She needed surgery to repair the defect and the intern hadn't picked it up when he examined her on rounds."

The nurse shook her head. "Alex, you're supposed to be resting, not working."

"I can't help it," the doctor grumbled. "I knew something was wrong with the woman. I couldn't just ignore it."

"Is she behaving otherwise?" Sandy looked at Regina.

The resident snorted and rolled her eyes. "If you don't count her throwing one of the phlebotomists out of the room last night, removing her own IV, and threatening Dr. Kelly with bodily harm unless he discharged her today."

"I don't need to be here and I'm tired of them sticking me with needles," Alex groused.

"Sounds like it's time for you to go home." Sandy sat down on the edge of the bed and dug into the pocket of her lab coat. "Here, I wanted to give this to you." She handed Alex a sealed envelope, which contained a card. The doctor turned it over before looking at her with uncertain eyes. "It's from everyone downstairs."

Alex looked at Regina who smiled and nodded at her to open it. The doctor's hands trembled slightly as she ripped open the seal and pulled the card out. Her eyes scanned over the hand-scrawled notes and she quickly closed the card. "I-I don't think I can read them all right now." Her voice shook slightly and she bowed her head, fighting the tears that threatened to fall. *Get a grip, Alex. It's just a bloody card. What the hell is wrong with you anyway?*

Sandy cleared her throat softly. "Alex, just know there are a lot of people here who care about you."

The dark head shook imperceptibly and Alex took a shaky breath before she looked up at Sandy. "Thanks," she whispered.

The nurse sat up straighter and blinked back tears. "Oh, Christ, now look. I am not going to sit here and start this shit." She wiped her eyes and stood up quickly. "You get your ass better and get back here. I'm not dealing with all these wet-behind-the-ears residents all by myself."

"You'll whip them into shape."

There was a knock on the door and the conversation stopped. "Alex?" Dr. Timmons stepped around the curtain. "I heard you caused quite a stir up here last night."

Alex shifted uncomfortably, feeling a dull ache returning in her chest. "If that doctor wanted banker's hours he should have gone into dermatology, not surgery."

The pediatrician raised his hands and waved them in front of him. "Whoa. I agree with you. Actually, that's not why I'm here." He looked at Sandy. "I need to speak to the two doctors here."

"I've got to go anyway." Sandy pointed at Regina. "Call me before you leave."

Dr. Timmons waited for her to leave and then turned to Alex. "How are you doing?"

Alex raised an eyebrow at the question and cocked her head. "As well as I can. Just another scar to add to the collection," she commented, trying to ease the tension she felt.

The pediatrician pressed his lips together and nodded his head. "I didn't want to leave without speaking to both of you."

Regina scooted to the edge of the chair and leaned instinctively closer to Alex.

"Alex, you take whatever time you need. I'll be managing the administrative duties in the ER while you're gone. When you're ready, the department is yours to run if you still want it." Dr. Timmons held up his hand at her protest. "Listen, I know it's a lot to throw at you so soon, but I'd have your entire department after me if I didn't tell you just that. You have a loyal bunch down there and they want you back."

Alex swallowed hard and blinked, trying to comprehend the significance of what he had just said.

"Dr. Kingston." Dr. Timmons focused on the blonde and gave her a warm smile. "You've left quite the impression on the medical staff."

Regina's eyes widened and her heart started to pound faster. "I-I—"

"There is a fellowship position available in surgery and one for pediatrics. Your choice, but I need an answer by the end of next week."

Regina stared up at the doctor in shock. She had been sure that Jameson's comment in the meeting would be her downfall at the medical center. "Y-You're offering me a fellowship position?"

"I believe that's what I just did." The doctor stepped back and looked at both of the women. "Take care of yourselves, ladies. Regina, you know where to find me. Alex, please think about what I said." With that, he inclined his head and backed out of the room.

Regina scratched her head and looked at Alex. "Did that just really happen or am I dreaming?"

Alex tilted her head back and stared up at the ceiling before gazing at the blonde woman. She touched Regina's face. "Nope, not a dream." Her eyes were solemn as she continued to look at her lover.

❖ ⌘ ❖ ⌘ ❖ ⌘ ❖

Regina stepped down out of the Jeep, and scanned the front entrance of the hospital. A smile touched her lips when she saw her fair-haired friend carefully pushing a wheelchair through the automatic sliding doors. Its occupant straightened slightly and blinked several times, her eyes adjusting to the sunlight reflecting off the snow. Alex's surgeon argued valiantly to get her to stay another day, but the recovering doctor flatly refused and threatened to sign herself out if he didn't agree to discharge her today.

The dark-haired woman grimaced slightly as the cold, damp wind buffeted her slender form and she shivered despite the layers of clothing that she was dressed in. A fleeting, tentative smile crossed her lips as she looked around her. Even though the cold air made her lungs ache, she inhaled deeply, trying to rid herself of the pungent, antiseptic hospital odor that she had come to loathe over the past week.

Sandy leaned over the taller woman's shoulder and pointed Regina out as she walked around the front of the Jeep. "There she is. Your chariot awaits, my friend."

There was a brief moment as Regina met Sandy's gaze and the two women smiled at each other. Sandy stopped, locked the brakes, and offered Alex her hand. With some effort Alex lifted herself out the wheelchair, ignoring Sandy's offer of help, and slowly straightened up before starting to walk toward the Jeep.

Regina approached the taller woman. "Do you need help?"

Alex shook her head, but rested her hand on Regina's shoulder anyway as they went to the taller woman's truck. Before she climbed up into the passenger seat, the dark-haired woman turned to the nurse.

"It's not enough, I know, but thank you." Alex clasped her hand and smiled into the woman's eyes. "You're a good friend, Sandy."

The nurse smiled back at Alex. "I'd hug you, but I don't

think that's a good idea."

"Rain check will do." The doctor nodded her head and then ducked into the Jeep, grunting as she settled herself into the seat. She felt a hand touch her arm and she looked at Regina, who peered at her with a worried look on her face.

"I'm okay," Alex murmured as she tilted her head back against the seat and closed her eyes. She had been ready to curl up somewhere alone like a wounded animal, but Regina insisted that she stay at her condo. Alex recalled Regina standing at the foot of her hospital bed the night before, glowering at the idea of Alex recuperating alone. *You weren't going to win that battle and face it, "no" was not an answer she was willing to accept.*

Regina smiled and shut the door. As she turned, Sandy wrapped her in a bear hug.

"Thanks, Sandy." She squeezed her back and held on for a few seconds before letting go.

"I'm going to miss you." The nurse pulled away, smiling.

"I'll be back. I want to be able to help Alex out and figure out what we're going to do after all this."

"Are you two going to be okay?"

Regina glanced over her shoulder at the profile of her lover, her heart lurching up into her throat as their eyes met and held. "I think so. Alex needs some time to deal with everything and so do I."

"Call if you need anything."

"I will. Go on; you're freezing out here."

Regina waved and went to the driver's side of the Jeep. She climbed in beside Alex and regarded her quietly for a moment. "You ready?"

The dark head nodded. "Just take me home."

❖ ⌘ ❖ ⌘ ❖ ⌘ ❖

A gripping, clamp like pain constricted her chest. Alex sat bolt upright in the bed with her heart pounding, and then collapsed slowly onto her side, gasping as she let the dream recede into her subconscious. *Easy, you're okay,* she told herself, willing the pounding beat of her heart to slow.

It was the same dream she'd had when she was up on the Cape, the same feeling of dread, hopelessness, and futility and now she knew its source. She'd dealt with mortality every day, her actions impacting the outcome of whether someone lived or died. Death was always there on the periphery, waiting patiently, always a grim reminder of how fragile the human body was.

In the past, she had kept it at arm's length; young, healthy, and at the peak of her career, it would not touch her, but now it had. She'd dealt with first her lover's death, miserably failed in her attempt to accept the impending loss, and now had come face to face with her own mortality and survived. Luck, fate, sheer will, and determination, Regina's heroic effort to save her had kept her alive to see another day and now it was up to her to put the demons aside and move on.

Quietly, so as not wake Regina, she eased out of the bed and crept out of the bedroom. Finally, almost two weeks after her surgery, she could walk without being bent over at the waist from the pain. She stubbornly refused to take any more of the painkillers and sedatives, secretly terrified that she would fall prey once again to her old addictions.

Alex settled onto the couch and turned on the lamp next to her. She tilted her head and stared up at the ceiling, turning her thoughts inward. It felt like she spent forever searching for someone to love. She thought she found that person with Lana, had learned to trust, even believed she deserved the happiness, only to have it slowly torn from her as she watched the woman she loved wither away. Now one tumultuous year later she'd been offered a second chance at life and love.

"Alex."

The sound of her name startled her. She turned her head and saw Regina, a blanket wrapped around her shoulders, standing by the edge of the couch. Alex sighed, seeing the soft, contemplative expression on her lover's face.

"Did I wake you up?" Alex asked softly.

Regina shook her head, and sat down beside her. "No. Did you dream again?"

Alex pulled her eyes away and stared down at her hands, her silence answering the blonde's question. Regina's fingers brushed her hair back over her shoulder, the comforting gesture bringing tears to her eyes.

Regina waited patiently for Alex to finally focus on her. When she did, Regina smiled and ran her fingers over Alex's face, wiping the tears away. "Talk to me, love."

Alex let out a shaky breath. "Regina, there's a part of me that wishes I'd just let him shoot Dana." There, it was out. She'd said what haunted her since she woke up and realized what had happened.

Regina moved closer, slipping her hand underneath Alex's arm. "I'd feel the same way, Alex. After what you've been through, most people would."

"I don't know if I can go back there. Just thinking about it makes me break out into a sweat. Even if I do, it may be months before I'm able to work again."

"Dr. Timmons said to take all the time you need before you come back."

"As medical director."

"If you want," Regina acknowledged quietly. It had been a shock to say the least, to see the gray-haired pediatrician in Alex's room the morning before she was discharged.

Alex turned her head and looked at her friend. "What if I can't do it?"

Regina caught the flicker of fear in those eyes. "It's too soon to worry about it. Give yourself time to get past all this."

"I don't want to let anybody down and it's not fair to you to have to be the one to deal with all this crap." Alex tapped her head and smiled sadly. The nightmares plagued her almost every night and frequently she would wake to Regina quietly holding her, whispering gentle reassurances in her ear.

"What are friends for, Alex? I just want to be with you, for better or for worse." Regina interlaced her fingers with Alex's, then lifted her hand up to kiss it. "I'm in love with you, Alex. Nothing changes how I feel for you."

"Regina." Alex bowed her head forward.

"Alex, I see your smile and it feels like I've seen it a hundred times before. It stays with me, makes me think of what you're doing when you're not here with me. I couldn't bear to lose you."

"I don't know what I can give you." Alex's voice cracked. "All I have is what I feel inside and I know that I'd be lost without you."

Regina moved closer and laid her head on Alex's shoulder. A thousand times in the hospital she felt the strength of the bond that drew them together. Not just as lovers, but as friends. Together they had seen each other through the darkest times in their lives, survived the worst and come out stronger in spite of it all.

There were still so many things for them to deal with, bridges that would need to be crossed. Derrick was still out there, most likely stewing over his last public rejection. Regina knew in her heart her parents would never accept Alex as her partner and the most important part of her life would go unacknowledged by them. It hurt, but not as much as the thought of losing the love she had found. The thoughts passed through her mind, and then faded when she blinked and looked up at her lover. She watched the facial muscles twitch reflexively as Alex stared back at her pensively.

"Alex, you're my best and truest friend, my partner and the love of my life." Regina slid from the couch and knelt at her feet. "I want us to share our lives, plan our future together."

Intense blue eyes edged with gray blinked back at her in surprise. "Are you asking..."

Regina lifted Alex's hands and kissed each palm. "Yes, I'm asking you to share your life with me. I want us to be together, forever." She sat back on her heels watching Alex's reaction nervously.

Alex scooted forward and raised her hands to Regina's face. She brushed her lips over her eyelids and along her cheekbones. Regina's lips were warm and soft. They opened, willingly taking Alex inside. Her tongue moved slowly, rediscovering and exploring Regina's mouth.

"I love you, Regina," Alex whispered through the kiss.

"Always," Regina breathed back, capturing the sweet lips again. She gasped as Alex lifted her up and guided her onto her lap. "Alex, you'll hurt yourself."

"Let me be the judge of that." Alex stretched her legs out on the couch and settled Regina against her. She pulled the blue and green-checkered afghan off the back of the couch, and laid it over their outstretched bodies.

Regina rested her head on Alex's shoulder. Alex caressed the blonde hair, tilted her head, and watched green eyes reflecting back the love she felt. She smiled and touched her lips to Regina's.

Finally, after all this, she found a companion for the journey ahead; someone who she knew would stand beside her no matter where the road led. Her heart raced as the love she felt claimed her heart and soul and she knew, as she kissed the woman in her arms, that it would never, ever let go.

Other titles to look for in the
coming months from
*Yellow Rose Books*

**Prairie Fire**
By LJ Maas

**Many Roads To Travel**
By Karen King and Nann Dunne

**Innocent Hearts**
By Radclyffe

**Strength of the Heart**
By Carrie Carr

**Tropical High**
By Melissa Good

**Northern Peace and Perils**
By Francine Quesnel

**Faith**
By Angela Chapman

Printed in the United States
15559LVS00003B/73-75